A Matter of

Happenstance

D0367100

Catherine Underhill Fitzpatrick

Plain View Press
P.O. 42255
Austin, TX 78704

plainviewpress.net
sb@plainviewpress.net
512-441-2452

ISBN: 978-1-935514-62-6
Library of Congress Number: 2010932900

Cover art: Rebecca Alm of Legacy Imaging and Susan Van Dyke
Cover design by Susan Bright

To Dennis

The love of my life

Reinhardt Family

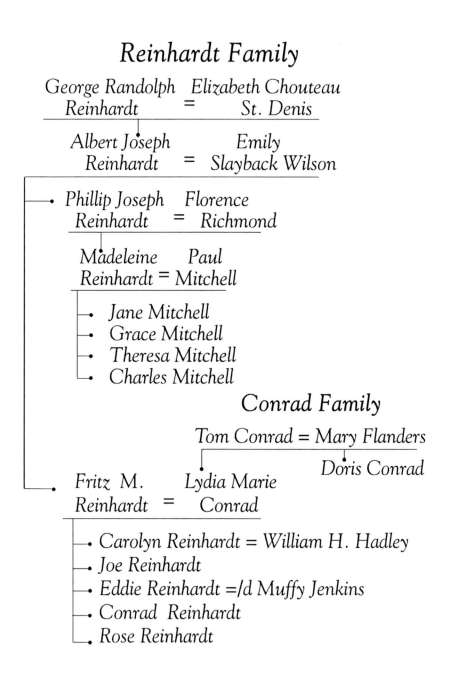

George Randolph Elizabeth Chouteau
Reinhardt = St. Denis

Albert Joseph Emily
Reinhardt = Slayback Wilson

Phillip Joseph Florence
Reinhardt = Richmond

Madeleine Paul
Reinhardt = Mitchell

- Jane Mitchell
- Grace Mitchell
- Theresa Mitchell
- Charles Mitchell

Conrad Family

Tom Conrad = Mary Flanders

Doris Conrad

Fritz M. Lydia Marie
Reinhardt = Conrad

- Carolyn Reinhardt = William H. Hadley
- Joe Reinhardt
- Eddie Reinhardt =/d Muffy Jenkins
- Conrad Reinhardt
- Rose Reinhardt

Hobbs Family

Theo Hobbs = Florelle Jones
- Sam Lee Hobbs
- Willie Hobbs
- Dalton Hobbs
- Charity Hobbs
- Sugar Hobbs
- Esmie Hobbs

Bordelon Family

Gatty Bordelon
- Palmer Bordelon
- Leroy Bordelon

Smith Family

Charles Smith = Rebecca Purchase

Leatham C. Smith = June Brennan

Brooke Smith

Gibaldi Family

Angelo Gibaldi = Giuseppa Verderame
- Vincenzo Gibaldi
- Salvatore Gibaldi
- Angeline Gibaldi

LaChapelle Family

Jan Gorecka = Hanna Badrykowski

Paul LaChapelle = Krystyna (Krysia) Gorecka

Sophie LaChapelle

Prologue

*L*evity, that blithe spirit. From daybreak to moonrise it scripted the story of Blenheim, as if scriveners had dipped quills in stardust and written on sheets of sky. For ten years the house seemed to float above harm's reach, cheating misfortune of its due. Ten years, an eternity, an eye blink, there and gone. On a July afternoon, under a flaring sun that rinsed the world of color, stilled verges of birdsong, and bowed the fevered heads of a thousand Old Garden roses, gravity slipped in through a door left ajar.

Fine Merchandise
1878

St. Louis

*R*edbuds spangled the city, crinkled branches that transformed winter-weary streets to scarlet pavilions. The carriage horse clopped along, oblivious to the display, bobbing its velvet nose low to familiar cobblestones. At the end of the line the driver rousted his last passenger. The dozing boy jolted awake and quickly patted his pocket. The telegram was there, safe. The boy backtracked on foot to Stoddard's Addition.

At the knock, George Reinhardt narrowed his eyes in the manner of a man accustomed to the swift arrival of bad news. He thumb-tossed the boy a penny and waved him off.

Too soon to be notice of eviction, George knew. Must be Pitzman. Sacked me last week right in front of the men. Now he's sent a wire. Made it official. God, I've got to tell Elizabeth.

George palmed the envelope, brooding. Maybe I should go to her father again and ask … nah, the old goat will choke before he gives me another nickel. Made that clear the last time. Grabbed me by the collar and tossed me out like a back-door beggar.

In his study, George stood with his back to the grate. He fired up an inexpensive cheroot and took a sharp draw, too preoccupied to notice its woody taste. Chandler Chouteau St. Denis, my esteemed father-in-law. Descended from a founder of the city and can't let a living soul forget it. Pompous ass. That man never did think I'd amount to anything. Ever since I married Elizabeth he's been itching for me to fail. Probably be delighted to see me off to debtor prison … Christ, he'll move Elizabeth back in with him and send our Albert packing off to boarding school, all before you can say "Jack be nimble..."

For the past week George had kept his desperate circumstances secret. He left the house each morning as usual, as if he were on his way to his desk at the municipal surveyor's office. Instead, he lounged on a park bench chatting with passersby and working up the courage to tell Elizabeth he'd been sacked from another crashing bore of another middling job. George jabbed an andiron at the fireplace, raising a flurry of sparks.

Denning turned me in, that ox, George thought. He could almost hear the conversation in his head … Reinhardt, sir? Why Mr. Pitzman, Reinhardt hasn't done a day's work in ages. George Reinhardt's a slacker, sir, always working out some cock-eyed plan to strike it rich. Thinks he's a cut better, too, married to a Chouteau and all.

George slit open the envelope. "Good God."

"What, dear?" It was Elizabeth, waiting in the dining room.

"Christ Almighty."

"Dear, the men at the survey office might have an ear for such language, but it is offensive to me."

George had come into a windfall, his second. Eight years ago, on his wedding day, he gained control of Elizabeth's substantial dowry. Each time his career hit a rough patch George had quietly liquidated one or two of Elizabeth's investments. The account had been bled dry. Now this. Thousands, no doubt.

From: First Continental Trust of Philadelphia. Stop.

To: George Randolph Reinhardt, St. Louis. Stop.

Your uncle Boyd Othman Reinhardt of Chestnut Hill passed away February 4, 1878. Stop.

Bequeathed entire estate to you, his sole heir. Stop.

Await instructions. Stop.

"Supper, dear."

George heard Elizabeth tapping her toe.

Elizabeth Chouteau was hardly more than a girl when a friend introduced her to George at an afternoon tea. She was drawn to the young man's languid manner, his heavy-lidded eyes, blue one minute and gray the next. She liked the way he looked at her from across the room, cocking his head as if bemused by some private observation. George came from modest means, Elizabeth knew that. How could she forget? Father brought it up endlessly. But George looked so splendid in a frock coat and top hat, and he had grand plans. Eventually, Elizabeth realized George's dreams were just that, dreams. She had come to accept George's inconsistencies, too. What she still found unsettling, though, was her husband's hunger for money and notoriety. Like many women born to wealth, Elizabeth regarded privation in abstract and naively romantic terms.

George helped her to a seat at the table. "You know, dear, St. Louis is growing by leaps and bounds. High time I invested in real estate."

"Mmm-hmm."

"Or copper mining. Basic industry. I've been looking into copper companies in Arizona. "

"George, do you know the first thing about mining?"

"Or a newspaper. Publish a newspaper and you're in a position to influence public opinion."

The housemaid ladled squash soup into Elizabeth's bowl and set a platter of roast beef on the sideboard.

George looked off into the middle distance and then brightened: "I suspect, however, the future is in dry goods. Dry goods on a grand scale."

"George, dear, eat your soup before it gets cold. Dry goods? Where did you get that notion?"

"Think about it. What if a man could try on six different styles of spatterdashes? What if he could see trousers in gray and brown and black, in gabardines and tweeds? See a dozen pairs of suspenders and give each one a good snap? What if you could poke your fingers into six pairs of gloves, don't you suppose you'd find a pair to your liking?"

"I suppose so," Elizabeth said. She knew so.

George waved his spoon for emphasis. "St. Louis has dozens of pokey little dry goods shops, but their selection is limited and the quality's spotty. Now Elizabeth, I've given a great deal of thought to the mail order game, but I keep coming back to the idea of a retail emporium. A dry goods palace. Think of it. Pinafores and dolls and tin soldiers. Shirtwaist dresses and French perfumes. Walking sticks and shirt collars. Chairs for the parlor. A dozen different departments and a hundred choices in each. Reinhardt's Retail Emporium we'll call it."

"It does sound like a wonderful notion."

That morning in the park George had picked a rose and pinned it to his lapel. Now, lost in thought, he tugged out the petals one by one. "Otto Krug's wife, down the street, what's her name? Herma? If Herma wants a new sofa, she could take the trolley to Reinhardt's and see sofas in brocade, even velvet. Carpets from Persia, too. Window curtains by the dozen! Reinhardt's will carry the necessities, but I'm going to specialize in the luxuries. Luxury, dear, that's the ticket."

Elizabeth rang for the maid. A beautiful beef roast, wasted.

Late that night George padded down to the kitchen and set a pan of milk on the range. His mind was spinning with visions of Reinhardt's Retail

Emporium. His son's new kitten tiptoed out of her basket and stretched before twirling figure-eights around George's ankles.

"I'll deliver purchases to any customer who lives close enough for a horse to travel there and back in, oh, say, half a day," George whispered to the cat. "I'll offer free delivery by rail for any item costing over $50. My customers won't have to guess about the price, either. Each item will have a label attached to it with a string, a little tab with the price written on it."

George stirred the milk and set the filmy spoon on the floor. Every August I'll reduce the price of leftover bed linens and furs, he decided. Clear out old inventory. He smiled. The kitten had licked the spoon across the room and lost it to the netherworld under the ice box. Then a disturbing thought occurred to George. The inheritance from his long-lost uncle wouldn't be enough. George would have to take on a partner, someone with deep pockets, someone who would stand back and let George make the crucial decisions. Someone like … Otto Krug.

Otto and Herma Krug lived a few doors down on Beaumont Street, in a blocky house fringed with square-cut bushes. A "Willkommen" mat greeted the few visitors who lumbered up to the door. Otto and George were merely neighborhood acquaintances, and in fundamental ways they were dissimilar men. George was a dapper dreamer who had married up, a personable but ineffectual risk-taker who had failed to find his true calling. Otto was a pinstriped banker with the constitution of a bulldog and the heart of a spaniel. For the past fifteen years he had served as vice-president of the German-American Bank of St. Louis, an institution that paid consistent dividends. Otto was lightning-quick with numbers, devoted to the minutia of his accounts and ledgers, and conservative to the bone.

George took a fresh spoon from a drawer and stirred extract of vanilla into the warm milk, mulling the prospect of Otto Krug as a partner. He decided to take his neighbor to lunch at the Planter's Hotel.

○

After the two men were seated, a waiter approached with cups of consommé. George noticed Otto smack his lips.

"I don't have to remind a man of finance about the benefits of diversified holdings," George began.

A few moments later, the server returned and moved to whisk away the cups. Otto held up a stubby finger. "Vasn't finished."

"And that's what I want to talk to you about today, friend," George went on. "Otto, we're poised at the dawn of a golden era, an era of explosive retail commerce. Now's the time for investment. Our city, St. Louis, is the place."

"Der place?" Otto said. A guarded look fell across his soft features.

"For a retail emporium." George speared a sliver of roast lamb, dipped it into mint jelly, and set down his fork. "Think about it. Think about shoppers choosing from dozens of silk parasols, hundreds of mother of pearl buttons, cabinets filled with twill corsets. Think about trousers, not one pair but two dozen pairs, in every shade of gray."

Otto's gaze strayed to the dessert cart. "Department stores, so low class."

George signaled a waiter to bring the sweets. "Buying in bulk will undercut the corner shops. We'll offer clothing, housewares and toys at a higher quality and lower price, and in a more enjoyable atmosphere."

Otto dumped several teaspoons of sugar into his coffee, but said nothing.

"St. Louis is the fourth largest city in America," George went on, careful to keep his voice low, calm. "We're booming, Otto. All the new banks on Olive and Locust, and the new hotels. Here, have another a tart. Scruggs and William Barr beat us to the punch, you know. Their dry goods stores are up and running. Ever been there? Brisk business. Brisk. And there's the Famous Clothing Store —"

"Ya. Dat one I know. Der missus goes there."

"We'll beat them both."

"How?"

"We distinguish ourselves. First-quality merchandise. A glamorous shopping experience. We build the finest department store in Missouri, in the whole Midwest. We treat customers like gold. And we sell things they can't buy anywhere else."

Otto scraped the last crumbs from his plate. He wiped his lips. He twirled the tips of his mustache, and fiddled with his watch fob. George fumed silently.

Finally, the banker folded his hands across his belly and met George's gaze: "Why shouldn't Barr have a little competition? Better you und me be winners dan Barr, eh?"

By the time the waiter slid the check under George's saucer, the partners had come to terms. They would purchase the city block bounded by Washington, Lucas, Sixth and Seventh streets, raze the existing structures, and erect a modern dry goods emporium, sumptuous in every respect. George would run the business with a slight majority stake. Otto would keep the books and hold sole minority interest. Otto Krug's name would appear after George's on every document, at every store entrance, in every advertisement, in perpetuity.

"Make der letters *hoch und felt*," Otto said, sealing the deal with a handshake. "Big and Bold."

Within two years the acquisition phase was complete, demolition was under way, and architects were fine-tuning structural and decorative details. In 1881, three years after George took his neighbor to lunch, project managers were supervising construction of a multi-story, 300,000 square foot building on the site. Otto had long since resigned from the bank and was devoting his considerable energies to keeping the project on budget. George was criss-crossing the country, familiarizing himself with the competition.

He started in Chicago, at Marshall Field's store in the Loop. After touring the store top to bottom, George decided he, too, should have a restaurant for Reinhardt & Krug customers. He'd offer interior decorator services, like Field did, and relegate old inventory to the basement, like Field's. With a chuckle, George decided to name it the Rock-Bottom Bargains Department.

He took the train to Salt Lake City and walked the few blocks to Zion's Cooperative Mercantile Institution. He found the shelves held a jumble of work overalls and cough medicines, pitch forks, baling wire, and cowboy boots. He stayed the night and boarded an east-bound train.

Three days after leaving Utah, George was in New York City. He joined a small crowd on Sixth Avenue that had gathered in front of Macy's fancy-goods store. He elbowed his way to the front and smiled. Macy had installed a litter of kittens in one of his display windows, kittens dressed in doll clothes.

It was rainy in Philadelphia, but George found Phillip Wanamaker's show galleries bright and airy. He made notes about Wanamaker's spacious aisles and plentiful gas lamps and ceiling windows. He recorded his thoughts about the display cabinets and gift boxes, the return and delivery policies, the size and security of cash drawers, the proximity to streetcar stops, anything, everything.

Sometimes George assumed the identity of a peckish shopper.

"This shirt is inferior," he told a clerk at Macy's. "Your colleague sold it to me this morning and it's missing a button. Kindly summon your assistant manager."

"Can you special order the trousers in gray?" he asked at Wanamaker's. "Why not? Kindly summon your assistant manager."

If he judged the assistant manager to be sharp-minded, George waited on the sidewalk. At closing time, he would draw the man aside and offer him a job as a full department manager at the future Reinhardt & Krug.

"How soon can you be in St. Louis? By the end of the week? Good. Start telegraphing order inquiries to your finest sources in London. Tweeds and herringbones. Only the finest."

Meanwhile, Otto Krug was keeping his thumb on the construction schedule and maintaining a log of expenses down to the penny. Krug had wired George with only three stipulations:

On Sunday the emporium would be closed, of course, and the sidewalk windows shielded behind curtains.

The inventory of undergarments must be stored in closed cabinets, away from the public eye. Individual items were to be shown to customers with discretion.

Female sales clerks must refrain from wearing lipstick, rouge, perfume, bracelets, earrings, and brooches. Small timepieces pinned high on the shirt, like the one Herma wears, excepted.

Otto and Herma yearned to have children but were not so blessed. Over the years, Herma began to suffer from chronic nervousness and low spirits. Otto often ended a tedious day at the office by saddling a horse and trotting off to a beer garden. He would part with a nickel for a stein of lager and a knockwurst sausage. When the oompa band struck up a tune, he'd sing along with the burly workingmen on the bench beside him. The city's beer gardens were happy places that reminded him of his boyhood in Bavaria.

Reinhardt & Krug opened its doors to shoppers in the autumn of 1884, six years after a man in imminent danger of losing his home, his wife, his son and his bold dreams, a desperate man, answered a knock at the door.

The day was warm and bright. Reporters from St. Louis, Chicago, Kansas City and Little Rock filed dispatches hailing the event as first-class entertainment. They called the grand Beaux Arts building an architectural gem. They described the bronze doors, the marble floors and swirling plasterwork, even the gurgling central fountain. They likened Reinhardt & Krug to a holiday resort. They quoted Chandler Chouteau St. Denis as saying he never doubted the capabilities of Mr. Reinhardt, his son-in-law. In noting St. Denis is descended from Chouteaus, the reporters took the opportunity to remind their readers about the city's founding in 1763.

A young Auguste Chouteau had accompanied his step-father, Pierre Laclede, on a journey upriver from New Orleans to establish a fur trading post. One day Laclede and the boy scouted out a timbered bluff that sloped away from the Mississippi's west bank. Oblivious to the howling wind, Laclede swept his gaze from wooded groves to meadows and willow marshes, drinking in the wild beauty, beguiled.

"I have found a situation where I am going to form a settlement which might become, hereafter, one of the finest cities in America," Laclede shouted.

Auguste Chouteau cupped his hand at his mouth. "Known by what name, sir?"

"By name in honor of Louis."

On Reinhardt & Krug's opening day 45,000 citizens, one-tenth of the St. Louis population, poured through the doors of America's newest retail emporium. Women inspected lengths of ribbon and fingered Directoire dresses. Gentlemen tried on silk cravats and took walking sticks for a stroll down the aisles. Youngsters dashed through the Children's Department, a storybook kingdom of china-faced dolls and scooters, tin soldiers and mechanical banks and play cooking sets.

The day's best seller was a rabbit boa, fluffy as snow. A chocolate-colored gabardine afternoon coat was a close second. Both were presented on walkabout models, one of George's novel ideas. A brief incident cast a shadow over an otherwise perfect opening day.

"Madam? Ma'am?"

"Yes?"

"Is that an item from the store you have there? Excuse me, just there?"

September sun poured down on the birdlike woman as she stood outside the main entrance. With infinite reluctance, she withdrew from the folds of her skirt a pair of lace gloves. "And who are you?" she said, her voice quavering at the tattered edge of dignity.

"Store security, ma'am. Afraid you'll have to come with me. I am informed the item has not been paid for."

"You are mistaken, sir. Remove your hand." She began to speak faster and flap the gloves at him. "I am a court stenographer. I have been employed by the court for some time. I have left my eye glasses at home and, unhand me, sir. Can't you see I was merely transporting the gloves to daylight to inspect them more thoroughly?"

According to a brief account in the *Globe-Democrat* the following morning, Miss Pauline Pennington, 46, an unmarried stenographer, was detained after exiting the Sixth Street door with a pair of gloves secreted on her person. Security guards summoned Mr. George Reinhardt, co-proprietor. After a brief consultation, Mr. Reinhardt declared the woman had won an unannounced store contest. Miss Pennington left in triumph, waving high the lace gloves.

That night George dreamed the glorious department store he founded would prosper down through generations of Reinhardts. He smiled in his sleep, envisioning his son and grandsons wealthy beyond measure, revered as titans of commerce, venerated as social philanthropists, regarded as avatars of high style. Toward morning, in the milky haze of dawning cognition, a draught of dread brushed his face like wind whistling through a window crack, and he realized a profound and fearsome thing:

Affluence, reputation and position will go a long way toward insulating a family from tribulation, but not far enough.

No Middling Matter
1885

Kerry Patch, St. Louis

*T*om Conrad recognized the kid slumped on a splintery porch, head between his knees, spittle dripping out the side of his gob. Patrick Malloy, all greenish and hung over.

"Sleepin off the fine effects of the mash now, lad?"

"The devil with ya, Thomas."

"Elbow-bendin, and on yer saint's day as well. Get to yer feet. Tis vomit yer sittin in."

"All royal blood and noble, are ya?" Patrick ground the sleep from his eyes with scuffed knuckles. He scanned the block and saw his younger brother. "There now, here comes a fine lad, and at a gallop, too."

Terrence Malloy skidded to a stop at the porch. When he caught his breath, he said: "Old man Murphy's garage is open as a barn door. Seen 'im with me own eyes, stashin a cash box behind some old paint cans. A fiver in there, I'll warrant."

Patrick took in the news. He cocked an eyebrow and looked up at Tom: "You with us?"

Tom dug his hands in his pockets. "I'm not enthusiastic on it," he said, kicking a pebble.

"Yer never enthusiastic on it." Patrick turned his attention to his brother. "Gimme that fag, Terrence, stuck in yer teeth."

The Malloys were almost to the end of the block when Patrick called back: "Thomas, a cash box ain't no middling matter."

"It breaks me heart to miss the shenanigans of the day," Tom shouted, "bustin into private property and all, stealin a man's hard-earned money and tossin a stink bomb for good measure."

"Me life's a miserable failure," Patrick wailed, rounding the corner.

Tom Conrad meant to be a firefighter at the Biddle Street Station someday. He wasn't going to gum up his chances by hanging around with the likes of Malloys, even though he was a Mick, like them.

The Conrad's story was common enough. Most every family crammed into the cold-water flats of Kerry Patch could recite a similar version. County

Cork, County Sligo, it was all the same. Back in the1840s, a silent enemy had blown across Ireland's emerald fields. *Phytophthora infestans*. Blight.

Seamus Conrad was Tom's grandfather. It was Seamus' habit to carry his morning mug of tea out of doors and blow it cool as he paced the rows. One morning he ran a gnarled hand over the plants and noticed lesions on the leaves, small wounds surrounded by a yellow halo. He sucked in his breath. Seamus had only these potatoes to sustain his family. He turned over the leaf and saw powdery mold. His heart sank.

Seamus called to Margaret and the children. They trimmed the plants and kneaded manure and peat to the soil, frantic to save a harvest all but smote. All that summer a stench lingered over the decaying crop. Each rainfall soaked the soil with spores that attacked roots and brought on more rot. The harvest was pitiful small. Seamus tossed the culls to the hedges, just as his father and grandfather had done on the same land.

That winter the Conrads went hungry. In spring Seamus planted his seed potatoes, damaged though they were, and reinfected the soil. Wind and rain and every swipe of his hoe spread the spores. Potatoes in the ground turned blackish. The Conrads starved.

Seamus sold his farm for a pittance and brought his family to America. With his last dollar he rented a shack in St. Louis, in the Irish section, Kerry Patch.

A Misery'd Back
1890

Yazoo Delta, Mississippi

*E*smie skittered to a corner. Daddy was fumin again, stompin around the cabin, goin on about why they gotta live like slaves when Mister Lincoln proclaimed coloreds free years ago.

By most any measure of self-determination, Theo and Florelle Hobbs lived in bondage, indentured to the Crowder Plantation. Tick Crowder inherited the land from his pappy by dint of being born male, and first. Theo and Florelle worked Crowder land from dawn to sundown in purgatorial heat for wages depleted by the rent they paid on a Crowder-owned cabin and the provisions they bought from a Crowder-owned store.

Each morning during the harvest, Florelle patted pork fat onto Theo's shoulder. By noon the burlap strap had laid open his flesh again, a raw wound that glistened pink under his damp shirt. In dwindling light, Theo dragged a last sack of cotton from the field and lifted Florelle aboard the mule wagon, as if she were light as air, as if he weren't exhausted. He'd smile at Charity and Sugar, their older girls, and kiss Esmie, the youngest, near asleep in Florelle's lap. Theo and the other field men trudged along, shoulders slumped, necks runneled with sweat, following twin grooves carved by the weight of generations of slaves transported down the same dirt path.

Charity nudged her mother. "Sit up, Mama. You leanin again."

"Chile, my back's cricked somethin awful."

Esmie woke up and rubbed her mama's knobby spine. A misery'd back was a constant, just like heat, bug bites, leg scratches, thirst, exhaustion. "Cricked back ain't bad, though," Florelle told her girls, more than once. Her boys, too. "Pain make a body forget it be hungry."

Esmie tugged at her mother's skirt. "How old am I, Mama?"

"Sweetness, you nearabouts three," Florelle said, running fingers through the child's hair. "Y'all keep by me tomorrow, hear? Mama tired o' watchin y'all wander off. Charity and Sugar, y'all see Esmie wander off, holler, hear? Rain comin tonight. Snakes be out again."

Six of Florelle and Theo's eight children lived through birthing. Sam Lee, Willie, Dalton, Charity, Sugar, and Esmie. Florelle was determined to keep them alive.

The following morning, Esmie toddled along after her mother. Florelle worked her way through the rows, tugging cotton from browning bolls, her hands working in the steady, natural rhythm of the harvest. Around midday she straightened up and shook her head like a puppy with an old rag.

"Feel dizzy, Sweetness," she said, her voice a husky whisper. A moment later she sank to her knees, her ninth pregnancy come and gone.

"Daddy! Come quick." Esmie watched, horrified, as clots big as chicken livers passed from her mama's grunting body and landed with a sickening plop, scarlet possibilities seeping into dark delta soil. "Daddy!"

Theo swatted aside sharp-edged bolls and dashed across the rows. He drew Florelle into his arms and staggered to the wagon. On the way back to the cabin, Esmie sat beside the driver. She searched the sky, looking for angels to come help her mama. Theo hovered over Florelle's bed a good hour. When she finally fell asleep, he hoisted Esmie to his shoulders and hiked back to the fields. Tick Crowder was a ways off, standing in his fancy buggy. Esmie worried when she saw him pull off his straw hat and mop his pasty forehead. When he spat a trickle of chaw, the child knew something bad was about to happen.

"Done had enough of this crap, Hobbs. Y'alls fired. Got an hour to git off Crowder land."

Charity and Sugar helped Mama to the main road. Theo, Esmie and the boys carried everything they owned strapped to their backs. The nearest town was five miles off, Chattooka, a miserable no-count settlement half-buried in the Yazoo Delta, a town with little to offer but more heat, privation, and bigots.

Each spring cotton plants unfurled from Chattooka in all directions, rippling to the horizon in rows straight as corduroy. By summer, the town appeared to be floating in a sea of green, its smattering of low roofs barely visible from the through-road. In autumn the bolls burst, a million downy puffs shining in the moonlight like opals. Chattookans were of two minds about the sight. Some folks claimed it resembled a blizzard, though they'd never seen a single snowflake. Others swore the dots swaying on twilight breezes were ghosts, come out to dance.

Chattooka's single macadam street ran parallel to a bermed stretch of railroad track that bisected the town like an old scar. A general store, a Baptist church, and a disconsolate schoolhouse presided over the north side of town. On the opposite side of the berm, paths trickled off to shotgun cottages so rudimentary in configuration a bullet shot through the front door would fly out the back unimpeded. The cabins lacked indoor plumbing, electricity, window screens, privacy, and on many a day, breakfast.

A monolithic cotton gin marked the southern edge of town. For fifty years the gin had maintained its owners in relative prosperity and kept its employees, an uneasy mix of freed slaves and poor whites, all but destitute. Now and then accidents occurred at the gin, events that, while somewhat regrettable, went all but unnoticed by authorities half a county away.

In the morning Theo and the boys traipsed over to the hiring shack. The foreman pointed Theo to the giant cylinders studded with teeth that separate fiber from seed pods. He gave the boys a hard look and then sent Sam Lee and Willie to the suction pipe and little Dalton to the balers. Charity and Sugar followed Florelle to the fields. Each member of the family, even Esmie, knew they'd work until they dropped, defeated by the grinding life of field labor, the perils of the gin, or night-riding bigots.

Prime Pleasure Riding
1887

St. Louis

*A*s the hour of graduation approached, Leatham realized how little a degree in economics meant to him. His temples throbbed. There was no turning back.

Students and parents filed into Washington University's ceremonial hall. Leatham considered bolting, but a chorale of B-flat and C trumpets had struck up a series of pompous, dirgelike chords. The low buzz of conversation faded.

Swallowing a wave of panic, Leatham scanned the risers. Why do all my friends look damned happy? They're marching off a cliff, a step away from a lifetime of, what? monotonous desk jobs in dreary offices. He felt a familiar knob of dread rising in his throat and he thought it must be what a fox feels after a trapper's clamp snaps around its foot. In stentorian voice, acting Chancellor Marshall S. Snow rang out the names of the graduating class of 1887. Leatham looked to the parent section and saw joy tears splashing onto his mother's bosom corsage, saw his father was shooting his cuffs, nodding to other fathers.

After the ceremony, Charles Smith suggested they flag a trap, but it was a short distance to home, the weather nice, and so they decided to walk. In the living room, Charles folded his Sunday coat with the precision of a statehouse flag and draped it over a chair.

Leatham thrust a sheaf of creamy paper at his father. "I know it isn't what you planned for me, but …"

"What's this, son? Your diploma?"

"It's an employment contract."

Charles' bushy eyebrows shot up.

"Father, remember all the hoopla about Buffalo Bill's Wild West Show coming to St. Louis? Well I went over to the fairgrounds yesterday and it felt like I woke up after a four-year sleep."

"Sleep? Is that what you call a college education?"

There it was, Leatham thought, the brittle voice, the neck flush. Father's furious.

"It's not forever. A year, two at most. It'll be an adventure." He paused, and then added, "I can't start at the bank yet. I can't —"

"You can and you will. Boatman's is expecting you. It's all arranged."

Leatham was an only child. A short and square young man, he had intense brown eyes and dark hair that swirled around cowlicks on each side of his forehead. He looked to his mother for support, but found only the familiar signs of pending hysteria. Rebecca Smith was breathing in rapid, shallow puffs. Her watery eyes darted around the room. Leatham knew she was picturing him under the hooves of a wild stallion, shot with Indian arrows, stampeded by buffalo, bleeding to death.

"For heaven's sake, Charles, do something," she cried. "Leatham's running away with circus people."

Charles took his wife by the arm. Halfway up the stairs, he turned and said: "Leatham, you and I will resume this discussion after your mother is settled."

Leatham heard the pop of a cork. Soon, he knew, his mother would be drifting on a fog of laudanum, staring with detached interest at the corsage on her bedside table, its petals already browning at the edges. He sat on the piano stool and twirled a few times. He plunked the keyboard, trying to drown out the sounds from above, the snap of Sunday suspenders shrugged off, the clatter of pocket change flung onto a bureau, his mother's warbled voice calling his name. By week's end he was gone.

Dear Mother and Dad,

If only you could see the show! Sitting Bull walks into the ring in kingly fashion, and let me tell you he makes an impression. Hair plaits all the way to his waist and a black and white feather sticking straight up from his head. Father, I think you'd get on with Sitting Bull. He's a dignified man, and he speaks with pride about the time he and Red Cloud and Spotted Tail got together with President Grant. And boy oh boy, when Annie Oakley comes blazing into the ring and shoots a bullet right through an ace of spades, Mother, you'd love it.

Buffalo Bill Cody's Wild West show was a raucous, nostalgic look at how things were a generation earlier, when the American West was still wild. Bill's Lakota braves beat tom-toms. His medicine men performed rain dances. His cowboys rode upside down and raced around barrels in figure-eights. And his herd of longhorns stormed the ring, raising clouds of dust. And just when it seemed things couldn't be more spectacular, Buffalo Bill rode into the ring on a magnificent prancing horse. The stallion flicked

24

its tail and flared its nostrils, as if preparing to leap a canyon and gallop distant mesas. Bill coaxed the animal to a polite bow, waved his cowboy hat, and informed the folks he surely did appreciate them coming out for the show.

That summer the Wild West Show was invited to London to join celebrations honoring Queen Victoria's golden jubilee. The crew packed up the tents, costumes and animals and sailed to England. Leatham went along as a trick-horse and bronco rider. Afterward, though, it was back to the endless hoist-ups and tear-downs of the circuit, to campfire oatmeal, midnight mosquitoes, and shirts that never quite dried. For Leatham, the show life had lost its luster. During a stop in Quincy, Illinois, he took a bad dive over the flattened ears of a bucking bronco. Splayed face-down in sawdust, he decided it was better to die of boredom at the Boatman's Savings Bank than get kicked to death by a horse.

Leatham decided to go home. If he couldn't return with his pride intact, at least he could show up with cash in his pocket. That night he paced the rows of tents until he came across a cowboy throwing a looped rope at an old box.

"Hiya, Frank."

"Leatham."

"Practicing?"

"Yup." The cowboy gathered up the rope and executed a near perfect flat spin, his hand cutting clockwise circles in the soft autumn air.

"Got me some buckskin chaps awhile back," Leatham said. "Broke in good and soft. Interested?"

"Maybe. Eight bits?"

"Nah."

"Four bucks, then."

"That'll do."

From a distance, show manager Nate Salsbury heard the exchange. He pointed to a matched set of nickel-plated pistols riding low on Leatham's hips. "Sellin them, too?"

"Nah. The Colonel gave them to me after the jubilee."

"What else ya got then?"

Leatham took off his leather vest and draped it over his arm like a warm flapjack. "This. Nice beadwork on it."

Salsbury took a dry draw on his pipe and thwacked the bowl against his boot heel. "Now that there's a beauty."

At the end of the St. Louis run, Leatham and Buffalo Bill shook hands and parted ways. Reluctant to go straight home, Leatham dropped his bedroll at a livery stable and walked to a nearby saloon. The bartender poured a glass of beer and jerked his head, calling Leatham's attention to a piano man playing in the shadows. "Colored boy got fire ants in his fingers tonight."

"He's lively. That's a fact."

"Have another?"

"No hurry."

The bar was empty except for a table of geezers playing desultory poker. The piano man lowered the lid and ambled off. Leatham ordered another beer. For a long while, the slap-down of a losing hand and hollow flap of a fresh shuffle were the only sounds. The bartender dunked glasses in a pail of murky water.

"Ain't my business, but something preying on you?"

Leatham thumped his fist on the counter. "The minute I get home my dad'll have me hog-tied to a desk, filling out loan papers."

"Don't sound like a bad thing."

Leatham grimaced.

A man pushed through the door, adding the treacly scent of French cologne to the more earthy aromas of the place. Leatham sized him up quick. A dandy, all done up in white. Boots shiny as Buffalo Bill's show saddle.

The man was bell-shaped, with small, darting eyes and wispy hair parted low and scraped to the opposite side. He ordered rye whiskey and took a sip, pinkie finger extended. "Looks like you and me the only thirsty fellas in St. Louie tonight," he said, sidling up to Leatham.

"Mmm-hmm."

"Got a minute, son?"

"Not your son, but sure."

"Son, I hail from the great city of Baton Rouge —"

Leatham took a long swallow. Haven't been back in St. Louis a day, he said to himself, and already I've acquired a second father.

"— and due to the pressin financial obligations of a client of mine stupid enough to sell a club-footed horse to Judge Virgil Pardo, I am authorized to sell a parcel of valuable property my client owns in the sovereign state of Mizzourah."

Leatham stared into his half-empty glass.

"Twenty acres, prime," the man went on. "Yonder west a ways, off a post road. Half-day ride, no more. I mention the price? Low. Barely gonna be sufficient to secure bail for my client, an esteemed citizen of Vermillion Parish languishin in a jail cell. And that ain't even countin what I need for jury persuasion."

Leatham and the bartender exchanged looks. Within minutes they learned the lawyer was a Southern Baptist, a gambler, a wayward husband, and the disheartened father of six buck-toothed girls. He was rattling off the names of each daughter, declaring Wanda Jolene his least favorite, when Leatham pinched his cowboy hat in place, nodded to the bartender, and pushed through the swinging doors. Sleep didn't come easy that night, though. Leatham tossed and turned on his bedroll, envisioning that piece of property just a half-day's ride from the city.

The following morning, he found the lawyer and they rode out to the property. The lawyer sat in the rented buggy, watching Leatham pace off boundary lines. Leatham was nearly out of sight of the post road when he came across an old Indian riding trail that looped through a field of purple coneflowers. He followed it until it forded a creek and mounted a challenging hill on the opposite side. By then, he was smiling.

 Prime pleasure riding, Leatham told himself, from spring turkey shooting straight through October.

The day was cool and clear. The air smelled of dried leaves. Breezes ruffled the tall, dry grass. Another month, Leatham thought, and I can tap those sugar maples. And that stand of pine over there, easy felling. Near the road was a small stone church. Presbyterian, Leatham decided. Been here awhile, too, by the looks of it. Graveyard and all. Folks coming to church, that's opportunity.

Leatham had brought a light lunch in his rucksack: a wedge of cheese, a few soda crackers, and a Bartlett pear. While pacing off the meadow, he ate the creamy pear and absently dropped the core. The heel of his boot sank four Bartlett seeds into the soft soil.

In the buggy, the lawyer made do with the last of the Flemish Beauty pears he'd brought from down home. When he finished, he tossed the core out into the tall grass. Eight Flemish Beauty seeds bounced across the loam, not far from the Bartlett seeds.

Leatham returned to the buggy and stood stroking the horse's neck. "How much?"

The lawyer cupped beefy hands around his lapels. "Son, this property's worth two, three times what we're askin. Were it not for my client's dire situation …"

Leatham tucked his chin and murmured to the horse.

The lawyer started over, his tone confidential. "Fact of the matter, y'all might say the place is ghostly. That there's the drift of it."

"Ghostly?"

"See them headstones yonder? Those souls is buried in consecrated ground, but I reckon that don't much matter. Where I come from, departed loved ones come risin on up again after every good gully-washer."

Leatham stifled a laugh. *Mr. White Linen's superstitious and I'm his only nibble.*

That night at the Planter's House Hotel, Leatham and the lawyer sealed the deal over a bottle of Kentucky bourbon, green turtle soup, and sirloin steak smothered in onions. The property cost Leatham most of his savings as well as the nickel-plated pistols.

During his summer with the Wild West Show, Leatham discovered he loved horses, their quiet nickering at night, the way their coats shine after a good curry combing, their delicate legs and lustrous eyes, their smell. Back at the livery stable, he sketched a horse and carriage and printed "Leatham Smith Stables" in a horseshoe curve. Satisfied, he turned the lantern knob until the flame died.

When they heard their son's plans, Charles and Rebecca Smith were stupefied. Leatham assured his mother he'd visit every other Saturday, but nothing he could say or do would mollify his father. With the last of his money, Leatham bought a mule, a cast iron skillet, and provisions to last the winter. At the edge of town he found his father waiting in a hired trap. Without a word, Charles handed his son two warm blankets, a fine handsaw, and a jar of twelve-penny nails.

During the long ride on the bony back of a mule, Leatham had plenty of time to think. *Came mighty close to being hog-tied to a bank desk. Guess I owe my freedom to a jack-ass lawyer and a club-footed horse. Best get post holes dug before the ground hardens. Sink a line in the shade, under the chestnut trees.*

The winter was mild but wet. Leatham slept in a canvas tent, spit-roasted squirrel and rabbit over an open fire, chopped wood, dug holes, set hitching posts, and lashed pine planks together to form a lean-to stable. Unseen, the pear seeds germinated and set down tap roots.

Each Sunday, country folk rode up the post road for services at the stone church. Leatham declined their invitations to join at worship, and they did not press. As winter wore on, Leatham and the church folk fell into a routine. He would bring pails of warm water and oats to their tethered horses, check the animals' teeth, clean pebbles from hooves, feel for windgalls and shin splints. The churchgoers, in turn, included him in their prayers and gave him a penny or two before they headed home. For Leatham, the sound of familiar hymns ringing through stained glass, the smell of saddle leather, and the sight of farm horses snorting clouds into the crystal air was payment enough.

In spring, a country doctor approached Leatham about boarding two pleasure horses. On Easter Sunday, Leatham tied a fat hare to his saddle, rode his mule to the city and had supper with his parents. The following morning he bought two brood mares at auction. Back in the country, he fenced off the pear saplings so the horses wouldn't nibble them down.

By the second winter, Leatham had enclosed the lean-to and filled seven stalls. By the third, Leatham Smith Stables was doing business out of a handsome Bavarian-style barn topped with a horse-and-carriage weather vane. Leatham never felt more alive than when assisting at difficult night foalings or leading a leggy colt to its first stilt-legged romp through his clovered pasture.

In April of the tenth year, the pear trees blossomed.

That fall Leatham invited the churchgoers to a picnic in his meadow. They sat at plank-wood tables, chatting, passing platters of roast pork and fire-grilled corn. A few intrepid souls dipped spoons into Mason jars filled with Leatham's homemade specialty: Nickel-Plated Pistol Pear Relish.

It Was All So Marvelous
1904

Portland Place, St. Louis

*T*he most stupendous event of the new century was unfolding practically in Albert and Emily's backyard. The Louisiana Purchase Exposition. The St. Louis World's Fair! Exhibitors, dignitaries, carpenters, electricians, plumbers, animal handlers, language translators, anthropologists, ethnologists, snake charmers, souvenir vendors, food providers and musicians started streaming into the city months ago. By opening day, tens of thousands of fairgoers had poured into town by rail, riverboat and horse. Hotels and boarding houses were putting up visitors on cots in the hallways. Restaurants, taverns, saloons and beer gardens brimmed with excited chatter.

Albert and Emily Reinhardt were determined to brave the opening day throngs. They had quietly decided to take little Phillip the following week. They would take George, Albert's ailing father, in his cane-seat wheelchair later in the summer; the heat would be worse, of course, but the crowds would have thinned.

"What a shame your mother isn't still alive," Emily said, securing her new spring hat with a long mother-of-pearl pin. Light streamed into the foyer through a fan-window over the door. "She was so proud of her Chouteau ancestors. She always said Auguste Chouteau helped make St. Louis a first-class city."

Albert beamed. "A world's fair city."

Albert was just thirty-two when his mother died of diphtheria. No one could fathom how she contracted the disease, but then no one noticed the sickly, wheezing dairyman delivering milk and cream to the Reinhardts' kitchen door, coughing phlegm into his hand and hastily wiping it off before grasping the lip of the glass bottle. After the funeral, George fell into a deep melancholia. Weeks dragged on. When finally Albert encouraged his widowed father to come live at Portland Place, the old man was so broken he put up little resistance. With infinite tact, Albert assumed control of Reinhardt & Krug, the department store George and the late Otto Krug founded with a handshake back in 1884.

Albert was expertly groomed for his new role. When he was still in high school, his father sent the boy to work on the loading docks every Saturday morning. After Albert graduated from St. Louis University, George assigned his son to a six-month stint in each department. Albert was a quick learner and diligent, a conservative visonary who took a keen interest in all things modern. One of his first decisions as president was to install moving staircases to the store's upper floors. He also offered incentives to anyone on the staff who proposed a newfangled item that turned out to be a best-seller. The employees who suggested safety razors, vacuum cleaners, and five-cent boxes of Crayola brand crayons had taken home a bonus in their weekly paychecks.

On a late April morning, President Roosevelt declared via telegraph the World's Fair officially open. Albert and Emily set out early. By mid-morning Albert had paid one dollar for two admission tickets and, gripping Emily by the arm, joined the crush of sightseers streaming through the gates. Organizers had warned against trying to see everything in one fell swoop. After all, the fairgrounds were spread across 1,200 acres and contained hundreds of exhibits. Albert made a beeline for the Palace of Electricity. An hour later he steered Emily to the Palace of Varied Industries, and then the Palace of Manufacturers.

At noon Emily insisted they join the long queue at the wireless telegraph exhibit, for she yearned to "speak by telegraph" to her aunt in Connecticut. Afterward, they lunched on platters of cold sliced pork and warm sauerkraut at an outdoor café. The afternoon brought more exotic activity. Albert suffered through a bumpy ride on a dromedary and tried to remain impassive while a strange little man wearing a turban draped a boa constrictor around his shoulders, rather like a woman's stole. To Albert's great relief, Emily informed the man they must go now, immediately, please remove the snake, they were due to meet friends in the Japanese gardens. Or was it the Tyrolean Alps?

They strolled along happily, with no particular destination, past a life-sized statue of a cow made of butter. At a replica of an Indonesian village Emily averted her eyes, for the villagers on display were completely naked. Albert stayed a long while at a log cabin that claimed to be the one in which Abraham Lincoln was born. Emily suggested they take a ride in an Irish jaunting car. They bought a commemorative Indian head penny for Phillip, a 1904 World's Fair paperweight for Albert's father, and a ruby-glass souvenir cup, for Emily. In the late afternoon, Albert handed a dime to a vendor and watched with dismay as the man scooped out a dollop of chocolate ice cream and sat it atop a cone-shaped waffle.

"What's this? No cup and spoon?"

"Don't need 'em," the vendor laughed. "This here's a World's Fair Cornucopia."

Albert asked Emily if she would enjoy a gondola ride in one of the Forest Park lagoons.

"Yes, love," she said, smiling, "I would. The perfect end to a fair-ly perfect day."

It was dark when Albert's Packard pulled up to the gates at Portland Place. Nanny had tucked little Phillip in bed hours ago. Old George was asleep, too. Albert lighted a lamp and climbed into bed next to Emily.

"I'll never get to sleep," she murmured, fingering a loose button on her nightgown.

"Nor I," he said. "Mr. Sousa's marching music is still ringing in my ears."

"That Observation Wheel, I'm not sure we should allow Phillip on that contraption."

Albert rose up on an elbow to face her. "Oh, I think it's safe enough. Besides, it's the only way to get a bird's eye view of the grounds."

"And did you see them cooking that beefsteak?"

"Well-done in less than six minutes!"

"What was your favorite thing?" she asked, her voice dreamy.

Albert clasped his hands behind his head. "It was all so marvelous. The flying machines, I suppose. You?"

"The sparkly lights on the Pike. Ten thousand! And seeing you, dear, trying to keep your dignity on top of a camel."

"Very funny," he said, stroking her hair. For awhile they relived the day's sights and sounds in silent reverie. Then they both spoke at once.

"That air conditioning exhibit, darnest thing I ever saw."

"The water cascades at Art Hill. Oh, and the aviary."

"Conditioned air. Do you realize that thing could revolutionize life in the tropics?"

"Parrots and macaws. And the cotton candy. Won't Phillip just love that?"

"Mmm-hmm."

Emily tossed off the sheet and walked to the window. The air was warm, the sky ablaze with stars. Moonbeams revealed the lush outline of her figure beneath her light gown. That night, she conceived her second and last child.

O

Shortly after Christmas, Dr. Burton paid a call at Portland Place. He concluded his weekly examination of Emily with a sigh, as if the matter was out of his hands.

"In light of your elevated blood pressure, my dear, I must insist on delivering the child at Mullanphy."

Albert kissed Emily's forehead and gestured for the doctor to join him in the hall.

"I'm not for it," Albert said after he closed the bedroom door. "My mother was taken to a hospital, and she died there four days later."

Dr. Burton tucked his stethoscope into his black bag. "Mr. Reinhardt, Mullanphy Hospital is the safest place for your wife, when the time comes."

"Hospitals are reeking death traps, sir. The places overflow with indigents spreading every sort of base disease. City Hospital is out of the question."

"I am not commending your wife to an unsanitary venue or a death trap, sir, and I am not suggesting City Hospital."

Albert was too worked up to hear a word the doctor said. He jabbed a finger at the man's chest and rambled on: "The original place was a horror. People dying of cholera in the wards. Charwomen from City Hall brought over to work as day nurses. And after hours, you know who gave the babies their bottles? A night watchman, that's who."

Behind the bedroom door, Emily plucked at the lace edging on her pillow case.

Emily Slayback Wilson was reared to fulfill a role no more or less important than the wife of a prominent St. Louisan. After years of home-tutoring, she was sent to Nashville, to a finishing school for young ladies. She took lessons in French, elocution, deportment, needlework, watercolor painting, and light poetry, a formal education constructed to avoid undue mental stimulation and infestations of radical notions.

At eighteen, Emily swanned into the welcoming embrace of society, and met Albert. A society wife was expected to be an accomplished hostess and an engaging guest, to join certain philanthropic committees but decline others, to engage in light badinage at luncheons and teas, to read romantic novellas, exchange recipes, supervise the help, and shop. In these endeavors, Emily surpassed all expectations.

Dr. Burton closed his satchel with an irritated snap. "City Hospital has been completely rebuilt, but I am referring your wife to Mullanphy Hospital. You must understand it is imperative to Emily's health, and the child's." With that, the doctor brushed past Albert and rapped on the bedroom door. He went in without waiting for a response.

"Emily, my dear, I'm sure you overheard. Rest assured. Mullanphy is a safe and modern facility. It services families like yours, dear. Only the finest. You will have a private room, and I will perform the procedure personally." He placed two fingers on Emily's wrist and consulted his pocket watch. He found her pulse slightly fast, but steady.

A week later Emily endured a brief confinement on an iron rail bed in Mullanphy Hospital, attended by wimpled Sisters of Charity. When delivery was imminent, orderlies wheeled her to a tiled surgery room. Dr. Burton administered the anesthesia personally, a quantity sufficient to render his patient unconscious. Frederick Maximilian Reinhardt slid into the world evidencing little inclination to be burdensome. With his first gurgling breath, the infant broke into a triumphant smile.

Emily remained hospitalized for the normal duration of ten days. Her private room began to resemble a flower shop. Beyond the window, however, the urban vista was monochromatic under low banks of ash-colored clouds. Emily liked to breathe on a window pane and trace the skyline, rooftops and steeples, bare-branched trees, even the ridges of stale snow marching along the curbs. She watched carriage horses trot smartly up to the hospital entrance and stamp their hooves as they waited; she laughed when they left droppings that steamed and quickly froze, and she wondered if everything was all right at home.

When the baby was a week old, Albert decided it was safe to take Phillip to visit his mother. He twined a cashmere scarf around his neck and stood at the front door, scanning the block. When he spotted Phillip, he smiled. The boy had rolled his hoop across the boulevard and almost to the gate house.

"Hitch up your socks, Phillip," he called. "We're going to see Mother and your new brother."

Stevens kept the family Packard in fine working order. Three mornings a week, he gave the sedan a good wash and buffed wax. Even so, Albert pulled a linen handkerchief from his pocket and wiped imaginary specks of dust from the head lamps. Phillip tugged off a mitten and searched for a smudge to wipe, too.

"Check the straps on the side-hamper son. Don't want it to fall off, right?" Albert said, hiking up to the driver's seat. Stevens turned the crank once, twice, three times, and the engine roared to life. Albert advanced the spark, smiling at the car's throaty purr.

"Hang on, boy! Here we go!"

At the hospital, Phillip stood beside his mother's bed, stiff as a toy soldier. "I've missed you, Mother. When are you coming home?"

Emily ran her fingers across the comb-ridges in Phillip's hair. My son is even more fastidious than his father or grandfather, she was thinking. "Look, darling, outside. Do you see Forest Park?"

"I think I do."

"Do you remember the things we saw last summer at the fair? The Mexican village? The soap-bubble fountain?"

Albert was arranging a fresh spray of yellow roses in a vase when clacking rosary beads announced Sister Hermita's approach. "Time to leave," she said, ending the visit with the surety of a guillotine.

Albert led Phillip down the hall. At the nursery window, he turned their heavy winter coats inside out, folded them over his arm, and hoisted the boy up until his toes gained purchase on the sill.

"Say hello, son. The baby's name is Frederick. Can you say Frederick?"

Phillip pressed his palms to the glass.

"What's the matter, boy? Cat got your tongue? Freee-drick."

Phillip balled his fists, straining to pronounce the troublesome word. "F-r-k."

Albert struggled to hold the boy. Come on son, he thought, I know you can say it. My father would have put me down and marched away by now. "Try again, son," Albert whispered. "Take your time."

"F-r-ritz!"

Albert hesitated. He and Emily disliked nicknames.

"Fritz!" Phillip twisted around and raised hopeful eyes to his father.

Albert patted his son's head. "Fritz. A fine name."

Even as a child, Albert had realized his father was a powerful force in a sophisticated world. But he yearned for just a regular dad, one who would march toy soldiers onto a pretend battlefield and roll toy trains along a track. One who could take a broken mechanical bank down to a basement workshop and fix it, or beckon a boy onto his lap and make up stories about pirates and police detectives.

Once a year, little Albert got his wish. Shortly before Christmas, George would lift his son into a sleek phaeton, pull a wool lap blanket across their knees, and draw him close. Albert would take in the rich, spicy scent of his father's cologne, and be happy. Then off they'd go, trotting along snowy streets toward Reinhardt & Krug. Along the way, George would instruct Albert on the importance of proper accessories.

"A man's pocket watch, his horse, his carriage, his wife, these are the most vital indicators of social position," George told the boy. "Choose well and you will be regarded as a cultivated person. Now, what are the four things?"

"A wife, a horse, a carriage, a pocket watch."

"Good. When we get there, be on your good behavior. You know how Mr. Krug loves his little holiday visits with you."

"Yes, Father."

Albert remembered his father observed, rather than participated in these annual visits with Mr. Krug. George would lean against the frame of Krug's office door, examining his fingernails, looking for flaws in the barber's buff. When Albert was young, he wondered if his father's partner might be Santa Claus, for Krug had a snowy beard by then, and evenings at beer gardens had produced an enormous belly.

"You been a gut boy, ya?" Krug always began, draping a thick arm around the boy's sloping shoulders.

"Yes, sir."

"No gambling?"

At that, George would chuckle.

"No, sir."

"Gut. Now stand straight and read plenty of books."

It was always the same. With an exaggerated wink, Krug would open a drawer and hand Albert a velvet pouch filled with quarters.

"The boy resembles you, George."

Albert did indeed have his father's lanky frame and gray-blue eyes half-hidden under thick lashes. He had his father's languid expression and engaging tilt of the head. In fundamental ways, though, Albert was altogether different. George hungered for wealth and created it; Albert was somewhat uncomfortable with the prosperity into which he was born. George yearned for acclaim and earned it; Albert regarded social prominence as a responsibility. George valued luxury; Albert's greatest treasures were his wife and children.

Having marched in lockstep after his father, Albert envied men with the freedom to chart their own course. He wondered whether he might have made a good lawyer, had his future at Reinhardt & Krug not been proscribed. A professor of history, maybe, or philosophy. What Albert took to heart from those long-ago holiday visits with Mr. Krug was the old man's simple advice: Read plenty of books.

At St. Louis University, Albert often plucked random volumes from the library shelves, brought them home, and read by lamplight long into the night. Critical reviews of the work of Pissaro in art magazines. Essays on politics. Astronomical charts and medical texts. Anything, everything. By his junior year, Albert could describe the function of the spleen, point out Orion in the night sky, and sketch intricate patterns of Gustavian design. Years of Jesuit education inculcated in him the resolve to live within the guidelines of a higher order, but adhere to a personal creed.

The Middle of Nowhere
1904

Yazoo Delta, Mississippi

*C*hile, git on over to the store and ask Moses Butters has he got work."

Theo swished a fly exploring his breakfast biscuit. On the subject of whether Esmie should get a paying job, he was adamant. The girl was fifteen, thereabouts. High time she stopped hanging around.

Esmie found Moses in his usual spot: out back of the store, hunkered on a wood crate, upturning the morning's first jug.

"Y'all done startin' early today. Y'all stink, too," Esmie said. To her way of thinking, Moses neither expected nor required civility, and certainly hadn't earned it.

The man was broadcasting a potent scent comprised of spit-up moonshine, spat-out chaw, body odor and lard-fried catfish, with musky undertones of piss. Moses didn't believe in hygiene. He disliked water, was suspicious of soap, and regarded bathing on an annual basis as sufficient. From one season to the next, Moses shuffled around Chattooka in the same overalls and armpit-rotted long underwear. Once in a great while, when he smelled so ripe even the dogs slinked away in search of sweeter air, his woman scraped off the filthy clothes and left Moses to stand buck-naked anywhere he liked while she gave the god-awful things a good creek rinse. Over the years, life had parted Moses from most of his hair, several teeth, and a thumb.

Esmie kicked at an open tin can, flustering a colony of ants that had been gorging on dried bean juice. "Moses, y'all got work or not?"

Moses squinted, sliding sideways as he passed a purgative blast. He didn't seem to hear the question, so Esmie went on, louder:

"I can read if the words ain't too big. Write my name and do sums."

"Up to what?" Moses said, rubbing trembly fingers in circles at his temples.

"I can make change for a dollar."

"Good enough. Nothin goes for more'n a buck or two."

According to every indicator of potential advancement, the Chattooka General Store was as far as Esmie would rise. She was a black girl with a sixth grade education acquired at a one-room Southern schoolhouse situated in the middle of nowhere. The classroom was ill-equipped for success. The teacher resorted to the Bible and the willow switch in equal measure. Behind her desk was a framed sketch of a long-dead president, a faded map showing 41 of the 45 states, and a droopy American flag tacked to the wall. The students sat on long wood benches, furniture that encouraged the little ones to swing their legs and squirm and doomed the older ones to slouching posture. They learned by sing-song recitation: alphabet letters, wars and presidents. They worked sums in chalk on slate boards which they wiped clean with their shirt-sleeves at the end of the lesson. The schoolhouse emptied at the beginning of spring tilling and did not open again until five months later, after the harvest.

The school, the dozy store, and a clapboard chapel formed the half-hearted hub of town. Each morning rheumy-eyed men took up residence on Moses' porch, content to watch the world whiz by an inch at a time. Mongrel dogs flopped at their feet. Children wandered over and snacked on paint chips flaking off the wobbly railing; toddlers born to Chattooka mothers and grandmothers roamed as soon as they were old enough to pull themselves upright. When the morning's diaper sagged with waste, they tolerated the inconvenience a spell and then simply stepped out of the thing, barely breaking stride.

Esmie cranked open the store's screen door. The rusty return coil screeched. While her eyes adjusted to the sudden gloom, she took in the familiar smells of the place — oats, peppermint candy, broom straw, coffee, pickles, dust.

Moses was negotiating the porch steps as if they were rafts on the high seas. "Ain't no purveyor of fancy goods. Ain't no sparkly big-city store. Only things I carry is things that sell."

Esmie frowned. She'd need to learn the store's barter system, or make up her own version. A dozen eggs for a tin of snuff, say? That sounded about right. Six stalks of rhubarb for a spool of sewing thread. A manure shovel for a plucked tom turkey. She glanced down the two short aisles as if seeing the store's inventory for the first time. Nails, cook pots, and bolts of cloth were piled in a clutter on wood shelves. Cotton work shirts and aprons dangled from pegs, one on top of the other. Brooms, rakes, spades, and fishing rods leaned into a corner. Barrels of flour and briny pickles too, with their lids half off.

"The tobaccy and shotgun cartridges is in these here cabinets," Moses went on. "Nobody gets at 'em without payin. Any questions, girly?"

Esmie tried to think. "How long my shift? What y'all payin?"

Moses was already gone. Behind him, the screen door shut with a slap. Esmie leaned her elbows on the counter and stared out at the street, scrunching her eyes against the blinding daylight.

Well Below the Water Line
1904-06

Licata, Sicily

*T*he child was named Vincenzo. *Conqueror*.

The winter following his birth, his father left the shadowed lanes and soft-sand beaches of his hometown in Sicily and boarded a ship for America. In Angelo Gibaldi's pocket was a $24 ticket for passage in steerage, ten dollars in cash, and the family grappa recipe. From New York, Angelo traveled by riverboat to Chicago. He took a three-dollar-a-week room in the city's Little Sicily neighborhood and found a job washing dishes at a Greek café. He could read and write in English decently enough, and he quickly started earning a few extra nickels writing letters for neighbors.

○

"Giuseppa, take your baby outside. Fresh air good for bambinos."

"Yes, Mama."

Giuseppa gathered up little Vincenzo. Wet again, she murmured. At the edge of town she chose a route that led up a steep hill. On either side of the path, she saw familiar olive groves, vineyards, and fields of artichoke quilting the countryside. It was autumn. Soon, she knew, farmers would gather the woody trimmings and dormant vines, and the morning air would smell of burning. Winded by the climb, Giuseppa rested a moment and looked to the teeming port below. Her heart was torn. She was terrified to leave her home and family, yet she yearned for Angelo. And when she thought of their new life in America, she felt a tingle of excitement.

Inside Castello St. Angelo, she set Vincenzo in a pew and rubbed her belly, round with another child. She dropped a coin into the collection box and smiled at the metallic clink. Blessed Virgin, she prayed, God the Father allowed you to live with your husband. Send me to America to live with my husband.

In the fall, Papa Gibaldi handed Giuseppa a letter. She tore it open. It was from America, from Angelo.

"He send the money?"

"Yes, Papa, he send."

Papa booked passage for Giuseppa, Vincenzo and the new baby, Salvatore. Giuseppa's eight-year-old brother, Francesco, was going to America, too. They made the eighty-mile journey to Palermo in a donkey cart. At the docks, Papa pointed to a steamship with black funnels emblazoned with Maltese crosses.

"That's her. The *Gregory Morch.*"

Giuseppa felt as if she had swallowed a stone. "I hear people talk about the diphtheria sickness on ships."

"Giuseppina, wipe that sick-dog look off your face," the old man snapped, using the elaborated form of her name. "The captain is a fine sailor. The ship, she is sound. You will be fine. Better than here."

"I know, Papa. But still."

"But still, now go. Go."

Giuseppa recited the Apostles' Creed out loud all the way up the gangplank.

"You're running the words together," Francesco said, shying away from crewmen standing by with buckets of disinfectant.

"Hush, brother. Pray yourself if you don't like my praying."

Giuseppa joined 1,763 third-class passengers who would cross an ocean in the rocking belly of the ship. For seventeen days she lived below the waterline, shared a single sour mattress with the three children, stood in line for ladled meals, for the fetid toilets, for a hurried sponge bath behind a curtain. She yearned for a glimpse of the sun.

One day, the ship's massive hull shuddered. The horn brayed and from the bridge came a series of piercing whistles. First class stewards knocked deferentially at stateroom doors. On the second class decks, butlers walked the corridors chiming bells. No discreet announcements greeted the passengers in steerage.

"Heavenly Mother, what is happening?" Giuseppa cried. "The engines, they growl like a bear."

A passing crewman clicked his tongue. "The captain's been making thirteen knots since Palermo. Now he's got to bring 4,800 tons of boat to a stop."

Giuseppa drew the babies close. "Francesco, we're in America."

"*Bravissimo!*"

"Go stand in line. See? There, where people are lining up? I'll change the baby and come stand by you."

The ship docked at the Battery. Stewards escorted thirty-eight first-class passengers to the main deck, elegant ladies and gentlemen who waved gaily to loved ones on the dock as they made their way down the gangplank, a fashionable parade of swishing silk taffeta, fluttering parasols, top hats and ivory-handled walking sticks. The twenty passengers in second-class emerged next. They took in the crisp harbor air and the magnificent skyline, and turned for a last look at the ship's enormous black and red funnels. At last crewmen herded the steerage passengers up interior stairways and shunted them onto tugboats for another, albeit briefer, water crossing. Whitecaps jutted from the dark swells. Giuseppa drew her shawl tight. Exhausted, confused, wrested from her momentary toe-hold on America, she and the children faced a protracted stopover at Ellis Island.

At three minutes before midnight on November 24, 1906, Vincenzo Gibaldi, age two, entered the land of opportunity. The boy was ravenous, pee-soaked, and wailing.

○

At three minutes before midnight on November 24, 1906, Frederick Maximilian Reinhardt was sound asleep in a spindled crib on Portland Place. The child was clean, dry, and contented. Earlier, little Fritzie's nanny had lowered him into a high chair painted with storybook scenes and fastened a bib over his sailor suit. A patient child, Fritzie twiddled the strings of his bib while Nanny offered him morsels of boiled chicken on a monogrammed silver spoon.

Ego te Baptizo
1908

St. Louis

When he applied for a job at the Biddle Street fire station, Tom Conrad tacked two years onto his true age. Afterward, he went to confession.

"Are ya sorry, Tommy-lad, for tellin a lie?"

"Yes, Father," Tom lied.

The fire captain knew, of course. The boy couldn't have been more than fifteen. Every weekend he hung around the station house, sweeping up, sharpening pencils, emptying waste cans. Once he even brought a sack of sugar cookies, still warm from his ma's oven. Over time, the captain saw young Conrad was a quick learner and eager to get ahead, unlike most of the Kerry Patch micks. As soon as he had an opening, the captain took Tom on.

Fifty-one steam engine companies served and protected the citizens of St. Louis. Tom started out at Biddle Street, transferred to a firehouse on Pine, then one on Market. He worked his way up from kitchen boy to stoker to ladder man. After more than twenty years with the department, Tom was district chief at a station on the near South Side, within walking distance of his house and miles from the old Kerry Patch neighborhood. The brick bungalow wasn't big or showy — couple of bedrooms upstairs, small garden out back — but Tom and Mary were thrilled. Doris, their little girl, was only a year old, but soon she would have to sleep in a youth bed with side rails. The new baby would need the crib.

The crowning of Lydia Marie Conrad's downy head was announced by her paternal grandmother, who assisted the birthing. Wrested from her mother's body, Lydia basked in beams of adulation. After Gramma Conrad transferred the infant to a bassinet, the house finally quieted. Doris toddled into her mother's room, peeked over the top of the bassinet, and burst into tears.

The baptismal day dawned cool and clear. Early daffodils speckled Mary's garden like dollops of butter. The scents of damp grass, thawed earth, and star magnolia drifted down the street on gentle air. During the short walk to church, Tom spotted a cluster of dandelions pushing up from sidewalk cracks, and he picked a bouquet for Doris. By the time they got to Our Lady of Sorrows, Doris had plucked off all the flower heads.

The Rev. Bernard Stolte dipped his thumb into oil of chrism and made the sign of the cross on the baby's forehead. *Lydia Marie, ego te baptizo in nomine Patris, et Filii, et Spiritus Sancti.*

Trussed in heirloom Irish lace, Lydia opened her cupid lips and yawned.

Disinclined to Tarry
1908

Storyville, New Orleans

*T*he residents of Storyville — permanent, occasional, and hourly—regarded Miss Alice Breaux as almost pretty, an assessment that was the God's honest truth. Save for the misfortune of an underformed chin and the sharp eyes of a raptor, Alice might have been a fair looker, once.

Breaux House was the most exquisite bordello in Storyville. Entirely legal and damned lucrative. Furnished with a courtesan's eye to sumptuous detail. Pastoral oils in gilt frames. Ferns cascading down pedestals. Glass display cases filled with curiosities. Torchiere lamps. Tasseled pillows. Even a blind piano man. And, most important of all, four-poster brass beds. Alice charged six dollars fifty cents for a fifty-minute session; by general consensus, Alice's mixed-blood "nieces" gave customers their money's worth.

"I ain't one to tolerate licentiousness," Alice was fond of telling first-time callers. "I demand it."

The fall of the House of Breaux occurred on an August night so thick a preacher man paid a dollar extra for a twenty-minute soak in one of Alice's claw-foot tubs. While The Rev. Amos Welk was marinating his privates in perfume water, Judge Harmon Guidry was in the parlor enjoying a mixture of banana rum, Grenadine and Amaretto. Judge Guidry drained his glass, teetered up to a receiving room, and set his cigar in a dainty ash tray. A few minutes later his companion, a stunning girl whose family was wiped out by the weevils, sat up in bed.

"That there smoke comin from your trousers, Judge?"

"Naw, dawlin. Now lay yo-self down agin."

The girl returned to her ministrations and hizzoner was soon rising to the occasion. Then he, too, sensed something amiss.

"Ivy, dawlin, is yo bedchamber blazin hot or is it me?"

Ivy giggled. "You hot as a poker, Judge."

The Hon. Harmon Guidry was delivering his verdict when a passing housemaid noticed dark tendrils of smoke coiling under Ivy's door and out into the hall.

"Fire! Fire!"

The judge's cigar had fallen onto the receiving room's thick carpet. In minutes, flames were racing across the dry fibers. To the window curtains. To an upholstered settee. To the hem of a silk dust ruffle. Fire rushed across the underside of the bed on a highway of wood slats. It rose through the soft mattress and voluminous bedclothes and found feather pillows and exploded. By then, Ivy and Judge Guidry were frantic, swishing Ivy's flimsy nightgown at it, making things worse, spilling the judge's brandy, turning a smoldering cigar into a conflagration.

Alice heard the alarm and raced from her private office. She was in the foyer, dumping water from a flower vase on flames licking the banister, when four of her most profitable nieces skittered down the stairs and ran out the door, slapping live cinders from their peignoirs, followed by four gentlemen callers, somewhat ankle-shackled by their trousers but wholly disinclined to tarry in a burning whorehouse. Alice lifted her petticoats and withdrew a small Derringer from her garter. According to a houseboy closely questioned by police later that night, Miss Alice got off two decent shots at Judge Guidry as he leaped from the landing window.

Alice repaired to Hilma Burt's place on Basin Street and spent a restive night. At daylight, sensing Hilma's hospitality had run its course, she freshened up in one of Hilma's marbleized bathrooms, snapped open her parasol, and departed.

Breaux House was gone, Alice saw that right off. Clots of gawkers were milling about, snickering, pointing, nodding. Policemen had cordoned off the premises with wire. Firefighters were still playing streams of water on the smoldering remains. Scattered about the yard were a few remnants of her elegant bordello, an iron boot scrape, a transom grille, a section of her rosette fence, her dolphin downspouts. Suddenly exhausted, Alice backed away and started walking. At Basin and Lafitte she paused, unsure where to go next, what to do first. Then she shouldered her parasol and continued on, determined to ignore the gargoyle-faced citizens tittering at their gates, eager for a glimpse of Alice Breaux in adversity.

Alice spotted one of her girls and frowned. Seraphine, the most gorgeous and marketable of all her Creole stock, was plopped spread-legged under a mottle-bark bald cypress tree. The girl was asleep, and snoring like a sow.

Alice kicked one of Seraphine's silk faille shoes which, she noticed, were muddy beyond redemption. "Wake up, girl."

Seraphine fist-rubbed her eyes. "Yes'm?"

Alice looked off. Her lifetime investment, gone. The proof of success achieved at the highest possible price, gone. The whole damned place, burned to a crisp. "I made me a boatload on Basin Street," she said to the girl. "Had some fun times, too. Maybe I best retire."

Seraphine struggled to her feet. "What we gonna do now, Miss Alice?"

"Goin to the bank, girl. Then goin to see a lawyer. And *then* we goin to Esplanade Avenue. Gonna buy that big ole house on Esplanade been for sale. The one what got them pillars out front and turret things on the roof. Buy me some respect, too." Alice wiped a smudge from Seraphine's cheek. "Stop wringin your danged hands, girl. Y'all can come along, be my upstairs maid or somethin."

A hot breeze blew down the street. Alice instinctively turned away and then, for no reason she could discern, turned back to face it. As the odd wind neared, she found she could see what was normally only felt, see the wind. It was thick with dust and soot and swirling, curling around itself, slowly at first and then faster, forming a tight coil. A few feet in front of her, it stopped its advance. Alice peered at the strange apparition and saw in it the dark ruins of her past. She held out her hand to touch it, and the twisting wind suddenly paled to a blue-white light in which Alice saw her future, saw herself living in splendor, saw denizens of the city nod to her as she took a morning stroll, saw a salver laden with invitations to mannerly luncheons and genteel teas.

The breeze died. The vision faded. But for long moments Alice's heart burned with desire and determination.

Alice Breaux was nothing if not a practical woman, and so she blinked herself back to reality and fixed her attention on the here and now. "Fix your damn hair, Seraphine. We goin to the real estate office."

"Miss Alice, I ain't had nothin to eat since —"

"Where my damn cook, anyhow? Cook! Get y'alls fat ass over here."

On her transforming journey from Basin Street to Esplanade Avenue, Alice brought along two remnants from Breaux House. Her cook, a doughy woman who could be counted on for mediocre meals and tasty gossip. And her prize girl, Seraphine, a lissome quadroon with the long neck, almond eyes, high cheekbones and dignified carriage of a priestess. Having nowhere to go, twelve-year-old Gattine Bordelon trailed after them. For a day and a night, the child crouched under azalea bushes in front of the Esplanade mansion. Eventually, hunger trumped fear and she crept to the porte cochere. Alice was brow-beating two draymen lugging crates into the house.

"No beggars," Alice barked when she noticed the girl. "Git."

"I ain't beggin. I be Gatty, from Breaux House."

"Who?"

Gatty grew up in the whorehouse scullery. Her earliest recollection was of curling up on a lump of soiled sheets that smelled of soap and semen, munching a stale beignet and being utterly contented. Whenever Alice's heels clicked along the back corridor, Gatty would hide behind the ice house. Alice had only vaguely known the child existed.

Gatty often wondered about her parents. Once she gumptioned herself to ask after them. Cook turned from a simmer pot on the stove and considered the question, trying to recall.

"Got a inkling your mama might have been one of Miss Alice's bedroom ladies. And your daddy, he either that cotton agent or that insurance man with the gold tooth."

"She pretty?" Gatty asked, but by then Cook was stirring her gumbo again. Gatty returned to the scullery closet and closed her eyes, trying to picture them. Her mama white or black? Her daddy Creole or Cajun? It was unknowable, so indistinct were Gatty's features and so dodgy everyone's remembrance of her conceiving. When Gatty looked into one of the gilded mirrors at Breaux House, what she saw neither pleased nor irritated her. The mismatches were a puzzlement to others, though. Pale brown eyes that upturned slightly at the edges. Gingery hair. Olive skin. Splayed nostrils and thin lips. Approaching puberty, Gatty still had the bones of a starling.

Had she lived elsewhere, or been a boy, Gatty's prospects might have been marginally more promising. If fierce enough, ambition and determination were creating wealth in cities such as Pittsburgh and Detroit. Grit and greed could bring prosperity out West, if a fellow was lucky. In the East, pedigree dictated a person's rung on the social ladder, which was the economic ladder, the fixed position of forbears passed down intact. But in New Orleans, purity of bloodlines was prized above all. Vague mixtures doomed the interbred to a coarse existence. Gatty's future being completely presumptive, she had no cause to hope otherwise and she didn't.

"Your scullery girl, remember? Miss Alice?"

After raining all night, a sharp breeze suddenly swept away the last lingering cloud. In the burst of sunshine, Alice felt something uncommon, a stirring of pity, and said: "There's a cot under the eaves for you, girl, and ten cents a week. Make damn sure y'all earn your keep." With that, Gatty was conscripted into what all assumed would be a lifetime of servitude.

During her brief residence on Esplanade Avenue, Gatty asked for nothing, received nothing, never complained and so expected nothing. Life had exsanguinated her of most human desires. What few sprouted, Alice pruned. Gatty's single aspiration, renewed each night before exhaustion gave way to the benediction of sleep, was to be overlooked. Safety in that.

Dark Eyes
1910

Chicago

Vincenzo picked up a bat. The outfielders instinctively moved halfway down the block.

That morning a kid who lived a few streets away had called Vincenzo a dago. The kid got in one good punch before Vincenzo decked him.

Even with his left eye swollen shut, Vincenzo was likely to smack a high flier and make it to the manhole cover with time to spare.

A Moment of Opportunity
1910

New Orleans

*G*atty had come of age in a whore house. At night, she had fallen asleep to the dark sounds inside a house of pleasure: the whispered requests of a fetishist, the moanings of men and women writhing with other men and women on a carpet, the slurred threats of a drunk vowing to blow the place to smithereens. These sounds were as familiar to Gatty as the whrrr of a toy train was to Fritzie, as familiar as the whoosh of a brush through a doll's chestnut locks was to little Lydia Conrad.

It was only now that Gatty came to know real evil, on Esplanade Avenue.

Another wracking blow was strafing Louisiana's mushy coast. Palm trees bent like willows. Magnolia leaves rattled. Hound dogs scuttled off to hidey holes. Cook and Seraphine took to their beds and slept through the storm but Gatty lay awake, staring bug-eyed at the dark eaves over her attic cot. A cabbage palm frond tore from its mooring and soared kite-like a moment before diving to the roof. Gatty bolted up, her bird heart thumping. She hurried downstairs to shut windows and sop rainwater from the sills.

Had it rained the night before or the night after, had the Lord Jesus permitted that branch to hang on a while, her life would have plodded along as before. Had Alice been able to climax a bit sooner or later, altering by seconds the leave-taking of the night's partner, the thread by which Gatty clung to the living world would have spooled out in a different direction. Had Gatty and the night-man missed one another, all that occurred later would not have. A moment of opportunity, a lifetime of consequence.

Gatty took rags from a cupboard and started to dab at rain water wetting the sills along the second floor hall. The man tiptoed from Alice's bedroom and lingered in the shadows, fastening his crotch buttons. Pitchfork lightning flashed. He saw the girl. His ruby lips curled.

Gatty recognized the man, his dirty yellow hair parted low to hide a knobbed head, his bushy muttonchops meant to hide pitted cheeks. At Breaux House, he had a reputation as a client who opened his wallet when offered the rare opportunity to snatch the innocence of a child, boy or girl, it mattered little. "Fancies hisself a boxer," Gatty once heard one of Miss Alice's nieces say. "Boxed me good last week."

Gatty froze. Without turning, without his eyes ever leaving Gatty, the man checked the handle on Alice's door. Then he walked down the hall and grabbed Gatty by the wrist. "Where's your bed, girl? Upstairs, I'll wager."

Gatty's mind whirred. She knew she couldn't call out. She knew Miss Alice would think it was Gatty's fault, would assume Gatty went after *her* night-man.

The man tossed her onto the attic cot and wrenched wide her trembling fawn legs.

"Damn you, stop twitchin." With a closed fist, he landed a swift punch between Gatty's thighs, and the breath whistled from her. The arch at the base of her belly was downy and thin, the tissue underneath delicate as rose petals. She threw back her head and for a moment zigzags of light played against the attic roof. She laid still, a doomed foal with a pistol to its head. The man unbuttoned his trousers and spat into his hand. He swiped the spittle across her most intimate part so her dryness won't chafe him, and then he shoved into her. She gasped at the reaving. Make it stop, she prayed. Make him go away.

The man withdrew and plunged deeper. He pulled out, thrust into her a third time, and exploded. Afterward he lighted a cigarette, and on his way out he tossed a small pennant from his pack of Egyptienne Straights onto Gatty's cot. "A gift," he said, much amused.

Within her, two eggs were descending a delicate, trumpet-shaped passage, on their way to scarlet sheddings that never came.

By autumn Gatty's condition had progressed from suspicious to certain. Alice brooded on the matter, determined to find out who was the jack-ass that bedded her scullery girl. "Hell, could've been that butcher boy hangin around all google-eyed all the time. Or my damn yard men, lazy fools."

"That so," Cook said.

"Gonna take the rug beater to that girl."

"Yes'm."

"Only way to find out who was the randy stud did this in my own house, right under my damn nose."

For most of her brief, disparaged life Gattine Bordelon had lived on grits, dirty rice, and the occasional bayou mudbug, which accounted for the girl being spindly as a salt marsh reed save for the ballooned belly she now hand-carried everywhere, her frame and constitution being insufficient to the task of child-bearing.

It's Louche
1911

New Orleans

*G*atty's confinement began on a spring evening so desultory gaslight flames stippling the city's verandahs rose unwavering. Out in the swamps, odors bubbled up. Cicadas fevered in the verges. At moonrise, Seraphine reported to Miss Alice there was little advancement of the girl's labors. Alice bestirred herself to send Cook for a midwife. "Don't come back with some Creole granny fixin to charge me a damn fortune," she warned.

Gatty never cried out. Not when the pains came in waves like bracky wash through a slough. Not when the sullen midwife pulled a boy child into the breathing world, dusky blue but alive, tossed the bloody rags to a corner, set the still-wet infant on Gatty's belly, and departed into indifferent night. Not when the pain flared again.

Some minutes later, soaked in sweat and wracked with visions of a pit viper feasting on her innards, Gatty called out.

Seraphine called down to Alice, who took her time negotiating the switchbacks and pinched her silk peignoir ankle-high along the way. When she reached the small room under the eaves, she saw Seraphine bending over Gatty's cot. Apparently, the girl had given afflictive birth to a second baby, another boy.

"Twins," Alice said, annoyed. "That damn midwife charged me a dollar and didn't even know there was twins in there." She started to caress one of the glistening infants, but yanked her hand away as soon as she noticed the baby's skin was lighter than Gatty's.

Alice measured absinthe into a glass and balanced a slotted spoon over it. With practiced movements, she placed a bit of sugar on the spoon, drizzled water over it, and stirred. The mixture turned greenish-white. "It's louche," she said. "Drink up. Them chores of yours ain't goin away."

Gatty drifted through the rest of the night in silken bliss, beyond life's variegated miseries, above the corrosion of despair, oblivious to serpentine demons, real or otherwise. Seraphine sponged her friend with cool water, but afterward Gatty felt neither sullied nor cleansed. Mewling babies cried out to be fed. She didn't hear. Borne to a place apart, she fixed on a single wish:

Let them live.

Cinderella Dressed in Yella
1911

St. Louis

*L*ydia Marie was in her most favorite place, the limelight. It was her third birthday, and the Conrad clan had gathered at Tom and Mary's bungalow to celebrate.

Lydia shoved her cake plate aside and toddled over to the mountain of gifts. Mary handed the child one present after another — a picture book, a box of chalk, a petticoat. But the moment Lydia tore off the wrappings, she tossed them aside. At the bottom of the pile was the biggest box. Lydia lifted its lid and broke into a dimpled smile.

"She looks like me!"

Mary beamed. The gift had cost a small fortune, and for the last three nights Mary had stayed up late sewing a doll-sized replica of Lydia's birthday dress. She even tucked a few tiny accessories into the box.

Lydia examined the miniature hairbrush, straw boater hat, and umbrella. "Look, Doris, it opens and closes."

Four-year-old Doris was counting the sticks of chalk and refused to look up.

Honestly, Mary thought, *my girls are only a year apart, but could they be any different?*

After the party, Doris clomped up to the bedroom she shared with Lydia and sat on the braid rug. With the nimble fingers of a pickpocket, she picked up a fistful of jacks and began to chant.

This old man, he played one, he played knick-knack on his thumb…

Lydia flopped on the low daybed and struggled to undo the tiny buttons marching down the back of the doll's dress. For a while, the sisters played in prickly silence.

When the dishes were finished, Mary came upstairs. "Bath time, girls."

"Me first, my birthday!" Lydia toddled after her mother, doffing clothes as she went. Mary sprinkled Ivory flakes under the tap and soon Lydia was chin-deep in bubbles. In the bedroom, Doris kicked away the jacks and picked up her jump rope.

Cinderella dressed in yella, went upstairs to kiss a fella…

Tom appeared at the bedroom door. "Not too much jumping, Doris. It's not good for little girls." He walked down the hall and peeked in the bathroom. What he saw warmed his heart. Mary was sitting on the rim of the tub, frosting Lydia's auburn curls with bubbles.

Doris suddenly stopped her sing-song chant. In the unexpected silence, she heard a snippet of conversation never meant for her ears.

"Lydia's turning out to be the pretty one, isn't she?" Tom said to Mary.

"Mmm-hmm," Mary answered, "Ten to one it's Lydia who makes the better match."

In the bedroom, Doris rummaged through Lydia's gift box. With a few harsh strokes of the tiny brush, the doll's lush curls were a tangle of wild crinkles. She kept brushing until the doll's hair was straight as straw, quite like Doris' own astringent pageboy.

Sighs of Purgatory
1911

New Orleans

$\mathcal{M}$a'am, Gatty need a doctor. That girl bleedin through the catch-rags."

Alice slammed down her hand mirror on the dressing table. Damn nation! Couldn't she even get herself dressed for the day without somebody bothering her about something? Alice picked up the mirror again. She decided to take her sweet time before answering Seraphine. She smoothed Jonteel cream into her neck wattles, and she tweezed the few black chin hairs that had sprouted overnight. Finally, she looked up and said matter-of-factly, "New mamas bleed some, girl. Tell Gatty to git up and empty the night soil basins. Polish them mirrors with a vinegar rag, too."

Seraphine half-dragged Gatty down to the billiard room and closed the pocket doors. Sunlight shot through the Venetian blinds, casting light-dark stripes on the game table's baize surface. Dour faces glowered from oval frames on the wall, portraits Alice picked up at auction and hung from ribboned hooks to give the impression of an esteemed lineage. The room felt close. The scents of cigar, brandy, sweet cologne, and lemon oil lingered in the still air. Gatty and Seraphine glared at one another across the table.

"Y'all got to stop mopin, girl," Seraphine said. "Git back to work or Miss Alice, she gonna throw y'all out the door." She tapped her toe, waiting on an answer. In the heavy silence, Seraphine ignored the creak of a floorboard in the foyer. "Well? You goin to work or not?" To her dismay, Gatty burst out crying.

"I can't do nothin! A cottonmouth snake done snuck up into my belly."

"What!"

"It coiled up in there, nasty."

The floorboard groaned again. This time Seraphine tiptoed to the pocket doors and flung them apart. It was Cook, pop-eyed as a calf at the chute.

Within the quarter-hour, Cook had served up Gatty's story to the kitchen maid next door. The maid passed along a spicier version to the butcher boy. The boy added savory ingredients and fed the tale to passengers on the Esplanade-Canal streetcar, who devoured it whole. By midday, news of Gatty Bordelon's voodoo snake was swirling like steam from a roux pot. N'Awlins was a city well versed in the chronology of sin: perdition, repentance, confession, and exoneration. Voodoo was a different matter, though, a fearsome, mysterious thing that lived by a different set of rules.

That afternoon, a passerby reported seeing Alice's hired man scrubbing the portico with brick dust. A woman dropping off laundry reported seeing a pin-stuck doll on Alice's stoop. The butcher boy, ever on the lookout for trouble, returned to the house and reported he saw a gris-gris bag tucked in the cleave of Miss Alice's pendulous breasts. By dusk half the city was discussing Gatty's snake and ruminating about what was in Alice's little sack. Fingernail pairings, some said. Feathers or armpit hair, others guessed. Bat wings and gouged-out frog eyes, perhaps. Flappish things plucked from briny ditches.

Late that night a black man stepped onto a backstreet stage. He lowered his bones to a chair set in a puddle of light. Eyes closed, he raised his trombone and commenced to blow blues mournful as the sighs of purgatory. Toward the rear of the room, a woman raised her arms.

"Luck," she moaned. "Lots o' things ward off bad luck."

"Amen," two or three folks answered.

"Some useful, some not," the woman shouted.

"Amen, sister!"

The music man pulled a handkerchief from his trouser pocket. He wiped the trombone mouthpiece and daubed sweat from the folds of his unbellowed cheeks, and left the stage.

The following morning Alice woke late. Still in her filmy gown and robe, she wandered downstairs and out to the side verandah. "Seraphine, where that newspaper? Bring out the *Picayune* and my beignets."

Alice loved her mornings on the verandah. The white wicker furniture. The lemon-sweet scent of magnolias. The sound of water trickling down the cherub fountain. Back at Breaux House, the garden area was used to hang laundry; there were always soiled sheets to be washed and hung. Now, in her new life, Alice found comfort in the oddest little things, the clatter of breakfast dishes, the whoosh of her butler's broom across her heart of pine floors. It was as if these everyday occurrences were proof of her newfound status, of the social acceptance that eluded her for most of her life. In the morning, on her verandah, Alice felt a palpable assurance that she would never again be what she once was:

A girl who thrice each night spread her legs on a ticking mattress crawling with bedbugs.

The sun was low but strong. With a start, Alice remembered that a burnished complexion was the mark of the underclasses. "Seraphine, where the hell's my bonnet? Bring that *Picayune*, too."

Alice strolled the verandah, rounded the corner to the front of the house and stopped short. There, in the lacy foliage of her potted fern, she saw a small black box. Alice smiled. Buckner Packwood had left chocolates, she guessed. No, more likely the postman had finally brought the doilies she ordered from a catalog store in New York. Might be a fresh supply of Belladonna plasters from the druggist … possibilities vanished as fast as they came.

Alice was close enough now to see the box nestled in her Boston fern was none of those things. It was a little coffin. A waxy black coffin. Alice opened the lid and gasped. Inside the coffin, somebody had placed a doll that looked astonishingly like Alice, a doll prickled with pins.

Alice stumbled backward and dropped the coffin. A note fluttered out and came to rest at her feet. Alice sucked in her breath and picked it up.

Blood turn black and flesh turn blue.
I will curse you if you force me to.

Alice flung open her mouth so wide her jaw hinges cracked, and screamed. All up and down Esplanade Avenue, heads poked out of windows and doors. In the house, Seraphine hurried to extrude a startled Tulane professor from Alice's bedroom. The butler hauled the yard men by their shirt collars to the foyer. Cook dragged the butcher boy off the back stoop, his legs wheeling in protest, and deposited him in the foyer, too. By the time Gatty roused herself and joined the others, Alice was pacing, her features twisted with rage.

"How that Black Coffin Death Spell get on my porch?"

Silence.

Alice squinted her eyes to slits. Abruptly, she slapped Seraphine. The blow left angry finger marks on the girl's cheek. She marched over to the delivery boy and cuffed him good, a closed-fist blow that sent the youth flying. Then she pulled a pearl comb from her hair and jabbed it at Cook's face, and Cook spoke up.

"Miss Alice, the trouble come on account o' Gatty."

Alice wrapped an arm around the woman's thick waist. "Why don't we settle ourselves in the parlor? Have a praline, dear?" Cook popped out the news of Gatty's snake infestation. The lineup in the hall quickly dispersed.

Gatty was doomed, and knew it. She retrieved her babies from the attic, wrapped them in a makeshift flour sack sling, and fled. With no plan, she drifted the neighborhood. The familiar sights seemed warped, like a reflection in a fun-house mirror. A nasty buzzing in her ears was drowning out the sounds of the city, reins slapping on horse rumps, vendors shouting to customers, draymen cursing, last night's rain trickling from downspouts. As she walked along, Gatty crooned to the babies but her voice sounded hollow and far, and she wondered whether she was really singing or imagining it.

The air smelled of flowers, fresh manure, spicy cooking and the wet-dog stench of river. Gatty hardly noticed. Piano music floated out an open door. She didn't hear.

She wandered through the morning, through midday and all afternoon. At dusk, she noticed lamps glowing through windows held aloft with sticks. She found herself crouched outside the back wall of Alice's garden. She cradled her babies close to her chest, for the world was spinning now. Spears of light whizzed in and out of her field of vision. She felt something warm and moist gushing between her legs. She stuck her arm through the iron twists of the back gate, pushed aside a few drooping peonies, and could not believe what she saw.

"Them's the yard men diggin a hole," she murmured to the babies. "Why they doin that?"

Gatty watched the men plunge shovels into the earth and toss the dirt high. The metal blades glinted in the moonlight like mirrors. She saw clods of dirt, grass and tangled roots soar into the air and fall, smothering Cook's peppers and asparagus, crushing tomato vines fixed with string to bamboo trellises. She rocked on her heels and whispered, "How Cook gonna make her turtle soup and gator-meat gumbo?"

After a while, Gatty heard Miss Alice tell the men to fetch firewood from the tool shed. They tossed their shovels aside and climbed out of the hole.

"Cook, y'all git out here," Alice shouted. The babies startled, their tiny fingers splayed. Gatty shushed them back to sleep.

Through the peonies, Gatty saw Cook and Seraphine lug the fish-boil kettle across the yard and set it next to the pit.

"Don't wake up, babies, hear?" Gatty whispered. "Don't make a peep."

The men tossed wads of newspaper into the pit and laid twigs and logs on top of them. Then they lifted the kettle and set it carefully on the logs. Alice struck a match. Gatty saw it fizzle and heard her curse. Soon, though, yellow-blue flames were licking the edges of the newsprint. Gatty looked up, following the sparks that swizzled into the night air. Seraphine and Cook backed away, she saw, but Miss Alice stayed at the brink of the pit, staring into the fire, enveloped in the steam. Gatty shivered, for in the strange orange light Miss Alice's face looked like a Mardi Gras mask. After a long while, Gatty heard the familiar burbling of water at a boil.

At Alice's signal, the yard men loped off to the tool shed and returned with a burlap sack. Gatty heard meowing, and suddenly the strange scene made sense. "She doin a cat-bone cure, babies! Miss Alice gonna find the one bone in that cat gots the power to make her invisible."

Alice reached into the sack and tossed the doomed, wriggling cat into the kettle of boiling water. Foam overran the sides of the kettle and hissed on live coals, up-spitting bits of liquid fury onto the matted grass. Hideous sounds strafed the night. Cook disappeared into the kitchen and turned off the electric light. Seraphine sank to her knees and vomited into a patch of hosta. Gatty clasped the babies to her chest.

Alice folded her arms and stared into the fulminating water, spellbound by the thrashings. Animal screeches finally gave way to rounded yowls, and then to awful silence. Fingers of smoke curled into the sky, animal agony turned to vapor. The fire started to die. Alice tossed on more logs. At last, she dipped a forked stick into the water and pulled out the carcass. Bits of fur and shredded flesh fell back into the simmering water. Alice dipped the stick again and fished out a section of spine, knobby reticulations the color of scrimshaw ivory. She plucked off a section and tucked it under her tongue.

"Tarnation! Damn thing's hotter 'n hell!"

"This here business my fault, babies," Gatty whispered, sick at heart.

Alice pinched a femur from the mass on the stick and waved it in the air to cool. Seraphine looked up, shook her head, and looked down again. Alice spat out the bone and tasted another, a rib bone curled like a smile. Still not satisfied, she cupped the cat's skull in her hand and held it to the moonlight, tracing a finger along threadlike cranial lines. She broke off the cat's saber teeth and then stuffed the skull whole into her mouth.

"Miss Alice!" Seraphine cried, on the edge of hysteria, "you invisible!"

Make Me Some Goofer Dust
1911

New Orleans

The following morning, Alice passed a hall mirror and swore. She was still visible.

Then, even more distressing news. The butler had discovered a black wreath tacked to the front door. Calm as a hangman, Alice summoned her yard men.

"Go," she said, handing over a scrap of brittle, yellowing paper. On it was a recipe written in spidery script. "Go wherever ya'll have to. Swamps. Them other places, too. Don't forget nothing." The men clomped out of the house, and Alice turned her attention to Cook:

"When they get back, y'all mix them ingredients in a pot, hear? Only way to get rid of this hex is a batch of Get-Away Powder."

Gatty and the babies had spent a fitful night behind the garden gate. Toward dawn, she slipped inside through the kitchen door and crawled up to the attic. By late morning she was hardly able to raise her head off the cot. Seraphine heard the faint sound of babies crying, and guessed her friend had returned. She snuck upstairs, changed the blood-soaked bedding and stuffed clean rags underneath Gatty. Then she picked up the babies, carried them next door, and gave the neighbor lady's wet nurse two pennies to feed them.

By early afternoon the yard men were back. The older man quietly turned over a small pouch to Alice. The younger man laid out the recipe ingredients on the table. Cook mixed Guinea red pepper, sulfur, salt, wild herbs and minced roots in a soup pot. When she finished, Alice snatched up the pot and walked out the back door. She was sprinkling spicy Get-Away Powder around the foundation of the house when the butcher boy came along.

"Whew-ee!" he yelped. "What a stink!"

Alice swatted at the boy and he scuttled off. When the pot was empty, she returned to the kitchen. Cook suspected Gatty was back. She caught her mistress's eye and nodded toward the attic stairs. Alice removed the small pouch from her skirt pocket and smiled as she twirled its drawstring.

Cook turned away, pretending to be busy at the sink. "Miss Alice," she said over her shoulder, "that be Goofer Dust you got in that bag? That be dirt from a dead girl's grave?"

Alice didn't answer. A minute later, she burst into Gatty's room, upturned the pouch and waved it back and forth. Powder swirled into the stale air. Gatty leaped up. Too late, for by then she was covered with gray-white film, fine as table sugar.

Alice tossed the empty sack aside. "Git, girl! Don't come back."

Gatty snatched up the babies and the flour sack slings. Then she raced downstairs to the kitchen. Seraphine was waiting at the back stoop. She tucked her life savings, five one-dollar bills and a few quarters, into Gatty's hand.

"Now run, girl," Seraphine said. "Miss Alice goin after her pistol."

Gatty was at the corner when Seraphine thought to call out: "What y'all name them babies?"

"Palmer," Gatty shouted over her shoulder. "Palmer and Leroy."

Spindrift clouds streaked the washed-out sky as if painted with a dry brush. The air was clammy. Gatty shambled along, clinging to the shoals of life. Blood trickled her thighs. Half-moons of perspiration darkened the sides of her cotton shift. She approached a house, but the doorman flicked her off like a fly. She passed a large clot and paused, looking at it, dazed. She wandered between two houses and snatched a petticoat from a line. Quickly, she wadded it into her underwear and set out again, stumbling, clasping the flour-sack sling to her chest. The babies were so small, passers-by assumed she was hugging herself.

Rampart. Dauphine. Bourbon. The streets all looked the same to her, smeary visions of horses, houses and strangers. Gatty jerked her head up, searching for the Monteleone Hotel; she remembered Miss Alice had once remarked on the enormous plates of food served at the Monteleone restaurant. It was hopeless. She would not recognize the Monteleone if she found it, and could not read the sign if she were looking at it. Blood soaked the back of her skirt. Faces in the crowd were stretching like rubber. Music danced in her head, off-key. Goose bumps pebbled her sweaty arms.

Canal Street. Gatty threaded a clamor of carriages, mule carts, electric streetcars, horses, riders, walkers. On the far side, a man motioned to her.

"Want to see a moving picture show, girly? Vitascope Hall, right here. Only a nickel. Cool inside, too."

The theater was dark and nearly empty. Gatty sank into a chair in the last row and leaned against the wall. Save for a man and woman in front, the hall was empty of patrons. For the first time in weeks, months, she felt safe. The silent movie flashed across the canvas screen, beaming grainy reflections of "Enoch Arden" onto her. She rested her head against the wall and gave in to the elixir of sleep. The babies slid from her lap like rolling pins and continued on, down her outstretched legs. Well-swaddled, they plopped on the floor without waking. When the film ended, a botanist delivered a brief lecture on the health benefits of home gardening. The couple in the first row listened politely. When the botanist finished, the house manager rousted Gatty with a nudge.

Out on the street again, the night seemed inordinately dark. Gatty shook her head, disoriented. "My brain buzzin with bees," she said to the babies. "The moon be rockin, and this here street is buckin. Don't matter. Know what, babies? I gonna be a parlor maid. Wear a dress with a lace collar and all. We gonna eat blood oranges and pecan pie. Gonna play pat-a-cake."

A pang flared from deep within her. She staggered into a gangway and braced herself against the clapboard siding. As soon as the pain ebbed, another started. She side-stepped the reasty remains of a raccoon and laid the babies on the bricks. Sinking to her knees, she gave in to paroxysm. Her lips peeled back in a grimace. She doubled over, fisting her hands, and rested her cheek against the cool, slick bricks. When the pain faded, she picked up the sack again and willed herself to her feet.

Her belly throbbed. The snake was slapping its flanged head against her vitals. She stuck a finger down her throat and gagged, but the snake drifted to the fringes of her mind and slipped away.

The babies' heads rested against her small breasts. Under ridges of bone, her chest felt like an empty cavity. She wondered at the uselessness of a heart pumping blood only to have it pool on the ground at her feet. If her heart stopped, she told herself, maybe the lower bleeding would stop, too. Then that thought drifted away, into the night.

Banks of blue-black clouds raced across the sky, born inland on angry gusts. The night was sticky, the heavens at rolling boil. Gatty trudged to the wharf. She saw a man and woman bend into the wind and hurry up a ferry boat ramp, and she followed, hoping the ticket-taker would assume she was their nanny. The man let out a beery burp and nodded.

Gatty stood at the stern. A thousand dots of light pinned the city against the ragged night. The ferry rumbled to life. She watched the dots slip away, vaguely understanding that her past, her every waking breath and every dreaming hope, was receding with the horizon.

O

Miles upriver, behind the gates of Portland Place, Albert kissed Emily lightly on the forehead and turned off the bedside lamp. Down the hall, a private-duty nurse handed two sleeping tablets and a glass of water to old Mr. George. In the children's wing, six-year-old Fritz ran his fingers across the pointed hands of his bedside clock, calculating time forward and backward in fifteen-minute increments.

Across town, in a neighborhood of red brick bungalows, Lydia thrashed in her sleep. In her dream, she had fallen down a rabbit hole and landed in a strange garden. Playing-card men were painting the roses red.

A half-day's ride west of the city, Leatham Smith squatted in his barn beside a brood mare, running a hand along her heaving flank, trying to determine why she was down. His son, Brooke, a short, muscular boy, hurried down the aisle, carrying a lantern and pail of warm water.

In Chicago's Little Sicily, seven-year-old Vincenzo sat cross-legged on the fire escape outside his bedroom window. High above, laundry drooped from lines that tatted over the alley like a game of cats' cradle. Vincenzo snapped the band of a slingshot and then lined up his stones. Soon, he told himself with a shiver of expectation, the rats would come out.

Winged Furies
1911

Algiers, Louisiana

*T*he ferry lumbered across the harbor to Algiers and sidled up to a dock. Eddies foamed in its wake, sending ghost-white curls across the inky water. Down the ways, Gatty saw a late night paddleboat spinning its wheel in drowsy circles. The decks reminded her of a wedding cake she once saw in a baker's window, and the railings were festooned with strands of white lights that twinkled on the choppy water, like stars. A musician pumped out 32-note tunes on a calliope. Gatty thought the music shrill and circus-like, but the partygoers on the paddleboat clinked their glasses in salute, their levity unmatched by the weary night travelers on the ferry.

By day, the Algiers waterfront was alive with stevedores and rope haulers and barrel makers. Roustabouts scrambled across bobbing decks. Teamsters hauled huge bales of cotton, coffee and bananas to weighing platforms. Steamship agents flailed papers. Rail yard supervisors gummed cigars. Every inch of the docks and yards bustled with industry. Now there was only the slap of water against sodden pilings, the squawk of a wheeling gull, and the far sound of the calliope.

Clouds boiled up from the south, bringing rain. Gatty glanced up and the angry splats struck her face and neck like needles. She waited until the last passengers moved off. Then, shivering with fever, she stumbled down the gangplank. The ground felt gelid. She stood at the end of the dock and swept her gaze across the vast, deserted yards, bewildered. A crewman crept up behind her and whispered something lewd. When she half-turned, he noticed the babies and moved quickly off. Gatty angled inland, through the sprawling rail yards, past the huge warehouses, utterly lost.

On Delaronde Street, bright balloons began to dazzle and explode in her field of vision. The babies felt so heavy her arms trembled. Somewhere on Seguin Street she saw a narrow open passage between two cottages, and stumbled in. Protected from the worst of the rain, she laid the swaddled infants on a patch of moss and sat, hovering, rocking in delirium. "One more storm," she told the babies. "This one gonna blow y'alls mama up to them pearly gates."

Pushed landward, the storm caterwauled through the passage like the out-whooshed breath of a leviathan. Gatty tightened the flour sacks around the babies. She tried to still her chattering teeth, and could not. Barely conscious, she finally relaxed. Her shoulders slacked. Her eyelids fluttered. She lowered herself to the ground and curled her body around the twins, a nautilus. She turned her face to the delta sky and in the blur of sheeting clouds she beheld winged furies, flights of them, come to avenge innocence lost to lust.

Toward morning the restless storm blew itself out. The last clouds scudded easterly. Pink tracers strafed the gloried dawn.

A woman hurried along Seguin Street on her way to the docks. Earlier that morning, Fleurise Hudicourt had bound her head in a colorful turban, tied an apron around her barrel waist, and walked to the ferry dock as usual. Fleurise worked as a laundress at the New Orleans Colored Waif's Home for Boys. At six, her no-good husband had wakened with a tooth ache and demanded oatmeal, soft-cooked, slow-cooked to mush, and in the aftermath of the storm, in the rising air pressure, the water had taken forever to boil, so she was late.

Fleurise heard a cry. Against her better judgment, she stepped into a shadowy passage between two cottages. Her gaze darted, alert for danger, but there was only a flop-eared dog sniffing a pile of dirty clothes. For a moment Fleurise thought she'd heard the mewling of a baby, but no. She was almost at the street again when the dog yelped and jumped back in surprise. Fleurise flapped her apron at the mangy thing, and what she saw next made her gasp: a hand, a thin, clay-colored human hand gripping a foot, a very tiny foot.

"Sweet Lord," Fleurise whispered, drawing back the rags. "What this nasty business? A little girl and a baby. Soaked in blood and jes about dead. God Almighty, two babies. Po-lice!"

Fleurise ran a hand across Gatty's forehead. The girl was oddly cool, her breath fast and shallow.

"Quick, police! Hurry, afore this chile passes!"

Fleurise cast a nervous glance over her shoulder, for she knew a thing or two about what happens to infants left in alleys. Loup garou, wolves from the dark side, swoop down on dying mothers and suck the blood from their unbaptised babies.

"Po-lice!"

The girl was whispering now though cracked lips that barely moved. With some effort, Fleurise lowered herself to her knees, straining to hear.

"Take 'em," the girl said.

"What?"

"Saved my babies from a she-devil. Saved 'em from a storm. Can't do no more."

Fleurise laid a hand on the girl's chest and prayed, helpless to do more. She watched her hand rise and fall, rise and fall, and finally still.

In that moment, in the crystal sky above Algiers, a morning star shook loose from its berth behind rosy ribbons of cloud. It drifted to Earth, to the narrow passage between two cottages, and settled in the cupped hands of a laundress. It bathed the woman, the girl, and the infants in a halo of golden light.

Gatty left the world as she entered it, in obscurity, her passing as hapless as a palm leaf striking a roof, as inexorable as the delta tide. By mid-morning her body was carted off. Police took statements, and when they finished Fleurise scooped the babies into the hammock of her apron, drew it high, and boarded a ferry. Two light brown heads flopped against the mound of her bosom, infants so listless she worried they, too, would die. She murmured in Creole and tucked the tip of her finger first in one tiny mouth and then another, and they did not die. Having abided with their mother for a matter of days, Palmer and Leroy Bordelon would live at the New Orleans Colored Waif's Home for Boys for the next fifteen years.

○

A notice appeared in the *Picayune*, buried on an inside page.

The Algiers community was saddened yesterday … unknown young woman … perished after a night of affliction in the elements … recently given birth to twin boys … all concerned in distress … discovered by a Mrs. Biggy (Fleurise) Hudicourt … the ill-fated mother now resides in the sweet bye-and bye …

It was Seraphine who noticed the newspaper story. It was Seraphine who snatched a silver candlestick from Alice's sideboard and marched off to a pawn shop. Seraphine who bought a pine casket and a plot in McDonoghville Cemetery, and wept as her friend was remanded to the Louisiana soil from whence she came. Seraphine who mourned the pity of Gatty's life and lamented her death. It was Seraphine who notified the New Orleans Colored Waif's Home for Boys that the twins had names. They were Palmer and Leroy Bordelon, mother orphaned, abused and deceased, father unknown, uncaring.

Alice never did find out who stole the damned candlestick off her sideboard.

The Power of a Uniform and Badge
1911

Chattooka

Charity and Sugar Hobbs were the prettiest girls in Chattooka, once, so quick to learn the Civil War battles the school marm allowed as how she might as well have two teacher's pets as one. They sang like angels at Sunday worship, too.

Esmie thought Charity and Sugar were the best older sisters in the whole world. When they sat under a shade tree making corncob dolls, they let Esmie sit close by, watching. When they walked to Lula Creek and took turns swinging out on the hemp rope, laughing so hard all their teeth showed, they let Esmie ride piggyback. Sugar even helped Esmie pick the leeches off her back.

That was before Bull Pinkney.

Esmie's sisters took a downhill turn when they got pregnant with Pinkney seed, the one sister within a month of the other. Charity was seventeen when Bull sweet-talked her into going behind the cotton gin one night, filled her with hooch from his uncle's still and then hiked up her skirt. Sugar was sixteen that summer, the summer Bull made two babies in two Hobbs girls and decided it might be time to get hisself deputized, be a sheriff like his daddy and granddaddy. That was the summer rumor had it Theo Hobbs was lookin for Bull.

Having fixed their reputations early and forever, Charity and Sugar quick-wed the only available men in the county at the time. Charity's husband was a roamer. On the few occasions he returned to Chattooka, he beat Charity with a doubled-over belt. Sugar's husband drank. Both men eventually decamped, leaving Charity, Sugar, and the younguns to fend for themselves. Every so often, Florelle would spoon leftover drippings into a hot skillet and make a hoecake, wrap it up with a ham hock and a couple of apples, and have Esmie carry the food across town to the side-by-side shacks where Charity and Sugar and their various children resided in squalor.

"Esmie, you boring," Sugar said one day, popping a piece of still-warm crust into her mouth. "All you do is work in that dang store. Ain't you almost twenty-five, girl? When you gonna get a man?" Sugar's little girl tugged at Esmie's skirt. Esmie broke off a piece of hoecake and handed it to the child.

Esmie had clerked at Moses Butters' store for as long as she could remember, counting out candy a penny's worth at a time, measuring cloth by the quarter-yard, stacking cans of beans and boxes of soap flakes in neat towers. At closing time she put away the cash box, padlocked the front door and walked across the bermed railroad track to her parents' cabin. She once told Mama she wouldn't mind stacking tins of Underwood deviled meat until the cows came home, a future that might have been worth betting on, were it not for Bull.

Of late, Mississippi's climate had been especially ill-tempered. Heat so nasty the splotches of tar out on Low Creek Road bubbled like pan gravy right through to sundown. Storm clouds billowed with promise and blew away. In the fields, soil puffed around the hooves of the cart mules as if the cotton had been planted in dusting powder. Bare-foot children snapped twigs of bone-dry bushes and drew pictures in the streets. Old men gave up their outdoor rockers and sought solace elsewhere. Mothers wiped sweat from the folds of fretful, chafed babies. Workers at the gin were exhausted by noon.

Esmie leaned against the counter and fanned herself with a month-old magazine. "Not one customer come by all mornin," she said aloud. Out front, a dog twirled two circles and flopped down in the street. "Even them porch fellas is gone, rized up like Lazarus and took off." Esmie chuckled. With no one to hear the joke, she started idly counting dimes in the cash box.

Bull kicked the dog to its feet and punched open the screen door.

The summer after graduating high school, which was the summer he impregnated Charity and Sugar, Bull was installed as Chattooka County's newest deputy sheriff. Pinkneys had been upholding their particular interpretation of law across 554 square miles of Mississippi Delta for years, so nobody was too surprised. In fact, had they thought much about it, they would have surmised Bull learned sheriffing from his daddy. In fact, Bull developed his own speciality: cuffing colored prisoners behind their backs and kicking the feet out from under them. Ever since pinning on a badge eight years ago, Bull had finger-raped more colored twat than he could count.

Esmie stood behind the counter and glowered as Bull helped himself to lemon drops from the jar. When he snatched a peppermint stick, she stalked off to the back of the store and started stacking cans on a shelf.

Bull twirled the peppermint stick in his mouth and examined Esmie's plump hips, trim waist, and fine ankles. "Girl, ain't you gonna say hello?"

"Don't need no hello, Bull. Y'all ain't shoppin, jes lookin."

Lookin at what, exactly? Esmie wondered. Last time this store had somethin new to look at was them Animal Crackers. Five cents a box. Esmie remembered the packages had looked like little circus wagons. Each package had had a loop of string so kids could hang it on their Christmas tree. Fool, she thought. Didn't Moses know folks in Chattooka ain't got five cents for no animal cookies? Ain't got money for no Christmas tree, neither.

Bull's eyes were small, deep-set in his fleshy face. They were glittering with interest as he assessed Esmie's strong points. He dropped the peppermint stick and crushed it under his boot, then sauntered down the aisle and nuzzled the back of Esmie's neck.

What occurred next happened quick as a flash of heat lightning across a summer sky. Esmie spun around to push Bull away, lost her balance, and tumbled toward him.

"Ain't you the pretty thang," Bull said, catching her in his arms, pinning her to him.

Esmie tried to wriggle free. Bull pinched her titty hard and then let her go. He moseyed around the store, taking the long route to the front counter, where he helped himself to another peppermint stick. "Be seein y'all again, real soon," he said at the door. "Got me a sweet tooth."

"Close that screen. Y'all lettin in flies."

Esmie brooded the rest of the afternoon, remembering the raw desire in Bull's eyes, thinking about the power of a uniform and badge. Back at the cabin, she shoveled cornbread and greens around her plate but had no stomach for supper. Florelle and Theo ate in silence, waiting. When the last chipped plate was washed and dried, Esmie announced she was leaving Chattooka.

"Ain't gonna hang around here and get knocked up by no Bull Pinkney," she said, blinking back tears.

Theo rose to his feet and slammed his fist on the table, upturning a salt shaker and sending two black flies zooming to the window. "Gonna kill that man," Theo said. "Squeeze the breath outa him with my bare hands."

Florelle lifted the dish pail out of the sink and pitched the water out the back door. Humming softly, she disappeared into the bedroom. For long minutes the cabin resonated with the low, throaty sound of Southern misery.

Esmie leaned against the sink and massaged her temples. "Didn't mean to fall right at him, Mama. I was tryin to push him off."

"I know, Sweetness," Florelle said.

Florelle carried an old pink sheet from the bedroom to the kitchen and laid it across the table. On it she set Esmie's spare cotton dress, a pair of white ankle socks, clean underwear, and a sliver of lard soap. She wrapped the last pieces of cornbread and a few hard peaches in a brown sack and set the sack next to the clothes. Still humming, she tucked five dimes and twelve fifty-cent coins in one of the socks. Then she drew the corners of the sheet together.

"Mama…"

"All I got, Sweetness."

Esmie had to go. They all knew it. They knew Bull would come back and take what he wanted. Theo was a peaceable man, but if Bull set on a third Hobbs girl, Theo would kill him. Maybe use a fish-gut knife, maybe the business end of a hoe. Somebody'd find Bull with his head minced like a Vidalia onion. A day or two later, Theo'd go missing. A day or two after that somebody'd find Theo hangin from a tree. And before nightfall, everybody in the county would know about the fire that had been lit under Theo Hobbs' dangling feet, the fire that was still smoldering when the field hands cut him down. "Smoked him like a ham hock," Bull's daddy would say, all proud-like.

Florelle kept her head down and packed a few last items into Esmie's travel satchel. Theo shuffled out the back door and stood at the line where the scraggly yard gave way to lush fields. He stayed a long while, facing away from the house, staring across an ocean of cotton. From the kitchen, Esmie saw her father's head dip. When he dug a fist into his mouth, she turned away.

"Go, Sweetness," Florelle said. "Daddy be fine."

When Esmie was out of sight, Florelle took her place beside Theo, whom she loved. They stayed at the far edge of the yard a long time, arms around each other's waists, determined to see nothing but another brutal sun melting into the green eternity of Mississippi.

Esmie hiked down Low Creek Road to Highway 61, aiming to head south to Clarksdale. A buggy drew near, and she picked up her pink satchel and stuck out her thumb. The driver snapped his whip, urging his horse to a trot. Esmie stood in clouds of cinnamon-colored dust and bladed her hand over her brow.

A while later a mule wagon approached from behind. She heard the driver give the reins a yank, and she turned to see. A bone-skinny woman in back waved. Two scrawny boys cupped their hands over their mouths and giggled.

"Y'all need a ride? Headin north, opposite to you, but still…"

Esmie shuffled her feet and looked away. Sensing her hesitation, the man clucked his mule. In moments the wagon was almost out of sight. The sun was hovering at the tree line. Mosquitoes were rising from the culverts, ravenous. Esmie wondered if she could walk all the way to Clarksdale, knew she couldn't, and felt the first stirrings of fear.

"Mister," she called, running, "I surely do thank you."

In the day's fading, Esmie rummaged her satchel for the daguerreotype she had taken from her mother's chiffarobe and tucked into the folds of her spare dress. She held it in her hands and smiled at the image of her parents on their wedding day, stiff, serious, rendered in sepia. She drew her thumb across their young faces and her heart bled remorse. Looking back, she could barely make out Chattooka in the lavender distance, the towering gin, the lanterns glowing in cabin windows, the twin rails of railroad track cutting through town, everything she knew and loved. Three hours after a chance stumble, Esmie Hobbs was one more drop of blind desperation in a great black river flowing north.

By the time she reached St. Louis her money had almost run out. She took a room at a boarding house for coloreds on Seventeenth Street. It was clean and safe. The landlady mentioned it was a short walk to Reinhardt & Krug, the famous department store. Esmie thought she'd rather like to see that, if they let coloreds in. The following morning, Esmie asked the lady if she knew about any jobs.

"Any work, any at all," Esmie pleaded, raising her voice over a racket outside. At the corner, a scrawny rat of a kid was bleating out the morning headlines. Beany Frazier had the vocal cords of an auctioneer. His usual corner was blocks away, but that morning the Hawley brothers laid claim to his spot so Beany relocated to a corner near the boarding house.

The landlady scowled. "Esmie, you got a nickel? Go get a paper, and tell that boy to shut his trap."

Esmie and the landlady sat on a porch swing, poring over classified ads in the *St. Louis Globe-Democrat*. Esmie was about to give up when she came across an item that seemed promising.

Private Housekeeper
Trained, Reliable

Able to prepare, cook and serve healthful meals for a family of four, supervise housemaid, manage provisions, and care for all aspects of domestic environs. Sunday afternoons and every other Thursday off. Uniform provided. Contact Albert Reinhardt, 71 Portland Place.

The landlady drew a map showing the route to Portland Place, and Esmie set out at once. The city was huge compared to Chattooka, but the morning air was fresh, the sky cloudless. Seven blocks to Jefferson. A few more to Olive. Eight blocks until Olive vectored off at Lindell Boulevard. Ten blocks down Lindell. Turn right onto Kingshighway. Two blocks, thereabouts. Portland Place would be on the left.

Esmie shoved the newspaper clipping through the gate. The guard waved her off and returned to his post. Esmie fixed her features in a pleasant expression. Fool man, she told herself, gotta get up in my face, act all high and mighty. "The Reinhardt family expectin their new housekeeper," she said. The guard reached through the gate, took the clipping, and held it upside down, pretending to read. Esmie stifled a chuckle.

"On the left," the man grumped, opening the huge gate. "The white brick."

At the side door, Esmie brushed street dust from her shoes and pushed the buzzer. A boy of about six answered, a beaming child with a crinkle-eyed smile so radiant it melted the ache in Esmie's homesick heart.

Enveloping Arms
1911

St. Louis

*T*he scent of yeast dough perfumed the house. Esmie punched down the mound in the mixing bowl and smiled. The divots made by her knuckles remained. "Leavin now, boys. This here gonna rise all night. Y'all let it be and tomorrow Esmie gonna make up some cinnamon rolls from the scraps."

Phillip shrugged. He had things on his mind, tomorrow's math test, and memorizing the new Boy Scout Handbook before the troop's next meeting. Fritz waved goodbye at the door.

"Go back inside, chile," Esmie scolded. "Catch your death."

Esmie scanned the lowering sky. "Storm comin," she said to the women at the streetcar stop, maids, cooks and nannies. "My boys gonna have them a snow holiday tomorrow." A sharp wind rustled the last of the oak leaves overhead. Esmie turned up her collar and held her handbag high and close.

The next morning, Phillip and Fritz awoke to the season's first snowfall. They tossed bathrobes over their pajamas and raced to the kitchen. Esmie set two bowls of steaming oatmeal on the table. Phillip picked out the raisins and tossed them into Fritz's bowl. When they finished, Esmie handed Phillip his parka and bundled little Fritz into his snowsuit and galoshes.

"Ten minutes, Fritzie-boy, that's all."

Outside, Fritz stuck out his tongue and caught a snowflake fat as a cotton ball. "Hey Phil, let's make snow angels!"

Phillip picked up a handful of snow and made a fist. "It's sticky enough for snow forts. Snow forts are better."

"Okay, snow forts."

Esmie stood at the kitchen window, watching. Worry lines furrowed her broad forehead. Shortly after she had arrived in September, Fritz had come down with strep throat. Complications set in, and the boy had developed rheumatic fever. Albert and Emily summoned doctor after doctor, but for days it was touch and go. Esmie sat by the frail boy's bedside, sponging his fevered arms and legs, reading his favorite story books, soothing him to sleep with gospel hymns. Fritz finally pulled through, but the doctors said the disease had damaged his heart valves forever.

Esmie tossed two empty fruit crates out the back door. The boys scrambled for the wood boxes and set to work building snow forts. Phillip built tall, thin walls and embellished them with crenellated ramparts, a flourish he'd seen in an illustrated novel about King Arthur. Fritz built a stubby fort and reinforced it with logs from the firewood pile. The battle was over in seconds.

"I won!" Fritz shouted.

"You did not. It's a tie." Phillip scooped up snow, trying to repair his delicate fort.

Fritz slogged across the battlefield and patted snow-mortar onto Phillip's guard tower. "Hey, Phil," he said, "let's make a snowman, a super-duper one. I'll roll the snowballs. You go get Father's top hat and walking stick. And a carrot for the nose."

Upstairs, Albert and Emily had nearly finished dressing. Albert swept back his hair with boar-bristle brushes and checked his collar studs. "Darling," he said, "did you know Esmie has trained the boys to fold their pajamas every morning."

"I know. She gives them little rewards."

"Money?"

"No, darling. A cup of warm cider or a carrot curl. She uses a paring knife and makes faces on apples, too. And darling, you should see our linen closet. Esmie has all the sheets and towels and pillow cases stacked in perfect piles, just like bolts of calico in a country store."

"She's a jewel, all right. She has me send part of her pay back to her family each week. Back to some God-forsaken town in Mississippi."

Emily began each morning in her conservatory, reading the newspaper, answering correspondence. It was her favorite room in the house, nearly tropical year-round for Albert had had heating tubes installed underneath the marble floor when he had the conservatory built. Emily's prized orchids and African violets grew wantonly in the near-constant sunshine and humidity.

Esmie brought a silver pot of coffee and poured a cup for Emily. As she turned to go, something out in the yard caught Esmie's eye. The hood of Fritz's snowsuit was down, she saw, flopping against his back. His hair was wet, too, and his cheeks were an angry scarlet.

Esmie marched to the back door and called to the boys: "Y'all c'mon back inside this here house now."

Phillip hid behind a tree. Fritz dropped to the ground and flapped his arms and legs, making a snow angel. When he finished, he lay in the soft depression of his body, utterly content. Suddenly, he lifted his head. He saw his mother in her conservatory, seated in her favorite peacock chair. She's a queen in a snow globe, he told himself. He saw his father walking out to the garage, drawing on his leather gloves. He noticed Stevens was shoveling snow from the driveway, and he saw Esmie on the kitchen stoop, hands on her hips, waiting for him. All the people I love are here, Fritz said to himself. Everybody is together here, and happy.

Esmie was fuming. "Boys, Phillip, Fritz, did y'all hear Esmie say to come whenever y'all gets around to it, or did y'all hear Esmie say *right this here minute?*"

Fritz ran to the house. In the back hall, he stuck out his arms and pretended he was a mummy while Esmie pulled off his soggy mittens and boots. Chunks of snow puddled on the linoleum.

"Stand by the stove while I go fetch dry clothes, and don't go peekin in my oven."

"Where's Mother?" Phillip said, pushing through the back door.

"Dunno," Fritz said.

Phillip looked over Fritz's shoulder. "Cinnamon buns done yet?"

"Nope."

When the boys were dressed, Esmie bent to the open oven and pulled out two baking pans. Heat rippled into the kitchen, raising beads of perspiration in the soft pouches under her eyes. The boys craned to see, but Esmie was blocking their view of the morning's treat.

"Wasn't much this week in the way o' scraps," she said, swabbing her face with a corner of her long apron. "Who wants the cinnamon roll?"

"I do!"

"I do, too!"

Esmie held her hands behind her back. Both boys tried to snatch the treat. Finally Phillip tapped Esmie's left arm and she handed him a cinnamon roll dripping with vanilla icing.

"You're the best maid we ever had," Phillip said, dancing off.

Fritz's eyes welled with tears. Esmie had been with the family only three months, but he had come to love her. Esmie baked bread every Monday, and every Monday she managed to have a bit of dough left over, just enough for two cinnamon rolls. The boys loved the treat, warm dough coiled around ribbons of buttery brown sugar, crushed pecans, and cinnamon.

Fritz turned away so Esmie wouldn't see his disappointment.

"Come now, Sweetness, your turn to pick," Esmie encouraged.

Fritz looked surprised. He wiped his nose with the back of his hand and tapped Esmie's arm. When she handed him a cinnamon roll, hot tears spilled down his cheeks. "Aw shoot," he said, "it's the waterworks again."

Esmie swept the child onto her lap and enfolded him in her arms. He buried his face in her neck. She felt the bird-beat of his weakened heart, and her thoughts bristled. Why this chile's mama not in here? Society folk don't know how to raise a young-un at all. And that Phillip, always knows best, always gotta be first, gotta have the finest. Fritzie ain't like that at all. This boy here jes pure happiness.

Esmie sat and rocked Fritz while he ate the cinnamon roll, but her mind was spinning. Life ain't all happy, even for rich folks. Some day this angel gonna find that out. Mm-hmm. That be the day little Fritzie gonna fall to pieces.

"Shush, Sweetness," she crooned.

Fritz loved these times, the quiet times with Esmie. He loved the feeling of her strong, dark arms around him, loved the smell of soap on her crisp uniform, the tunes she hummed, bible hymns learned in a Baptist church in Chattooka.

Emily had finished her correspondence and was peering into the beveled mirror of the hall tree stand. She arranged a fur stole over her tailleur suit and then pierced her smart felt hat with a mother-of-pearl pin. "Esmie, is Stevens back yet? Tell him to bring the car around, would you? I won't be home until four or so. It's bridge day again. Did you order the brisket? Esmie?"

"Yes, ma'am. It lookin nice and tender."

Fritz ran to the foyer and stood on tip-toes. His mother gave him a kiss, and then was off for the day.

"Drive along Lindell, Stevens, would you? And then Olive," she said, sliding open the privacy glass. Even though Emily was anxious to see the city's newest landmarks, the basilica cathedral and the huge public library, she might not tell Albert she'd done so. Municipal construction was hardly a suitable interest for a woman of her stature.

At Washington and Sixth, Stevens glided the sedan to within a few feet of Reinhardt & Krug's entrance. Each time Emily walked into the gorgeous store she thought about Albert's father, about what a shame it was that George was too frail to see all the modern improvements.

George had been unwell for some time. Shortly after the turn of the century, his wife had passed away, plunging George into despondency. Months passed, and when George showed no signs of improving, Albert took over as president of Reinhardt & Krug. Then another blow: old Otto Krug died in his sleep. Having no children, Krug left his equity in the store to Albert, the descendant of his faithful partner. Now, at age thirty-two, Albert was in sole control of the largest department store in the Midwest.

At supper that night, Emily was keen to discuss items in the morning newspaper, topics the Topping Ridge Country Club ladies had received with cool reserve. "Albert, I read that Emma Goldman has delivered another radical speech about —"

Albert jabbed a carving knife into the roast. "Mmmm."

"Darling, you're sawing Esmie's brisket like lumber. And did you hear about the train robbery?"

"Yes, Emily, I did. Phillip, pass me your plate." Emily went on: "Masked men boarded a Missouri Pacific express car and terrorized all the passengers. Goodness."

Fritz was enthralled. "Neat-o. Was anybody shot to death?"

Albert returned the carving knife to the platter with more care than necessary. "Darling, accounts of female anarchy and railway thieves are hardly occurrences for review with the children. Fritz, hand me your plate before this roast is stone cold."

Emily cleared her throat. "I drove past the new library this morning. I'll be so happy when we can all go there. My, how many books we'll read."

Albert chewed thoughtfully. Once again he was overcome with a sudden melancholy, a yearning for what wasn't to be. Albert had inherited a future quite different from the one he might have chosen, the contemplative life of a professor. His world was his father's creation, the ever-changing flash and gleam of Reinhardt & Krug.

Small Demonstrations
1911

St. Louis

Phillip frowned at the dry smear of copper-colored blood staining Fritz's cheek. He turned back to his work and said, "Your honker's bleeding again, brother."

"Aw, darn." Fritz wiped his nose on his cuff and grimaced. That afternoon, a boy on the playground had made fun of his name. "Freed-rich, Freeed-rich!" the boy taunted. Fritz socked the kid in the stomach and got a sharp punch in the nose in return. From across the playground, Phillip saw the ruckus. By the time Phillip and a couple of older boys drew close, Fritz and his opponent, Teddy, had reached a painful stalemate. Teddy was holding his stomach and bawling like a baby, and Fritz was gushing blood like faucet water.

Fritz pinched the bridge of his nose, "It's a tie, wight Teddy?"

Phillip and his friends glared at Teddy.

"Right, Fritz," the boy said.

That evening Fritz worked on his Christmas list while Phillip wrote letters informing his teachers he wished to be called Phillip, never Phil.

Fritz decided to ask Santa for a monkey. "Hey, Phil, what are you asking for?"

"More soldiers. Lead, not tin."

The following morning Emily found the boys' lists on the hall table. She glanced at them and then waited to catch Albert before he left for the day.

"Your younger son is asking for a live monkey," she laughed, "a monkey and thirty dollars in coins and small-denomination bills."

"What? What does Fritz intend to do with thirty dollars in small bills?" Albert knew, though. Fritz wanted enough bills to practice addition, division and multiplication with real money.

When Fritz was four he could count to ninety-six, by sixes. Last fall, when the boy was starting first grade, he could add a column of two-digit numerals in his head and arrive at the correct sum. Albert and Emily were dumbfounded.

"The issue isn't the money, darling," Emily said, laughing, "The issue is whatever would we do with a live monkey?"

O

Each Christmas Eve, Albert and Emily hosted a glittering party for their friends and neighbors. On the day of the gala, caterers and decorators poured into the house, an assault that overran the kitchen and sent Esmie scuttling to the basement.

Despite the tumult downstairs, Emily remained serene. In the early afternoon she stepped into the master bathroom for a calming soak. Ingrid, her personal maid, had filled the tub with warm, lavender-scented water. Ingrid was a gift from her mother on Emily and Albert's wedding day, and had stayed in the family's employ ever since. Ingrid altered Emily's suits and gowns, ordered Emily's favorite soaps and creams, hand-washed her silk underthings, dressed her hair, brought cool compresses on headache days and warm compresses on monthly complaint days.

At her dressing table, Emily stared passively into the triple mirror while Ingrid brushed and brushed her hair, and finally swept it up in a glorious mass of loose waves. When the last hairpin was in place, Emily held out her foot and Ingrid smoothed sheer ivory stockings up her legs, fastening the tops to a satin suspender belt.

It was late afternoon by the time Ingrid lifted Emily's evening gown from the bed, a Poiret kimono that had arrived from Paris two days earlier. The dress was a sweep of green silk that rippled from shoulder to floor like falling water. Ingrid disappeared into the closet and returned with Emily's jewel case. Emily fingered her treasures and finally settled on an emerald and diamond brooch the size of an apricot. Ingrid pinned the brooch to a low sash knotted at the front of the gown. She fastened a slim black ribbon around Emily's head and tucked three ostrich feathers into the back. Last of all, she retrieved elbow-length evening gloves from a shallow glove drawer.

At six sharp Emily gave over the bedroom to Albert, took a last glance in the mirror, and walked down the hall. "Put on your velvets now, dears," she said, rapping slightly on the boys' door. "It's time."

Soon, the first guests were ringing the bell. Hired valets parked cars up and down Portland Place while Stevens escorted the guests inside, took their wraps and showed the way to the third-floor ballroom. On their journey up the stairs, the visitors marveled at life-size angels made of plaster of Paris,

Della Robbia swags festooning the windows, crystal stars dangling from the high ceiling, and in the ballroom an enormous balsam tree that glowed with hundreds of candles and beaded ornaments.

"Emily, where did you find the fabulous baubles?" a neighbor asked, fingering a tiny windmill hanging from a low branch.

"They're glass, imported from Gablonz."

A string quartet played selections from Handl, Bach, and Corelli. Waiters wove through conversation groups, holding aloft trays of champagne in crystal flutes, paté-stuffed figs, apricot brioches, mushroom tarts, and coconut crusted prawns. By nine o'clock the dance floor was a swirl of tail coats, beaded gowns, diamond tiaras, and exotic feathers.

At ten Albert signaled the musicians to take a break. On cue, the waiters retreated. The happy din of conversation quieted, and Albert summoned everyone's attention.

"My sons, Phillip and Fritz, have prepared small demonstrations for your pleasure," he told the guests. "Will you kindly indulge them?"

A chorus of merry voices answered: "Here, here!"

"Right," Albert began. "Someone pick a letter of the alphabet, any letter."

A man with a monocle spoke up: "The letter S."

"S it is. Whose last name begins with S? Ah, yes. Blaine and Ellen Shaw, would you come forward?"

The crowd parted. The Shaws appeared uncertain, but walked to the center of the room. Albert beamed. "Now Phillip, what can you tell us?"

Phillip stepped to his father's side and appeared to study the Shaws. Under the scrutiny of a ten-year-old boy, Blaine and Ellen appeared uncomfortable. After what seemed an eternity, Phillip spoke. "I can tell you, Father, that Mr. and Mrs. Shaw have exquisite taste."

Blaine and Ellen relaxed.

"Mr. Shaw," Phillip went on, "arrived tonight in an exquisite evening cape over a peaked-lapel coat and drill waistcoat. The outseam of his custom-tailored trouser is silk braid. The square-cuff shirt has a stylish winged collar. His studs and links are moonstone, and his footwear is varnished calfskin."

Phillip ignored the polite applause. "Mrs. Shaw's pleated gown is one of Fortuny's successful Delphos creations. The Spanish designer created the look to resemble robes worn by aristocrats in ancient Greece. My congratulations, madam."

Ellen Shaw bobbed her head with delight while the other guests applauded with enthusiasm.

Next, Albert called Fritz to the center of the room. A butler brought a light carry-table scattered with dozens of cashew nuts. The guests grew still again.

"Someone, please select a fractional number," Albert said. "Any fraction. Let's see what my boy can do with it."

A tall, slender man spoke up. "Sixteenths. Let the lad try that."

Fritz flashed his signature crinkle-eyed smile and began separating the nuts into rows. In less than a minute, the six-year-old boy had arranged one hundred cashews into sixteen rows. With a flourish, Fritz popped the remaining four cashews into his mouth. Guests rang out a chorus of bravos. Musicians struck up "Jingle Bells." The ballroom swirled with dancers.

O

From time to time, Albert enjoyed calling his sons to his study and challenging them with number games or word quizzes. The boys basked in the attention.

On a drab winter Saturday a few weeks after the party, Albert devised two new games. "Phillip, Fritz, see if you can make exactly one dollar using these nickels, dimes, pennies and quarters. If you can, I'll let you keep the dollar. That's right Fritz, good boy. Phillip, catch up, now. That's good. Oh, you boys will have me a pauper soon."

Albert quickly realized the game was too easy and he moved on to a more difficult one.

"Got your chalk boards? Good boys. All right, continue this sequence as far as you can until time's up. Ready? One plus one is two. Two plus one is three. Three plus two is five. Five plus three is eight." The Fibonacci Sequence.

Oak logs popped and sizzled in the fireplace. The mantle clock chimed the quarter-hour. At twenty-five past, Albert double-checked the time against his pocket watch and told the boys to lay down their chalk.

Phillip held his board aloft. "Got all the way to 233, Father."

"Excellent, Phillip. Now Fritz, what've you got to?"

"Did okay, Father," Fritz said, turning his board face-down.

Phillip hooted. "Ha! Beat you again."

Esmie rapped at the study door. "Mr. Albert, you know of any chile wants a roasted marshmallow sandwich?"

Esmie had learned to cook at her mother's side, watching Florelle stretch a scrawny chicken and a mess of greens to three suppers. For a few weeks after she came to the Reinhardt house, Esmie was overwhelmed. The kitchen was so large, so modern. The food budget was virtually unlimited. Half the fancy dishes Mizz Emily wanted prepared, Esmie couldn't even pronounce. But the Reinhardts were kind and patient, and before long Esmie was turning out meals that combined the essence of Southern cooking with the elegance of a society chef. Breakfasts of fried eggs and bacon, grits drizzled with sorghum, and coffee so strong Albert claimed his feet didn't touch ground until noon. But suppers were Esmie's specialty, and she soon established a delectable routine. Mondays, slow-roasted brisket with onions. Tuesdays, fried chicken. Wednesdays, lamb chops and mint jelly. Fridays, skillet-fried catfish. Saturdays, beef steak and buttered potatoes. Sundays, country ham studded with cloves.

On Thursdays, Esmie's day off, Stevens drove the family out to Topping Ridge for supper. "Lest we all starve," Albert said, every time.

Phillip and Fritz tossed their chalk boards aside and raced to the kitchen. Esmie handed Phillip a sack of marshmallows and slabs of dark chocolate. She sent Fritz off with a packet of graham-flour crackers.

"Go on, now. Stevens done made a trash can fire out back. Fritzie, y'all start wheezing, come right back inside here."

Before long the boys had licked the last of the melted marshmallow from their fingers and were playing sword fight with the sticky twigs. Watching from the study window, Albert thought his heart would burst with love. As a child, Albert had yearned for the camaraderie of a brother, even a sister.

When Phillip and Fritz ran off to roll hoops, Albert turned from the window and picked up the boys' chalk boards. He examined Phillip's first. The boy had filled his slate with columns of calculations up to 233. Good boy, Albert thought. Phillip's got a good head and he's fastidious like my father. He'll run the store someday, it's a perfect fit.

Albert picked up Fritz's tablet and his eyes widened in dismay. Why, the child must have done all the computations in his head, he told himself. There was a single number on the board, and no erasure marks. Fritz had calculated the Fibonacci Sequence to 4,181 … in his head.

Valiant Efforts
1914

St. Louis

*B*ells rang out across the spring night, rousing muddled citizens from sleep and sending them to the windows. The discordant clamor bounced across city rooftops and raced down dark streets. Lights winked on. Fear leached into the air and traveled house to house like graveyard fog. These banging clappers were no Sabbath knells, no holiday chimes or cheery declaration of peace, no reverent tolling for the dead. What then? Had drunken students climbed campaniles? Had rascals taken over the church towers?

On it went, the ominous clanging, as if the great city of St. Louis was on fire, which it was.

Tom Conrad and his crew hitched skittish horses to a steam engine. The driver slapped reins and off they galloped toward an ugly orange-yellow bloom staining the underbelly of low night clouds.

At Third and Washington the driver reined his horses to a rearing halt. Tom felt a mighty blast of heat, as if he'd opened a furnace door and peered in. It was the Missouri Athletic Club, he saw, engulfed in flames. A sizzle of fear raced up Tom's spine. He quickly shook it off. Best not to think, he knew. He jumped from the engine and ran toward the club. The fire had a nasty head-start. Tom saw club members dangling bed-sheet ropes from smoking windows. Other men, he saw, were stumbling pell-mell down blazing hot fire escapes.

Tom and his crew watched three men try to leap to the roof of a nearby feed store. The first made a clean, long jump to safety. The next man got across the abyss, too. Tom and his crew watched, entranced, horrified. The third man backed up, ran to the precipice and hurled himself into the air. He was older than the others, heavy and clumsy, and he failed to clear the distance. For a gut-wrenching moment, the man clung to a narrow overhang. Tom turned away, helpless. He'd seen men wheel through air. Heard them scream as they fell to their death, spread-eagled, coattails flapping like tattered wings, earth rushing up at them as they fell.

Gunshots cracked from somewhere inside the building. Tom sprinted to the door, ignoring the flames and groaning timbers. "Come lads," he shouted to his crew. "They're taking their own lives in there."

"Tis death, Tom," a buddy called out. "No use goin for it. No use at all." By then Tom had vanished in clouds of black smoke pouring from the entrance. A long minute passed. Finally he emerged, dragging a coughing man to safety.

By then the streets surrounding the club were in chaos, a tangle of firefighters, policemen, trucks, ladders, buckets, doctors, stretchers, and gawkers. Wild-eyed horses stamped and jangled in their traces. Streams of water arced through the air and fell on fire-licked doors and windows. A brick wall collapsed with a thunderous crash. Sparks sizzled high into the sky.

For a long while the blaze raged out of control. Fresh waves of smoke boiled out windows. Every so often flames burst through burn-holes in the roof. At each new eruption, onlookers pointed and groaned.

Back at the bungalow, Mary watched the hideous glow, soon sick to her stomach. She scooped up her two little girls and carried them to her bed, but the children sensed her fear and grew fidgety. Doris traipsed back to her own bed. Lydia danced after her sister. Beneath the blankets, Mary curled into a tight ball. Her girls were too young to know the danger their father faced that night. Tom had pet names for his daughters. Doris was Lanky-Doodle. Lydia was his Little Flapdoodle.

Dawn breasted the horizon, bathing the city in a pearly glow, plating it's great river in silver. The fire had reduced the Missouri Athletic Club to piles of charred bricks and smoldering timbers. A chimney stack stood stark against the pale sky, like an obelisk. Cinders gathered in gutters that gushed with run-off water. The acrid stench of fire was everywhere.

At midday Tom sent his exhausted crew home. Mary found him on the stoop and wondered how long he'd been standing there. He appeared stunned, unable to cross the threshold. He pulled off his soft cap and turned away. He's mortified, Mary guessed, ashamed about his tears. Mary put an arm around his waist and urged him indoors.

"We couldn't get at them, love. Everything was on fire, the rugs, furniture, everything. Flames licking the walls, running across the floorboards. "

"You tried, Tom. You tried your level best."

"They were sleeping at their club. No harm in that, was there?"

"No harm in that." She kissed his forehead.

"Stairs were gone. Elevator shaft was a furnace."

"You did your best, Tom. That's all anybody asks."

Tom had rushed the building three times and managed to drag four men to safety. He dove in one last time, seconds before a wall collapsed. When he didn't reappear, his crew sprinted in with a ladder and found him in the choking hell of an upper floor, down, unconscious. They hauled him out moments before another major collapse. Two men propped Tom up against the truck and clapped him on the back until he started breathing.

Mary brought a pan of warm water and wiped the soot from his bloodied knuckles. He lay back on the sofa and closed his eyes. Mary saw his eyelashes were singed. The buttons on his jacket had started to melt. He smelled of fire. She dipped the rag again and drew it across the lines riming his forehead.

O

Albert had rushed to the hall telephone as soon as he heard the bells, assuming it was a fire, terrified Reinhardt & Krug was burning. Stevens drove him into the city, but they were forced to take a wide detour around the disaster site. Stevens stood alongside Albert through the night. Soon, in ones and twos, R&K clerks and managers appeared. They formed a bucket brigade around the store to douse any live cinders that might fly that far. At dawn Albert returned to Portland Place. Esmie handed him a cup of coffee. Emily brought the morning newspaper. Bold, black headlines marched across the front page.

Terrible Fire
Missouri Athletic Club Blaze Claims Many Lives
Crème de la crème lost
Valorous efforts

Albert rattled the coffee cup to the hall table and wandered to his study. He felt as though he were sleep-walking through some awful dream. Emily came in, and he looked at her with bewildered eyes. "I play billiards with these men. They're friends of mine, of ours."

"I know, darling."

"I play squash with them in the club's gymnasium on Thursdays. We swim laps in the pool."

Emily eased the newspaper from his shaking hands and scanned the article. "The paper says they have five bodies at the city morgue. It says there could be twenty-five more in the rubble. Allen Hancock. James Reilly. Oh darling, how awful."

City fathers declared a day of mourning. At the station houses, dignitaries presented medals to the crews who fought the disaster.

"Every day you risk your lives for others," the city fire chief said at Tom's station house. "We hold you to lofty standards. We expect you to disregard your personal safety. We expect you to serve our noble city, and you did not let us down. Thomas Aloysius Conrad, you and your crew have demonstrated what it means to be a hero."

That morning, Albert and a dozen M.A.C. members met at a downtown restaurant to discuss forming a committee that would oversee construction of a new club. They agreed to finance the project by selling bonds and lifetime M.A.C. memberships. A brewer named August Anheuser Busch was one of the first to buy the bonds.

I'm the Winner
1915

St. Louis

*T*he April morning was clay-gray. Overnight showers had turned the vest pocket park near the Conrad bungalow into a sea of mud. Teeter-totters angled the way they were left. The rain had reduced sandbox castles to rippled drifts. Swing seats waggled in the breezy air.

Doris and Lydia set their Easter baskets on a patch of grass and sat on side-by-side swings. They toe-kicked back and forth a while, taking care to avoid the puddles below their swing seats. Doris proposed a race.

Lydia perked up. "What's the prize?"

Doris paused, as if mulling it over. "Whoever swings highest gets two eggs from the other person's basket."

Lydia leaned far back and began to pump her little legs. Soon she was so high the tension on the chains broke at the far end of each arc. She looked down, delighted at what she saw: Doris was trailing badly, hardly trying. "I'm winning!" Lydia crowed. "I'm the prettiest and I'm the winner."

Doris hopped off and grabbed Lydia's Easter basket. Lydia looked down and saw Doris skip around the playground, setting one of Lydia's colored eggs on each swing seat.

"Stop it!" Lydia called, frantic to slow down. "Those are mine."

Before Doris ran off, she grabbed each empty swing and gave its wood seat a yank. One by one Lydia's Easter eggs tumbled off and landed with a sickening crack.

Wipe It Off
1916

St. Louis

*A*lbert tossed a log onto the grate, sending clumps of orange-yellow embers into sizzling ecstasy. It was time, though Emily certainly didn't think so. Nevertheless, he had made his decision. It was time to begin grooming Phillip for the responsibilities he would one day shoulder — guiding a great American retail institution through the 20th Century.

Albert gave the log a couple of pokes and then replaced the poker. He turned to Emily and said: "The boy's got to prove himself. That's imperative. He's got to start at the bottom."

"Yes, darling, but he's only sixteen —"

"I was fourteen when my father started me on the loading docks, and I can't say I suffered any permanent damage."

The following Saturday, Stevens drove Phillip downtown and deposited him, as instructed, at the receiving docks. The foreman had been alerted. He put the boy to work alongside the union men, hoisting crates off trucks, wheeling steel dollies to and from the dingy holding bays. For a boy accustomed to roaming the glamorous display floors, a boy who at a glance could tell a Prince Albert frock coat from a tuxedo, a Norfolk jacket from a Mackinaw, hauling freight through the gritty bowels of the building every Saturday was going to be unmitigated hell. The first day, when he thought nobody was looking, Phillip licked his finger and scrawled "*Omnes relinquite spes*" on the side of a dusty truck, Latin for "abandon all hope." Phillip was admiring his handiwork when the foreman tapped his shoulder.

"What's that, sonny?"

Phillip froze. "Nothing."

The foreman cracked his knuckles. "Then wipe it off."

Albert got word of the incident, of course. That night at supper he gave his son a vivid warning.

"Never belittle the men, Phillip. They're Teamsters, most of them. They work hard and their diligence deserves your respect. Their world is rough, and sometimes dangerous. You know Montgomery Ward? Yes? Well Montgomery Ward held out against a Teamster strike a while ago, and before it was over twenty-one men lost their lives."

After that, Phillip worked Saturdays on the docks without complaint. Not because he feared the roughnecks, though he did, and not because it pleased his father, which it did. Phillip worked hard because he knew it would hasten his rise.

Hungry for the Ring
1918

Chicago

A fellow once asked Vincent whether he was Sicilian or American, and he paused before answering. Vincent's world was Little Sicily, a slice of Chicago marinated in hope and saturated in poverty, a world that teemed with tensions that flared like a thumb-flicked match.

At an age when most boys were sneaking cigarettes and trading Honus Wagner baseball cards, Vincent was skipping school and hanging around seedy South Chicago boxing gyms. Sometimes blood spattered from the ring onto his face. He liked that, wiped it off and licked his fingers.

Vincent had sold his sling shot to his little brother. He didn't need it anymore, didn't sit on the fire escape knocking off alley rats with stones. He owned a BB gun now and took it to deserted places he knew, weedy railroad sidings, vacant parking lots behind abandoned warehouses, places where birds gathered on overhead wires. He savored the moments just before he fired. He'd train his sights on one bird and then another, deciding which would live, which would die. It sent ripples of pleasure through his belly, all the way to his crotch. After he took a shot, he'd watch the terrible flapping with clear, cold eyes, then cock the lever and take aim again.

One day a boxing club organizer noticed Vincent working out at the gym. What he saw, and he recognized this right off, was a strong, determined kid hungry for the ring, a kid who might have the makings of a top welterweight. The man decided to let Vincent train as long and hard as he wanted at the gym. He even offered the kid a $10-a-week job at the biscuit factory he owned.

"What's your name, kid?" the man said.

"Vincent, but I'm thinkin about changing."

"Yeah, to what?"

The words spilled out: "Somethin less wop, more like a boxer. Jack, maybe. Jack McGurn. No, *Battling* Jack McGurn."

Precious Little to Gain
1919

New Orleans

*T*he mission of the New Orleans Colored Waif's Home for Boys was noble: reconstitute delinquent character traits and inculcate the virtues of industry, obedience, sobriety and thrift. The Home went about these laudable goals by providing scanty nutrition and ample doses of corporal discipline, a paradigm that led to the swift elimination of under-motivated foundlings but instilled in boys of a more proactive disposition qualities that might be regarded as entrepreneurial.

After eight years at the Waif's Home, the twin sons of Gatty Bordelon were artful scroungers. Palmer always led the way; their aggrieved birthing in Alice Breaux's attic had left Leroy slow in more ways than one. Most days, Palmer headed to the Vieux Carre, to the back doors of hotels and restaurants that served mouth-watering cuisine in quantities diners couldn't possibly finish.

"Pee-yewie, this one a whole lot o' nasty," Leroy said, head-down in another trash can. His voice sounded hollow and tinny. The boys had been scrounging for two hours, with little luck. The sun was a high, orange ball pasted to a cloudless sky. The air was soupy.

"Pinch your nose, brother. Them slops is a might putrid."

Leroy let go of a maggoty pork bone and came up for air. "It all covered with white bugs and blue-bottle flies," he whined, gasping.

On a good day, Leroy might resurrect a ham hock without too much gristle, a griddlecake, even a handful of shrimp, and for a few hours the boys would know the pleasure of a full belly. Today wasn't a good day.

Palmer sat on an oak barrel. Hunger gnawed at his gut. "We needs to try somethin different. Knock on the back door, see?"

"Where?"

"You see me pointin, Leroy? That one there, behind the Patio Royal. Tell the man there be a lady conked out in the alley and she moanin somethin awful."

Leroy squinted into the blinding morning. "What lady? Ain't no lady."

"It's a trick, see? Keep jawin about the lady till the man goes see. That way, I can slip inside the Royal kitchen and snatch us some food."

Leroy pretended to examine a crack in the pavement, hedging. He swiped a hand across his sweaty armpit and took a whiff. "Then what we do?"

"Then we run like hellfire damnation."

"I talk about a moanin lady, ain't that tellin a lie?"

"It ain't a lie, Leroy, jes a fib. Lyin's about big stuff. Fibbin's about little stuff. Fibbin ain't good, but there's times it come in handy."

Leroy stuck out his lower lip. "We ain't liars."

"We scroungers. It's what we is and what we gotta be. Now go."

Leroy knocked at the door. A kitchen dog scratched to its feet and let out a series of rifle-shot barks. The twins ran like rabbits.

The following day Palmer found an abandoned pull-cart. Perhaps abandoned, Palmer didn't wait around to make the distinction. He raced back to the Waif's Home half-rolling, half-dragging the rickety cart by its handle and hid it in bushes behind a small outbuilding. That night Palmer lay awake, thinking, planning. After breakfast, he whispered his plan to Leroy.

"We get a piece of wire, see? We stick the wire in that honey pot in the pantry, and then…"

Palmer took Leroy by the hand and led him through the French Quarter to Jackson Square. He pushed through the great doors of St. Louis Cathedral and steered Leroy to a side aisle. The boys shuffled along in silence a bit. When Palmer saw a collection box bolted to a tall column, he stopped.

"Leroy, y'all still got that sticky wire? Poke it on down."

Leroy inserted the wire in the slot and poked around. The scratching sound seemed alarmingly loud, but no one came to investigate. Finally, Leroy broke into a nervous grin. "I feel somethin!"

"Shhh. Okay, pull it up real slow."

"Aww. It done dropped."

"Try again, brother. Keep fishin."

A few minutes later the boys hurried out into blinding daylight. In Palmer's pocket was a sticky, crumpled dollar bill. A few minutes after that, they were retrieving Palmer's cart from the bushes.

Come springtime, Louisiana farmers trundled early crops to the Halle des Legumes. Strawberries and leaf lettuce appeared first, but by mid-June there was all manner of produce being dropped off at the great Halle, as well as at neighborhood markets and street-corner stalls. At a fruit stand in Back O' Town, Palmer handed their dollar to the vendor in exchange for ten melons.

Leroy scratched his head. "We can't eat that much, brother. What we goin to do with all them melons?"

"Make money. We businessmen now, Leroy."

"Businessmen?"

"Y'all know that boy at the Home, the one got ears stickin out a mile?"

"Yeah."

"He say cooks at fancy houses pay extra if a melon come to the door, so's they don't have to lug it home from the corner."

Palmer and Leroy loaded the watermelons onto their cart and pulled it to the Garden District, calling out the rhyme they heard other sellers sing:

> *Watermelon! Watermelon! Red to the rind*
> *If you don't believe me jes pull down your blind*
> *I sell to the rich*
> *I sell to the po*
> *I'm gonna sell to the lady standin in that do.*

The brothers soon realized the vendor had overcharged them. Eventually, though, they sold all but one melon. By then, Leroy was exhausted. He sat on a curb and rested his chin on his knobby knees. "Sunball turning my head to a fry skillet, Palmer."

"All right, brother. Let's get this here wagon back to the hidey place. We gonna need it again tomorrow."

At the Home, Palmer carried the last melon to a shady bench and checked to see if anybody else was around. Nobody was. He took out the small knife he always carried in his trouser pocket and sawed the melon in two. Soon the boys were gorging on sweet, ruby watermelon.

"Life sure is fine, right Palmer?"

Palmer lined up eighteen pennies on the bench, chastising himself for the day's small take, determined to not be duped a second time.

Leroy spat out a seed. "We goin back to that church, right?"

"What for?"

"Put back the money."

"What?"

"Palmer, we ain't no stealers. We's businessmen."

"Dang, brother. We ain't puttin back the money. We gonna buy more melons tomorrow."

O

They made her acquaintance on one of those rare June mornings when the air was pure and the sky blue as glacier ice. Leroy spotted her first, down the street, yanking a balky two-wheeled cart piled high with pale green melons. In the absence of definitive information, Leroy called her the Honeydew Girl.

"Look, Palmer."

"I knows it."

She was skinny as a sapling, with a splash of freckles across her nose. Her hair was a mess of tight, flat braids. A blue checked shift hung from her bony shoulders like a tablecloth on a line.

Leroy elbowed his brother. "Looky, that nanny-lady stoppin the girl, see? She buyin a melon off that girl."

"Shut up so's I can hear."

The woman dropped a nickel into the girl's hand and took two melons. "Ballast," the woman chuckled, lowering the melons into a huge black perambulator. "Smooth the ride so this here cowlick-child stops his squalin."

Across the street, a house cook called to the girl: "Get on over here a'fore I change my mind."

Palmer spat. "Damn. This our corner. That girl stealin our customers."

"Damn." Leroy said, too. Leroy hated confrontation. He picked a nit from his hair, examined it, and flicked it away. By then the cook was lugging two honeydew melons down one of the shady, herb-lined paths that separated the block's large homes. As soon as the kitchen door slammed shut, Palmer hollered to the girl:

"How much you sellin those crappy little things for?"

"Two and a half cents apiece. That way, folks buy two. And they ain't crappy."

Palmer admired the girl's shrewd pricing. Honeydews are smaller by far than watermelons, and yet she got more money for her melons than they had. "Are too crappy. Damn near dead, theys so white."

The Honeydew Girl planted a hand on her waist and glared. Leroy noticed the girl's hipbone poked against her loose pinafore.

"Shut up a minute," the girl said. "Let me think."

Palmer shrugged.

"Y'all got a knife?" the girl asked.

"What for?"

"Give it over. I'll show y'all what for."

Leroy pinched the corners of his mouth to keep from snorting. Leroy always snorted when he saw something funny and a skinny, bare-footed girl barking orders at Palmer was powerful funny.

Palmer fished in his trouser pocket for his knife. The girl shifted her weight from foot to foot while she waited. Her gaze skittered off and back. In time the boys would be accustomed to that. In a city of drawlers, the Honeydew Girl communicated in clipped phrases. In a city of shufflers, she darted like quicksilver. By the end of that summer, they understood she was quick to accuse, slow to forgive and unable to trust, a girl with nothing to lose and precious little to gain.

Palmer handed her the knife. "Ain't no chicken. I can take that back anytime I want."

"Stick the carts in there." The girl pointed to a tall magnolia bush dotted with waxy blossoms. She squatted between the carts and took a melon from her wagon. She signaled Palmer to take one from his cart, too. Palmer chose the smallest.

"Gimme your shirt," she told Leroy. Leroy kicked the dirt a few times and then crawled into the bushes and unbuttoned his shirt. The girl snatched the shirt, laid it flat on the ground, and set her melon on it. Then she took the watermelon and set it next to the honeydew.

Palmer's knife was small but sharp. Starting with the watermelon, the girl made four quick incisions and removed two L-shaped wedges. With the precision of a surgeon, she cut the red flesh from the wedges and carved out the lower half of the watermelon. While the boys watched, she chopped all the meat into cubes. She worked intently, edging the hollowed-out watermelon with angular cuts so it resembled a basket with zigzag trim. Finally, she cubed the green honeydew flesh and mixed it in the basket with the red watermelon.

Leroy grinned. "Nice."

"Ain't done." The girl sneaked down a narrow passage between two houses and returned with a handful of mint leaves.

"Tear these into bits and sprinkle 'em over them melon chunks," she said.

When the basket was finished, the girl set it in her cart and took off down the street.

"Wait!" Palmer howled.

"Follow me," she hissed. "Not too close."

Before long, the boys spotted a housemaid ambling down the street. The woman was holding ribbons attached to the wrists of a little boy and girl. They toddled along beside her, tow-headed twins dressed in blue look-alike outfits. The Honeydew Girl cut Palmer and Leroy a look and they retreated. Palmer pretending to kick a stone down the street, but he kept an eye on their new partner.

The transaction was over in a minute.

Leroy snorted: "You see them prissy white kids pesterin for a bite outa our fruit basket?"

Palmer gave the Honeydew Girl a hard look. "What'ja get?"

"Ten cents. Seven for me, three for you."

"No fair!"

The girl pursed her lips. "I gets more on account of the basket was my notion. From here on, we join up, make baskets, and split the money even."

That spring they sold dozens of fruit baskets. Palmer and Leroy pocketed more money than they'd ever seen.

One day in late June, the girl took a small, round watermelon off Palmer's cart and started shaving off bits of the green skin. Gradually, she made deeper and deeper crescents that eventually exposed the red pulp. Palmer and Leroy watched as the melon took on an uncanny resemblance to a blooming rose. A sous chef paid fifty cents for the rose melon. It was a banner day.

When farmers came to the city with cucumbers, the girl told Palmer to buy the biggest ones, the cukes that sold for a penny apiece because they were more apt to be tough and bitter. She sliced each cuke in half lengthwise, hollowed out the rind and filled it with diced cucumber meat, chive, red pepper, and day-old beignets from alley bins. In a single, record day they sold sixteen cucumber boats.

In the afternoons they would divvy up the cash. Then the girl would pick up her cart handle and walk off. She never said where she was going and the boys never dared ask. The Honeydew Girl could be prickly.

"Somebody got at her awhile back, that'd be my guess," Palmer said one night. He and Leroy had been chasing lightning bugs, pulling off the lights and sticking them on their fingers, like rings.

"You see her today?" Leroy asked. "Yard man touched her shoulder and she done jumped like a cat. That girl livin purely on the streets."

Palmer considered this. He's noticed she wore the same blue plaid dress every day, noticed it was getting sort of ripe. He had also taken note of the girl's single glorious attribute, her fleshy, fruit-stained lips.

One afternoon when the carts were empty and the profits divided, the girl grabbed the front of Palmer's shirt. She drew him into the thick cover of an Indian azalea and kissed him full on the mouth, an intimacy so unexpected and astonishing Palmer liked to keel over. The girl was halfway down the block before Palmer realized what had happened. He licked his lips to taste the fruity kiss again.

That night Palmer lay awake a long while mulling over that kiss, hoping the Honeydew Girl would repeat it. He thought next time he might put his arms around her. He hoped she might put her arms around him, too. He imagined how nice that would feel. Palmer could not recall anyone ever wrapping their arms around him, except Leroy, and a hug from Leroy didn't count.

There was no second kiss. The Honeydew Girl never grabbed his collar and pulled him into the bushes, never again kissed him with her luscious lips, her cherry breath.

One day, when the plums and blackberries were done and the squash crop almost finished, the boys waited at the meeting spot but the Honeydew Girl never came. That night Palmer pulled his scratchy blanket to his chin. He lay awake a long time, chewing the inside of his cheek.

"She turn up," Leroy whispered in the dark. "Next spring. Soon as them strawberries come in."

"I knows it," Palmer said.

"Probably wearin that same danged blue dress, too."

Palmer smiled. It occurred to him that maybe he loved the Honeydew Girl.

Clear Running Streams
1919

St. Louis

*T*he boy jabbed his arm in the air. "Father Frank, can we pick our topic?"

The Rev. Francis Michael Cochran tapped a stub of chalk against the side of his nose, as if considering the request, which he was not. The research paper counted for half the semester grade. It always had. The topics would be assigned randomly. They always were.

Father Cochran had been doling out World Literature essay assignments to freshman boys at St. Louis Academy for years. The priest's once-thick head of hair was wispy as spun sugar. The pads of his fingers were puckered. Lavender veins wormed up the side of his shiny forehead. But his eyes were clear and bright, his mind the match of any seminarian's.

"Ah, lad, the answer is no. However, I shall devise a process by which each of you selects a topic by your own hand."

The students groaned. With a shrug, Father Cochran indicated the decision was out of his control. My boys, he thought. My last class of boys, frisky as colts, counting the minutes to the bell.

The next day Father Cochran brought a glass fish bowl to the classroom and set it on his desk. The boys leaned forward, curious about a bowl filled with bits of folded paper.

"Come, lads. Single file. Claim your assignments."

The first boy plunged his hand in the bowl and plucked out a piece of paper. "Thomas Hardy," he told the others. *The Return of the Native.*

The next boy drew Kipling and seemed pleased, but the third student glanced at his topic and pretending to gag.

Father Cochran's brows shot up. "Peter Vogel, whom have you chosen?"

"Do I have to say?"

"Loudly and clearly."

Peter stretched out his arms as if crucified, and sighed, "Thy will be done. It's the Brontë Sisters."

The room erupted in boos and catcalls. By the time the old priest managed to get the classroom under control again, Fritz had pulled a piece of paper from the bowl, returned to his desk, and slipped the assignment into a textbook. Peter Vogel reached across the aisle and grabbed the book.

"Reinhardt got a pope! Some ancient pope named Alexander."

Fritz leapt to his feet. Flashing his signature smile, he pointed at one friend and then another, shouting: "I challenge any papal naysayer to a duel. Epees or pistols, your choice. Men, know this: I shall defend my dead pope to the death!"

Four boys made a chair of their arms and carried Fritz around the room. A parade of classmates followed. Father Cochran brought up the rear, steadied by a blackthorn walking stick.

A week later, Albert called Phillip to his study. "Son, you had Cochran back at the Academy, didn't you?"

"Everybody did, freshman year."

"See if your brother needs help with that term paper, will you? I believe it's due Monday, and your mother tells me Fritz is off to a slow start."

Phillip was now Reinhardt & Krug's assistant First Floor manager. At his father's urging, he agreed to take night courses at St. Louis University, but Phillip found the business of luxury retailing far more stimulating than textbooks.

Albert could not fathom why anyone would spurn the opportunity to further his scholastic knowledge. Albert had dropped out of St. Louis University only reluctantly, and only because his father's debilitating depression made it clear Albert would have to assume the presidency of Reinhardt & Krug far sooner than expected.

Given the choice, Albert would have earned an advanced degree and then perhaps taught. Sometimes, especially in the morning, a sort of wistful melancholy would sweep over him, like the feeling of plunging into a warm pool. He'd be driving downtown or riding the escalator to his office, and suddenly he'd find himself back in the campus library. He could see the shafts of light that slashed from high windows onto the study tables, could smell the scent of old paper and leather book bindings, could hear the flap of turning pages and the scratching of pens, and his contentment was, for the moment, complete. Albert lacked his father's entrepreneurial zeal, but he was a competent man, diligent and kind, the sort of person who inspired employees to perform better.

"Slow start? Father, Fritz is off to no start on that essay. Who did he get?"

"Fritz is under the impression it is a pope named Alexander. I rather suspect it is Alexander Pope. See if you can find a copy of Pope's *Essay on Man*, will you?"

The following night Phillip brought home four books from the St. Louis Public Library. He found Fritz stretched out on his bedroom floor, strumming an invisible ukulele and singing "Doo-Wacka-Doo." Fritz finished the tune and gave Phillip a cheery salute.

"Aww, dry up," Phillip said, wheeling on his heel.

"All right, Philly-boy. Hey, don't be a wet blanket. Open one of those books. I'll write my darn paper about whatever I see on the page."

Phillip tossed a book onto Fritz's bed and walked off in a huff. Fritz picked up the book and read:

Oh Happiness! our being's end and aim!
Good, Pleasure, Ease, Content! Whate'er thy name,
That something still which prompts th'eternal sigh,
For which we bear to live, or dare to die

"Hey now," Fritz said, though nobody was near, "this might be the only pope who actually talks turkey." An hour later Fritz was at his desk, hunched over an Underwood typewriter. Albert smiled at the sound of keys clacking like Morse code.

Within a few days Fritz had finished his essay, a meditation on four lines chosen at random from a body of work written by an author drawn at random. "I regard the poet Alexander Pope as a visionary," his paper began. "His goal in life is happiness. His ideal world is a world of leisure."

Fritz pontificated for five pages and finally drew his thoughts to a dubious, looping conclusion. "In a way, Pope's world is quite like mine. We Reinhardts live in a bubble of pleasure and ease, a bubble that shields us from harm and heartache. The analogy is imperfect, however, for a bubble is a complexity of math, chemistry and physics, but its membrane is a millionth of an inch thick. Whereas our house on Portland Place is made of brick. It's sturdy and durable, but still it is a bubble. As long as nobody removes the 'e' from Pope, the Reinhardt bubble won't pop."

That afternoon Fritz rode his bicycle to a sporting goods store and bought a split bamboo fly rod. Back at home, he threaded line through the guides and attached a lure. He scissored the edges of his term paper until it resembled the rough outlines of a fish and stuck the hook through each page. He wrapped the essay, the hook, line and the fishing rod in brown paper and rode his bike to school. At the rectory, he left instructions at the reception desk to give the package to Father Cochran.

The old priest hadn't received a gift in years. With eager, fumbling hands, he tore off the wrappings and let them fall to the floor. He glanced at the fish-shaped essay papers and carefully removed them from the hook, thinking: What had one of the lads done? How did he know?

Father Cochran grasped the rod with the overhand grip of an expert and executed a forward cast. The line flew down the long rectory corridor and plunged into an imaginary brook.

Francis Cochran grew up on his family's dairy farm. The work was never finished, but on Sunday afternoons his father waved him off and Francis hiked to his favorite spot, a clear, running brook at the far edge of the farm. He would sit for hours on a flat outcrop of rock and cast a line into the rills. On good days he would fill his metal pail with crappies and panfish. Casting in solitude, the youth observed how the sun sparked on ripples, how wildflowers pushed up from mud banks and leggy water bugs skimmed the surface, how mosquitoes loved to whine at his ears and how speckled fish passed over the shoals, smooth as dirigibles. He regarded these wonders as proof of a benevolent God, a God who made the smallest things magnificent. Father Cochran hadn't fished since the day he turned seventy, at a surprise outing put together by his fellow Jesuits at the Academy. That was nine years ago.

These days, the old priest didn't bother to hide his failing health. Two fingers fit easily between his Roman collar and the corrugations of his neck. His cassock drooped at the shoulders. He had taught freshman boys for as long as he could remember, leavening Shakespeare and Hardy with a measure of Kipling and Moliere. He treasured each day, each class, each boy. Most, anyway.

Back in his small room, he took up a red pencil and wrote "B" on Fritz's essay. The lad did analyze Pope and clearly benefited from doing so, he told himself. But the essay ended with capricious piffle, as usual. "Precisely why my colleagues regard the boy lightly," he said aloud. "If they'd only look deeper, they'd see something truly remarkable."

Father Cochran carried the fly rod out to the garden and lowered himself to a stone bench. His joints throbbed in the cold. His nose dripped. He ignored these small discomforts, preferring to occupy his mind with the Reinhardt boy's thesis. A bubble is among the most fragile of physical constructs, he knew. The slightest breeze whisks it away. The prick of a pin destroys it. Inevitably, gravity will pull it down by its own infinitesimal weight and it will collide with something, anything, the smallest thing, to its doom.

Father Cochran cast the fly rod, revisiting the streams of his youth. In a short while, though, the effort tired him. He rubbed his chest. "I've watched that boy for months now," he murmured, though no one was near. "Under his sporting shell I sense something profound. But what? Goodness? Yes. The boy has a natural benevolence, an innate desire to give of himself. No, a *need* to give of himself. Is he a jokester? Bah, that's only his immaturity. One needs to look deeper to see the boy's true self, to understand how rare he is. Men yearn for proof of God's existence, but failed to recognize His hand reaching out to fill the heart of a boy with grace."

The old priest tried to stand and faltered. He had left his blackthorn stick in the rectory. He dropped hard to the bench and sat there, dazed. From somewhere far off he heard the burble of children laughing. A breeze ruffled his snowy hair and he smelled tendrils of scent. Soup. His grandmother's barley soup. He hadn't smelled that since he was a boy on the farm. He looked across the schoolyard to bare-limbed trees in the far distance and found to his surprise that he could pick out purple finches, flickers, and starlings in the branches, could clearly see each feather, even their darting eyes. These things he noted affectionately and without a sense of loss, for by then his body had slipped to earth, and his soul had swept up to the embracing sky.

Askew
1920

New Orleans

Leroy spotted her before Palmer did. The boys had spent another morning roaming the city, pushing aside brush, poking into cluttered carriage houses and moist, unholy alleys. She lay askew, crumpled on flour sacks alive with maggots, her skinny limbs flopped at impossible angles. The flies had found her, Leroy saw that right off. Something had gnawed her foot, too. Alley rat, he guessed. In the smirchy light, her skin was the color of the faded burlap sacks.

"She here! The Honeydew Girl!"

Palmer ran into the shadows.

"She dead," Leroy said, his voice flat. He bent over and gripped his knees, triangulated. "Look like somebody wrenched her."

"I knows it." Palmer shoved his fists into his pockets. A muscle worked in his jaw, as if he was chewing something small and hard. All fall, all winter, Palmer had looked for her.

The girl's chin was resting against her collar. A bone jutted from the paper-thin skin below her ear, like a tongue poked against the inside of a cheek. Leroy tugged off his soft cap and held it over his heart. After a long minute, he laid a hand on Palmer's shoulder and said, "Ain't nothin y'all can do for this here Honeydew Girl."

Palmer squatted beside her body and traced his finger down her arm.

"Gotta go, brother," Leroy said. "Police come by, we cooked."

Palmer took out his knife and cut a strip of fabric from the hem of the girl's pinafore. He closed his eyes and held it to his face, breathing the scent of her. Then he tucked the fabric in his pocket and walked out of the alley. Golden daggers of sunlight pierced his heart.

Bold Vision
1920

St. Louis

*P*ops, don't throw that newspaper out."

Albert lowered his chin and looked over his spectacles. "Got another fish to wrap, Fritz?"

"Nah. Just want a look."

Albert handed over the *Wall Street Journal* and Fritz took it to his bedroom. For weeks he'd been poring over stock tables, scribbling notes and making calculations in a moleskin booklet. Every Friday he made three theoretical stock picks. At the end the month, he verified his hunches.

A year ago, during his sophomore year at St. Louis Academy, Fritz combined his Christmas money with his winnings from schoolyard math games and, under Albert's signature, bought four shares of stock at $3.50 a share. By spring, Fritz's holdings had turned a $2.75 profit.

Now, at 17, Fritz owned stock in a motor car company, a copper mine, a shipping line, and two railroads. He researched his picks carefully, selecting big businesses that were financially solid and that produced tangible goods of lasting value. He researched the companies' leaders as well, making sure to pick firms guided by men of bold vision.

A Double Windsor
1920

St. Louis

Albert looked out his office window and noticed his son's car speeding down the street. He picked up the phone on his desk and dialed the extension for the loading dock supervisor. "Fritz showing a positive attitude yet?"

"Couldn't say, Mr. Reinhardt. Your boy's wandered off again." The supervisor spat a caramel stream of chaw and went back to work.

This time, Fritz wasn't going far. He rounded the corner and double-parked his roadster at R&K's Washington Avenue entrance. When he reached the top floor, he shot Albert's secretary a wink and walked straight into his father's office.

"I'm dying down there, Pops. The only part that's, what would you call it, formative? is the jokes. Man, those drivers roll in with some juicy ones. Hear the one about the... "

Albert cleared his throat.

"Anyway, I've been down there every Saturday since Hector was a pup. Isn't it time you moved me up? Say, men's suits? Or neckties? Neckties would be acey-deucey."

Two weeks later Albert re-assigned Fritz to Men's Furnishings.

O

"Good afternoon, madam," Fritz said, "Can I help you?"

"A necktie for my husband, Mr. Herbert W. Heumann."

The blue-haired matron wore a feathered hat, a lizard handbag, and a beady-eyed fox stole. A small terrier perched in the crook of her arm. Fritz willed himself to not laugh, and launched into the script Phillip had prepared for him.

"Madam, as you appear to be a person of exquisite taste, I'll show you Reinhardt & Krug's finest selection."

The terrier yipped.

"Shush, Bartley." Mrs. Heumann pursed her liver-colored lips into a pucker and kissed the dog's forehead.

Fritz fanned ties across the counter. "These came directly from France, ma'am, designed by Mssr. Patou."

Mrs. Heumann glared at the ties, and then at Fritz, and then pronounced Cubism to be crude and said that the ties looked like her granddaughter had painted them.

Fritz kept his expression neutral. He brought out a dozen more ties, conservative stripes and small-scale prints. Mrs. Heumann fingered them with gloved hands.

Fritz hoped to scoot out early enough to make his two o'clock tee time at Topping Ridge. "Should I try one on?" he said, slipping a tone-on-tone tie around his neck. He finished the look with a four-in-hand knot.

"No," the woman sniffed. "Not that."

He removed the tone-on-tone and tried on a rep stripe, tying it with a Double Windsor knot. "This one's a beaut, right Mrs. Heumann?"

"Don't use slang with me, young man," she said. Bartley bared its tiny teeth and growled.

Eventually, Fritz showed Mrs. Heumann every tie in the case. He tied Shelby knots, Kelvins, and four-in-hands. Minutes passed slow as faucet drips.

"Try the first again," Mrs. Heumann pouted.

Fritz leaned across the counter, swung the knotted tie like a lasso and roped in Mrs. Heumann. He raised the knot until it neared the fleshy netherworld between her second and third chins. Then he dashed off toward the store's Sixth Street doors and freedom. Mrs Heumann screamed for help. The dog leaped from her arms and ran cirlces around her, barking as loud as it could.

At supper, Albert re-introduced a variation of his favorite guessing game: he proposed they try to name each of the twenty-eight presidents, in order. Turns went round the table until they got to Wilson. Emily declared that of all the presidents, the one she most admired was John Adams. Fritz announced he was resigning from Reinhardt & Krug and relinquishing all future interests in the business. Forks clattered to plates. In the thundering silence, Fritz looked at his father and then at his mother. "I'm going to make more money and be much happier doing something else."

Phillip lobbed a biscuit across the table. "More money? Says you."

"Says me. I intend to make heaps of it. And I won't be sticking dimes in a cash register all day, either."

Phillip took offense. "They're Tiffany cash registers. Grandfather George had them designed especially for us."

Fritz went on. "I have it mostly figured out, Father. I just have to be a little better than the next guy."

Albert wiped his mouth and sat back. "That's the key, is it?"

"That's it, Pops. The horse that wins the race wears the roses, but he only has to win by a nose. Even if he wins by a whisker, he takes home ten times more prize money than the nag that came in second. After I graduate from the Academy, I'm going to be the best stock broker in St. Louis, a nose in front of all the other guys."

"Betting a lot on your schnoz," Phillip chided.

"Bet you an ace-spot, brother. Everybody's in the market these days, but darn few of them are smart investors, and a lot of them are suckers. I heard about a guy over on Delmar who convinced his parents to put three hundred bucks into RCA Victor. Listen to this. So the parents paid ten percent of the share price and a bank loaned them the rest on some half-baked installment plan, putting up the stocks they were buying as collateral. They call that buying on margin."

"What's so bad about that?" Phillip asked.

"Those people could only scrape together ten percent," Fritz explained. "That means they bought ten times the number of shares they could afford. Everybody thinks the market is going to keep on appreciating forever. Everybody expects to sell at one hell, oh, sorry mother, at one heck of a profit."

"Isn't that just playing the market?" Phillip said.

"It's greedy and it's dangerous. Playing the market is fine and dandy during a bull market. But when the market turns sour, which it eventually will, the schnooks who bought on margin are in for a shellacking."

"Here's my wager," Phillip countered. "I'll bet you come crawling back to the store with your tail between your legs."

"Philly-Boy, you've always wanted to be the big cheese. As of tonight, I'm officially stepping out of the way."

Albert had been listening in silence. At times he rather enjoyed a good back-and-forth during supper, provided the topic was appropriate for mixed company. Besides, he had already made his decision about Fritz. After the menswear manager phoned upstairs with word of Fritz's appalling outburst, Albert had jabbed the lever on his intercom.

"Miss Simmons, have Stevens bring the car around. Then ask Ferguson in Menswear to gift-wrap six neckties and put them in the car. Conservative ties, not those Patou things. And get Topping Ridge on the phone, the pro shop."

By the time Albert got to Topping Ridge, the club pro had retrieved Fritz from a sand hazard on the third fairway. Back in the car, Albert and Fritz sat as far apart from one another as they could and rode the distance to Lafayette Square in chilly silence. At the Heumann home, Fritz carried a gift box to the door.

"For Mr. Herbert W. Heumann," he said, handing the box to the housekeeper, "with Reinhardt & Krug's deepest apologies."

Now Albert looked down the length of the dining room table, and he was alarmed to see tears welling in Emily's eyes. She assumes Fritz has disappointed me, he told himself. Quite the opposite. The boy is doing what I yearned to do and could not. Albert set aside his napkin and rose to his feet. For a long moment the dining room crackled with tension. "Fritz, you're young, not even finished with high school," Albert began. "It isn't too early, though, to fix your course to a worthy pursuit. Whatever road you choose, son, I want you to know the decision is yours to make."

Emily relaxed, and Albert raised his voice over the boys' excited chatter. "I'm going to level with you. I had hoped you both would join me downtown. Phillip, you've made me a proud man and I expect you will continue to do so. And Fritz, there will always be a position for you at Reinhardt & Krug."

"Thank you, Father."

Albert dipped his fingers into a small vest pocket and brought out his gold watch. "It is half-past eight. I think it's time for a revelation of my own."

Emily and the boys leaned in. Albert was a man of great dignity; the notion that he had been keeping a secret was hugely intriguing.

"At ten o'clock each evening I make an accounting. I ask myself whether I have used the hours given to me for worthy endeavor. I review the day, determine whether I have improved myself or the store, whether I've bettered the lot of our customers or my employees, or merely refreshed myself in order to further these goals the next day. If so, I retire unencumbered. But if I find the day wanting —"

"Thirty lashes with a wet noodle," Fritz laughed.

Albert scowled and went on. "Each day is precious, son. Each dawning presents a once-in-a-lifetime opportunity. I am far from perfect, and on the days I squander that opportunity, I cannot rest until I put the waning minutes to use."

"How?" Emily asked, genuinely bewildered.

"I say the Lord's Prayer, asking forgiveness. I say the Nicene Creed for faith and the Hail Mary for intercession on behalf of those whom I have failed."

"I never knew," Emily murmured.

"What, not on your knees, Father?" Fritz chuckled. "Sorry, pops, doesn't count."

"Son, I've suspected you would pursue a career in finance. You show interest in it and a remarkable ability for it. The world of finance is a worthy choice but rife with temptation. Remember, honorable men adhere to an absolute morality. Deciding right and wrong based on circumstances or potential gain will blight your soul. Most importantly, be accountable for your decisions, society places a high value on that."

Phillip glanced at Fritz and silently mouthed the word, 'Whitman.'

Albert walked around the table and stood behind Fritz's chair, mentally reviewing passages from his favorite authors. Whitman, he decided. Whitman, when one is at a crossroads.

Albert rested his pale hands on Fritz's shoulders and cleared his throat, a willow of a man trying for the resonant tone of an archbishop.

"Oh to be self-balanced for contingencies,
To confront night, storms, hunger, ridicule, accidents, rebuffs..."

"Darling," Emily interrupted, "you don't think Fritz will confront ridicule and rebuffs?"

Albert was abashed. "Why no, certainly not. Whitman was speaking of generalized bedevilments. I, on the other hand, have only angels at my table."

Fritz flapped his arms like wings. "No, Father. Archangels!"

Most Eligible Bachelors
1921

St. Louis

*A*n invitation to the Veiled Prophet Ball. In St. Louis, it was the gold standard of status. For the third year in a row, Phillip would be dancing at the city's signature society event. This year, Fritz would, too.

Crimson maple leaves drifted like confetti outside the conservatory's glass walls. Emily leaned back in her wicker chair, dreamy-eyed. My boys are the most eligible bachelors in St. Louis, she assured herself. Then a slight frown darkened her lovely features. Oh, Phillip isn't what you might call dashing, but he's tall and fit, and he's advancing at the store. He converses well enough, too. Phillip isn't as witty as Fritz, but who is?

Emily knew her sons as only a mother does. Phillip commanded a room, Fritz enlivened it. When Fritz walked into a party, the air felt suddenly charged. Lights burned whiter. Musicians picked up the tempo. Dancers whirled faster. Everyone felt gayer, lighter, brighter, better. She had witnessed this a dozen times, Fritz's charisma.

Emily sipped her coffee, lost in pleasant reverie.

In autumn, St. Louisans celebrated the Veiled Prophet festivities with a public parade and, later, with a strictly private ball. In the morning, working families bundled up their little ones and gathered four and five deep along the parade route, jostling for position. Fathers hoisted toddlers to their shoulders as soon as they heard the marching bands, and everybody oohed and aahed as dozens of lavishly decorated floats rolled by.

For families like the Reinhardts, the Veiled Prophet festivities didn't begin until dusk, at the start of the invitation-only formal dance introducing young women of society to society. Each new debutante dressed in a billowing white gown and glided into the crystal ballroom on the arm of a handsome young man whose job was to steady her as she made a low bow before the enthroned Veiled Prophet.

Emily smiled, remembering her debut, years earlier. "I practiced that curtsy for weeks," she murmured. "My girlfriends and I were so afraid we'd fall. And oh, how we tried to guess who the Veiled Prophet was, sitting on that throne, hidden behind that sparkly veil. It was all so mysterious, so beautiful."

"My, oh my," Esmie said, trickling fresh coffee into Emily's cup. "That must have been something, Mizz Emily."

Emily glanced at the clock. Albert was playing a chilly golf game at Topping Ridge. Next Saturday he'd start exercising at the Missouri Athletic Club, swimming laps in the indoor pool, following up with cigars, cards, and Scotch.

Emily consulted her appointment book. A luncheon and a tea on Monday. Committee work on Wednesday and Thursday. The Portland Place Horticultural Club lecture series, she'd have to get started planning that, organizing her committee. Each day she wrote a few more solicitation letters for the St. Vincent de Paul Society's annual fund drive. And soon she must turn her attention to the family's holiday party.

The house was quiet. Phillip was off early in his Bugatti, off to Karlsruhe again.

Phillip was the third generation of Reinhardts riding to hounds at Karlsruhe, a European-style hunt club situated on wooded bluffs overlooking the Missouri River. Emily smiled, envisioning her son galloping across the countryside. Phillip cut a dashing figure on horseback, in his crested jacket and twill jodhpurs, his back ramrod straight and his heels nicely down in the stirrups. Soon, she knew, he'd advance from junior status to fully vested membership at Karlsruhe, at Topping Ridge and the M.A.C. In a few years the clubs would welcome Fritz, too. Albert's friends would submit formal proposals. Letters of invitation would arrive. Albert would quietly write each club a large check. The votes, cast by secret ballot, would be unanimous. Phillip and Fritz were Reinhardts. Membership at Karlsruhe and Topping Ridge was not predicated on social connections or affluence. That was taken for granted. For clubs at the apex of the city's social ladder, admission was a matter of genealogy.

Fritz had left the house, too, to join his buddies for rummy at Topping Ridge. "Laphroaig, my man," he said, striding into the Grille Room.

The barman drew a pilsner. "Your father left instructions. Only beer, Mister Fritz, and only one. You're barely sixteen – what you doing drinking Scotch?"

"And a mountain of club sandwiches for my friends over there. Say, Luther, you know what a man eats when he's stranded in the desert? The sand-which is there! Get it? Sandwich."

Fritz roared at his own joke and waved to his friends. The fellows at the game table were a few years older than Fritz but they'd all grown up together at Topping Ridge, ordering kiddy cocktails, diving splashy cannonball-style into the pool, taking golf and tennis lessons, squiring debutantes to the club's swanky dances. One of the guys was already working full-time at his uncle's bank. Another fellow was headed for the family business, manufacturing fuses. The third was on the fast track at Ralston Purina.

Fritz rounded the table, ostensibly to shake each friend's hand. The guys wisely breasted their cards. Luther brought over a tray of triple-decker sandwiches and the Ralston Purina fellow grinned. "Looks like great chow."

"Sir?" Luther said.

"That's what we call it at Ralston. Remember Mr. Danforth served in France during the war, right? When he got back, he wanted to try out some of the lingo he'd heard the doughboys using. Over there, they called food 'chow.' So now Ralston's putting 'chow' on all every sack of feed we make."

"Hey Luther," Fritz said, "toss a log on the fire, will you? It's awful chowly outside."

○

A sharp cold snap had powdered Chicago with dry snow. Frosty gusts sent litter swirling in miniature cyclones that skipped along the sidewalks. Helena DeMore was helping her mother chop pork shoulder and mince garlic for homemade salami. Maybe for the last time, Helena thought, tingling at the secret. She and her new boyfriend planned to elope that night.

Helena was sixteen and new to the neighborhood. The boy was seventeen, a school dropout, a biscuit-factory worker who knew his way around Little Sicily. His name was Vincent, he told her. Conqueror.

Vincenzo, Vincent, Jack McGurn. Future welterweight champion of the world. Future assassin.

The Same Shade of Gray
1922

St. Louis

Albert had a surprise for Phillip. It was the large corner office on the uppermost floor of R&K that had been vacant since Otto Krug passed away. "Your new quarters come with a request, son," Albert said. "Would you take a drive out to Topping Ridge, say one Thursday a month?"

Phillip's smile melted. "Father, Thursdays are Ladies Day."

"Exactly. The Topping Ridge ladies are some of our most loyal customers. Engage them in light conversation, even if it's just for a few minutes. Think of it as marketing, or research. I expect we'll benefit from your outings."

Phillip hated the idea of exchanging pleasantries with blue-haired matrons at Topping Ridge, but he saw the logic in it. On Thursday, he drove out to the club. The women playing contract bridge were delighted to offer their opinions about everything from Persian rugs and roasting pans to pop-up toasters and silk scarves. After a quarter-hour, Phillip left them to their bidding auctions and returned to the cloakroom. Howell, the attendant, was behind the half-door, as usual. Just as Howell passed Phillip's cashmere overcoat across the divide, a young woman rounded a corner.

"Howell," she said, stopping abruptly, "are you giving away my coat?"

Howell fumbled for the hanger tag. "My mistake, Miss Richmond. Your wrap must have been right next to Mr. Reinhardt's."

"I see," she said, softening. "And both coats are the same shade of gray. Howell, don't you think Mr. Reinhardt has excellent taste?"

Phillip was uncharacteristically flustered. "I'm sorry, have we met?"

"Briefly. Last year at the Veiled Prophet Ball."

"Right. You were with Garrison Simon.

"And you escorted..."

"Just now I can't recall. But I remember you. Florence Winter Richmond."

Phillip held her coat and in the moment it took Florence to glide her arms into the sleeves, Phillip undertook an evaluation of her that was swift and sure as a diamond merchant raising a gem to the light. Her dress was stylish, he saw, sashed below the waist. Her shoes were fashionable T-straps.

He noted Florence had arranged her hair in loose finger-waves, eschewing the odious short chop all the new-fangled flappers were sporting. Though her back was to him, he had noticed her features were lovely, especially her porcelain complexion. He found himself tempted to run his finger down the knobs of her long, slender neck.

Back at the store, Phillip gave considerable thought to Florence Winter Richmond and concluded she was worth going after. She was chic but conservative, sophisticated and yet ladylike, educated, but not overtly opinionated. These were qualities he admired in a woman. More to the point, her family belonged to Topping Ridge and she'd made her debut at the Veiled Prophet Ball, so she came from the right kind of people. Six months after their chance meeting at the cloakroom, Phillip and Florence exchanged wedding vows at a small stone church near the banks of the Mississippi River, a site dedicated a century and a half earlier by Pierre Laclede, the city's founder.

The honeymoon was both a romantic getaway and a foraging expedition. In Venice, Florence bought yards of lace and six pairs of leather gloves. In Portello, Phillip ordered a sporty Alfa Romeo. In Paris, Florence visited couturiers on the Rue du Faubourg Saint-Honore and Phillip toured the Citroen plant on the Quai de Javel. In Belgium they purchased bed linens at Libeco Lagae.

Soon after they returned to St. Louis, Phillip drove Florence out to the suburban Village of Ladue, to see a magnificent Tudor on Barnes Road that had come up for sale. Phillip was careful to appear ambivalent during negotiations, but the timbered gables and tall setbacks impressed him. Phillip envisioned the four-bay garage filled with his burgeoning collection of luxury cars. Florence envisioned filling the five bedrooms with their children.

In the eighth month of her first pregnancy, Florence felt a series of sharp pains. The baby was coming early and fast, and, though she could not know it, the baby was presenting rump-first. The doctor arrived at the house just in time. Afterward, he found Phillip pacing the upstairs hall.

"Congratulations, Mr. Reinhardt, you have a beautiful daughter. She's a little small but otherwise healthy. Your wife had a difficult delivery, however. Florence will require bed rest for at least two weeks." The man then took Phillip by the elbow and moved away from the bedroom door.

"What is it?" Phillip asked. The doctor was frowning and refused to make eye contact. Phillip knew these were worrisome signs.

When the man finally explained his concerns, he looked at Phillip straight on. "Florence lost a lot of blood. She's very weak. Another pregnancy will kill her."

Phillip appeared stunned. From his expression, the doctor was concerned Phillip had not fully understood him. "She will die carrying a second child," the older man added, and then, enunciating each word crisply, he said: "You must make absolutely sure that doesn't happen. Do you follow, sir?"

Phillip raked his hand through his hair. "I, well, I'm afraid I don't."

The doctor stepped closer and squinted into Phillip's face, but said nothing.

"No more children?" Phillip said, sputtering. "We're Catholic. We cannot use... How are we to live like that?" Phillip's gaze darted, seeing dull years spinning out, nights in separate beds, separate bedrooms, seeing a lifetime trapped in a platonic marriage. He paced the hall, chewing the inside of his cheek. He barely noticed the doctor quietly let himself out.

Behind the bedroom door, tears spilled down porcelain cheeks and landed on linens woven on fine Belgian looms.

You Won't Fall
1922

St. Louis

Rosati-Kain was in a frenzy of excitement. The girls giggled and whispered and passed notes in class, too distracted to open a book and far too keyed up to study. The teachers were restless and temperamental. The switchboard jangled with phone calls from parents. Posters had been up for a week. Fliers were in the mail. This year's Spring Play would be the biggest and best ever. Ever!

Peter Pan
A Spectacular, High-Flying Extravaganza of Ultra-Aerial Proportions

Art students were creating scenery — an Edwardian nursery and a swashbuckling pirate ship. The sewing club was whipping up elaborate costumes. The science teacher volunteered her Newfoundland dog. The drama coach, Sister Anna Joseph, took it upon herself to hire a professional rigging crew. It was a shameful expense, she knew, but the two lead actresses would actually fly. Tickets sold out in three days.

Mary Alice Whitfield would be Peter Pan, of course. With years of acting lessons under her belt, Mary Alice was scheduled to make her triumphant debut that summer in the Muny Opera production of *Geisha*. It was a minor role, non-speaking, a tea house servant girl. Still, Mary Alice would appear on stage in Forest Park. That was something.

Lydia Marie Conrad was only a freshman, but her long chestnut curls, her Cupid's bow lips and adorable dimples won her the coveted role of Wendy. Sister Anna Joseph assigned Doris Conrad to the stagehand crew, unwittingly rubbing fresh salt into an old wound. For weeks the Conrad bungalow had simmered. Lydia flounced from room to room, script in hand, reciting her lines aloud. Doris ricocheted from sullen silences to peevish outbursts.

On opening night, six hundred students, parents, siblings and boyfriends poured into the gymnasium. Behind the stage curtain, the rigging boss chomped a dry cigar and barked at his assistants as they buckled Mary Alice and Lydia into their flight harnesses. "Lash the straps well, men, or the girls will break their necks. Remember, they'll be fifteen feet in the air."

Peter Pan's costume was simple, emerald green shorts, blouse, and tights. Wendy wore a long ruffled nightgown that covered Lydia from shoulder to ankles. Sister Anna Joseph stayed nearby as the crewmen adjusted their straps and buckles under the girls' costumes.

Lydia fussed with the cuffs of her nightgown. "Sister, you're sure I won't fall?"

"Yes, dear. The crane is really sturdy. That wire looks thin, but it's plenty strong."

"You're sure?"

"Yes. And besides, your sister will be right next to the man operating the crane. You won't fall. Now run out on stage. It's time."

The first act went smoothly. When the three Darling children started a pillow fight in their nursery, feathers flew on schedule. Wendy stitched Peter's shadow. Finally, Nana the dog romped on the beds, diverting the audience's attention while Mary Alice and Lydia dashed behind the curtains at the rear of the stage. The rigging crew quickly attached Kirby wires to the harnesses. In a wink, Mary Alice and Lydia were in the spotlight again.

When it came time for the girls to fly, Sister Anna Joseph gave the signal, the men cranked their winches, and Mary Alice and Lydia rose into the air, as if by magic. They whirled across the stage and back three times and then soared out above the first rows of seats. The audience was ecstatic.

Weeks earlier, during rehearsals, Doris had discovered a large electric fan stored between the layers of tall curtains offstage. Now, working quietly in the dark, Doris plugged the cord into a socket and crouched unseen next to the machine. She rested her cheek against the silent motor and watched her sister, a white ruffled angel. The audience was on its feet, clapping and cheering. Twin spotlights were sweeping smooth paths, following Peter and Wendy as they sailed along. Lydia flew toward Doris and flashed her sister a triumphant smile. Then she pivoted in mid-air and flew to the far side of the stage again.

Doris gave the control knob a sharp twist. The fan blasted air across the stage. Mary Alice was flying toward Doris, facing the wind head-on. Lydia was flying in the opposite direction. The strong airflow puffed out her nightgown like a balloon.

Doris twisted the knob again, to the highest setting. The concussive blast hit the ruffled nightgown, flipped it inside out and sent it whooshing over Lydia's shoulders.

Folding chairs clattered and collapsed. The audience rose to its feet, the gymnasium plunged into mayhem. Grandparents gasped. Parents groaned.

120

Sleepy toddlers wailed. Rosati-Kain girls squealed and clutched one another. High school boys pointed and guffawed. Nuns watching from the fringes shut their eyes and made hasty signs of the cross. The rigging boss bit his cigar in two.

For a minute, maybe more, Lydia continued to fly in the turbulence, unable to help herself. Strung up by a wire, shackled in ruffles, legs wheeling, arms waggling, she soared across the stage and back. Against the blue velvet backdrop, her underpants blazed like a comet.

Taste of Blood
1923

Chicago

*O*f all the collectors for the Black Hand, Orazzio Tropea was the most sadistic, disposed to inflict pain, indifferent to the suffering of his victims, a torturer whose weapon of choice was an ice pick.

Angelo Gibaldi was a decent man, a father, good husband, and an industrious worker. He now owned the café on the edge of Little Sicily where he started years ago as a dish washer. The small restaurant served gyro sandwiches, hot soup, and small jars of hooch. "Why not make a few nickels selling grappa under the table?" Angelo told his Guiseppa, when she worried. "Some my best customers, they cops."

The Black Hand had no problem with Angelo so long as he made tribute payments, regular. But now there was a problem, and on a bitter cold January morning Orazzio Tropea was sent to fix it. Tropea spoke briefly with Angelo and then left the cafe. Late that afternoon, Tropea and two other thugs returned. Tropea drew a shotgun from his coat and pulled the trigger. The first blast hit Angelo in the chest. The second blast ripped open his head. Angelo was dead before he hit the floor.

Vincent — now called Jack McGurn — decided to stop at the café on his way home from the biscuit factory. He'd put in an hour at the gym later, for sure. McGurn liked punching the Everlast heavy bag, but what he really loved was going a round or two in the ring, sweating like a pig, dancing like a damn bull fighter. At some point, he'd feel a strange rush, a tingly mix of euphoria and rage. That's when he'd start slugging like a piston. He loved the lightning attacks, the dodgy defenses and copper-penny taste of blood, the roar in his ears. He loved it. Craved it.

McGurn reached the café moments after the get-away car sped off. The place was in chaos. When he saw his father's body in a pool of blood on the floor, he collapsed in anguish. Silently, he vowed revenge.

Within months of Angelo's murder, Orazzio Tropea and the two thugs with him at the café, Jimmy the Bug and Willie Altierri, were murdered. Word spread. Vincenzo Gibaldi — Jack McGurn — would soon be the top bodyguard for Chicago's most notorious mobster. Having graduated from slingshots, to BB guns, then to pistols and shotguns, McGurn would master a new and far more lethal weapon: a Thompson submachine gun.

Developed for military use, it would be marketed to policemen, yet available at street corner sporting goods shops. It was thirty-one inches long and light as a feather. It fired 100 rounds a minute. At close range, the bullets would pierce steel.

Soon McGurn would become a dead-eye shot at fifty yards.

Catherine Underhill Fitzpatrick

A Small Brass Key
1924

Chicago

*P*hillip boarded an early train for Chicago. He lunched with business associates at the Drake Hotel and spent a productive afternoon touring display booths at a retailers' trade show. At five, he flagged a taxi and headed for one of the luxury apartment buildings that form a glass and limestone escarpment along Lake Shore Drive.

"Good evening, Mr. Reinhardt. Nice to see you again," the doorman said, opening the elevator cage. "Miss Valerie is at home, sir, in the penthouse."

I should think so, Phillip said to himself, I'm paying for the place. As the elevator rose, Phillip rubbed the small brass key in his trouser pocket.

Social Calls
1924

St. Louis

I'm here about the job."

The receptionist looked up, startled. "The job?"

"The job for which I am perfectly suited."

A month after graduating from St. Louis Academy, Fritz launched his new career. He drove to Clayton, a growing community seven miles west of the city, and showed up at a brokerage house. On the basis of the Reinhardt name, a senior partner agreed to see him. That afternoon at the management meeting, the man brought up Fritz's surprise visit.

"It was unorthodox, to say the least," he said. "And I'm a little suspicious. Why isn't the boy at Reinhardt & Krug?"

"I have no idea," another partner said. "In terms of a position here, he hasn't one iota of experience. Besides, I heard him in your office, and let me tell you, the incessant jokes will drive clients away in droves."

The others rustled their papers, ready to move on, but the firm's silver-haired senior partner spoke up:

"If I may, a personal anecdote. Gladys and I live on Portland Place, as all of you know. For years we've been guests at Reinhardt Christmas parties. Big shebangs. Back a ways, when the boy was still in knee pants, he performed the most incredible feat of mathematics I've ever seen. I know Albert Reinhardt, he wouldn't raise a fool. I say we get the boy back here and find out what's in his own portfolio, if he has one. That should tell us a great deal."

Within the week, Fritz was hired on a trial basis. At first, he struck the senior partners as spending an inordinate amount of time with their pretty young secretaries, regaling the office girls with funny stories and limericks. Soon, though, the partners realized Fritz's cavalier methods belied a blade-sharp mind and solid instincts.

Fritz woke each day at five-thirty, rode the banister down the stairs, and retrieved the newspaper from the stoop. He brewed strong coffee and left enough in the pot for Esmie, who took the bus to Portland Place and arrived at six. Back in bed, Fritz combed columns of stock listings looking for trends, noting surprises, tracking fluctuations.

At nine or so he finally strolled into the office. For the rest of the morning, he chatted on the phone with prospective clients, cajoling them with knock-knock jokes and funny stories, all the while threading ticker tape through his fingers. By the end of the second week nineteen-year-old Fritz had forged a base of twelve clients.

"And that," he bragged to Phillip, "is without pestering Father's friends for pity business."

Fritz's first clients were his buddies from St. Louis Academy, college-bound fellows who were too young to have much to invest, but too loyal to their pal Reinhardt to turn him down. On a foundation of $8 and $10 portfolios, Fritz began to build their holdings, and his. Three months after joining the brokerage house, he resigned. That night the family gathered at the M.A.C. to celebrate Phillip's twenty-third birthday. After dessert, Fritz made an announcement.

"Father, I need you to co-sign some paperwork. I took a year lease on a swell office over on Maryland Avenue. I'm starting my own investment firm."

No one spoke. The clatter of silverware was deafening as waiters cleared the table. Albert removed his steel-rimmed spectacles and wiped the lenses, struggling for control. "Isn't this hasty, son? You've hardly been there —"

"Tarry in haste, repent at leisure. By the way, Philly-boy, I'll need a desk and a couple of chairs from R&K. Got any to spare?"

Emily broke in before Phillip could explode. "What will you call your new company, dear?"

"Thanks for asking, Mother. I'm calling it Fritz M. Reinhardt & Associates."

Albert looked bewildered. "You have associates? Already? Who?"

"Just me, so far. Sounds classier, though."

Emily waited a week and then had Stevens drive her to Clayton, to Fritz's small office on Maryland Avenue. She found her son with his feet up on the desk, chatting on the phone. Ticker tape littered the floor of the cramped room. A cigar butt smoldered in a saucer overflowing with ashes.

"Pig sty," Emily said, turning on her heel. By the time Fritz got off the phone and ran out to the street, his mother's sedan was gliding around the corner.

That afternoon Emily rang an employment agency. "I require a clerical secretary. She must not be too young, and she must not be the least pretty."

At eight sharp the following morning, Miss Betty Foley arrived at the office of Fritz M. Reinhardt & Associates. In her handbag were three lead pencils, two notepads, and a dust cloth. She knocked. She tried the knob. Undaunted, she tapped the tip of her umbrella on the sunny pavement, and waited.

In time, Miss Foley learned that what seemed like social calls were actually business calls. Fritz took a meandering route to the central point of the call. He might dissect Jesse Haines' blistering fastball or tell a Silent Cal joke. Sometimes he sang a few bars of the latest Gershwin tune or brought up the closing of Ellis Island and the discovery of Pharaoh Tutankhamun's tomb. Once he passed along, confidentially, of course, the juicy news that R&K was pea-green about Macy's popular Thanksgiving Day parade.

Miss Foley chuckled when her young employer brought toys to the office — a model airplane, a snow globe, a saucy rubber statue of a Hawaiian girl with a penis under her grass skirt. And yet she had seen him juggle a dozen market variants in his head while fine-tuning a client's hundred-dollar portfolio.

Fritz still lived with his parents on Portland Place, but they seldom saw him. After work, he'd pick up a date and zoom out to Topping Ridge or down to the Statler Hotel for supper. Afterward they'd hit one of the city's members-only nightclubs, sip martinis and dance. *Yes! We Have No Bananas* was the year's hot tune, and Fritz loved to see and be seen on the dance floor.

Later, after he dropped off his date, he'd sometimes head down to the riverfront, to a shadowy back room in the Cherrick Building where stone-faced poker players hunkered around a barrel, men who took him for what he was, a rich kid on the slum. Men who mistook him for ripe pickings.

"Hear the one about the French maid and the cream puff man?" Fritz said one night, in great shape before the draw. For hours he'd been parlaying so-so hands into a mountain of chips, tracking every card. Around four in the morning, he made a point to start losing.

Fritz had lost his virginity in one of the old brick buildings on the riverfront, lost it to the wife of the bartender. The husband had fought in The War to End All Wars and had come home badly wounded below the belt. The wife was happy to dally with a handsome young man in the apartment above the pub. Afterward, Fritz told her she was beautiful and she'd turned her head and wept. He briefly considered leaving money. Instead, he set his expensive wristwatch on the nightstand and quietly left.

○

Phillip's butler pulled two chairs out to the edge of the patio. A few minutes later he returned with tumblers of Scotch and bowls of cashews. It was a golden Saturday. Phillip and Fritz watched warm breezes shower the lawn with orange-red leaves. Florence and a friend were volleying on the clay tennis court beyond the patio. Florence was an agile player; her one request after the wrenching birth of their daughter, Madeleine, was to have a private tennis court built.

Phillip's calculated ascent in business and social circles was well underway. He was now the senior vice-president at the city's most prestigious department store, a business that employed hundreds of St. Louisans and attracted shoppers from throughout eastern Missouri and southern Illinois. He had married a chic debutante and had sired a cute, obedient daughter. He owned an impressive Tudor home on Barnes Road in Ladue. He sat on two civic boards. Each evening at seven, Phillip's butler poured him two fingers of single malt Scotch, which Phillip drank while scanning the afternoon paper. At eight, Phillip escorted Florence to the dining room. When they were seated, a nanny presented little Madeleine for good-night kisses.

"What is it tonight?" Phillip often asked, pulling a starched napkin from a silver ring.

Saddle of lamb. Tenderloin of beef. Salmon filet with capers. It mattered little. He and Florence dined at the ends of a table bedecked with a massive central floral arrangement. Tapers burned in silver candelabra too, flames unflickered by a breath of passion.

On the patio, the brothers sipped Scotch and chatted, idly watching Florence and her friend volley.

"I don't need a girl who's brainy," Fritz was saying, "and I don't mind the quiet ones, either."

Phillip signaled the butler to bring more cashews. "What about the one who stuttered? How'd that go?"

"Bought her a triple-scoop ice cream cone and told jokes for a solid hour."

Phillip chuckled.

After a pause, Fritz turned serious: "When I dropped her off she actually got out a whole sentence. She said it was the best night of her life."

Phillip looked to the tennis court, suddenly wistful. Ah, Fritz, he thought, you always did know how to make the best of anything. Wonder how you'd make the best of my situation, my marriage? "What about that girl who lived near Mother and Dad on Portland? Weren't you soft on her?"

Fritz grabbed his crotch. "Soft as steel."

"Did you connect?"

"Not exactly. I wandered over, hoping she wasn't back at boarding school. She was. The grandmother gave me the word. Remember her? Old lady sat on the front porch swing that whole summer. Anyway, it's a gorgeous night and I'm dateless and the grandmother's yakking about the moonlight and stuff."

Phillip watched Florence's friend stretch to return a lob. "So?"

"So I wind up asking Granny to go out with me."

"Good God, Fritz. What did she say?"

"She says where do I intend to take her, and I say the grand opening shindig at the Tivoli."

"Shindig! You said shindig to the grandmother?"

"That old gal took me for a bucket of popcorn and three cherry fizzes. By the time I got her home it was midnight. Gave her a peck on the cheek and remanded her to the custody of her furious son."

Phillip looked off, lost in thought. Typical, he told himself. Fritz could turn lemons into lemonade. Well, I've made some lemonade myself, in Chicago.

"Florence can't have any more children." Phillip said, his voice flat.

Fritz took a hard swallow. "What?"

Phillip's gaze had wandered to his wife's friend again. He answered without taking his eyes from the tennis court. "Well, she could conceive if we, you know, but another pregnancy would kill her. Or so the good doctor told us after Madeleine was born."

"God, Phillip, I'm sorry. So, uh... "

"Florence is reading Jane Austin. I've found other diversions."

"You're kidding."

Phillip snapped. "Everything's a joke to you, isn't it?"

Fritz squinted into the sun at Florence, a darting silhouette in crisp tennis whites.

A Knock-Out
1926

St. Louis

Doris ran to answer the phone. It was a former classmate from Rosati-Kain, one of the school's most popular and stuck-up girls.

"I know we haven't seen each other in a year, but Doris I'm in a bind. You heard I'm getting married on Saturday? No? Well I am. And Martha Pfeiffer — you remember Martha — she was going to be my maid of honor, but she's got some horrid virus. I called Marie Dwyer, but she's sick as a dog, too. Ellen Hunt and Frances Schaefer are in Michigan, and I'm on the outs with Betty and Rita. Golly, Doris, you're the only one I could think of who'd be available on such short notice. Would you be an angel?"

"I don't... "

"Wait. Don't say a word. This is a tickle: Fritz Reinhardt, you know, the younger one, the *unmarried* one, he and Alec were high school buddies, sort of. Anyway, I convinced Alec to ask him to be best man. Fritz Reinhardt would be your date!"

"Oh," Doris said. After a calculated pause, she added, "I suppose I could do it, as a favor."

"Swell. Your sister can come, too, as a guest."

At 10 o'clock on Saturday morning Fritz stood in front of a church altar and scanned the pews. He saw one or two familiar faces, Alec's friends from the Academy, not exactly his group. Then he spotted her. Fourth row, bride's side. Achingly lovely. Absolutely the cat's pajamas. Fritz tossed the girl a wink. She batted her eyelashes like a plantation belle and lowered her missal far enough for Fritz to glimpse her Cupid's bow lips curled in a coy smile.

Doris traipsed down the aisle, a wash of bile green chiffon and yellow jonquils. "Good God," Fritz whispered to the groomsman next to him, "it's a bird dog with the scent of quail in the air."

"See the one in the fourth row?" the groomsman said. "That's the sister of the sourpuss in green. The *younger* sister."

"How young?"

"Reinhardt, like you ever cared."

At the wedding reception, Lydia and Fritz danced a torrid tango. On the sidelines, Doris fumed. When the music stopped, she followed Lydia to the ladies room.

"Just what do you think you're doing?" Doris hissed, whacking her bouquet against the sink.

Lydia played the innocent. "Why, what do you mean?"

"You know good and well. You've been flirting with Fritz Reinhardt all day. I'm the maid of honor. He's supposed to be paying attention to me."

Lydia checked her lipstick in the mirror. "That I cannot help."

"You always get everything, don't you?"

"And you always want what I have," Lydia shot back. "Well, I appear to have gotten Fritz Reinhardt. He's already asked me out on a date. We're going to dinner Saturday at Topping Ridge Country Club."

In the reception hall, Fritz was waiting with a couple of the Academy guys. "Look at those gams, fellas," he crowed. "Bet she does a mean Shimmy."

Lydia planted herself at his side and giggled. "Fritz, honey, zip it."

Fritz took a sip from a slim flask. "Zip it? Baby, I'm having a hard time refraining from un-zipping it."

Lydia giggled again, and turned her heart-shaped face so Fritz would notice her dimples.

Elite Jobs
1926

New Orleans to Chicago

*I*t had rained. Spring leaves sagged, freighted with water. Runoff pouring down in a thousand downspouts played metallic tympanies. The day wore on. Sunlight muscled through the clouds. Steam rose from city sidewalks. For two hours, Palmer and Leroy had been dragging a wobble-wheeled cart of strawberries, asparagus and early lettuce through Gert Town. The darn thing seemed to find every pothole. Palmer's trousers were splashed to the knees.

Leroy snorted. "Look like y'all pee'd in your pants."

Sweat trickled down Palmer's cheek. He wiped it with the back of his hand and kicked at a half-dead frog. "We ain't never gonna get ahead in this danged city, Leroy. I heared there's easy work in Chicago, heared a man say they pay three times what a colored can make in N'Awlins."

"Uh-huh." Leroy picked up the frog and slipped it into his shirt pocket. Leroy had followed Palmer out of the womb by eleven minutes. He'd lived in Palmer's shadow fifteen years at the Waif's Home. If Palmer was going North, Leroy was going, too.

"Somethin stinks," Leroy said, pinching his nose.

"Got that right. Must be a viewin." The stench from Parfitt's Funeral Parlor was making his eyes water. "They needs to get that body to the bone yard."

"It do have a fragrance," Leroy said.

Palmer set down the cart handle and leaned against a lamp post. "Y'all remember that Honeydew Girl?"

"Uh-huh. Can't hardly picture her face no more."

Palmer picked up the handle again and shuffled down the street. "Try picturin snow, brother. Buildings so high the tops is in the clouds."

That night, Palmer lay awake finalizing his plan. He roused Leroy before dawn and they lit out, waifs traversing a still-slumbering city. At Antoine's, Palmer raised a rear window and boosted Leroy through the opening. Leroy soon reappeared, his pockets stuffed with boiled rice and roasted yams. At Broussard's the boys filched a whole roasted chicken, a string of pork sausage links, a jar of green tomato relish, and a handful of oysters. At the rail yard, Palmer hiked up into an empty boxcar and stuck out a hand for Leroy.

Fifteen years after Esmie Hobbs hitched a ride on a mule wagon outside of Chattooka, Palmer and Leroy Bordelon hobo'd out of New Orleans in a boxcar, lured by boastful fliers tacked to fences and telephone poles.

Leave the hellish South! Good jobs for everyone

Ford Motor Company, hiring!

Armour - Opportunities!

The boys feasted on oysters, yams and spicy relish. Afterward they laid back, rocking with the train as it chugged northward, leaving the fruit cart and the Waif's Home behind.

"It be so dark in here, Palmer, I don't gots the foggiest idea what I ate." Leroy's voice was edged with fear. He had never been beyond the city limits.

Palmer slid open the door and stared at fly-by scenery. Its newness thrilled him. The Indian-red dirt. The droopy swamps giving way to picturesque fields, little groves of hickory and gum trees, creeks dotted with sandbars.

Leroy was groaning now. "Palmer, my belly don't feel - -" Leroy twisted sideways and vomited a sour burst of half-digested oysters.

Palmer slid open the door all the way. Fresh air poured into the boxcar, along with the roar of cycling wheels.

That evening, Palmer lay down in a slat of moonlight near the boxcar door and motioned for Leroy to scoot next to him. The twins fell into an uneasy sleep as the train followed the river through Memphis and on into Illinois. Palmer woke once and crawled to the half-open door. Switching towers and trestles passed before his eyes, farm houses painted ghostly white, silos poked up in silhouette against night sky. By now he was oblivious to the revolutions of the wheels, the long whistle blows, and piercing blasts of exhaust. He felt at peace. Felt the stirrings of hope.

Sometime that night Palmer's old dream returned. He and Leroy were walnuts nestled in a shell, mirror images separated by the thinnest of membranes. In the dream, stubby appendages elongated, and became pale brown arms and legs. Faces emerged. One walnut twin was bigger and stronger than the other. Suddenly, a huge hand cracked the shell and it burst open. The bigger baby popped out safely, but the monster snatched the smaller baby. Gigantic fingers raised the little walnut baby up to a huge mouth dripping with saliva. Palmer jolted awake, bathed in sweat. He felt in the dark for Leroy and relaxed some.

Suddenly, a voice out of nowhere said: "Checkerboard crew tonight."

Palmer jerked around. In the blink of light from a passing watch tower he saw a figure in the far corner. A white boy. The whitest white boy he'd ever laid eyes on. Sickish white hair. Eyes so pale and blue they made Palmer's flesh crawl. Must've slipped in during one of the whistle-stops, Palmer guessed.

Palmer slipped his hand in his pocket and felt the smooth, reassuring handle of his knife. I could take him, he told himself, come to that.

"I don't much mind shines," the boy continued. He shrugged off a makeshift blanket of old newspaper, and yawned. "Got a fag?"

"Nope."

Palmer glanced at Leroy. Good. His brother was still conked out.

"Any gump then?" the strange boy asked. "Ain't ate nothing but hundred on a plate since the barrel house."

Palmer had no idea what the boy was talking about. He turned sideways, but kept the kid in sight.

The boy stroked the downy beginnings of a mustache. "Headin up the line?"

"Yep."

"Dumb-ass."

"What y'all callin me?"

"I said dumb-ass, dumb-ass."

Palmer stood and planted his hands on his hips. "You itchin for trouble?"

"Don't go gettin all hot. I seen a thousand coloreds go North, thinking it's on the plush up there."

"So?"

"So it ain't like that. Ramblers like you and your friend here ain't got a clue. Up North, people just as hateful to coloreds."

"That's baloney," Palmer said.

"All right, friend. I ain't lookin for no pokeout anyways."

Palmer lay down near Leroy, pretending to doze, but he kept his eyes open a slit, just in case. A dozen worries had pecked at him all night. Now there was another worry, a white boy in their boxcar, a white boy who wouldn't shut up.

"… at the car plants in Detroit, coloreds get hustled off to a separate line. Takes 'em half a day to get up to the hiring shack. Most don't even get taken on. If they do, it ain't good work."

Palmer twisted around to face the boy. He hated to egg him on, but he was curious. The boy scrooched closer.

In Pittsburgh, the white-haired boy said, talking in excited bursts, steel mill bosses made coloreds do the most dangerous work, pouring vats of hot metal into molds, grinding steel parts. "Little sharp bits fly all over, prickle your skin, get all up in your eyes," the boy said, blinking furiously. "Detroit ain't pretty, friend, but other places ain't no rosier."

"Like where?"

"New York. Boston. Ain't nothing there for coloreds except be a shoe shine boy."

The boy's features twisted with sick glee describing tenements that crawled with rats and roaches, old women who coughed through the night, drunks on the stoops, thugs and rapists who preyed on kids for the fun of it.

Palmer shuddered. "What about out West? Maybe we goin there, be cowboys."

The strange boy looked nonplussed. "In the West, coloreds just plain got lost. Nothin but miles and miles of purely open space out West." He swept his arm in a half-circle, for emphasis. "Ranch bosses fling the coloreds out to mend fences, way out. Them prairies stretch far as the eye can see. And the mine bosses, they pick the coloreds to work the deepest veins."

The boy looked off, as if he could see men cleaving the wilderness with axes. "Lumber bosses truck the coloreds to outback camps. Gangs of white men in them camps got picks, steel pincers too."

Palmer took a deep breath and chucked up his chin. "We goin to Chicago."

The boy spat a stream of spittle. In Chicago, he said, coloreds live in Black Town, cold-water walkups, families crammed all together along South State. The men work at the slaughter yards for Swift and Armour, the boy went on. "Work like dogs. Stand all day in animal drippings, suckin in disinfectant with every breath. And all the time, right behind you, the old crank-crank-crank."

Palmer shrugged, as if he didn't care, and asked, "What the old crank-crank-crank?"

"The carcasses, big old animals hung on hooks, moving along a overhead line. Sounds like your mammy pullin her clothes line around, except it ain't." The boy paused and then added, "That ain't all you hearin, neither. You hearin cows and pigs and sheep and such shoved through the chute, screamin and squealin, bellowing like they at the gates of hell, which ain't far from true."

Palmer felt a wave of nausea. "Shut y'alls mouth! My brother and me's tryin to sleep."

The boy wouldn't stop. "The Poles, the Irish, they do okay slaughterin. But a fella like your friend there couldn't take it. Wind up cuckoo in the head. I knowed a man once, tramped with him in Arkansas. He told me about them slaughter houses, didn't hold nothin back, neither. They poke them cows and sheep up the chutes with sharp sticks. At the top, a guy whacks 'em on the head with a baseball bat. Then —"

"Shut up."

"— they tie up the legs with wire and hoist em up on hooks, hangin there, all drippy while they movin along the line."

Palmer could hardly believe such places exist. "Your friend done that?"

"Said he did."

The boy plucked a piece of straw from the floor and stuck it between his teeth. "They knife the throats, you know? Scald off the skin. Saw off the heads. Guts spill out like spaghetti, only guts is all blue and purple and don't smell good like spaghetti."

Leroy whimpered.

Damn, Palmer said to himself. Leroy been awake the whole time, heard everything.

"We ain't goin to no slaughter house," Palmer told the strange boy. "Ain't goin that way at all."

Wedding Caps by Firelight
1926

Hannibal, Missouri

On her tenth birthday Sophie LaChapelle received a hand-made booklet bound in oilskin and tied with twine. In it, her parents had recorded the facts of their ancestry, as best they knew. Sophie swallowed a knob of disappointment. She'd expected a middy blouse. A blouse and a doll. She'd dog-eared the pages in the Sears Roebuck catalog. In a reedy voice wrung of gratitude, she thanked her mother and father and carried the gift to her pouting spot, a rope swing dangling in the shade of a shag-bark oak. Squirrels fretted in the heights, anxious to resume their vertical errands. An hour later the child turned the last page.

"I'm descended from dirt-diggers," she sighed, tossing the booklet aside. With the toe of her shoe, she scraped a fissure in the soft dirt. "I come from salt miners and pigeon keepers and I'll be stuck in Hannibal forever."

A breeze picked up, a gentle zephyr that bore the scent of river, mowed grass and line-dried towels. It rustled the leaves above Sophie like a thousand moths impelled to wing, then swooped down and skimmed the hood of the car parked next door, Officer Corcoran's Model T runabout. He always left it in the driveway backwards, facing Bird Street, ever ready for hot pursuit. Before continuing on to wherever summer breezes go, the wind fluttered the pages of the booklet, as if curious.

The last name of Sophie's great-great-grandmother was lost to time, but her first name and her story were passed down like an heirloom teapot. Hanna.

Hanna grew up in the early 1800s on a farm in Upper Silesia, grew up without a mother and so at a young age and by a quite natural process took to mothering those she loved. Each evening after the last crumbs of poppy seed cake were pinched from the plates, Hanna's father and brothers trooped out back without a word. Hanna rose, too, lifted an iron pot from the hearth and poured water into a tarred tub. Steam ribboned up in the night air, provoking the girl's hair to unruly contortions. She bound it into a bun secured with tortoise pins, the ones a lady placed in her palm the day they buried her mother.

When she finished the dishes, Hanna took up her lace-making hook and tatted wedding caps by firelight. Once in a great while she worked exquisite trim destined for the robe of a bishop or cardinal, but most nights she made wedding caps, dainty things to grace the heads of rich men's brides. Her fingers flew, stopping only to draw another length from the skein on her lap. She sat in silence but for the occasional hiss of a log, taking pleasure in the sounds of evening, the far, hollow barking of dogs, the footfall of work boots on packed earth, the raked squeal of hinges yearning for oil, her father's pigeons rustling in nest boxes.

How Hanna met Jan Gorecka was lost to time, too. According to the booklet, Jan worked near Krakow hewing rock salt from earthen labyrinths. Hanna and Jan Gorecka married, that much is known, on Sophie's mother's side.

Sophie's father wrote sparingly of the facts and guessed at some, for little was passed down except this:

In 1824, a French Canadian youth named Paul LaChapelle met a girl named Hanna Gorecka, a girl with long, delicate fingers and rippling hair. Her family had emigrated from Poland. In every generation, it seemed, one of the girls was named Hanna.

Paul was a digger. His arms were thick as barn beams for he worked eleven-hour days clawing out sections of the trench for the Lachine Canal, near Montreal. For years, French Canadians and Irishmen had labored in the nine-mile trench, gouging mud, hacking rock, hauling detritus up and away with nothing but shovels and determination. Paul froze in winter and sweltered in summer. It was back-breaking labor that paid a pittance. When the dedication speeches and fancy ceremonies faded, the diggers were fired.

Paul wrote to relatives in America. A reply came almost immediately.

Dear Cousin Paul,

Your letter arrived Tuesday last informing of the turn matters have taken. It appears our Northern neighbors issued no Mercy to faithful employees. We are in Good Health, thanks be to the Creator, except Mother is troubled with boils and Jane's baby has the colic, though we heat a bag of cornmeal each night and lay it on the child's stomach.

We shall soon be preparing our fields for the Harvest. We anticipate a good yield, for we put our seed in the ground at the first call of the whippoorwill. Hannibal is but an hour's walk, a fair city with clean Air and honest Governance. I will inquire on your behalf as to employment at the lumber mill, the soap and candle factories, the quarry and the river front (though the latter can be an undesirable locale).

I conclude in hopes you will soon abide with Family in Missouri, for I am not young and not so brisk as before. Surmounting any perils of journey, we shall expect to see you in the course of one month hence.

By the time they reached Hannibal, Paul was destitute and Hanna was heavy with child. At night, they lay on quilts under the pitched roof of the cousin's garret, surrounded by old trunks and lame-legged chairs. Paul pointed out the Big Dipper winking beyond a dormer window. Hanna loosed her thick braid and rested her head on his shoulder, oblivious to mice skittering through walls and the low buzz of paper wasps tip-toeing across umbrella-shaped nests.

"The river here ..." she said one night, her voice velvet with sleep.

"What is it, love?"

"It make me think of the Vistula."

"Could you be happy here in America?"

She didn't answer. By then she was asleep, lulled by heart sounds stolid and true.

The Promised Land
1926

Chicago

*P*almer slid open the door and pushed Leroy out. "Roll, brother, like I taught y'all!"

Leroy tumbled from the boxcar into the brilliant afternoon. Palmer squatted and jumped just as the train rounded a last curve and huffed into the Union Station yards. The boys shielded their eyes against sun flares glinting off ribbons of track.

Leroy had landed awkwardly. Now he poked a finger through a jagged tear in his trousers and explored the raw skin beneath. "Dang, Palmer, I done laid open my knee."

"Ain't nothin. But y'alls a sorry sight."

Leroy stuck out his lower lip. "Y'alls got sight from sorry eyes."

Palmer chuckled. Leroy never quite got things right, he said to himself. That why he always gonna need me. Leroy'd do the same, if he'd been first born, if I'd come out puny cuz he done took up too much space inside our mama.

Palmer gave Leroy a shove. "We fix that knee later, brother. Right now we gotta find Black Town, like the boy on the train told us. Gotta find the Olivet Baptist Church. That be where the train boy said coloreds go, if they got no place to light."

The boys plucked across lines of track as fast as they could. They were near the edge of the rail yard when a sharp whistle froze them in mid-step. Palmer dropped to a crouch and swung around to see who had spotted them. It was an old hobo sitting at the base of a bridge stanchion. He whistled again at the boys, then stuck out a finger rimed with grit and pointed off to the south.

The boys sprinted in that direction.

"Palmer," Leroy said, after a while, "I thinks I got the lice."

Palmer stopped to examine his brother. Blades of straw clung to Leroy's trousers and his hair was frosted with dust. Palmer sniffed and crinkled his nose; Leroy smelled like old oyster vomit.

"Brother, I knows you got the lice," Palmer said, walking on. Suddenly, he stuck an arm out to stop Leroy. "We here. We at the Olivet Church."

Leroy shook his head. "That ain't it. The white boy say the church ain't barely big enough to fit all the Sunday folks. This here church is big."

"I knows it. But the boy said folks stand in back and spill out onto the street every Sunday."

The sanctuary was dim and cool. Dark wood pews formed a semi-circle around a raised stage. The boys stood in back, framed in the doorway.

"Smells good," Leroy whispered, "like lemons and flowers."

"Shhh. See that man up there? He the man we supposed to see."

Dr. Lacey Kirk Williams glanced up from his notes for Sunday's sermon and saw two tall, gangly boys in silhouette. Afternoon sun streamed through high stained glass windows onto them. Rev. Williams laid down his notes and folded his hands on the lectern. Their faces were in shadow, but he guessed they were fourteen or so. Underfed, too. He saw that right off. New to the city, scared.

"And still they come," he said softly.

Rev. Williams looked to the balcony behind the lectern. "I'll be back, by and by," he said. His voice was clear and rich, the kind of voice that carried words to the rafters. A woman seated at a beautiful pipe organ nodded and went back to her sheet music.

Leroy wrung his cap. "He gonna chuck us over to the police."

Palmer moved in front of Leroy and said over his shoulder: "He look okay, brother. Dignified, you could call it."

The minister started up the aisle. He could see the boys better now, see their eyes, sunk in dark sockets. They were tired, scared, and hungry, but he knew to be cautious. They could be after money. They could spook and run off and then how could he help them? "Got a place to light?" he asked, drawing near, keeping his voice calm.

Palmer tucked in his shirttail. Leroy hiccoughed.

"Come along then."

Rev. Williams led the boys to a boardinghouse around the corner. The place was cheap but decent. At the front desk, the minister paid in advance for three nights.

"Come to services Sunday morning," he said, brushing dust from Leroy's hair. "Nine o'clock sharp."

The landlady showed the boys to a small room on the third floor. It was furnished with a cot, a chair, and a three-drawer chest. A bare bulb dangled from a cord in the ceiling. The room was stifling. After the landlady left,

Palmer tried to open the window. He managed to wrench it up a few inches, but no farther. Leroy lay on the cot, scratching.

"What you see out there, brother?"

Palmer pressed his forehead against the glass. "Nothin. Alley. Side of the next building."

Leroy fluffed the pillow. With a sigh, he kicked off his shoes and wriggled his toes. "Truly …"

"Truly what?"

"Truly Chicago be the Promised Land," Leroy said, already half asleep.

Palmer settled himself head to toe with his brother. He was bone-tired, too, but his thoughts wouldn't stop churning. We needs jobs, he told himself. Who gonna hire two colored boys? What if somebody hires me but they don't want Leroy? Do we ask for one paycheck or two? Palmer waggled the pillow from under Leroy's head, gave it a couple of punches and stuffed it under his neck. He stared at the ceiling. The rust-colored water stains reminded him of clouds he used to watch with the Honeydew Girl, laying side by side in sweet grass after the fruit carts were empty, calling out animal shapes in the sky.

Sometime after midnight, Leroy jabbed his brother in the ribs. "Palmer, wake up! My belly's thwackin."

"I knows it. Me, too. Let's go scroungin."

For the millionth time, Palmer wished their mama had lived. Or their daddy had come to fetch them.

Halfway Presentable
1926

Chicago

Y a'll wash up first, Leroy. Water's in that pitcher."

Palmer sat on the edge of the bed and rubbed his eyes. Gonna be tricky, he knew, finding food. Don't know the city, can't tell what parts are safe. Gotta make sure I don't get us lost, too.

"Leroy, freshen up. We gotta look halfway presentable. Coppers see us lookin like bums, they haul our sorry asses to the slammer. And gimme that towel."

Leroy snapped the towel at his brother. "Let's go. Ain't y'all starvin?"

"First we find somethin to eat. Tomorrow we gonna see about jobs."

Leroy's broad face brightened. "How about we be streetcar drivers? I seen a million streetcars today."

"Leroy, since when do you know how to drive? No sense tryin for a job where we gotta do somethin if we don't know how. And ain't no use goin after a job bossin white folks, neither."

"Uh-huh." Leroy pondered this a full minute and then said: "What left?"

The boys crossed the tracks at 30th Street and headed south on State, Black Town's main artery. Even at that hour, the wide street was bright with headlights and lighted signs. Palmer and Leroy melded into the stream of late nighters.

Leroy rubbed his throbbing belly. "We needs food, brother."

"I knows it. Once I get the lay of the land we can be delivery boys, deliver things, how that sound?"

Leroy grinned. "Delivery boys ridin fancy bicycles. Flyin along."

"Or hotel porters. I heard a colored fella tell a girl he was a porter at the Drake Hotel. That girl was a looker, and the fella was no sap, neither."

Palmer smelled a familiar aroma: barbecue sauce. He ducked into an alley. A minute later Leroy was head-down in a garbage bin, fishing out short rib bones. Suddenly, Palmer yanked him up.

"Duck!" Palmer hissed. He shoved Leroy behind a row of barrels and tucked in next to him, close. The hiding place was barely wide enough.

Palmer's heart clattered in his chest. He peeked out and saw an open door in a building near the entrance to the alley. A burly man had grabbed a guy by the shirt collar. While the boys watched, the big guy let go and the skinny guy fell to the ground like a dropped puppet.

"Lush," the big man growled. "That's the last time I see your mug at the Vendome, hear? Think you was working for pushovers?"

Palmer clapped a hand over Leroy's mouth. "Wait here. Don't say nothin till I give y'all the signal."

"What signal?"

"Cripes, Leroy, just don't say nothin."

The drunk got up and staggered off into the night. Palmer tucked in his shirttail, rose, and walked to the center of the alley. "Sir, me and my brother here, we's willin to do that fella's job."

The burly man whirled around. "Where'd you boobs come from?"

"We come from State Street, sir. And there bein two of us, we can do twice the work as that souse in half the time."

The man lit a cigarette and blew spume of smoke, considering. Palmer started to worry. The man was big as a bear.

"Clean-up boys," the man said, appearing to think things over. He took another long draw and then flicked away the cigarette, as if he'd made up his mind. He sauntered over and grabbed the boys by the back of their necks. "You might do. How about we go see the owner, Mister O.C. Hammond."

It wasn't a question.

Inside the enormous building, the bouncer told the boys that O.C. Hammond owned the Vendome and several other movie palaces in Black Town. He shoved Palmer and Leroy into a pool of light under wall sconce and squinted hard at them.

"You boys is colored, ain't ya?" he said, taking in the boys' broad features, wiry brownish-blond hair, light brown skin and big green eyes.

"Colored enough," he concluded. "Only coloreds work at the Vendome."

Precisely the Effect
1926

St. Louis

*L*ydia Conrad danced a mean Shimmy. In the sixth year of the Bone-Dry Years, the sight of Lydia in full-body vibration was intoxicating to Fritz and the other argyle sweater boys at Topping Ridge, which was precisely the effect Lydia had in mind.

"I believe the lucky guy is Fritz Reinhardt," Mary Conrad told Tom that afternoon. "Doris is at a picture show. She said she couldn't stand her sister one minute longer." Mary raised the back of her hand to her forehead and dipped in a melodramatic swoon. Tom chuckled, then turned serious.

"Make sure Lydia's wearing something decent, will you honey?"

"You mean *can* I? She's eighteen, Tom. The way that girl is changing, I can't be sure about anything. Did you know she plucked her eyebrows completely off and penciled in new ones?"

"What!"

Earlier that month, at the wedding reception of Doris's friend, Lydia had danced with Fritz six times and written her phone number on the palm of his outstretched hand. For six days she had starved herself, trying to whittle her curves into the boyish shape that was all the rage. With money from her job at the Switzer licorice factory, she bought a short, sexy dress. She made a salon appointment and had the beautician cut her lush auburn curls in a short, sleek bob; the straightening solution was strong enough to melt steel. Each night, Lydia practiced the latest dance steps in front of her bedroom mirror.

Lydia, daughter of a firefighter, great-granddaughter of Kerry Patch immigrants, was determined to rise to the pinnacle of St. Louis society. "This is my chance," she told her mother. "If I don't grab it, if anything goes wrong, I'll wind up hitched to some dull bloke, scrimping and saving so someday we can move from a dinky apartment to a piddling bungalow. I'd be nothing, a nobody."

Without a word, Mary kissed her daughter on the forehead and left the room.

When the band finally took a break, Fritz steered Lydia to a corner and spiked her lemon squash. Lydia called him a scamp and puckered her lips in a dimpled pout. Fritz waved his pals over and told them Lydia Marie Conrad was too wild for a fellow as modest and mild-mannered as he. The Topping Ridge crowd went off into gales of laughter and right then Lydia knew she had him.

The following Saturday Fritz took Lydia to Tower Grove Park. He paid a lightning-sketch artist two bits to do a likeness of his new girl. Lydia sat on a high stool and crossed her legs at the knee. Behind his easel, the man picked up a stub of chalk. With quick, short strokes he depicted his subject in Fauvist abstractions. When he pivoted the finished sketch with a smile and a flourish, Lydia jumped off the stool and stormed off. How dare that man, she fumed. And why didn't Fritz stop him? Lydia considered tormenting Fritz with a brief but effective sulk, but decided otherwise. There would be time for sulks, later.

"Fritz Reinhardt, you knew all along," she purred, willing a rosy blush to her cheeks. "You're a shameless rascal."

The next week Fritz took Lydia on a boat ride in the big lagoon at Forest Park. She wore a flowered dress of cotton lawn, demure white stockings and white ankle-strap shoes. Twenty-two years after Albert handed Emily into a skiff on the opening day of the World's Fair, Fritz paddled his new sweetheart across the same placid lagoon. Lydia reclined in the bow and opened a Chinese parasol. She rested the cane handle on her shoulder. The white paper circle framed her face like a moon, a halo. She knew this. She'd thought it all through.

Fritz rang again and off they went, to a roller rink on Cherokee Street. When he knelt to lace her skates, Lydia ran her fingers through his hair. Soon they were gliding arm in arm around the rink. Skaters rushed up from behind and overtook them. It occurred to Fritz that Lydia might be the right girl for the rest of his life. It was a conclusion Lydia had reached the moment she peeked over her missal at him, the moment Doris, swathed in pea green chiffon, started to march down that church aisle.

Fritz and Lydia circled the rink, smooth as glaziers. As the music played on, they silently scripted their melded future, unaware the plots differed. After a while, Fritz's thoughts turned dark. For the first time, there was trouble at work.

A few months earlier Fritz had taken on a new client, Pete Shelley's father. Pete was one of Fritz's many buddies back in high school. Mr. and Mrs. Shelley had seven kids; Pete was the oldest. He'd gone to St. Louis Academy on a hardship scholarship. The Shelleys had managed to build a small nest egg of about two thousand dollars which they kept in a lock box behind the flour bin in their kitchen pantry. Until recently, Mr. Shelley had a decent job, driving a truck, delivering lumber to construction sites. Three months ago, a load of two-by-fours shifted, and when he got out of the truck to secure the straps, the load broke loose and crushed his legs. The doctors said Mr. Shelley would be in a wheelchair the rest of his life.

The Shelleys knew they needed to make their savings grow, they just didn't know how. Pete called his old friend. The following night, Fritz sat across from Mr. and Mrs. Shelley at their kitchen table.

"I'll put your money to work," he said, after Mr. Shelley laid out their situation. "I'll spread it out over six to eight companies. Don't worry, they'll all be solid. I'll pick the stocks myself. Trust me, they'll produce."

Herb Shelley wrung the back of his neck. "You got one heck of a reputation for making money, but you're awful young. Just so's you know, we're counting on that money."

Fritz rose and shook the man's hand. "It'll be there. I'm proposing solid investments that will maximize your gain."

A few days later Fritz returned to the Shelley's house. He told Herb and Mrs. Shelley he had decided to invest their nest egg in Diamond Match and Mengel Co., American Tobacco, and Goodyear Tire & Rubber Company. He made a few remarks about each company and finished up quickly. No one said anything for a long moment. Mrs. Shelley spoke up first.

"I don't think much of putting our money into puny match sticks," she said, fiddling with the collar of her housedress. Mr. Shelley didn't like Goodyear, either. Goodyear's dirigibles reminded him of those god damned German Zeppelins, he said.

In a mortified whisper, Pete Shelley told Fritz that his mom and dad would never invest in a cigarette company. "Ever since my little sister got so sick with the asthma, my parents can't abide being around tobacco."

Fritz sat back and spread out his hands, palms up. Silence seemed to suck the air out of the small kitchen. An overhead light hummed. The faucet dripped, each drop producing a plink so loud it might as well have been a steel pellet. Mr. Shelley cleared his throat. He and the misses had done their own research, he said. They had picked three stocks, too: Zeus Auto Body Corporation, Plains Farm Equipment, and Brennan Mills. Fritz had never heard of the companies. He urged them to go with his picks, but the Shelleys were insistent. Fritz put their every dime into Zeus, Plains, and Brennan Mills.

Three months later, on the morning of Fritz's roller skating date, Mrs. Shelley showed up at the brokerage house in Clayton. Her hair was disheveled, Fritz saw, and her handbag had come unsnapped. The woman seemed to not notice.

"What have you done, boy?" she cried.

Fritz led her through the lobby, into his private office. He beckoned to a chair, but Mrs. Shelley was too agitated to sit.

"Have you checked the financial pages? The stocks are down. Way down. Our money's nearly gone."

She let out a long breath of air. Fritz watched her run her fingertips across his desk top. At the rubber statue of a Hawaiian girl, she stopped. She ruffled the doll's dried-grass skirt. When she saw what was underneath, she snatched her hand away.

"I hear you like jokes," she said, drawing herself up to leave. "Is this a game to you? Because it's hardly a joke to us."

When she was gone, Fritz wracked his brain, trying to remember the last time he'd checked on the Shelleys' stocks. He closed his office door and sat at his desk a long while, devastated. Why hadn't he persuaded the Shelleys to go with the stocks he'd picked? Why didn't he explain the risks more clearly to them? He picked up the ridiculous Hawaiian toy and threw it against the wall. And why in hell didn't he bird-dog their dicey investments? His father's words rang in his ears:

Hold yourself accountable for your decisions. The world places high value on a man's judgment and integrity.

Skating beside Lydia, Fritz resolved to recoup the Shelley's money even if he had to divert some of his own holdings to their account. He glanced up at the spinning mirror ball and winced at the dazzling flashes. It occurred to him that he could pay them their $2,000 that afternoon, if he wanted. It wouldn't kill him, he told himself. Christ, I'd barely feel it. I've been playing with my clients' money like it was a numbers game in Father's study. I won every time, until now.

The roller rink organist played on, moving seamlessly from an up-tempo number to a slow, lilting tune. The lights dimmed. Lydia rested her head on Fritz's shoulder. He stroked her hair absently, lost in thought. Truck drivers. Carpenters. Street sweepers. Waitresses. Plumbers. People who stuff their life savings in a coffee can. People with a damn slim margin between making the mortgage payment, or not. People with no safety net. Tons of people live that way, on the razor edge of ruin. Well, not *my* neighbors, not the sterling silver Portland Place crowd.

Fritz took a corner too fast and veered sharply. Lydia seemed not to notice. The lights were blue now, the music soft. Fritz's thoughts turned inward again. Ever since I graduated from the Academy I've done just one decent thing, he told himself, started a business. But it's been more like a game to me than a business. And the rest of the time I'm just circling. Heading for a picture show, or a dance, or a round of golf. Pretty damned pointless.

The music rose to a crescendo. Lydia twirled a reverse and skated backward, facing him. She held out her hands and Fritz took them in his. Her beauty, her innocent sensuality stirred his soul. He gazed at her in the blind, moony way lovers do. Look at this girl, he said to himself. A spectacular beauty with a sweet, giving personality. She probably hasn't a single expectation beyond a South Side bungalow, a couple of kids, and a meat loaf in the oven. God, I love her. I *love* her. She's the one. This girl's going to be my lifetime investment.

"My lifetime investment," he said aloud.

"What?" Lydia laughed.

Fritz released her hands and she started to wobble.

"Help, Fritz! I can't see where I'm going."

He drew her close and cradled her face in his hands. "I can. Trust me. I know exactly where you're going." Skaters winnowed past, a blur of shapes, colors, snippets of conversation. Sparks glinted off the mirror ball and danced across the ceiling, the walls and floor. The organ played on.

The following week they went to a movie, and by the time they got back to the bungalow it was late. They sat on the porch swing and slowly rocked back and forth. The moon was high in the sky, mottled and milky, the air heavy with the scent of lilacs. Lydia traced her fingertips along feathery figure-eights at the back of Fritz's neck. He pulled a small box from his pocket and dropped to one knee.

"Here, Baby. It's for you. The biggest rock in the quarry."

Lydia snatched the box and opened it. Nestled in satin was a platinum ring set with an Asscher cut diamond. Four and a half carats. She slipped the ring on her finger and waggled her hand under the porch light. For weeks she had played it just right. Now, triumph.

"Mister, you have done yourself proud," she said, angling the ring this way and that.

Then they were on their feet. Fritz took Lydia in his arms and she kissed him lightly on each closed eye, an intimacy he found exquisitely arousing.

She leaned into him with her whole body, and he kissed her deeply on the lips. His hand strayed to her breast, and she pulled back.

"Sorry, Baby." He moved his hand lower and tickled her ribs, secretly pleased at her modesty.

"Go ask my dad, Fritz, right now."

Fritz punched the doorbell. He knocked, and rang the bell again. Up and down the block, porch lights flashed. Lydia's father thrashed out of bed with a start and took the stairs two at a time, as if the city were on fire, which it wasn't. Through the peephole, he saw Fritz smiling that crinkle-eyed smile. Tom was dumbfounded. The boy was snapping his fingers, practically dancing.

"Sir," Fritz shouted, "may I have your daughter's hand?"

Tom raked his stubbled cheek and opened the door an inch. "Son, come see me in the morning."

On a lilac-scented evening, a young woman two generations removed from a County Sligo potato farm welded her future to a young man sired by a merchant prince.

The Conrads dutifully invited the Reinhardts to supper. Over corned beef and boiled potatoes, the two families searched for common ground.

"Looks like we have a date," Tom began. "The first Saturday in August, right?"

Albert nodded. "That's my understanding."

"Our Lady of Sorrows. I've talked to Father Stolte."

Tom sensed he'd dropped a bomb. What did they expect, he thought, the cathedral? Give these Reinhardts an inch and the budget will go right through the roof. "You know, Emily, may I call you Emily? Our Lady of Sorrows is so pretty. Ever been there?"

Mary Conrad had been observing Emily, the woman's elegant dress and fashionable shoes, her cool control, and now, the way her finger tapped the handle of her dessert fork, almost imperceptibly.

Tom slogged on. "Mary's going to bake the wedding cake here at home. We'll bring it to the church hall the morning of the ceremony."

Mary chimed in: "We'll put little bouquets on the tables, and paper streamers. The church and hall will look beautiful."

Tom scraped the last of the corned beef from his plate with his fork. Doris coughed. Albert reached for his pocket watch and drew himself up, as if to speak, then thought the better of it, and folded his hands in his lap. Lydia glanced anxiously at Fritz and he smiled back at her, a pie-faced grin that showed her he was completely oblivious to the tension in the room. Finally, Tom delved into an even thornier thicket.

"Lydia and her mother are working on the guest list. We'll have to hold it to a hundred people, fifty couples, twenty-five for you and twenty-five for us. That's seems fair. Emily, could you get your names and addresses to Mary in the next few weeks? Good. Well, I think everything's settled."

Tom sat back and gave his wife a satisfied look. Mary could have strangled him.

Under a veil of well-practiced composure, Emily churned. How on earth? Twenty-five couples? It can't be done. There's Portland Place, the neighbors. The Topping Ridge crowd. Albert's M.A.C. friends. And Karlsruhe. There's all the Reinhardt & Krug people, the board, the executives, their wives. There's Phillip and Florence, and little Madeleine. Madeleine will be the flower girl, of course. And my side of the family. All of them. And Fritz's friends. Heavens, he has so many. Twenty-five couples. It's absurd.

Albert cleared his throat. "Sounds wonderful, Tom. Would you do us the honor of allowing Emily and me to take care of the reception arrangements? Topping Ridge has a fine ballroom and a gorgeous view, and the pastry chef out there does a special wedding cake."

"Five layers," Emily added, rather too quickly. "The chef pipes the prettiest white roses around each layer."

The mantle clock struck eight. Mary retreated to the kitchen and returned with a pound cake and a bowl of ripe strawberries.

○

A few hundred miles north of the Conrad dining room, Palmer and Leroy were lounging in the Vendome's basement maintenance room, sprawled on mouse-chewed theater chairs. While they waited for the movie to end and the auditorium to empty, they snacked on stale popcorn and half-eaten candy bars and leafed through old comic books, as happy as fifteen-year-old boys can be.

Seven hundred miles south of the Conrad bungalow, Alice Breaux was in her formal dining room, a solitary figure at the head of a table meant to accommodate a dozen guests. She dined by candlelight, carefully gumming each spoonful of strained peaches.

Back fifteen years or so, right around the time of that evil hex business, Alice had suffered an attack of nerves that manifested itself in unseemly rashes, heartburn, and voracious dreams. Alice began to grind her teeth at night. Over the years she ground and ground until she was left with nothing but nubs.

You Boys Show Up
1926

Chicago

*P*atrons left the grandeur of the Vendome Theater reluctantly, in dribs and trickles. When Mr. Frank Hammond, the son of the owner, finally gave the signal to blink the house lights, the last ticket-holders moseyed out and lingered on the sidewalk, prolonging their return to reality. Most nights Palmer and Leroy couldn't start sweeping the 1,400-seat auditorium until after ten o'clock. At first the maintenance chief kept a close watch on them. But by the end of summer he trusted the boys to do their work and lock up.

Their routine seldom varied. First, they swept the theater's long, canted aisles. Then Palmer would take a whisk broom and dust pan to the seat crumbs and Leroy would scrape up globs of Wrigley's gum and Bit-O-Honey from the floor. After that, Palmer would wipe down the retiring rooms. Each night he told Leroy not to worry. Each night, as soon as Palmer was out of sight, Leroy worried, he'd hear the chandeliers tinkling high above, hear the lobby's marble lions growl, see a shadow flicker in the balcony. Within minutes, Leroy would be jumpy as spit on a griddle.

"Palmer, the ticket men gone?"

Palmer called out from the gentlemen's retiring room: "Ticket men, candy girls, usherettes."

"Mister O.C. too?"

"All the Hammonds. Done drove off in their fancy cars."

"Where to, Palmer?"

"To The Fountain or the Phoenix. Probably listenin to Doc Cook and the Fourteen Doctors of Syncopation right now."

Leroy sighed. "That man blow like Angel Gabriel."

One night, Palmer finished the retiring rooms early enough to spin his brother a yarn. "Hey Leroy, Mister O.C. parkin under the El tracks, right now."

"Why he do that?"

"He walkin up to a door and knockin. A little window in the door is openin up and Mister O.C., he sayin, 'Little warm tonight ain't it, One-Eye?'"

"Who One-Eye?"

"Nobody. One-Eye's the secret password. It be a speakeasy, see? They got gangsters in there with Tommy guns in violin cases." Palmer had left the Ladies' retiring room and was standing at one of the arched entrances to the auditorium.

Leroy leaned his chin on the broom handle, picturing the scene. "What else?"

"It all smoky. Flapper gals is dippin cocktail glasses in a bath tub filled with high-test hooch."

"No-o-o."

"That so, brother," Palmer said, warming to his subject. "In back they playin craps, lettin their gals kiss the dice. Uh-oh, po-lice is stormin the speakeasy now. Watch out!"

Leroy dropped the broom. A look of terror flashed across his broad face. Palmer roared with laughter.

"You jes foolin, brother," Leroy said, sticking out a pouty lower lip.

"I foolin."

Leroy knelt, probing under a theater chair for litter. "Where you gonna be, Palmer?"

"You think about it now, cuz you knows. Cleanin the gentlemen's smokin room."

Leroy picked up a wrapper from the floor. Baby Ruth, his favorite. He smoothed the wrapper in his palm and licked it clean.

Usually it was after midnight by the time they finished. In the basement, Palmer tossed the dry trash into the furnace and poured the pails of gray water down the floor drain. Leroy wrung out the string mops and picked goop from the broom bristles. On the short walk back to the boarding house, Palmer always whistled a soft tune.

Every Friday, before the nightly show, Mister O.C.'s older son, Frank, handed out pay envelopes to the Vendome staff. Usually, Mister Frank left the twins' envelope with the maintenance chief. But one Friday Frank stayed late, and happened to be in the lobby when the boys came up to clean.

"You boys show up," Frank said, pinching a handsome fedora onto his head. "You don't drink and you don't smell. I like that."

Palmer glowed. Then and there, he decided that working at the Vendome was the best job ever. Best job, best bosses. Especially Mister Frank. Look how snappy that man dress, Palmer said to himself. Sharp. Pinstripe suit, two-tone shoes, and that yellow fedora. Mmm-mm.

Each night Mister Frank and Miss Cherie, his fiancée, put in an appearance at the theater. A quarter-hour before curtain time, Mister Frank would take a seat in the shoeshine chair out front and leaf through *The Defender*. Miss Cherie would occupy herself applying fresh lipstick and checking to see that her stocking seams were straight, a task that never failed to draw Mister Frank's attention from the news of the day. If the shoeshine man dallied, Miss Cherie would pop her gum to the snap-snap of his rag. Eventually Mister Frank would fold his newspaper and tell the man sorry, better hurry it on up.

Mister Frank liked to say Miss Cherie and her mama were close as ivy on an oak tree. Miss Cherie's mama operated a two-chair beauty parlor, wig restoration service, cosmetology school and scalp rejuvenation center out of her front room. Twice a week, Mama reinvigorated Miss Cherie's scalp and then coaxed her daughter's coiffure into artistic finger waves that hugged Miss Cherie's skull like a bathing cap. Mister Frank added to his fiancée's pleasurable appearance by presenting her with a fur stole, which Cherie wore all summer in defiance of Chicago's near-tropical climate.

"What you fellas plan to do with all this moulah?" Mister Frank asked Leroy, making conversation before he handed two pay envelopes to Palmer.

Leroy tipped his cap. "We spend some and save some."

"Good idea. All right, you boys enjoy the weekend. Summer's fierce but it don't last long in Chicago."

Mister Frank took Miss Cherie in his arms and they performed a flawless Quickstep across the lobby. At the door, he dipped Miss Cherie low and she buckled her knees and clung to her man, even when the fox stole slipped off her shoulder. Outside, Miss Cherie glided into the front seat of Mister Frank's new Pierce Arrow and scooted across to the middle, smooth as a butter knife across hot toast.

A week earlier, Palmer had asked the maintenance chief what a swanky motor car like Mister Frank's cost.

"Mister O.C. bought it as an engagement gift. Set the old man back three G's."

In the last few months, the boys' lives had settled into a comfortable routine. Two meals a day at the boarding house. Clean sheets every other week. Baths on Tuesdays and Fridays. In July the landlady loaned them an electric fan, on account of that sticky window.

One night late that summer Leroy stretched out on the cot and clasped his hands behind his head. "We got it better than most folks," he said.

"Got it good, brother," Palmer added, swatting Leroy's pungent toes away from his face.

Don't Close Your Eyes
1926

St. Louis

*A*n August wedding. In St. Louis. What were they thinking?

The morning of the wedding was hot enough to peel paint. Nevertheless, Fritz and Lydia pledged their troth in formal attire before 354 guests sardined in the pews at Our Lady of Sorrows, a church built to accommodate 150. After Mass, members of the Ladies Sodality served chicken cacciatore, buttermilk biscuits, and slabs of cherry Jell-o. When the happy couple cut the first slice of wedding cake, Mary smiled; she'd been up half the night baking and frosting the layers in her small oven at the bungalow.

Albert rose to give the first toast. Emily held her breath.

"My most fervent wish," he began, holding aloft a cup of punch, "my most fervent wish is that through the years Fritz's and Lydia's love for one another grows ever stronger and deeper, and that in the autumn of their lives they look back and regard this day as the moment they loved each other the least."

The guests clinked their cups, but Albert wasn't finished. "From the Bible we know that love is patient and kind, not jealous or boastful, not arrogant or rude. We know that love bears all things, hopes all things, and endures all things. And we know love never ends. Fritz, Lydia, may your love never end." Albert flapped the tails of his morning coat and took his seat. Emily patted his hand.

○

Twelve years of Catholic education had ill-prepared Lydia for her wedding night. Some weeks earlier, her mother brought home a pamphlet describing in vague terms a wife's nuptial duties. Lydia waved it away, leaving Mary to wonder whether her daughter knew everything or wanted to know nothing.

At the Chase Hotel, the bellboy showed Fritz and Lydia to the honeymoon suite. While the boy busied himself stowing suitcases in the closet, Fritz repaired to the bathroom. As soon as he heard the bellboy leave, he strode into the bedroom naked, and hard as iron. Lydia was already in bed. She had pulled the sheet and blanket up to her chin.

"Fritz, honey," she said, "I'm tired. Let's just get some sleep."

Fritz was stunned. He distinctly recalled that right after they got engaged Lydia indicated — not in so many words, but clearly indicated — that after they were married she would be an adventurous lover. Through the long, hot summer, Fritz had anticipated couplings in baroque, possibly Oriental configurations.

Fritz grabbed a towel. It's kind of cute, he told himself. Anyway, in about two seconds Lydia won't feel tired, I can guarantee that. He sat at the edge of the bed and switched on a low table lamp. Lydia turned away. She's scared, he told himself. First time. Virgins! Tell a joke, rub her back, she'll loosen up. Fritz ran his fingers through her hair. At his touch, he heard her inhale sharply. He lay down next to her and tried to snuggle, but she curled into a ball with her back to him.

Good God, he thought, what's going on? All the sexy suggestions she whispered in my ear. Did she think she'd get married and stay a virgin? Is she frigid?

Fritz sat up. A terrible realization rushed through him, dark as river water. Did he happen to notice Lydia peeking over her missal at that church, or did she arrange to sit up front, to be noticed? Did he ask for her phone number, or did she offer to write it on his hand? Was it his idea to take her out on that first date, take her dancing at Topping Ridge, or had she sort of suggested it? Who said 'I love you' first?

Had she *ever* said she loved him?

In gathering despair, Fritz recalled that after their engagement was announced, Lydia appeared bored when they were together. Oh, she was endlessly fascinated by his family's wealth and social connections, the homes and expensive cars, the private clubs, the parties and trips. And she adored waltzing into Reinhardt & Krug and walking out with boxes of clothes rung up on the family account. But now that he thought about it, she wasn't at all interested in the Shelley family fiasco. In fact, she'd tossed it off, said Herb Shelley's losses were his fault and his problem to fix, not Fritz's.

Christ, he though, his face twisting in anguish, I could have married a dozen girls. But I fell for a gold-digger. Phillip warned me about girls like her. God, how could I have been so gullible?

For a brief moment he thought about wrenching Lydia onto her back and forcing himself on her. Or putting her in a taxi and sending her back to her father. What he really wanted to do, though, was sweep her off to an exotic island, lie with her in warm sand, hold her forever. He clenched and unclenched his fists, aching with anger and yearning.

He lay back, not knowing what to do. While he thought things over, he stared at the ceiling fan pushing rondures of sluggish air. He fell in love too quickly, he understood that now. He'd mistaken infatuation for love. Lydia Conrad was so beautiful, so sweet and naïve, it never occurred to him she was anything but what she seemed. He had convinced himself she was a treasure, a jewel dropped into his hands, commended to his care. He realized now she was a clever, trifling girl who came into his world by chance and captured his attention by design, who sensed his vulnerability at the skating rink and turned it to her advantage.

Lydia had stopped trembling. He looked at her, awash in affection, and realized that he still loved her, that he might never fall out of love with her, that he'd never leave her. Having half-given his heart to dozens of girls, he had committed fully to Lydia. But that wasn't it. He'd never leave her because he'd never want to.

He discovered he felt no sense of betrayal. He hadn't lost anything, he realized, because Lydia had never given herself to him to begin with. In a perverse way, she was the ideal wife for him, he decided. She was an insatiable taker. Lydia would take and take and give little in return. And he was a giver, he knew. He'd pour out endlessly and need little in return. Ever since he was a kid he'd felt more alive, stronger and more worthwhile when he was making someone happy. When he walked Esmie to the bus stop. When he bought that split bamboo fly rod for the old priest. Bought an ice cream cone for a girl with a terrible stutter. Took a lonely grandmother to a picture show. Over-tipped a caddy. Turned over his interest in the store to Phillip.

There's always one who cares more, he told himself. Always. I'll be the one.

"Turn over, Baby," he said.

She didn't move.

"Turn over, look at me." His voice was a lullaby. She turned, clutching the coverlet to her throat.

"Kiss me," he said.

She raised herself on one elbow. He licked her lips lightly and she raised herself higher and kissed him.

"Don't close your eyes," he said, covering her mouth with soft kisses. "Look at me, Baby. Look at your lover."

He felt sure Lydia had never kissed with her eyes open. He suspected it felt both wicked and delicious. He slid the case from a pillow and tossed it over the lamp, dimming the glow. He traced a finger along the strap of her satin nightgown and then cupped her face in his hands. Her eyelids fluttered, and he tucked the tip of his thumb in her mouth.

"I want to see you," he said. "Will you let me do that?"

Lydia lowered the sheet to her waist.

"You're so beautiful. Show me your secret places."

With infinite patience, he peeled away the sheet. "Lie back. Watch my face."

Lydia scrunched lower and was still.

"What do you want?"

She said nothing.

"Want me to touch you? Put my hands on you."

She nodded.

"Say what you want."

She hesitated. "Touch me."

He traced his fingers down the shallow furrow that ran from her throat to her belly. "What do you want?"

She looked down.

He bent until his shadow covered her. When he took her in his mouth, she arched her back. "Open your legs, Baby," he said, finally. "Yes, like that. Don't close your eyes. Look at me. Watch me."

Afterward, Fritz lay awake long into the night, caressing her winged shoulder blades, the tiny bumps and divots of her spine, drowning in love and loss. At dawn he kissed her awake. She shrugged into a thick hotel robe and dashed to the walk-in closet.

"Baby," Fritz called from the bed, "come back. Let's have another good time before we catch the train. Lydia? Baby? You in there?"

She jangled the wire coat hangers and shouted at him through the door. "Don't ever ask me to do it like we did it last night. It was sickening."

Fritz ran a shower. He stood under the jets, head down, palms braced against the tiles. He had married a coy and feckless girl. He had offered her his heart, his gilded life, and a rather stupendous diamond, and she had taken them without a moment's hesitation, without a shred of affection. Warm water splashed his shoulders, ran down his arms and sheared off. He stared at the eddy circling the drain. Steam wheeled to the ceiling, thick as smoke from a pyre.

At the train station, Fritz bought his wife a strawberry ice cream cone. Lydia pecked him on the cheek and said she was happy as a sunflower in July even though it was August. A porter showed them to a first-class compartment. After a while they went to the dining car, shifting side-to-side with the rolling gait of the train. They lunched on lamb chops with mint jelly, Pommes de terre Dauphine and crème brulée. Between courses, a waiter brought finger bowls filled with lemon water.

Back in St. Louis, the bride's father was starting a shift at the firehouse. The bride's mother was making a list of the wedding gifts, circling the mountain of creamy boxes on her dining room table. The bride's sister was in her bedroom, peering into a hand mirror, wondering if she should chop her long pageboy into a pert bob, like Lydia's.

On Portland Place, the groom's parents were sleeping late. Stevens, the chauffeur, was waxing Albert's sedan. Esmie was scouring oven racks encrusted with brown sugar.

In Ladue, Phillip was packing for another business trip. Chicago again. Florence was practicing tennis serves. Little Madeleine was chasing after the balls.

In Chicago, Palmer and Leroy were sleeping late, too, situated head to toe on a narrow cot.

Jack McGurn was in a dingy flat, sitting in his boxer shorts and strappy undershirt on the edge of an unmade bed, cleaning the barrel of a Tommy gun.

In Plaquemines Parish, Louisiana, the once-beautiful Seraphine was rocking on a porch chair. A dog had flopped at her feet, raising a cloud of fleas. Once the most sought-after Creole girl in Storyville, Seraphine was gaunt, with the haggard in-sucked cheeks and smudged eyes of a woman on the steep downslide.

Alice Breaux always suspected Seraphine stole that candle stick off her sideboard. Shortly after Gatty disappeared, Alice tossed Seraphine out. Unprepared to fend for herself, Seraphine took several swift, hard landings. One morning she woke to find herself in bed with a ropey oysterman. He told her he had a place in the bayou, said she could stay as long as she liked. He helped her into his small boat and took her to the swamp, to a shack in a wilderness of brown, lapping water, spongy soil, cypress trees dripping with moss. At sundown that first night, Seraphine saw muskrat nests in the muck. At nightfall she saw alligators, nasty, silent things, skimming the brackish slough just beyond the yard. In fulsome night she heard birds squawking in their shaggy rookeries. Vapors rose from the oysterman's viscous yard.

The following morning, the oysterman put Seraphine to work tending nutria he bred in cages out back, and then he left. He returned at irregular intervals, sometimes with a sack of cornmeal, always with the expectation of sex. When she begged him to take her back to the city, he beat her.

O

"Penn Station! Pennsylvania Station!"

Porters set down foot stools. Steam clouds hissed from the train's underbelly. Soon Fritz and Lydia were admiring the New York skyline from a taxi. Then they transferred to Cunard's floating palace, the *Aquitania*. Lydia said she wanted to explore the Palladian lounge and garden cafe. Fritz went directly to their quarters, a three-room suite filled with bouquets, chocolates, and ridiculously lavish fruit baskets.

The crossing was pleasant, the sameness of calm seas relieved by shuffleboard at noon, caviar at five, and midnight tangos. In London, they enjoyed the same view from their window at the Savoy that Monet had when he painted four pictures of Waterloo Bridge. Five days later, on the motorway to Stratford, their driver eased the Silver Ghost to the side of the road and held open the back door for them.

"Look up, sir, ma'am. You won't see the likes of this anywhere but here."

Fritz and Lydia crunched across gravel and threaded their fingers through the iron lace of a gate. At the crest of a rise, a palace of buff-colored limestone shimmered in afternoon light. Blenheim. The ancestral seat of the dukes of Marlborough. Fritz took in the dimensions of the place and tried to fathom the cost of its upkeep. Lydia gazed in thrall a moment and then reached for her Brownie box camera. She was not a sentimental woman, but she shot five pictures, ratcheting a small wheel to advance the film until it would go no farther. The chauffeur nattered on about Blenheim's rose gardens and rococo staterooms, about long-ago hunts and feasts. Then a frown puckered the man's pointy chin and he said:

"This place was nearly the ruin of John Churchill. His family, too. A cautionary tale, it is."

Lydia tossed the camera into the car. "Yes, well, let's hit the road. How far did you say, to Stratford? Fritz, honey, get in. There's a vodka tonic with my name on it at the White Swan Inn."

The driver took it slow along Evesham Road so the young Americans could savor the scenery. Fritz opened the privacy window and tapped the man's shoulder. "What's the story about the place?"

"Your hotel in Stratford's just up the road, sir. I'll have to nip off a good bit of detail. Let's see now. Yes. It all began back in August of 1704 ..."

Twilight in Bavaria. Heat rises from the loam to meet cooler drafts hovering above. The air is alive.

John Churchill, commander of the British and Imperial Army, strides into an empty church. The sanctuary is fragranced with burnt wick and wet stone. For a strange moment, Churchill thinks he hears someone in the nave, hears whispered petitions. He shakes it off and twines up the belfry steps. From the vantage point of an eagle, he raises a spyglass. Through its ocular, he sees rivulets elbowing through summer marshes, crops drowsing between hedgerows, lanes embroidering a hamlet. By tallowy moonlight, he sees the French army tented for night.

Returning to the ground, Churchill notes a change. The air has thickened with droplets.

At daybreak, the French cavalrymen hike into the mist to gather sweet grass for their horses. A youthful attendant draws back a tent flap and rouses Camille de Tallard, commander of the army of Louis XIV, Sun King of France. Tallard yawns. With visibility clouded, he assumes Churchill's horsemen, dragoons, foot soldiers, and gunmen are marching north to resupply. They are not.

The sun crests the horizon and warms lavender earth. Gravity pulls moisture to ground. The fog vanishes. To his horror, Tallard sees Churchill's forces advancing, a thundering column of scarlet coats and tricorne hats. Trumpets sound the alarm.

The French are fighting with superior numbers of soldiers and munitions, but their horses are ill with glanders, a febrile infection that forms bacteria in the soil and lodges in the animals' lungs. And Tallard had made a single foolish assumption, with enormous consequences.

Churchill has made sure his armies are well supplied, and he has deployed them brilliantly.

Day-long attacks and repulses scatter the dead where they fall. Wounded soldiers crawl to stream banks. Scarlet water gushes into the Danube. At dusk, Churchill rides into the town of Blindheim astride a white stallion. He has been in the saddle since daybreak, but he pauses in the village square to dash off a note to his wife.

I have not time to say more but to beg you will give my duty to the Queen and let her know her army has had a Glorious Victory.

Queen Anne grants Churchill a royal manor in Oxfordshire and pledges to have a palace built there. Blenheim, the English version of Blindheim. She decrees Churchill and his heirs may live at Blenheim forever, in splendor. Royal promises, fragile as bubbles on infant lips.

In life's twilight, a war hero like Churchill should retire content. He does not. His heart was broken years earlier, when his only son died of smallpox. Court intrigues vaulted him to eminence and plunged him to disgrace. Battles took a physical toll. Squabbles during Blenheim's protracted construction took an emotional toll. In 1719 a portion of the palace is ready, finally. Churchill and his wife move in. He is old and tired. Three years later he suffers the last in a series of strokes, and dies.

Symphony and Cacophony
1926

Chicago

*D*amn, I love this city!" Palmer jingled the coins in his pocket and checked to see if Leroy was following. He was. It was two in the morning. They were finally done cleaning the Vendome. Chicago, city of sideways blizzards, incessant wind, and shimmering heat, Chicago was momentarily ambrosial.

Palmer held a coin up to a shaft of moonlight sluicing into the Vendome alley and turned his palm until it caught the light. Tomorrow he'd take Leroy to Maxwell Street, buy his brother a pair of socks. A pair of socks and a root beer float.

Back at the boarding house, Leroy went straight to the cot and felt for the loop of string he kept under the pillow. "Y'all countin money again, brother?"

"Y'all playin cat's cradle again, brother?"

Every Friday night, Palmer stashed some of their pay in a cigar box at the back of the lowest dresser drawer. By the end of the summer, the box contained $38.20.

"We got enough for another picture show?" Leroy asked.

"You always pesterin. Ain't we at a movie house every night? And didn't we see a picture show at the Oriental a while back?"

"I knows it. 'Tramp, Tramp, Tramp' with Miss Joan Crawford."

"You are pitiful," Palmer said. He thought it amusing that Leroy had a powerful crush on Joan Crawford.

"I ain't pitiful, jes a little dizzy about the dame."

Palmer snatched the pillow. It was Friday, *his* pillow night. "Sure was a good time, we seen that picture show at the Oriental. Them ushers gussied up like sheiks of Arabee. Paul Ash and his men changin their costumes, fast as a whistle."

"The Rajah of Jazz," Leroy added, drawing out every syllable.

South Chicago was beginning to feel like home. Just like in New Orleans, twilight sent strange winds down the streets of Black Town. Colored lights flickered on, washing sidewalks in rainbow hues. Buses rumbled along faster, keeping pace with roadsters, coupes and runabouts. Paper boys shouted out the evening headlines. The air felt charged. Every breath took in the scent of sizzling chops, home-brewed beer, hair pomade, perfumed wrists.

Symphony and cacophony blew out open doors and windows, swept along South State and took wing to the rooftops. Tunes smooth and mellow as honey poured from saxophones and E-flat clarinets. Ragtime plinked across piano keyboards. Blues poured from battered guitars. Nervous riffs skittered from every blow into a harmonica, every squeeze of an accordion. Marquis lights blazed over the Vendome, the Deluxe, Sunset Café, Dreamland, booked solid with the star-power bands of King Oliver, Phillip Dodds, Jelly Roll Morton. A block of two off The Stroll, smaller venues took on lesser bands and, sometimes, pure unknowns, teenage soloists straight out of their mammy's church choir, wiry hopefuls who cobbled together fiddle, banjo and washboard into a band, into a show, a two-night gig, a chance.

One evening at dusk, a club doorman tapped Leroy on the shoulder.

"Hey, kid, wanna hear somethin strange?"

"Guess so."

"Last night I seen a jazz man toss a fiddle straight up in the air. Threw his bow up, too. You know what? That damned fiddle flew up to the Pearly Gates, playin tunes the whole way."

Palmer tugged his brother's sleeve. "C'mon Leroy, he pullin our leg." And yet, Palmer half-believed the man.

The boys liked to get to the theater early, relax in the basement maintenance room, listen to Erskine Tate warm up his Vendome Symphony Orchestra, one floor above them.

"Tate on violin tonight," Palmer said, turning his ear to the ceiling.

Leroy was pulling clean, dry rags from a line strung between two ceiling pipes. "Jimmy Bertrand doin washboard and drums. Mister Earl Hines and Fats Waller up there, too, I'm thinkin."

The boys fell silent. For an hour, syncopated rhythms ricocheted off the auditorium walls, seeped through the floorboards, and settled in the souls of twin boys raised on the mournful, joyful sounds of the South.

Chinaman Blues
1926

Chicago

*T*he landlady passed out blankets on Thanksgiving morning, one per room. Still, Leroy griped that his fingers and toes were near froze off. Palmer agreed to buy those wool jackets they saw the week before in a shop window on Maxwell Street.

"That it?" Leroy asked, his voice high and squeaky. "Brother, we need gloves. Boots, too."

"I knows it. Can't spare more."

Leroy cut his brother a dark look. "That basement at the Vendome the only place my bones is warm."

During their first week at the Vendome, the boys discovered sound carries through the building. They set about furnishing a corner of the maintenance room as their private listening spot. Leroy contributed two old theater chairs with mouse-chewed seats he found upturned in an alcove. Palmer added a fruit crate to use as a foot stool and filched a lantern from the landlady's parlor. Leroy overlooked the lantern, but when Palmer turned up with a braid rug slung over his shoulder, Leroy took issue.

"Where that come from?"

"Nowhere," Palmer said, defensive. "Mighta found it hangin on some old lady's porch rail or somethin."

"Y'all gotta go back, leave that lady a dime, at least. We ain't no thieves, brother. We businessmen, remember?"

Winter had come on hard. The brothers passed the dreary late afternoons in their basement listening spot, leafing through old magazines swiped from a Black Town barbershop, bathed in the butter glow of a kerosene lantern, enjoying some of the finest music in America.

"Chinaman Blues," Leroy said one night. "Mister Tate in fine form."

Palmer pushed his chair against the wall between the maintenance room and the furnace room. Waves of radiant heat seeped into his spine. "Brother, did y'all know Mister Armstrong growed up in N'Awlins?" Palmer said, strumming an invisible banjo.

"Naw-w-w."

"I heared one of the sidemen tell Mister Frank. Louis Armstrong done lived a spell at the Waif's Home. His daddy done lit out like ours done."

"His mama a whore like our mama?"

Palmer smacked Leroy hard upside the head. "Our mama ain't no whore. No whore at all."

Over the years Palmer had created an idealized vision of their mother, denied her death, rationalized her absence, remade her as the woman he wanted her to be. "Our mama a fancy waitress at Antoine's," he informed Leroy. "She real pretty, too. Wasn't no children allowed at Antoine's, so she had to give us up. Made her real sad. She probably got lots of money by now. Probably tryin to find us, but we gone."

"How you know all that?"

"Knows it, is all."

"Why Louis Armstrong at the Waif's Home if he had a mama?"

"He done shot off a pistol celebratin New Year's. Coppers caught him and stuck him in the Waif's Home. That where he learned how to blow horn."

Leroy scoured his memory, massaging his forehead with his fingertips. "I do not recall no Louis Armstrong playin horn at the Home."

Palmer sighed. Sometimes his brother was so danged frustratin. "We was babies back then, Leroy."

Leroy jumped to his feet and waved his arms, celebrating the news. They grew up with Louis Armstrong!

Palmer grabbed him by the shirt. "Hush up, brother. The maintenance chief gonna come down here. I wanna rest a spell before we start cleanin. Damn, this heat do feel fine ..."

Palmer dreamed he was a child again, back at the Waif's Home. Mister Armstrong was there. He raised a horn to his lips. His cheeks puffed like bellows and he blew notes that jumped off refrains and hit high A's. The man held notes a year and then built layers of rhythm that swooped from joyful to soulful and back. In his dream, Palmer applauded the black man, a waif risen from the gutter to the stars.

A Smoke-Filled Room
1927

St. Louis to Chicago

*T*he bull market was on a rampage. Factories were churning out consumer products, everything from Monitor Top Refrigerators and Kleenex Cold Cream Kerchiefs to Kool-Aid Drink Mix, Burma-Shave, and cans of Green Giant vegetables. Corporate earnings bedazzled investors. Stock prices acted like hot-air balloons snipped from their tethers. Speculators wagered on the slenderest of margins.

For the third time, Fritz Reinhardt & Associates expanded. The brokerage house now occupied an entire block of Maryland Avenue and employed fifteen associates.

Lydia assumed she and Fritz would celebrate their first wedding anniversary with a fabulous trip. Greece, perhaps, or Acapulco. Phillip had taken Florence to Acapulco, and they raved. But Fritz put the kibosh on a major trip. Too much market activity, he said. The office would fall apart.

When Lydia went into a royal sulk, Fritz relented, and arranged a weekend getaway to Chicago.

"Stay at the Blackstone," Phillip advised. "It's classy, right on Michigan Avenue. Get an east-facing room so you've got a view of the park and the lake."

The taxi pulled up to the hotel and Fritz broke into a broad smile. "Phillip steered us right, Baby. Look up. Twenty-three stories."

"Your brother's a know-it-all. Come on, Fritz. My suitcases are getting into the hotel before I am."

When the bellman learned they were newcomers to the Blackstone, he went into his spiel.

"The Blackstone has seen more than its share of United States presidents, sir. Theodore Roosevelt and Woodrow Wilson stayed here. But our biggest day was June the eleventh, nineteen hundred and twenty. That was when Warren Harding got the Republican nomination for president, right here at the Blackstone. A group of big shots were in one of our rooms conferring, smoking cigars and such, trying to decide who to nominate."

"Probably hitting the brandy, too," Fritz chuckled.

"A newspaper man wrote up the story and called it a smoke-filled room. That was his words. Smoke-filled room."

"Well this room isn't smoke-filled, it's scrumptious," Lydia said, running her fingers over the gray silk coverlets and yellow satin curtains. She paused to smell a spray of yellow roses, unaware Fritz had phoned ahead to order them. The bellman stowed the luggage and opened the banks of windows. An August breeze, cooled by its journey across Lake Michigan, wafted into the room.

"Let's dance tonight," Lydia said. "I want to cha-cha-cha. No, I want to Charleston."

"Baby, we've got front row seats at the Blackstone Theater, remember?"

"Oh," she said flatly. "What's playing?"

"Haven't the foggiest."

"Excuse me sir, ma'am," the bellman said. "Could be a show came straight here from Broadway. The Blackstone had Miss Helen Hayes a while back. Ethel Barrymore, too."

Fritz handed the man a dollar, drawing a sour look from Lydia.

After the door closed, Fritz said: "What the heck, the guy knew his history. Say baby, how about a rumba, right here?" Fritz rolled his hips in sexy pantomime. "I hear it's all the rage in New York."

"I know. Greenwich Village. The El Chico. I'm not dancing like that and you aren't, either, buster."

"Kill-joy. Hey, while I've got my wallet out, take this." Fritz handed Lydia a one-hundred dollar bill. "Stick it someplace safe. If we get separated, you'll have plenty of dough to get yourself back to the hotel." She wasn't surprised; Fritz had made a similar gesture a year ago, when they got to the Savoy.

Lydia tucked the folded bill behind the grosgrain ribbon banding inside her new hat.

A Tour
1927

Chicago

A breeze off the lake swept the August heat and humidity inland, where it tormented prairie farmers harvesting a universe of Illinois corn. Miss Cherie, resplendent in a tangerine halter dress and matching sun glasses, dipped into the front seat of Mister Frank's Pierce Arrow and slid over to the middle, smooth as a swan, a diversion lost on her fiancé. Frank was struggling to lower the car's canvas bonnet.

Cherie scanned the sidewalk. "Hey Frankie, isn't that the boys who clean up the theater?"

Frank looked up. "Sure is. Palmer, what's cookin?"

"Not much, Mister Frank. Mighty fine day for a ride, though."

Frank snapped the last canvas rivet. "How about a ride, boys? Plenty of room in back."

Palmer couldn't believe his luck. From the time he first laid eyes on that car, he'd dreamed about it. He and Leroy hopped into the rumble seat. Miss Cherie tied a chiffon scarf around her hairdo. Frank revved the engine.

The boys waved like royalty to passersby. A few blocks from the theater, Frank pulled to the curb. "Cherie's mother's place," he explained to the boys. "Cherie and her mama live in each other's back pocket. We got sixty minutes to kill before that woman is sufficiently beautified." Frank draped an arm over the seat back. "How about a tour?"

Frank moved into the flow of traffic, driving with one hand, pointing with the other as he directed boys' attention to drug stores, barber shops, music stores, photography studios, restaurants and green grocers. "All colored owned," Frank said with pride.

At State and Washington, Frank told Leroy to check out the large bronze clock on Marshall Field's department store. "Look like a giant eye, don't it, Leroy. What time that clock say?"

"Summertime, Mister Frank!"

Frank crossed the Michigan Avenue bridge and slalomed between the streetcars and taxis, sedans and buses making their way up Chicago's signature street. "There's the new Tribune Tower," he told the boys, pointing. "Thirty-six stories."

Leroy craned his neck. "What those things way up there, Mister Frank?"

"Buttresses," Frank called over his shoulder, and the boys hooted with laughter.

When Leroy finally stopped snorting, he asked Mister Frank if they were going to see Cubs Park.

"It's got a new name, Leroy. Calling it Wrigley Field now."

"No kidding. Like the gum?"

"Like the gum. Cubs playin the Robins today, I believe."

Palmer had been following the Cubs all summer. "Sparky on first," he said. "No, maybe third. They got that man playin two bases."

Frank looped around the ballpark, headed south a while. Eventually, he pulled to the curb at the Art Institute. "Gotta go, boys. You get back all right from here?"

Leroy hopped out of the car, pulled off his cap, and bowed. Frank leaned across the front seat and extended his hand for a shake.

"Go on," Palmer prompted his brother.

Leroy clasped Frank's hand, tentative as a schoolboy.

"Firm it up, Leroy," Frank called, revving the engine.

Grant Park stretched along the Lake Michigan shoreline like a caterpillar. Shade trees dappled the grass. Softball players sprinted around makeshift bases; their wives busied themselves on the sidelines, setting out picnic hampers and jugs of lemonade. Children pedaled tricycles on winding paths. Old men dozed on benches. Dogs strained at leashes.

"Palmer, see?" Leroy pointed to three policemen rousting a black man bivouacked in thick shrubbery.

Palmer winced. "Ain't our business. Let's go, brother. Y'all c'mon now."

"Stop yankin, Palmer."

"Then c'mon."

"We the only coloreds here, brother," Leroy said, wringing his cap again.

Palmer shrugged. "Look sharp. Might get the bum's rush."

"There's the fountain!" For weeks Leroy had been pestering to see Chicago's new Buckingham Fountain. "A hundred and thirty-four jets, you know that, Palmer? Them jets stay on twenty minutes and then go off, and then go on again and…"

"I knows it, on account of y'all told me a hundred times," Palmer said, turning his back to Leroy.

Heady New Realities
1927

Chicago

*L*ydia stepped out of the elevator cage. She had changed into a twinset and swing skirt, ankle-strap heels and a cloche hat. Heads turned.

A year of marriage had transformed Lydia. No more hand-me-downs from Doris. No more cheap dresses run up on her mother's Singer sewing machine. Among the heady new realities to which Lydia had effortlessly adjusted was an unlimited expense account at Reinhardt & Krug. For a girl who couldn't attend the Rosati-Kain winter formal because she couldn't afford a gown, taking home a dozen dresses, hats and handbags each month from the swankiest store in St. Louis was rapture.

When they returned from their honeymoon, Fritz had bought a four-bedroom brick house on Lake Forest Drive, a new neighborhood on the outskirts of Clayton. Fritz had given his bride free rein to decorate the place, and Lydia went to town. She was learning how to drive, too; Fritz had bought her a Chrysler coupe. Every now and then Stevens would stop by and take her out for a driving lesson. Best of all, Lydia had a new circle of friends, chic young wives and mothers who played golf, tennis, and bridge, women who had bowed at the Veiled Prophet Ball and graduated from snooty Eastern colleges. Women who had opened their social circle just wide enough for Fritz Reinhardt's blindingly pretty bride to wriggle in.

In elemental ways, however, Lydia was unchanged. Instead of a nascent generosity, there was still insatiable greed. Instead of security, there was continuing self-doubt. At the core, she was still Lydia Marie Conrad, petulant, vain, shallow, guileful, and grasping.

Fritz was waiting for her in the Blackstone lobby. "You're a looker," he said, grinning broadly as she left the elevator. Lydia tucked her chin and rewarded him with a coy smile. Her standard come-on, he told himself, the one that meant nothing.

Lydia was wearing her new hat, a linen cloche that fit her head like a bowl. The hat's brim was embellished with silk hydrangeas and satin ribbons. An older gentleman waiting for the elevator touched the handle of his walking stick to his forehead and nodded at Fritz.

The hat is like the woman wearing it, the gentleman silently observed, expensive confections in which function follows form at considerable distance.

Mist
1927

Chicago

*L*eroy was whirling in the fountain's cool mist like a tipsy ballerina. Around him, vapor rose and fell, transforming the scene into a dreamy watercolor.

Palmer kicked off his shoes and sat on the lip of the lowest basin, watching his brother. A few moments later he pivoted and dipped his feet in the water. The din of the jets was as loud as an airplane at takeoff. Behind him, Leroy danced in widening circles.

Fritz chose a path near the shore and took Lydia's arm. In the distance, they saw the stately fountain wreathed in diaphanous mist. Fritz started a joke about a sailor and a barmaid. At the saucy punch line, Lydia pursed her lips and pulled away. Perhaps it was that sudden movement, or the sudden, sharp wind, that sent her new hat sailing.

Fritz sprinted off, shouting over his shoulder: "I'll get it, Baby."

Lydia's hat bounced along the path a ways and then soared, kite-like. Light as a feather, it dipped and rose on currents of cool air, glanced off a lamp post, and finally tumbled to the ground. Lydia hobbled after Fritz as best she could in high heels, but he was soon well ahead, and the hat well ahead of him. It cart-wheeled on its brim a few revolutions and then another whiffet sent it into the air. It blew inland, changed course, and veered to the waterline again. Fritz thought it was a goner, but the winds were unpredictable, and a new gust sent the hat to the ground, reeling toward the fountain in a series of crazy somersaults. Fritz was breathless and losing hope when the hat finally rolled to a stop at the feet of a teenage boy.

Fritz slowed, watching the boy scoop up the hat. He guessed the kid was about sixteen or seventeen. He was tall and well-built, a colored boy, sort of. Now the kid was holding the hat upside down, peering inside, and shouting.

"Palmer! Hey, Palmer!"

Apparently the kid's friend couldn't hear over the roar of the fountain. Fritz moved forward in small steps. He figured the hat and its secret stash of emergency money would be gone for good if he spooked the boy. He drew closer and stopped a few yards from the boy, close enough to see the kid had kind of a goofy look to him. Christ, Fritz thought, why hadn't Lydia clamped a hand over her damn hat?

The boy was poking his finger in the crown now, twirling the hat like a top. "Palmer," the kid shouted again, "a space ship from Mars done landed!"

The other boy swiveled around. Panic flashed across his face. Leroy was holding a hat, a fancy lady's hat. Clearly, the white man wanted it back. Palmer rose and started toward Leroy. He saw Leroy's finger snag on something, saw Leroy turn over the hat and look inside again, saw his brother grin that big, horse-toothed smile of his.

"Palmer! Somebody done hid money in here!"

The jets stopped. The last drops fell to the basin in graceful lines, like pearls unstrung. A gull wheeled overhead, screeching at the afternoon sky. A girl bounced a red ball. An old man whistled to his dog. Palmer heard his pulse in his ears, a cyclic hiss. He stumbled to Leroy's side and faced the man, the three of them frozen in a speck of time. Finally, the man held out his hand for the hat. Palmer looked at Leroy, his almost mirror image, his other self, and understood from his brother's rubbery features everything that was registering in Leroy's mind and heart. Confusion, at first. Dawning comprehension. Then disappointment and resignation. And then, to Palmer's surprise, childlike joy.

What happened next occurred in an instant, the time it took a trick horse to toss its rider to the ground. The time it took a palm frond to thwack a rooftop, a hitchhiker to jump onto a mule wagon, a dimpled girl to peek over a missal. In that instant, Leroy placed his wind-given toy in the man's outstretched hand and bent his lanky frame into a courtly bow.

"Well here's my hat." It was Lydia. "Lucky that boy didn't make off with it, huh honey?"

Fritz cut her a sour look, lost on Lydia, who was inspecting her hat for smudges. "It's a little beat up, but none the worse for wear. Fritz, honey, you got here just in time. Another minute and these two galoots would have made off with it."

Palmer pulled a wrinkled cap from his trouser pocket and slapped it on his head, tugging the visor low. "Sorry sir, ma'am. My brother didn't mean no harm."

Leroy's smile melted away. He looked confused again, and suddenly miserable.

Lydia turned on her heel and started to walk away. Fritz clamped a firm hand on her arm and held it. Fritz Reinhardt had made a fortune based in great measure on intuition, and he decided to go with his intuition now. He turned back to the boys and said, "Guess you're expecting a reward."

Leroy piped up. "No sir. We not expectin nothin. We ain't stealers. We businessmen."

Fritz chuckled and relaxed. On a hunch, he drew out his wallet and handed a small card to Palmer. "I'm inclined to give you a reward anyway. Here. It's my business card. Keep it. Anytime you want to collect that reward, you'll know where to find me."

Palmer read the words printed in raised letters on the card.

Fritz M. Reinhardt & Associates
Equity Acquisitions, Financial and Estate Planning
Maryland Avenue
Clayton, Missouri

Had the wind been decisive that day, had it blown steadily toward lake or shore, had the youth been surly or the rich man inclement or the wife the least bit gracious, how different things might have been. By some strange alchemy, a breeze and a bonnet melded four lives. In those few moments, coincidence intersected with the signet of character.

A stroll in the park is a commonplace thing. A wind-blown hat is unremarkable. And yet ordinary events carry the seeds of profound consequence. They can fell armies as silently as bacteria rising from soil. They can attack a scullery girl as quickly as the click of a door latch in a night hall. They can uproot a loving daughter as inadvertently as a misstep in a grocer's aisle. They can redirect the lives of boys as indistinctly as mist shearing off a fountain. They are unpredictable, these matters of happenstance, in every way save one:

Come they will.

Barely Contained Patience
1928

St. Louis

𝒫hilip was deeply frustrated. Reinhardt & Krug's competitors were surging into the future. The St. Louis department store had prospered nicely under his father, Albert. But in an era when New York and Chicago stores were opening lucrative branches in outlying areas, Albert was resisting expansion. He feared it would drain business from the flagship store. But the city was congested and sooty, and sparkling new suburbs were beckoning.

Phillip waited with barely contained patience for the day when he would take the helm. In the meantime, he quietly assembled a team of executives to draw up plans for branch stores. The committee recommended opening R&K branches in Clayton, Crestwood and Hazelwood. Each store would anchor a cluster of smaller, low-rise stores. While the plans weren't even off developers' drawing boards, the concept was well-researched: shopping centers, surrounded by acres of parking spaces, located alongside major transportation routes. Wives and mothers who were relatively inexperienced drivers would find it easy to shop right in their own neighborhood.

Philip's secret transition team proposed an even more startling change: Fill the branch stores with basic household items, all the modern conveniences suburban consumers were coming to regard as indispensable. Ditch the sumptuous luxury that had been R&K's mainstay since its inception.

Phillip's day would come, sooner than expected. Within fifteen years, R&K would own and operate six branch stores in St. Louis County and two more in Southern Illinois. In so doing, behemoths like Reinhardt & Krug slew legions of quaint mom and pop stores.

Gangsters Rule
1929

Chicago

*T*he law was slippery. Politicians wrote it. Judges quoted it. Lawyers danced around it. Ward bosses sold it. Union bosses bought it. Cops broke it. Mobsters simply ignored it.

Two paranoid, dangerous men — Al Capone and Bugs Moran — presided over powerful illegal empires, money machines that included the rackets, bootleg booze, gambling parlors, prostitution joints, nightclubs, speakeasies, and tenement stills. Mob hits were a dime a dozen.

Palmer and Leroy had been working at the Vendome almost two years. One night before the eight o'clock show, they heard Mister Frank and the maintenance chief talking.

"Moran's horning in on Capone territory worse than ever," the chief said. He was bent over the engine of Frank Hammond's Pierce Arrow, searching for the source of a ping Cherie heard earlier that day. The chief's voice sounded hollow.

"Yeah, the papers say Moran's knockin off Capone guys like ducks in a shooting gallery."

"Moran's a fool, taking on the Outfit." The chief wagged his monkey wrench in the air behind him, for emphasis. "Capone never goes anywhere without protection. Machine Gun McGurn might be a slick dresser, but he's a bad-ass."

Palmer hurried Leroy along. "C'mon brother. Ain't none of our business."

O

Valentine's Day dawned windy and bitter cold. As planned, lookouts hired by Jack McGurn spotted Moran men entering a garage on North Clark Street. Moran's big whiskey deal was going down. Moments later, a phony squad car carrying McGurn triggermen screeched to a stop out front. Four goons dressed like cops waltzed into the warehouse and ordered Moran's boys to line up facing a brick wall. It was over in seconds.

The killers made a clean getaway. McGurn, the mastermind of the St. Valentine's Day Massacre, had an ironclad alibi: he was in a Chicago hotel room that morning, making love to his latest mistress.

Black Headlines
1929

United States

$\mathcal{A}$ decade of bull markets was coming to a crashing end. A decade of wiseguys flipping stocks like tiddly-winks, of school teachers plowing their life savings into the stock market, of machinists and welders, plumbers and electricians passing along hot stock tips to their friends. Finally, the superheated market erupted.

> *Stock Prices Slump*
> *Stampede to Unload*
> *Many Accounts Wiped Out*

Big-timers put pistols to their heads, or opened the oven and turned on the gas. Panicked citizens rushed the banks, frantic to withdraw their money. Billions in wealth vanished in a month.

A few investors profited during the downturn, though, men like Jesse Lauriston Livermore, Floyd Odlum, Joseph P. Kennedy, and Fritz Reinhardt.

Fritz was a schoolboy when he dove into the market. At first, he bought shares in firms that made things he knew about. When Postum, the breakfast cereal company, went public, Fritz bought $100 worth of the stock. Cereal, Phillip had scoffed, you put a hundred bucks into a cereal bowl? That year Postum's gross revenues were flat. But the following year revenues jumped and the stock split. Each original and new share earned a $3 cash dividend. Two years later the stock split again.

Fritz and most of his clients weathered the Great Depression by staying faithful to the conservative guidelines he established after he repaid Mr. Shelley, the disabled lumber trucker. He restricted his buys to rock-solid companies and did meticulous research beforehand. He didn't hang onto proven losers, hoping they'd pop back up. He didn't shuck a winner out of fear it might decline. He traded during clear bear and bull markets, when stocks moved in a predictable direction.

People began to call Reinhardt "the smart money."

Rat-a-Tat
1931

Chicago

*L*eroy was being silly again, dancing, just like four years earlier when he did that stupid ballerina thing around the fountain in Grant Park. Only this time he was holding a string mop, like it was his partner, doing a dumb tango in the Vendome basement. It was the dead of night. Palmer snatched at the mop, and missed. Leroy glided away.

"Knock it off!" Palmer shouted. His words echoed and faded in the warren of musty, cavernous rooms. He upturned the last bucket over the floor drain. Dirty water splashed his trousers and he cursed.

Palmer twisted the tap over the standing tubs, plugged the drain, and sprinkled Fels Naptha in the water. He rinsed out the rags and hung them over a wood rack. He heard Leroy, off somewhere, having a grand time. Twenty years old, Palmer said to himself, and my brother still actin like a damn kid. Ain't he ever gonna grow up?

Palmer traipsed to the boiler room, looking for Leroy. The basement was suddenly so quiet his own footsteps sounded a tap dancer's. Damn, Palmer thought, soon as I go to fetch that boy he shuts up. If he hidin in this basement, I ain't never gonna find him.

"Whoop!"

It was Leroy, in the supply room.

Palmer felt along the wall. He heard a scraping noise, like fabric on metal, coming from the supply room. He figured Leroy was playing on the delivery chute, crawling up the ramp and sliding down.

The supply room had two doors. A service door opened to stairs leading up to the alley. A large delivery door opened to the alley, too, by way of sliding steel panels at the top of the ramp. The delivery door was open only when trucks pulled into the alley to disgorge cartons of candy bars, paper napkins, soda syrup, popcorn kernels, ticket coils, film canisters, all sorts of supplies. In the gloaming, Palmer saw his brother. Leroy was squatting at the top of the ramp. Behind him, the delivery door was open a few inches. Moonlight angled down over Leroy's shoulder and glinted off the steel ramp.

What happened next occurred in an instant. Leroy started to slide down the ramp. In the alley, a staccato rat-a-tat shattered the pitchy night, causing Leroy to lose his balance and tumble over the side of the ramp.

"Somebody poppin popcorn up in the alley," Leroy giggled, sprawling on the cement floor.

Palmer made a lunge for his brother and clamped a hand over Leroy's mouth. Quickly, he grabbed Leroy in a headlock and scuffled into the shadowy triangle beneath the ramp. "Ain't no popcorn," Palmer whispered.

For long minutes they crouched under the ramp, backs pressed against the wall. In the musty silence, Palmer feared his every breath sounded like wind from a clapped bellows.

Another burst of gunfire. Six sharp cracks and then the brothers heard a man's voice:

"Take that, ya sap."

Leroy squirmed but Palmer held him fast. After a little while, Palmer leaned out and looked up through the opening in the sliding panels. A shadow moved across the shaft of moonlight. Fear shot through Palmer's gut like sparks flying off flint. He sucked in his breath and wrapped Leroy in a vise-grip.

The barrel of a Tommy gun poked through the opening. An instant later, hot lead whizzed down into the supply room. Shells bounced off the floor and ricocheted off walls. Palmer felt Leroy's tears splashing onto his hand.

Then another burst. Bullets sank with sickening ease into cardboard boxes and wood crates. Finally, silence. The shadow moved off.

The brothers hunkered under the ramp, hardly daring to blink. From above, they heard awful moaning. To Palmer it sounded like a guy in terrible pain. Palmer fixed his eyes on the underside of the ramp, as if he could see through it, see whatever horror lay bleeding in the Vendome alley. He heard a faint wet gurgling and then the scratch and flare of a match. He heard the quick heel-toe tap of footsteps on paving stones. Then a car door clicked open. Keys jangled. The engine turned over and purred to life. He heard the raspy clack of gears changing and, finally, tires screeching into the night.

Palmer waited five minutes. Finally, he let go of Leroy and dipped his face into the lacings of his fingers, trying to still his pounding heart. "What y'all see, Leroy?" he demanded.

"Nothin."

"What ... y'all ... SEE?"

"Two men."

Palmer looked up at the opening between the sliding doors. "And?"

"One had a Tommy gun, just like the pictures in the paper."

"And?"

"The one with the gun, he wearin real nice clothes."

"Like what?"

"Spiffy."

Palmer's heart clattered in his chest. Capone's bodyguard. Machine Gun McGurn. The maintenance chief told Mister Frank that McGurn was bad to the bone. "Look at me, Leroy. That was a gangster, a hitman. He plugged a guy right up there."

Leroy was blubbering, wiping away snot and drool with the back of his hand.

Palmer grabbed him. "He see y'all?"

"No."

"Did … the man… SEE you?"

"Might've. Can't tell. I skedaddled. Went down fast and fell off the slide."

Palmer held his head. His thoughts reeled. Can't count on Leroy keepin his fool mouth shut. Tomorrow that boy be braggin. Word gonna get around. McGurn, he be gunnin for us next, and he know right where to find us.

Palmer pulled Leroy to his feet. "Come on, brother."

The brothers edged around the body in the alley, keeping their backs pressed against the Vendome's brick wall. Soon, they were back at the boarding house, collecting their clothes and their savings. By dawn they were heading for the rail yards, crossing streets that had become familiar, streets that had seemed safe.

The great city of Chicago fanned out from Lake Michigan across two hundred square miles of prairie. In 1931, several million people called Chicago home. A total of 36,000 of them would die that year. Most would pass on of natural causes. Some would be crushed by falling objects. Some would be done in by fire, electricity, or the odd strike of lightning. Some would perish under the wheels of streetcars, or drown, or hang themselves. A number of Chicagoans would be murdered by deranged spouses or jealous lovers, by furious neighbors or strangers. They would be rendered lifeless during routine surgery, poisoned at a neighborhood restaurant or at their own kitchen table. A number would be snuffed out by the Mob. Despite frequent, lurid headlines, the chances of Palmer and Leroy witnessing a gangster hit were infinitesimal. And yet it happened.

The twins fled Chicago as they had arrived: riding a boxcar alongside hoboes, jackrollers and low-down drunks.

"This train goin to St. Louie?" Palmer asked.

The bum was half-asleep. "Possible."

Palmer laid his head on his bedroll and listened to the train's long whistles. He recalled the rich man's business card, the words he memorized years earlier.

"Good," Palmer said. "We got connections in St. Louie."

That A Child a Daddy Now
1932

St. Louis

The infant took her first breath in the rosy dawning of an April day. A nurse found Fritz where she'd left him, in the waiting room of the maternity ward. He was at the window and staring out, as so many other young men did when the wait was long, when worry gave way to boredom and boredom gave way to restless exhaustion. During the night, Fritz had tracked the moon's arcing journey to the horizon. He'd counted winking stars and traced constellations until the pinpoints waned. He squinted into the brightening and saw the redbuds had burst into bloom overnight, jeweling his city in carnelian gorgeousness.

The nurse showed him the way to his wife's private room. Lydia was asleep, so he tiptoed out and stood at the nursery window, scanning the bassinets until he found his daughter. Through the glass, he examined her as best he could, her plump cheeks, her delicate eyelids, tiny as the petals of an alpine flower. When she opened her lips and yawned, his heart melted with love. After a while, another new father showed up at the nursery window. The man pressed his face to the glass and made ridiculous cooing noises. Fritz backed away and sprinted to the public telephone in the hall, suddenly wild to spread the news.

In the firehouse, Tom gave the bell three swift pulls and then dashed down the street to Woolworth's. "Where are the dolls, the ones with the candy hearts?" Before the clerk could answer, Tom had bolted halfway down the wrong aisle.

In the bungalow, Doris took the call at the telephone niche. Afterward, she dialed a girlfriend. "… and I just know the baby's middle name is going to be Doris."

Mary sat on the sofa and stared dreamily into space. After a while, she reached for her knitting bag. Soon long, thin needles were clicking like typewriter keys, whisking up lengths of pink yarn into a nubby layette blanket.

On Portland Place, Emily had been waiting by the phone. After receiving the happy news, she pressed the buzzer for Stevens. Emily was determined her granddaughter would be appropriately outfitted. She had Stevens drive her downtown to R&K for satin receiving blankets, silk booties, infant caps and day gowns.

In the kitchen, Esmie hummed softly as she penciled new items onto her weekly shopping list: flour, brown sugar, and pecans. Fritzie, a daddy now, she said to herself. Gonna make my boy his favorite treat, fresh batch o' cinnamon buns.

At the flagship store, Phillip capped his fountain pen and summoned his assistant. "Watkins, pick out a teething cup and rattle, to send to my niece. Sterling, not plated. And have it monogrammed."

Albert hugged his elderly secretary, gathered himself, and asked the astonished woman to put through a call to his banker. "It's a girl, Hastings," Albert boomed into the receiver. "Fritz and Lydia have a daughter. Yes! We'll need another trust fund. Her name? Carolyn Elizabeth Reinhardt."

A week later, Lydia and the baby went home to Lake Forest Drive. The following morning, Esmie filled a wicker hamper with a fine pork roast and a dozen cinnamon rolls. Esmie had nursed Fritz through rheumatic fever, bandaged his scraped knees, dried his tears, and taught the boy all six verses of "Amazing Grace." She intended to take a city bus to Lake Forest Drive and deliver those cinnamon buns to her boy in person. Get a good look at that new baby, too.

Stevens appeared unexpectedly at the kitchen door. He picked up the hamper of food and carried it to the garage. Esmie peered out the kitchen window and glared squint-eyed at Stevens as he loaded her hamper into the trunk of Emily's Cadillac. Then the chauffeur did something that seemed unthinkable to Esmie – he opened a passenger door and stood next to it, just like he did for Mizz Emily, only this time he was motioning for *Esmie* to come on out and get in the car!

At the conservatory window, Emily smiled. Stevens was doing just as she had told him. She had visited her son and daughter-in-law a day earlier and she would do so again that afternoon. This was Esmie's time.

The drive to Clayton took less than fifteen minutes. When they got to the house, Stevens honked at two men in the yard. One was mowing the lawn and the other one was planting alyssum and purple salvia along the driveway. Hydrangea bushes marched across the front of the house. By midsummer they would burst into softball-sized blossoms. At the front door, the yard men had planted pink petunias and vinca vines that cascaded from Chippendale planters.

"It's the new gardeners," Stevens told Esmie. "Twins, I think. They've only been here a month or so, but they've got the place looking like a flower shop."

After the alley shooting, Palmer and Leroy hoped to get to St. Louis by train, to find the man who gave Palmer his business card, and collect their long-overdue reward. But the train was heading north to Milwaukee. Palmer knew McGurn would have no trouble driving up to Milwaukee and finding them so he and Leroy hitchhiked farther north. By late July they were in the orchards of Door County, and it was cherry-picking season.

"Seven thousand on every tree," the farmer warned them. "Not sweet, neither. Like to make a mouth pucker."

"I knows it," Leroy said, his features scrunched in a grimace. "Found that out."

They stayed in Wisconsin through apple picking season and then they angled south and west. In Nebraska they harvested soybeans, and when that work petered out they hitched a ride to Iowa. They were shuffling along a two-lane road, cold, hungry and bewildered, when a farm wife flagged them.

"Looking for work?"

Palmer motioned for Leroy to keep to the far side of the road. The woman looked worry-pinched. Her jacket was too big, too, more like a man's size. Her thin hair blew across her face like corn tassels. Palmer observed she didn't brush it back, like she didn't care.

"Maybe," he said.

"My husband got a broke leg. I sure could use help with the milking."

By Christmas they had made their way to California – Leroy said he'd always wanted to live in California, and Palmer was too disheartened to disapprove. They found jobs at a Nob Hill hotel, working the night shift. Leroy was the doorman. Palmer operated one of the hotel elevators. They wore red jackets and pillbox hats. Palmer said they looked like toy soldiers, but Leroy liked the uniforms. One night, Leroy suggested they exchange jobs, and Palmer reluctantly agreed. That was the night Leroy nodded off at the controls and Mayor Rossi experienced a near free-fall from the top floor to the lobby, the night the hotel manager fired them.

After that, they hitched half-way across the country and wound up in the back of a truck delivering supplies to Hannibal-LaGrange College. When they awoke, the truck was parked in front of a diner 100 miles north of St. Louis. Flat broke, cold to the bone, Palmer and Leroy traipsed around to the diner's back door and asked if they could wash dishes in exchange for a hot meal.

Snow had come early and hard that winter. It collected in ravishing layers that pillowed on fence posts, drifted against garages, and drooped from eaves. Telephone lines took on the look of delicate lacings. That first afternoon, the brothers scrubbed pie pans and rinsed coffee cups at the Huckleberry Diner until their fingers puckered. At closing time, a woman built like an elephant had offered them plates of spaghetti, glasses of milk, slabs of apple pie, and full-time jobs at the diner.

In time, Leroy developed a severe crush on Sophie LaChapelle, one of the Huckleberry waitresses. Sophie was in her early twenties, Palmer guessed, sort of pretty and real friendly. One afternoon Sophie had confided to Leroy that although she liked working at the Huckleberry, she yearned to live in a big city. That afternoon, Leroy had traced a heart on the fogged window over the sink. Inside the heart he wrote LB + SL. Palmer quickly wiped it off and cuffed him good.

They finally got to St. Louis in late April, almost a year after leaving Chicago. They made their way out to the suburb of Clayton, and Palmer eventually found the address he'd memorized, the offices of Fritz M. Reinhardt & Associates. On Maryland Avenue, Palmer reminded Leroy what the man in the park had said. *Anytime you want to collect that reward…*

O

Palmer and Leroy followed Stevens to the kitchen door and watched him carry the hamper inside the house. Esmie followed at close range.

"Gonna be busy around here, now there's a new baby," Leroy remarked.

Palmer cut his brother a sharp look. "Don't go mindin about that. Babies be none of our business. Our business is —"

Leroy sighed. "Mowin lawn, trimmin bushes, tendin flowers and vegetable gardens. I knows it."

"For who, Leroy?"

"For Mister Fritz and Mizz Lydia."

"Who else?"

"The Kellers, the Simons, jes about everybody on Lake Forest Drive. Y'all knows it, Palmer, why you askin?"

"Makin sure you knows it."

Leroy brightened. "Best job we ever had."

"Vendome was the best job we ever had," Palmer said ruefully.

Leroy hung his head. Palmer wouldn't let him forget that his stupid tango dance and sliding game made them leave Chicago. After a bit, Leroy said, "Gardenin for Mr. Fritz and Mizz Lydia gonna be the best job we ever had. Y'all wait and see."

Winter Fields
1935

St. Louis to Chattooka

*E*mily read the name in the telegram's glassine window. A shadow of concern crossed her face. "Esmie, it's for you."

Esmie carried the envelope to the kitchen, holding it between her thumb and middle finger, as if it were a snapping turtle. She set it on the table and occupied herself rinsing cups at the sink. The house was silent. In the parlor, a mantel clock struck the hour. Esmie startled at the noise and then stared out the kitchen window awhile. An early snowfall was dusting the still-green grass. The wind was up, blowing leaves into knurls under twiggy mock orange bushes. Esmie finally took up a paring knife and slit open the envelope.

Mama real bad. Stop.
Come quick. Stop

It had been more than twenty years since Esmie stumbled into Bull Pinkney's arms, since her Daddy had said he'd go after Bull if he tried anything more, which everybody knew Bull would, years since she left Chattooka and found her way to St. Louis, to Portland Place. That first week, Esmie had rearranged the Reinhardts' linen closet, and convinced the boys to fold their pajamas, and baked cinnamon buns.

Then Fritzie took sick, the younger boy, the boy with dreamy eyes and the smile of an angel. Esmie wrapped ice chips in clean towels to cool his forehead. She steeped peppermint candies in warm water and held the cup to the child's cracked lips. She minced apples with ground cloves and spoon-fed the slurry to him. She made clover blossom gargle to soothe his raw throat and eased his swollen knees with comfrey leaf poultices and massaged castor oil into his elbows, and Fritz improved.

In a fog, Esmie passed the telegram to Emily.

Emily went straight to the telephone. "Albert, dear, Esmie's mother is dying. Come home. No, stop by the bank first, would you? Esmie will need cash for travel." When she returned to the kitchen, Emily put a kettle on the stove. "I wonder," she said, opening and closing cabinets, searching for tea cups, "have you something to put traveling clothes in?"

"Never had no need, Mizz Emily."

Emily left the kitchen and phoned R&K again. "Luggage Department? This is Mrs. Reinhardt, Mrs. Albert Reinhardt. Would you send a suitcase to the house right away? The blue leather. Large, I think. I need it here within the hour. Good. Now, would you put me through to the Women's Department?"

Stevens drove Esmie to the railroad station. On the way, she took off the smart new shoes Emily had ordered for her and tucked them in the smart blue suitcase. She eased her feet into the old lace-up shoes whose bulges seemed to expand in synchrony with her bunions. The money Mister Albert gave her was safe in the zippered compartment of a new handbag.

At Memphis, she transferred to a Greyhound bus and dozed in the rear until it hissed to a stop at Low Creek Road. Dirty-bottomed clouds were shedding a cold mist onto the winter fields. During the fifteen-minute walk to Chattooka, Esmie reassured herself. Goin back to St. Louie, soon as I can. Mister Albert and Mizz Emily, what they gonna do without Esmie? Who gonna bake a whole ham every week? Who gonna keep that cleanin girl in line? Goin back soon as Jesus see fit to take Mama home.

Jesus took his sweet time. In the meantime, there was only Esmie to care for her mother. Sam Lee had gone off to Alabama, got a job at the Florala Saw Mill Company. Dalton still hung around, but Dalton was worthless. Nobody'd heard from Willie in ages. Sugar hardly ever left her trailer, just dozed on that old sprung couch of hers. Charity was fat as a sow.

One raw morning in January, Sugar showed up at the cabin. She was skunk-drunk, waving a half-empty bottle, pacing the front yard like a zoo tiger.

"Y'all hear what happened after you lit out?" Sugar hollered. Esmie appeared at the door. "You ever know? Daddy went tellin every damn soul he gonna kill Bull Pinkney."

Esmie wished her sister would go away.

"The gin boss was a Pinkney, you might recall." Sugar's voice dripped sarcasm. "One day he shut off the power. Said the lint cleaner was clogged up. Boss told Daddy, 'Stick yo hand in there, boy. Clear out that machine.' What Daddy gonna do, Esmie? Ain't got no choice. Daddy shoved his hand in the machine, tryin to find a clog."

The tang of breakfast vomit burbled in Esmie's throat. She leaned against the jamb and closed her eyes, dreading what Sugar would say next.

"Guess what, Esmie? The power come on."

"It was a stroke!" Esmie wailed. "I got a letter from Dalton. Daddy died of a stroke."

"That what Dalton told you, girl? Two weeks after y'all skipped town, our daddy died and you took it to be a damn stroke?"

Sugar's words hung in the forlorn air. Esmie's face twisted into a grimace. "Dalton's letter said don't come. He said y'all done buried Daddy already so don't come."

Sugar laughed bitterly. "First them steel teeth chopped off Daddy's fingers, but he couldn't wrench free. Then they whacked off his hand. And then they ground up his whole damned arm."

Esmie sank to her knees. Mist settled on her graying hair like a cap of sequins. Sugar went on, relentless.

"Silas Lum heared the screamin. Daddy was stuck in that machine all the way up to his shoulder before Silas could get to him. Time they drove Daddy to the hospital, he done bled to death."

Esmie choked. Every breath was a struggle. The buzzing in her ears drowned out the sound of her own voice: "I never knowed. Nobody never told me."

"You never asked! You too busy sashayin around up North, doin for them rich folks."

Sugar took a last pull on the bottle. She heaved it at Esmie and it shattered against the side of the cabin. Sugar swore, and backed away into the thick morning.

A day after Mama's funeral, Sugar took off and never came back. Dalton moved in with Charity, the both of them sick as dogs. A lifetime working the intake pipe had shredded Dalton's lungs. A lifetime of sloth had made Charity severely diabetic. Esmie stayed on. That summer, Jesus called Charity and Dalton to the afterlife they'd earned.

Esmie scrubbed the old cabin a last time. She'd doled out the few bits of crockery and some furniture to neighbors, and she was bending low, reaching under the bed for her blue suitcase, when she felt nauseous and clammy. Her left arm prickled. She stood up, but a crushing pain sent her to the floor. It felt as if an ox were standing on her chest. The terrible pain radiated to her throat, and she curled in a ball and closed her eyes for the last time. Without a sound, she sang her favorite hymn.

Through many dangers, toils and snares … we have already come

T'was Grace that brought us safe thus far … and Grace will lead us home

The Hit
1936

Chicago

McGurn never saw it coming. Capone was in the slammer doing hard time. The Mob leadership was changing. Inch by inch, they'd squeezed him out. But he never saw the hit coming.

According to the death certificate, Vincent Gibaldi, age 32, aka Jack "Machine Gun" McGurn, died at two minutes past midnight in a Chicago bowling alley, in the presence of twenty witnesses, none of whom saw a thing.

A Hush Falls Over the Crowd
1936

Huntleigh, St. Louis County

*L*eatham turned over his business on the Old Post Road years ago to his son, Brooke. The stables were in good hands: Brooke grew up mucking stalls and hanging tack, and he loved horses as much as a man could love anything.

When the weather accommodated, Leatham would drag a chair out and tilt it against the side of the barn. Once situated, he'd lean back, lower the brim of his cowboy hat, and give himself over to the scent of summer wildflowers and the buzz of honeybees. And then nod off …

The bleachers are awash in denim and calico. Fifteen thousand fans are cheering the buffalo hunters and barrel riders, rooting for stage coaches pursued by marauding Indians. Annie Oakley rides into the ring, little bit of a thing on a galloping horse, and shoots a hole through the ace of spades. More cheers, louder.

A hush falls over the crowd. Leatham Charles Smith, star of the Wild West Show, thunders into the ring on a magnificent horse. His belt buckle throws off sun sparkles as the stallion jackknife-kicks around the ring. Leatham's ice-white hat sails off. His legs flap in the stirrups. His backbone bends and straightens. Somehow the man hangs on. The crowd is ecstatic. Leatham clucks his tongue and the frothing bronco prances backward on the diagonal, like a startled kitten. To the crowd's amazement, Leatham Smith, star of the show, stands in the stirrups and grazes his spur against a flank. The animal lowers its head and takes a bow, pretty as you please. The crowd is levitating now, youngsters bouncing on the risers, mothers clapping their hands above their heads, fathers and grandfathers whistling through their fingers.

High above the arena a passing crow squawks, waking Leatham from his nap.

Integrity Above Question
1939

St. Louis

Department Store Magnate Dies
End of a Glorious Era
Son of 'Retail Emporium' Founder

"Albert Joseph Reinhardt, 71, former president of Reinhardt & Krug department store, died at 7 o'clock Tuesday evening of heart failure at the Ladue home of his son. Mr. Reinhardt was a public-spirited citizen who enjoyed a splendid standing in the community as a board member of the St. Louis School System, a trustee of St. Louis University and the St. Louis Public Library, a member of the Sewerage and Water Board, and several private clubs. As president of the downtown establishment that bears his name, Mr. Reinhardt was regarded as a man of integrity above question. The only son of George Randolph Reinhardt …"

Proof of Ancestry
1940

Hannibal

*I*n the winter of 1940, on an afternoon thick with snow, the future of Sophie Hanna LaChapelle veered off its predictable path. Ever after, Sophie would remember the day because such a small thing, shoe laces, changed her life.

Sophie was twenty-four. Locals regarded her as malleable in temperament and palatable in appearance. It was rumored her hair, when loosed at night, cascaded in lush rivulets to her waist, a sight none but her family could confirm. Back in high school, Sophie worked part-time at the Huckleberry Diner out on Highway 61. When she wanted extra money, she knitted woolen sweaters which she sold at Junie Lyn's Dress Boutique, or tried to. "This here's a thing of beauty," Junie Lyn would say, fingering the intricate cables. "Ain't but a handful of gals in Marion County got a plug nickel to spend, though." Junie Lyn regarded window shopping as somewhat akin to watching a racy picture show, that is, pleasantly diverting but not near as worthwhile as the real McCoy.

After Sophie graduated from Hannibal High, folks expected she would advance to full-time employment at the Huckleberry, and she did. Waitressing was widely regarded as Sophie's one true calling. In her heart of hearts, though, Sophie held several versions of her one true calling, and none had a smidgen word about Hannibal or the Huckleberry.

A customer pushed through the door and brushed snow from his shoulders. Like a thousand nameless fellows, he hung his rumpled coat and hat on the metal rack and eased onto a stool at the counter. Like a thousand fellows before and a thousand to come, he rested a foot on his briefcase and studied the menu with the fervor of a divinity student parsing Leviticus.

Sophie pulled a pencil from the thick coil of hair at the nape of her neck, and smiled at the man. "So mister, what brings you to Hannibal?"

"Shoe laces, among other small items of great import."

The man ordered pie, same as most men who shuffled in and out of the diner, in and out of Sophie's life, which is not to say the Huckleberry didn't have its regulars. Old Artie Granger, right there in his usual spot. Sophie had a habit of pouring free refills for Artie until Dorothy hollered from the kitchen wasn't it high time Artie got on home, hadn't he got a wife and grandkids? And Pete Hackett. Every Wednesday Pete polished off meat loaf, whipped potatoes and a wedge of pie without dislodging the toothpick at the corner of his mouth. It's a wonder, Dorothy said, jowls wagging like dewlaps.

Men who traveled northeast Missouri in winter knew to take it slow and easy on Highway 61. Black ice was everywhere. Inching along, they stayed out of the ditches and had ample opportunity to read the billboards posted at quarter-mile intervals along the roadside.

> *Home-Baked Apple Pie Every Day!*
> *Hand-Dipped Cones – One Scoop or Two!*
> *Chicken-Fried Steak and a Side of Friendly Service!*

The diner's oval windows glowed through the winter gloom, cheery as holiday strands. Most drivers passed by. But plenty of fellows were sick and tired of oncoming headlamps and backward-whizzing telephone poles. They down-shifted and veered off the road, tires scrunching across frozen gravel. Hollow-cheeked truckers. Salesmen in shiny suits and dull shoes. Face-creased travelers chasing a dream or running from reality. All of them on the way to somewhere else. They ordered coffee and the special, or coffee and pie. The dreamers ate in reclusive silence, but the salesmen always chatted away, to the guy on the next stool, the couple in the next booth, the waitress, to anyone who expressed a glimmer of interest in the ways and means of term life insurance, genuine linoleum floor tiles, encyclopedias, shoelaces.

Now and then a fancy sedan would pull onto the lot. Over the years Sophie learned a thing or two about rich fellows -- they enjoy jawing with a nice-looking waitress, same as the down-at the-heels boys.

The snow was falling harder. The tinny plink of silverware rippled over the booths. Somebody plugged a nickel in the juke box and "Summertime" drenched the Huckleberry in Southern misery. Dorothy reached into her uniform and yanked the strap of her mail-order brassiere back to its shoulder groove. "Three Specials, up!"

Sophie lined the plates along her arm and walked the food to a booth. Back at the counter, she poured the Shoelace Man a cup of joe and handed him a slice of pie. He tucked the newspaper behind the napkin holder and took in the aroma of baked apples, rising like wood smoke in winter mountains.

"Sure you don't want a square meal?" The man looked like he hadn't eaten in a while. "It's Tuesday. Country-fried steak."

"No thanks, Miss."

Sophie didn't press. Lots of fellows ran near on empty, nothing in the wallet but a sawbuck and a snapshot of the wife.

The Shoelace Man watched Sophie with detached interest. Pete Hackett plugged another nickel in the juke box and punched the buttons for "Brother, Can You Spare a Dime?" Sophie grimaced. Just what we need to lighten things up around here, she thought. A moment later she realized the Shoelace Man was talking.

"… and this briefcase here doesn't just contain shoelaces."

Sophie nodded. These fellows, she said to herself, all it takes is a smile and they open up like a clam. "No? Not just shoelaces?"

"Oh no, Miss. I got laces, of course. Cotton laces in black, brown and white. Short little laces for baby shoes and real long ones for ice skates."

Sophie rested her elbows on the counter and smiled at the man. "Mister, you've sure got an interesting job."

Dorothy peered out from the kitchen and shook her head. "That Sophie," she told the boy washing dishes in the annex, "she's one in a million."

The Shoelace Man was still rambling. "You know how many kinds of shoelaces there are?"

Sophie swept a crumb from the counter. "I have to say I'm curious."

"There's leather, suede, flat, round, waxed."

"Is that right?"

"It's a fact. I also got shoe polish, shoe horns, and aglets."

"Aglets," Sophie laughed. "What the heck are aglets?"

"Miss, you're asking a frequently asked question. Aglets are the little tips on the ends of shoelaces. They make it easier to thread through the eyelets. See? Small things of great import."

"Aglets. Who would have thought they deserved their own special word?"

The man scraped the last bits of pie onto his fork. "How about I teach you how to tie a seven-step Freedom Knot?"

"I'd like that, but see that fellow over there? His supper's ready and he won't wait on any seven-step Freedom Knot. Another cup, for the road?"

"No thanks." The man shrugged into his damp coat. "Miles to go before I sleep."

"Happy travels, then. Take care."

Snow blew through the open door and danced in the air. The man bent into the wind and disappeared into the night.

Sophie started to clear away his dishes. The Shoelace Man had left his newspaper behind. She ran to the door and wiped a circle in the fogged glass. Through the blowing snow she saw red tail lights receding in the dark.

Dorothy poured Sophie a glass of buttermilk and took a slice of cake from the display round. "Anything left this time of day ain't worth the space it's takin."

"Not so and you know it." Sophie tossed a hand-knitted sweater over her shoulders. She tucked the Shoelace Man's *Globe-Democrat* under her arm and carried her snack to a booth. Chewing slowly, she opened the newspaper to the classified ads.

Sophie's father was a quarryman, a digger like generations of LaChapelle men. It was her father who insisted on the name Sophie Hanna. Every generation of LaChapelles has had a Hanna, he told her mother. Years ago, back when Sophie's father worked a ten-hour shift at the quarry, he had collapsed on a bed of crushed limestone, and died. Sophie's mother opened their house on Bird Street to boarders. Sophie started leaving her tips on her mother's bureau when she returned from a shift at the diner. College for Sophie was out of the question. Everything but the Huckleberry and knitting cardigans was.

Sophie skimmed the want ads. Licensed Hospital Nurse. Automobile Mechanic. Part-time Music Teacher.

French Maid

Society Woman Seeks Personal Attendant.
Duties include assistance dressing for teas, dinner parties,
receptions and balls.
Experienced at maintaining extensive wardrobe
and the art of coiffure.
French woman preferred.
Letters of reference and proof of ancestry, upon request.

Contact Mrs. Frederick Maximilian Reinhardt
St. Louis
Woodlawn 2-687

Sophie squinted. The last number was barely legible, but she finally made it out. Still she hesitated. *My father's people were French Canadian. Does that make me French? Is French Canadian even French?* She nibbled her cuticles, worrying over every word of the advertisement. *What if I'm ironing a fancy ball gown and I singe the daylights out of it?*

Dorothy emerged from the kitchen, daubing a napkin at perspiration beading her upper lip. "Flop two's up. Flop two, up!" Dorothy let out an exasperated sigh. "Cyril Kaspersen, get on up here and fetch yer own durn eggs."

Sophie tucked a stray curl behind her ear. *The art of coiffure? I can do pony tails and braids, maybe a bob, and a bun. No, a* chignon. *Okay, what about proof of ancestry. Sophie Hanna LaChapelle did not come into the world with a French birth certificate.*

Sophie twirled the glass, watching buttermilk helix up the inside. She was determined to get this job, to move to a big city and have a more exciting life. So yes, she'd give Mrs. Frederick Maximilian Reinhardt proof of ancestry. She'd resurrect the little oilskin booklet from the back of her closet and bring it to St. Louis, to wherever Mrs. Reinhardt lived. She'd read it out loud. Everything. The complete record of Sophie Hanna's descent from lacemakers and pigeon fanciers, salt miners and canal diggers. Every page bore testament to the tensile bonds of family. Every word brought back to the breathing world the people of Sophie's past. Motherless girls who sat beside hearths, crocheting in contentment. Strapping young men who walked away from farms and went to work deep in the earth. Parents and children who crossed an ocean in restless hope of betterment. Who joked and prayed, worked and played, who sang hymns, baked bread, danced under the moonlight, fell in love, married, made children and nursed them through illness and taught them what they could, who delighted in grandchildren, grew old and died. They were no different from anybody's forbears. Anybody's.

Sophie had been a girl of ten when she first read about them, when she shuffled out to the rope swing and skimmed their stories and begrudged them. But after a thousand shifts at the Huckleberry, a thousand fragmented connections with customers who shuffled in and out of the diner, in and out of her life, men and women occupying every point along the continuum from pick-up truck to Cadillac sedan, she knew they all wanted the same thing: a slice of pie, a cup of joe, a drop of undivided attention, and a friendly smile.

Sophie slid out of the booth and scooped her late-day tips from the counter. When the juke box fell silent, she stuck a coin in the pay telephone in the corner.

"Long distance, please."

Dorothy shouted from the kitchen: "Shingle with a shake's up."

Sophie cupped her hand around the receiver. "Yes, operator, I'll wait."

○

Miss Foley picked up the ringing phone. "Mr. Reinhardt, a call for you."

"Take a message, would you? I'm tracking GE, Ford and gold, and they're all on the move."

"It's a young woman. She says her name is Sophie. Sophie Something-French-Like-a-Chapel. She's calling about the advertisement Mrs. Reinhardt placed in the *Globe-Democrat*."

Fritz looked up. "Put her through."

"Hello? This is Sophie LaChapelle. I'm calling about —"

Damn, not a trace of a French accent, Fitz thought. "You're not French."

"No."

"Not from Paris?"

"Not even close. I'm from Hannibal."

"How soon can you start?"

"First of January?"

"Here's a piece of advice, play up the French name. And here's the address …"

New Year's Day dawned so cold puddles of slush froze solid. Palmer and Leroy took an early bus to Clayton to get a head start on salting the driveways and sidewalks along Lake Forest Drive. When Sophie's taxi crawled up the Reinhardt drive, Leroy dropped his bucket and waved.

Palmer pulled off his wool cap. "Y'all remember us, Miss Sophie? We washed dishes at the Huckleberry a while back."

Sophie broke into a wide smile. She was so relieved to see familiar faces she almost forgot to pay the driver. Her dream had finally come true, but the tall buildings and whizzing traffic, the store windows brimming with smart clothes and the crowds were more than a little intimidating.

Lydia flung open the front door. In a wink she was bustling her new French maid to an upstairs bedroom at the back of the house. Before Sophie knew what was happening, Mrs. Reinhardt was rushing around the room, showing her how to adjust the lights, the window, the radiator, opening and closing all the bureau drawers. When Mrs. Reinhardt reached for Sophie's valise, flung it on the bed and began working the latches, as if she meant to unpack the girl's things, Sophie let out a small gasp.

"Mrs. Reinhardt, I'll ..."

Lydia looked up, startled. In her haste to get Sophie settled, she had reversed the roles. It was a ghastly blunder. How could she have been so stupid? If her society friends heard she had actually waited on the hired help, they'd close ranks. She'd be dumped from the smart set. That's what they were waiting for, wasn't it? A blunder. Lydia Reinhardt had it coming, they'd say. A fireman's daughter who vaulted from a job at a candy factory to the apex of St. Louis society. A Rosati-Kain girl who married up and bored into their world like a beetle tunneling into heartwood. They wanted her out, these rail-thin women with their degrees from Smith and Vassar, their salon hair and five-bedroom homes, wanted her to say or do something so déclassé that they could be done with the charade of friendship. She'd been dancing at a precipice, and now she'd stumbled. The French maid would talk. St. Louis was a big small town. Word would get around. Sophie had to go, immediately.

Sophie blushed, searching for a diplomatic way to get past the moment. "Ma'am, you are too kind. I feel at home already."

"Good, fine. Sophie, is it?"

"It is. Shall I call you Mrs. Reinhardt?"

"That will do. Take a few minutes and then meet me in the dining room."

Lydia took a seat at the head of the table. When Sophie arrived, she motioned for her to sit at the opposite end.

Sophie clasped her hands in her lap and leaned slightly to the left so she could see Lydia through the centerpiece of tall flowers. "Mrs. Reinhardt, I should clarify a few things," she began.

Sophie opened the small booklet on her lap and started to read. In a firm, clear voice she told of her mother's ancestors from Poland, a farm family of lace-makers and pigeon-fanciers. She told about her father's people, who dug the Lachine Canal and, afterward, dug rock in a quarry near Hannibal. And her mother, who took in boarders to make ends meet. She described the Huckleberry Diner, and Dorothy, and the Shoelace Man.

Lydia listened in icy silence, her Cupid's bow lips a thin line of disapproval. Each new revelation drove Sophie LaChapelle further from Lydia's vision of a French lady's maid.

"I'm so sorry if I misled you," Sophie said. "I'm used to hard work. I don't smoke or drink alcohol. I don't even date. I'm not French, but I learn fast and I'd love to take care of anything you need."

A child's voice broke the tension in the room. "Isn't Hannibal where Tom Sawyer and Becky Thatcher lived?" It was Carolyn. She was standing in the doorway, twirling a tennis racquet. A stretchy bandage circled her left wrist.

Carolyn looked anxiously from her mother to Sophie, then went on in a rush: "That's one of my very favorite books, the one about Tom and Huck. Daddy gave me that book last summer. I'll bet you like that story, too," she said. Carolyn moved to stand beside and slightly behind Sophie's chair. She laid her right hand, her good hand, on Sophie's shoulder and smiled sweetly across the table. "Mother, I'll bet Sophie – it's Sophie, right? – I'll bet Sophie could tell me and Joe and Eddie all about where Tom and Becky live. Daddy probably knew that, didn't he? Oh mother, we're going to love having Sophie here with us."

Lydia regarded the Hannibal woman with a newly critical eye and then turned her attention to Carolyn. "What happened to you?"

Carolyn took a deep breath. "It doesn't hurt, Mother. I chased one of the balls down that ravine at school. I slipped trying to get it. But Mother, look at Sophie's beautiful hair, she's done it up so pretty. I bet Sophie can do lots of fancy hairdos. I'll bet she can knit and crochet, too, just like the poppy seed girl. Mother, aren't you glad we have Sophie now?"

By then Lydia was wearing the satisfied expression of a milk-fed cat. Tomorrow was ladies day at Topping Ridge. I'll show them, she thought, holding out a hand to examine her new ruby red manicure. Always gloating about their European cooks and their English nannies. Wait till they hear Lydia Reinhardt has a French lady's maid.

Then an even more satisfying thought occurred to her.

Wait till I tell Doris.

Guess Who It Is
1940

St. Louis

*T*he jewel sound of hand bells rang through the snowy afternoon. On city streets, holiday swags drooping between lamp poles took on the look of evergreen smiles. Fritz double-parked at the main doors of R&K and the doorman tipped his cap. "No Sunshine Turret-Top roof today, Mr. Reinhardt?"

Fritz laughed. "Maybe I will crank it open. Neither snow nor rain nor hail nor gloom of winter shall stay the owner of a Turret-Top Cadillac from the swift completion of his appointed rounds."

Fritz found Arthur Weissman in his usual spot, seated by a window in the Alterations Department. The master tailor was relocating the last of twenty-three buttons on a gown one size smaller than the woman who purchased it.

"Weissman, how's the nimble-thimble business?"

"We're on pins and needles," Weissman said, his standard line. The man's assistants looked up from their work and smiled.

Fritz sometimes appeared in the workroom, stayed long enough to tell a joke, and left. But today he had come with a request. "Any chance you could whip up a Santa Claus suit for me? Got to have it in a hurry, though."

Weissman punched his spectacles back to the bridge of his nose. It was early December, a frenetic time for his department.

"Gotta be a first-class job," Fritz went on. "Real velvet and fur trim."

Weissman winked. "To fool the little ones at home, eh?"

"You got it. To fool the kids."

Fritz returned at the end of the week. "Ho-ho-ho," he boomed, emerging from behind the fitting room curtain. The costume was perfect. "What do you know? It's a quiz show and I'm not van Gogh."

Weissman and his staff waited for the punch line.

"I'm not John Doe and I'm not Jim Crow," Fritz coaxed.

Weissman caught on to the game. "Not Ivanhoe or Romeo?"

Fritz grinned. "Not even Geronimo. Answer quick or answer slow, but make your guess before I go."

An elfin tailor spoke up. "Michelangelo?"

"Hell's bells no!"

"Edgar Allen Poe?" a seamstress guessed.

"No, no, eat crow!" Fritz bellowed.

"Your name sir, do bestow," Weissman said. "And conclude this holiday show."

"Good grief, man, don't you know? Santa Claus, to friend and foe." Fritz clapped Weissman's shoulder, sending the man's spectacles gliding down his nose again.

Fritz quietly handed Weissman a paper sack. "Fine job on short notice. Wish the family Happy Hanukkah for me, and here's a little something to pass out to your staff."

After Fritz left, Weissman opened the sack. In it were small leather boxes, one for Weissman and each member of the staff. Inside each box was a twenty dollar bill.

O

Fritz drove to Goode Avenue and parked at a nondescript frame building, an orphanage for colored boys. A middle-aged man answered the door.

"I phoned earlier —" Fritz began.

"Mr. Reinhardt. I remember," the man said, stroking a thin goatee.

The director called the boys to the front hall. A dozen or so solemn-faced lads formed a line, shortest to tallest. The director kept them waiting pointlessly, a show of control that struck Fritz as cruel. Fritz recalled his St. Louis Academy days, the disorganized clumps of boys jostling one another in the hallways, each struggling to be first, refusing to be corralled, boys born and bred and destined to lead, not brow-beaten so they followed like lambs.

The director snapped his fingers. The youngest boy toddled into the parlor. Fritz beckoned the child to come closer and drew him onto his lap. "What would you like from Santa this Christmas, my good man? A puzzle?"

The boy looked up with wistful brown eyes.

"A toy truck?" Fritz encouraged.

The director produced a wood ruler and rapped the child's knee. "Come, come, don't keep the man waiting."

Fritz shot the director a withering look and then turned back to the boy. "It's all right. Santa has all the time in the world. A stuffed bear, maybe? Yes, I think a stuffed bear."

Afterward, at the door, the director pulled Fritz aside for a confidential chat. His breath was sour but Fritz refused to back up. "It is a difficult calling," the man said, "molding something from nothing. So many are the offspring of deviates. It takes firm discipline and --"

"Here," Fritz said, handing the man a check. "This should cover the gifts and a Christmas supper for the boys. I'll have my assistant follow up."

Dusk was drawing a gray veil over the city. Fritz drove to the St. Louis Blind Girls Home, a stately red brick building on Page Boulevard. He hadn't called ahead, and he hoped he wasn't interrupting their supper. A short, doll-like woman opened the door.

"Oh, my" she trilled, taking note of the velvet Santa suit. "Girls! Come quickly. We have a visitor. Can you guess who it might be?"

Four little girls made their way down the twin stairs, fingertips lightly touching the banister, and walked into the grand hall, counting their steps. Fritz stood still while the oldest girl ran her fingertips across his features. She patted his beard and fur collar, and her face wrinkled with confusion.

"Do you believe in Santa Claus?" he asked.

"Yes," she said, understanding now.

"Good. Would you like a china doll for Christmas? A pretty dress? Maybe a stuffed rabbit?"

The house mistress took a scrap of paper from her pocket and noted each child's request. A half hour later Fritz opened the trunk of his car and brought in a box filled with dolls, stuffed animals and dresses in several sizes. The house mistress started to weep.

"We're so grateful. I don't even know your name. How can we thank you properly?"

"Ho-ho-ho," Fritz called, opening the car door. "You've got it wrong. I'm the one who's grateful."

The weather was worsening. For once, Fritz drove with caution. The streets were slippery and congested with holiday shoppers. While waiting for a long red light to change, his thoughts wandered.

Offspring of deviates, my ass, he said aloud. They're kids, boys abandoned on a doorstep. Now I get it, why Dad reminded Phillip and me a million times how lucky we were. I've got to start hammering that into Carolyn and the boys.

By the time he turned onto Lake Forest Drive, Fritz had decided to make return visits to the orphanage and the blind girls' home. I'll have Weissman make an Easter Bunny suit, he said to himself. And a Halloween costume, nothing too scary, though. New shoes for all of them. New parlor furniture, too. I'll get Phillip to send a sofa from R&K. And what was with those pails in the hall? Damn, I bet the roof leaks.

Lydia saw headlights in the drive and went to the door. "You're late," she said, her pretty features tinged with irritation. "We ate hours ago. And what's this get-up you're wearing?"

Fritz stomped snow from his boots and twirled the tips of the Santa mustache like a silent film villain. "So, Mrs. Claus, what would you like for Christmas?"

"Oh you. Go upstairs. The children are already in bed."

Carolyn's light was on. Fritz peeked in. "Ho-ho-ho! Santa wants to know, have you been a good little girl?"

"I think so, Santa," she answered, tucking her injured wrist under the blankets so her father wouldn't see. Carolyn had been warned time and again about sliding like a skater on the school playground.

"How old are you now, little girl?"

"Eight."

"And just for the record, where do you live?" It was their private call-and-response.

"In my daddy's heart."

"Where in his heart?"

"In the heart of his heart."

With infinite care, Fritz unclasped a tiny barrette dangling from Carolyn's hair. He set it on the bedside table and said, "Go to sleep, sweet baby. Tomorrow you can make out your Christmas list. Mommy will help you."

Carolyn blew him a kiss. "I can do it myself, Daddy … I mean Santa."

The following morning Lydia found Carolyn's Christmas list on the kitchen table.

> *Orange hot pad*
> *1 blue apron*
> *Garden Gloves*
> *Garden Gloves*
> *White Gloves*

A nice hanky
The Yearling
baby rattle
red necktie
Dorothy Gray dusting powder

"What is that girl thinking?" Lydia said, reading the list again as she poured herself a cup of coffee. Then she remembered something, and all was clear. The other afternoon, Carolyn had sat on the carpet and watched Lydia get ready for a party.

"Shoot," Lydia had muttered after pulling the lid from a box of dusting powder. It was Dorothy Gray Floral Fantasy, her favorite. "I'm almost out."

Lydia guessed Carolyn had watched each member of the household to see what they might need or want. Then the child had made out her list. Orange hot pads for the cook. An apron for the cleaning lady. Garden gloves for Palmer and Leroy and white cotton gloves for Sophie. A handkerchief for the nanny. A storybook for little Joe. A rattle for Eddie. A tie for Fritz.

"And Dorothy Gray dusting powder for me," Lydia reported to Fritz a while ago. "That child asked for things she means to give away."

Fritz pushed aside his plate of eggs and took the list. As he read it, his heart burst with love.

"Well?" Lydia demanded. "What do you make of it?"

"She's a giver," he said. Something you'll never be, he added, silently.

Lydia picked up Fritz's toast and took a bite, chewing thoughtfully. "I guess you think that's just ducky? Well, Carolyn's not getting hot pads for Christmas, thank you very much. I've already bought her ice skates, and a skating outfit, and a Sonja Henie doll. They're all wrapped --"

Fritz interrupted. "I know. I know. Carolyn's generous, and that's a wonderful quality, but she's too impulsive for her own --"

Lydia was working herself into a stew. "-- and a Wolverine play refrigerator, and a play stove, and a new tennis racket, and one of those cute new --"

"Too impulsive," Fritz told himself. A shadow of concern swept his face.

Your Home Will Outlive You
1945

Huntleigh, St. Louis County

*T*hirteen years after a hire-car driver made an impulse stop near Stratford-on-Avon so that his honeymooning passengers could glimpse Blenheim, Fritz bought a parcel of land on Coach Lamp Lane in Huntleigh on the outskirts of St. Louis County, and commissioned an architect to design a replica of the Baroque English palace. Despite wartime shortages of materials and craftsmen, the mansion was now nearly finished.

During months of construction, Fritz took to leaving the office early and driving out to Huntleigh. He watched bulldozers carve Blenheim's massive footprint and scour out the enormous hole for the basement. He watched caravans of cement trucks rumble up the lane, spinning their giant bellies. He found music in the rasp of saws and the ping of hammers. He took in the various scents — the old-penny smell of turned dirt, the pungent odor of milled lumber and the smoky perfume of stone dust. Cranes lowered steel I-beams into place. Carpenters crawled like spiders over the studs and rafters. Bit by bit, he saw his home gather form and substance, rising in pickety relief against the Missouri sky.

One day flatbed trucks had arrived with blocks of buff-colored limestone quarried in Indiana. He ran his hands across the blocks and frowned, for it seemed some blocks had small imperfections.

"These aren't flaws," a mason explained. "They're voids, indents left by plants or bugs, even shells. That one? A streak of calcite, perfectly normal. And there? Pit holes. Limestone has character, Mr. Reinhardt. The men who built the world's great cathedrals and universities used it."

Fritz still appeared uncertain.

"The stones will age to a uniform color," the mason said, turning back to work. "Your home will outlive you. It'll outlive your children, even your children's children."

Fritz rubbed his thumb across one of the shallow depressions. He wondered if it had been left by a shell washed up from some vanished sea, or an insect that flew and fell in a single summer and cast its image in stone for a millennium. He remembered the day many years ago when he and Phillip played in the snow at Portland Place. Esmie had called them indoors but

Fritz had stayed on, lying in his snow angel. He remembered looking from window to window and realizing everyone he loved, everything precious to him, was safe in that house.

Recently, a strange foreboding had leeched into Fritz's dreaming mind, stirring misgivings, about what he couldn't say. One night he dreamed a hand was tossing diamonds into a waterfall. Another night it was ambulances racing across a canted, brooding city. A typhoon bearing down on a tiny island. An old woman foot-shuffling her wheelchair to the edge of a cliff. He would jolt awake, filled with thumping, unformed dread.

He hired a graduate student, a brainy kid eager for a quick, paying research project. "I want something to put on Blenheim's cornerstone," Fritz said. "Start with the Greeks but don't stop there. Authors, poets, philosophers. Anything about a man's home."

The student had heard about Blenheim, of course. The Reinhardts' notoriety was second only to the Busch family's. In June, the *Post-Dispatch* had run a two-page spread about the palatial home nearing completion in Huntleigh.

"Mr. and Mrs. Fritz Reinhardt's 16,000 square foot home is the signature work of St. Louis architect Carter Stanton," the article began. "Interiors and furnishings by Bernard et Fils of Paris will showcase a collection of Renaissance ceramics, 17th century Italian paintings, and English porcelain procured from antiques dealers in New York.

"On the main level, a marbled foyer with sweeping split staircase divides wings housing a grand salon, formal dining room, a kitchen suite, paneled study, and jaunty Hawaiian Room. On the second floor, a central corridor gives way to tributary passages that lead to six bedroom wings. The third floor consists of an opulent ballroom with a barrel-vault ceiling and raised dais for musicians. A fourth floor has sleeping quarters for twelve servants."

Architect Carter Stanton was quoted as saying he designed the home in homage to a stunning palace in England built for John Churchill, 1st Duke of Marlborough. Stanton told the reporter the floor plan of public rooms and functional areas allows servants to go about their duties virtually unseen.

According to the news report, the mansion was situated on five rolling acres at the terminus of Coach Lamp Lane, and so approached head-on. In front, a half-circle drive would soon be in place, flanked by an allee of teardrop linden trees. In the grassy center of the motorcourt, a life-size statue of Venus de Milo would hold forth, pried a decade earlier from an Italian villa whose owners had fallen on hard times and wept as she left. At the rear of the house, terraced grounds would sweep away from a brick patio in a series of outdoor vistas that unfold like scenes in a play. The focal point of the parklike grounds would be a 15-foot-tall mermaid fountain surrounded by swirling beds of Old Garden roses.

○

Fritz parked in a patch of shade. It was late August. The sun was beating like sticks on a drum. "We're here. Everybody out."

"Daddy, can I stay in the car?" Carolyn begged. "Nancy finally got to the moss-covered mansion."

"Nancy Drew," Lydia explained, rummaging in her straw tote for a tube of lipstick. She added: "Fritz, go on ahead. Joe, Eddie, you go, too. Jesus, it's hot. Thank heaven we left the baby home with Nanny."

The boys romped like colts across the wasteland of packed dirt that would become the motor court. Fritz walked up to the house and leaned against one of the Corinthian columns. For a while he watched masons setting the last of the bluestone slabs in place on the portico. Then he unfolded the university student's report and scanned it.

Joe and Eddie were racing toy trucks across the hardpack. Fritz smiled, as if he could see happy years to come. Someday, he thought, my boys are going to shoot off fireworks right out there. They'll roar up the drive in their sports cars. They'll sneak beer and play pool with their buddies in the rathskeller, and make out with their girlfriends out in the garden somewhere. And Carolyn, she'll sweep down the stairs in her Veiled Prophet gown. Conrad, my little dare-devil, maybe she'll go for pony rides at that old stable down the road. Lydia and I might even have another kid, who knows?

The boys were squabbling. Joe accidently mowed over Eddie's truck. Eddie kicked dirt at Joe. Fritz remembered being sick with rheumatic fever when he was just about Eddie's age. Phillip had bounced on the bed, thinking it would cheer him up, but it made his joints ache worse. Esmie swept him onto her lap and massaged his knees and sang his favorite song.

> *Swing low, sweet chariot*
> *Coming for to carry me home*

Fritz folded the report and shoved it in his pocket. He'd already decided the cornerstone phrase. He came across it years earlier on his twenty-first birthday. His father had given him a limited edition of T. E. Lawrence's autobiography, *The Seven Pillars of Wisdom*. It took Fritz a month to get through the thick book, but he found Lawrence's courage deeply moving. The title of the book is from Proverbs, his father had told him, adding: "It refers to Wisdom hewing seven pillars to build her house."

Carter Stanton's initial blueprint of Blenheim featured eight Corinthian columns marching across the front elevation. "Change it," Fritz said. "I want seven."

"But it won't be symmetrical," Stanton had argued.

"I know, but it'll be proverbial."

Stanton sighed, and quietly resolved to hide the seventh column behind one of the others.

The phrase for the cornerstone is from Lawrence's dedication, a poem he wrote to an Arabian boy who died of typhus. Fritz didn't care one way or another about Lawrence's rumored relationship with the boy; the words crystalized why he built the home.

> *I loved you*
> *So I drew these tides of men into my hands*
> *And wrote my will across the sky*
> *In stars*

Every Catty Little Thing
August, 1945

Huntleigh

*A*t age thirty-seven, after carrying four children to term, Lydia's beauty remained intact. The girl who wore hand-me-downs from her sister was an arbiter of style now, and never dared be seen in anything the least unfashionable. For a rather routine family drive from Clayton to Huntleigh, Lydia wore a chic halter dress and peep-toe high heels.

At the construction site, a trace of disappointment crossed her face, as if comparing this Blenheim, her Blenheim, to the palatial English estate she photographed years ago. She comforted herself with the thought that sixteen thousand square feet of house and five acres of land isn't exactly chump-change.

When Lydia was a sophomore at Rosati-Kain, two popular girls had sidled up to her in the cafeteria line. She was delighted, assuming they were going to invite her to join their table, their crowd. Instead, they plucked at her ill-fitting blouse, making fun. Lydia never forgot it. Now, twenty years after marrying into one of the wealthiest families in America, Lydia couldn't stop yearning to get somewhere better, have something more, be someone else, all just out of reach.

"Carolyn," she said, "put away that book. The decorator's waiting and so is Daddy."

Lydia leaned against the car and lighted a cigarette, lost in thought. I'll make those women regret every catty little thing they ever said. They can drop hints like crazy; once we move in, I'll take my sweet time inviting them out here.

Although Lydia hadn't kept up with the Rosati-Kain crowd, she found herself anxious to show off her mansion to her old classmates. She smiled, envisioning them ripping into invitations mailed with a single-word return address: Blenheim.

I'll show off Carolyn in her tennis whites, she decided. I'll have Joe in jodhpurs and a little Karlsruhe Hunt Club blazer, like his Uncle Phillip's. Joe can take lessons at that horse stable down the road. I'll put Eddie and Conrad in look-alike outfits, pale blue, with cherries embroidered on the collar. "Carolyn, what's that horse stable called?"

"Leatham Smith Stables, Mom. I think."

Lydia started toward the house, savoring victory in a war that was only hers to win. Behind her, Carolyn danced across the hood of the car, arms spread wide like a tightrope walker. Fritz looked up, and his face puckered with concern. "Carolyn, get down before you break your neck!"

Lydia was halfway to the portico when she stopped and scanned the grounds for her decorator. Where was that beetling little man?

Mssr. Mathieu was the fourth interior designer to have a go at Blenheim. Bernard et Fils created ravishing interior spaces for the bluest of bluebloods and for months, Mathieu had been foraging for treasures with which to litter Blenheim. Now, with everything coming together at a fever pitch, Lydia was tormenting him with change orders.

"The foyer has to be torn up and reset."

"The marble tiles, madam?"

"I want them on the diagonal. And rehang the grass cloth in the dinette, I can see every seam."

"Madam, grass cloth is thick. The seams —"

"But I do like the Chino-serry mural in the dining room."

"Chinoiserie, madam. Shin-WA-ze-ree."

Today Lydia intended to tell Mssr. Mathieu he must immediately change the coffee table inlays from walnut to macasar. And the finials, from pineapples to fleurs-de-lis. And ask about the bullion trim. Was four inches skimpy?

At the moment, Mathieu was poking into boxes and crates at a South St. Louis warehouse, making sure the tapestries for Blenheim were safe and dry, checking Oriental lamps and Baccarat chandeliers nestled in excelsior, measuring Venetian glass mirrors, counting English clocks and Italian statues.

Lydia hobbled across the dirt yard, avoiding construction debris. "Carolyn, stay by the car," she called over her shoulder. "If you see Mssr. Mathieu, tell him I'm inside."

The stairs from the motor court up to Blenheim's front portico were a ziggurat of deep treads and short risers. Just as Lydia planted a peep-toe shoe on the first step, a breeze caught the hem of her skirt and lifted it. One of the workmen glanced up and winked.

Lydia's vision clouded with black thoughts. Who did this lunk think he was? Who did he think *she* was? Some candy factory girl? If Fritz wouldn't yak with the masons all the time, all pally-pally, they wouldn't act so familiar. Lydia glared at the man, and in so doing she misjudged the next step.

What happened next seemed to everyone at Blenheim that day to occur in slow motion. Lydia toppled backward and hit the ground hard. She landed with a low grunt, a jumble of arms and legs, and swirling sun dress. Her sun glasses clattered off. Her necklace came unstrung. Pearls bounced merrily across the dirt.

Fritz rushed down to her. He knelt, cradling his wife in his arms. Lydia sank her face into his shoulder, mortified.

"Where's it hurt, Baby?"

"My foot. I might have conked my head, too."

Fritz asked again, this time in a sing-song voice. "Where's it hurt, Baby?"

Lydia knew the routine. Fritz used it to distract the kids when they scraped an elbow or knee.

"It hurts here, for starters," she snapped, rubbing her ankle.

He poked her knee. "There?"

"No. *Here*. My ankle."

Oh, there." Fritz massaged her wrist. It was part of the game.

"Not my arm."

"Your nose, you say? How'd you fall on your nose, Baby?"

Lydia struggled to her feet. She brushed the dust from her dress and Fritz gave her backside a playful swat. The masons picked up their trowels and went back to work.

Lydia limped into the house. Focused on her throbbing ankle, she was unaware of a far more threatening injury. When she fell, her head had struck a bit of limestone half-embedded in the dirt. Now, a sizeable knot was rising behind her ear.

She bent to examine the checkerboard squares. They were spinning like water circling a drain, then fast as debris in a tornado. Lydia looked up. The whole foyer was speeding round and round. She grabbed a newel post and closed her eyes until she was sure she wouldn't fall again, wouldn't embarrass herself again.

With a single misstep, Lydia's remarkable social ascent had peaked, and begun a protracted decline.

A Flash of Bravery
October, 1945

Clayton

"Two men here to see you, sir."

"I told you, Miss Foley, no appointments this morning. I've got six active files on my plate and I'm meeting Phillip at the club in an hour."

Fritz ruffled the folders on his desk. At the top of the stack was a file labeled "Finlay."

Bice Finlay was a vice president of McDonnell Aircraft, and Fritz's best friend. Peacetime was about to put McDonnell in a tailspin, with a big backlog of unsold planes. During the good years, Bice had bought a six-bedroom Tudor on Lindell Boulevard, a beach house in Lauderdale, part interests in a silver mine and a race horse, and two framed Maxfield Parrishes. Fritz was putting together a plan to shelter Bice's assets in ways that wouldn't raise a red flag with the tax boys.

The file labeled "Pills" was a consortium of pharmacy owners. "Chair" manufactured up-market furniture. Fritz had been trying to convince Chair to start mass-producing cheap dinette sets and sell them to returning servicemen and their brides.

But today the files would wait. Fritz was eager to get out of the office and onto the golf course. He intended to make par on the killer tenth before the season ended. The tenth at Topping Ridge was a five-shot bear, a 220-yard carry over a bog with a cattail creek down the left. Players who chipped onto the green found it sloped away from the pin to a twelve-foot sheer drop into sand. All summer, Fritz had been chipping golf balls onto the green and watching them roll into the sand.

"No interruptions, Miss Foley. I've got Finlay, Pills and Chairs and one hell of a mess out at Blenheim."

"Sir?"

"It rained this morning. Blenheim is wallowing in mud. When it's sunny, Blenheim wallows in dust. I have no grass, Miss Foley. I have weeds, ruts, rocks, ant hills and gopher mounds, but I do not have a single blade of grass. My wife's driving me nuts."

"But you only moved in two weeks ago."

"I can tell a vice president at Ralston where to invest his money, but I can't get those East Coast landscapers to hire somebody here to slap down sod. The roses aren't in yet, either. Lydia's mad as a hornet —"

"I can imagine."

Miss Foley had been with Fritz for twenty-one years, ever since his mother had phoned an employment agency demanding a not-too-young, not-too-pretty secretary for her son. Miss Foley was accustomed to overhearing Fritz's off-color jokes, but his ill-humor today was worrisome. It seemed to her Blenheim was proving to be one big headache.

Lydia had insisted the grounds be designed by landscape architects at Fairsted, the Massachusetts firm founded by Frederick Law Olmsted. As soon as they accepted, she began peppering them with dozens of fantastical suggestions. For sport, a newcomer to Fairsted included in a packet for Lydia's approval a sketch for a rustic potting shed based on Marie Antoinette's garden cottages at Versailles. Blind to the humor of insiders, Lydia had gleefully approved the design.

The main house was finished and occupied, but it seemed to rise out of bare ground. The motor court was paved, but the statue of Venus was stored in the garage. In back, the brick and bluestone patio was finished and the mermaid fountain was installed, but the other features – the pie-shaped beds of roses, the arbors and pergolas, the marble reflecting pool and Japanese Tea House and lily pond – hadn't been started. Lydia was wild.

"The two men here to see you," Miss Foley prompted. "They're Palmer and Leroy."

Fritz leapt up. "Christ, tell them to come on in. What's it been, four years?"

Palmer fired off a crisp salute.

"Looks like the Army taught you a thing or two," Fritz said, grinning.

"Yes sir," Palmer said, "and a might more." Palmer stood at parade rest, feet slightly apart, hands clasped behind his back, chest out, shoulders back.

Fritz was impressed. Palmer's been discharged, but he's still a soldier, Fritz saw. At his gesture, the brothers lowered themselves to chairs and sat flagpole straight.

Fritz clipped a cigar and flicked the flint wheel of his Dunhill lighter. He took a few puffs, studying his former gardeners through clouds of blue smoke. He noted the crinkled gray hair at Leroy's temples, the creases in Palmer's forehead. "So gentlemen, what've you been up to?"

"Enlisted the day after Pearl Harbor, sir, as you know," Palmer began.

"I remember." Fritz exhaled a stream of smoke. For the hundredth time, he cursed the childhood illness that had damaged his heart and forced him to sit out the war. Like many men who couldn't serve, Fritz regarded the war as the chance of a lifetime, the chance to be a hero. It was a chance he would never have, never be able to offer his life in a great war, never know the terror of being wounded on a faraway battlefield, fearing his singular, gallant sacrifice would be swallowed up in the panorama of victory or defeat. There would be no memorials erected in his name by a grateful community, no testing of his zeal, of his courage or cowardice, his mettle. He wondered if he would have known a flash of bravery. He envied men who did.

"See any action?" Fritz asked, though he doubted they had.

Palmer shifted in his chair. "Not much, sir."

Leroy shot his brother an astounded look. "Did too."

Fritz set the cigar in an ash tray. "I got time."

"Well, sir," Palmer said, "they trained us like crazy at a camp in Louisiana, then another one down in —"

"Texas," Leroy cut in. "Texas was hot as N'awlins. They made coloreds train longer than whites, too. Whites got to fight after two months."

Palmer laid a hand on his brother's arm and Leroy fell silent.

"We shipped out with the 761st," Palmer went on. "Pretty quick we got sent to France. Pulled them tanks right onto the beach. Before we knows it, General Patton hisself climbs up on one of our tanks and starts talking to us."

"Lots of us," Leroy put in, "all colored."

"Is that right?" Fritz said.

Palmer went on: "General Patton said he don't care what color we is, just so we kills the Kraut sons o' bitches."

Leroy cut his brother a worried look.

"S'cuse me, sir," Palmer said, "but that's how the general talked."

Leroy shook his head at the memory. "We didn't believe it, him thinkin us was equal and all."

Palmer picked up the story. "We fought a hundred eighty-three days straight. Felt like a thousand."

"Was that the worst?" Fritz asked.

Palmer pinched the bridge of his nose, stalling. "Lots of worsts."

Fritz waited.

"Well," Palmer said, "there was the time our unit came across an American tanker..."

They assumed it was abandoned, though they couldn't see why, the exterior showed no sign of being hit. The commander ordered Palmer to open the hatch and call to the crew inside. No answer. "Find out what the hell's going on in there," the commander yelled to Palmer. Palmer lowered himself through the hatch door. At first all he could see were the legs and boots of four crewmen. He took a deep breath and squatted. At eye level with the tank crew, Palmer's blood turned to ice. They were dead, all of them, sitting up as normal as you please. On every cold, soulless face was a look of utter surprise.

Leroy told Fritz about their buddy, a guy named Crecy.

"Sgt. Warren G. H. Crecy, baddest bad-ass GI ever lived," Leroy said. "One day, one of our units was bein attacked pretty bad by a Kraut ambush. We come along and Crecy, he hops into a tank, gets it goin and busts through their lines, blastin them with everything he got. Kraut Panzer comes over the hill next, and nails Crecy's tank with a rocket."

"What happened," Fritz said. "Did they get him?"

"Not by a mile," Leroy said. "Crecy, he jumps out of the tank, it all on fire, and he flips out, he so mad. Hops into a Jeep, gets ahold of a .30 caliber machine gun and starts a-pickin off the enemy one by one. That ain't all. Next day, Crecy's tank get bogged down in the mud. So Crecy hauls his ass out — Krauts shootin all hell at him — and starts scoopin mud outa the track, tryin to get the tank going again. He notices some of our guys is pinned down, bad, so he gets a big-ass .50 caliber gun this time and smokes the whole damn Kraut offensive, couple of machine gun nests, too. Come time it all over, me and Palmer and some of the guys had to pry Crecy's hands off that machine gun."

"You fellas make me proud," Fritz said.

"Our battalion done got eleven Silver Stars and sixty-nine Bronze Stars," Leroy said. After a pause, he looked down and added: "But now we back, and we nothing again."

Palmer filled the awkward moment. "Sorry sir. Leroy and me, we's lookin for work again. The two of us, together."

Fritz tapped an inch of ash from the cigar and took an exploratory puff. "Yard work?"

"Any work. We do twice the job in half the time."

Fritz leaned back. "Nice line, Palmer. Use it often?"

Palmer smiled. "Yes, sir."

"Got a place to stay?"

"Just got discharged. Came right to St. Louie."

Fritz took two twenties from his wallet. "Get some civvies, work shirts and pants, sturdy shoes. Outdoor gloves. We're not on Lake Forest anymore. Catch a bus going west out Clayton Road or Manchester. Ask the driver to stop at Old Post Road and then walk to Coach Lamp Lane. You fellas can stay in the rooms above the carriage house. It's nice, a sitting room, little kitchen, bedroom, shower. I thought Lydia's parents would move in there, but I can't pry that damned fireman out of his bungalow. Anyway, fifty bucks a week and I'll throw in a used car."

Palmer and Leroy were speechless.

"Just get the damned sod laid, soldiers. And plant the roses."

Rhapsodic Coverage
Christmas, 1945

Blenheim

Gleaming limousines conveyed two hundred of the city's finest through the graceful allee of lindens, spangled now with holiday lights. Fritz and Lydia's Christmas Eve ball was the event of the social season, Blenheim's official coming-out party.

Mssr. Mathieu had suggested the theme, a reincarnation of Queen Victoria's 1842 Bal Costumé. Lydia commissioned replicas of the medieval outfits Victoria and Albert wore a century earlier. Back in November, after her final fitting, she had folded the magnificent gown into a Louis Vuitton steamer trunk and boarded a TWA flight to New York, where the camera of up-and-coming fashion photographer Richard Avedon recorded for posterity the mistress of Blenheim, resplendent in orange velvet and a glittering crown.

On Christmas morning, the morning after the party, the *Globe-Democrat* landed on doorsteps with rhapsodic coverage.

"Financier Fritz M. Reinhardt and his socialite wife, Lydia Marie, last evening christened palatial Blenheim, their Huntleigh manse, with festivities unmatched in local history ..."

Contented
1948

Blenheim

$\mathcal{F}$ritz loved each of his children — Carolyn, Joe, Eddie, Conrad, and the new baby, Rose. He loved them in the fierce way fathers ever have loved. But his firstborn, his angel Carolyn, was the child he held fast in the wellings of his heart.

Carolyn had inherited her father's magnanimity and her mother's beautiful chestnut hair, winsome dimples and Cupid's bow lips. But Lydia was petite and slender, while Carolyn was growing up tall and athletic. Lydia's sparkling personality was laminated over boundless greed. Carolyn's appeal was intrinsic.

On Carolyn's sixteenth birthday, Fritz gathered the family in Blenheim's formal dining room. The staff had set an Edith Wharton table -- tapers glowed over Grandmother Reinhardt's sterling epergnes, Limoges china and Waterford crystal. After the birthday girl blew out the candles on her cake, servers rounded the table with champagne. Carolyn lifted her glass, and peered inside. "What's this?"

"It's a key, darling." Fritz's face shone. "You'll need that to start your new car. It's out on the motor court, a brand new Buick Super Convertible."

In Cognitive Decline
1950

Blenheim

$\mathcal{D}$raw Lydia's morning bath. Help her wash. Help her dry. Help her into a fresh nightgown and robe. Bring up tea, toast, a vase of fresh roses. Take out her pin curls. Brush her hair. Help her to the chaise lounge for her morning nap. Bring up lunch and a magazine, *Ladies' Home Journal* or *Look*, anything with pictures. Wake her at three. Win a game of gin rummy and lose the next five. Make an appointment with the salon to touch up Mrs. Reinhardt's roots.

It had been ten years since the Shoelace Man forgot his newspaper at the Huckleberry Diner. Back on Lake Forest Drive, Sophie had been responsible for maintaining Lydia's fabulous wardrobe, dressing her mistress's hair in flattering styles, and keeping track of a social calendar filled with garden parties, card parties, pool parties, holiday parties, cocktail parties, dinner parties and civic events. Sophie lived the life she'd dreamed of, lived it vicariously through Lydia. It was enough. She was happy.

Now, five years after the move to Blenheim, each day had become indistinguishable from the next. Lydia's dizzy spells, memory lapses and confusion had reduced Sophie's world to a blur of mundane tasks.

At first Sophie noticed small things. Lydia misplaced her car keys, forgot Carolyn's tennis match, Eddie's parent-teacher conference. Then she noticed Lydia napping longer, practically dozing half the day away. One day, Lydia returned from a luncheon at the club, opened the refrigerator, and deposited a $6,000 bracelet on a roll of Braunschweiger. The cook went to Sophie. Sophie went straight to Fritz.

"Have you noticed Mrs. Reinhardt seems listless, sort of flat?" Sophie asked.

Fritz sat back and sighed. "I have, yes."

"Her memory's bad, and she gets bad headaches, too."

Fritz rocked his head, trying to loosen the knots of tension in his neck that were always there. He stared through the study's tall Palladian window at the statue of Venus. "I think I know when it started. Masons were putting in the last of the bluestones out front. Lydia stumbled on the steps. She was embarrassed, so I joked about it, trying to buck her up. We knew she'd twisted her ankle. She mentioned she'd bumped her head, too, but we … well, the men were gawking and Lydia was embarrassed, so I joked about it."

He turned away, but not before Sophie glimpsed a ferocious regret fall across his face, its features deeply lined, as if etched in dry-point.

By that first autumn at Blenheim, Fritz suspected his wife wasn't quite herself. By the second autumn, Lydia was vague, less mindful of the children. In time, when she couldn't hold her own in social conversations, her engagements dwindled to hair appointments, therapeutic massages, the occasional luncheon date with Florence, the rare visit from Doris.

The Conrad sisters were never close. From its earliest hours, their relationship was steeped in a jealousy that over the years had grown strong and bitter as tea in a forgotten pot.

A fitful child, Doris was barely a year old when Lydia burst into her world, all apple-cheeked and dimpled, haloed with chestnut ringlets. Doris had plummeted in status from only child to older child, from the darling daughter to the difficult daughter. Dethroned, Doris sulked and threw tantrums. Resentment was predictable, revenge probably inevitable.

Lydia never forgot her sister's get-even tricks, the swing race, the blowing fan when she flew across the stage at the school play. Lydia retaliated in the most effective way possible: she married well. On Lydia's wedding day, the fragile balance of power took a seismic shift. During the years Lydia whisked from the designer room at Reinhardt & Krug to Topping Ridge for lunch, dinner dances at the M.A.C. and charity balls at the Chase Hotel, Doris was typing and filing in a South St. Louis office, coming home to a small apartment and a rough husband.

Now the Conrad sisters were middle-aged women, and the balance of power had shifted again.

Adversity and an iron will had kept Doris whippet thin. She wore her straight, ash-blond hair in a pageboy swept away from her high forehead and held in place with a simple headband. Her features were too angular to be pretty, her brows dark and thick, her nose sculpted as a Dachshund's. Doris underplayed these debits with a touch of coral lipstick and a well-edited wardrobe of slim skirts, tailored blouses, and soft cardigans. She looked good.

Lydia did not. She had grown haggard and puffy. Her lush chestnut curls had given way to limp tendrils dangling from a scalpy side part. Stale breath and a dullness about the eyes prompted her children to back away.

She rarely initiated conversation. Her responses were brief and tended to trail off. Changes in routine agitated her: A warm shower instead of a bath, a new nightgown, lilacs instead of roses.

A few days after the bracelet incident, Lydia had awakened in a rage. "You've got a pistol," she screamed at Sophie. "You're going to shoot me in the back. You hid a butcher knife under the bed, too. Whore. Murderer. Murderer!"

Sophie rushed to the phone.

"I'll be there in twenty minutes," Fritz said. "Call Dr. Sherman. Get him out to Blenheim."

After the doctor finished upstairs, Fritz saw the man to his study and poured two tumblers of brandy. "Lydia's mother's a little senile," he told the doctor, "but Lydia's so young..."

Dr. Sherman set down the glass. "This can strike early, Fritz. We just don't know much about --"

"-- and it takes a hell of a toll on a marriage."

"Bring her in next week. I'll give her a complete workup."

A white-capped nurse showed Lydia and Fritz to an examining room.

"The latest pregnancy was normal?" Dr. Sherman asked Lydia. He held the chest piece of his stethoscope in his hands to warm it while he waited for her to answer.

Fritz answered. "Smooth as butter. Another girl. She's almost a year old now. We named her Rose, after Lydia's little flower patch."

The doctor ignored the joke. Blenheim's gardens were nationally famous. "Lydia, have you experienced any seizures," he asked.

Lydia's expression clouded.

The aging family doctor recommended vitamin tablets.

Within six months Lydia was visibly worse. She only occasionally ventured beyond the master bedroom. She slept ten hours at night, dozed in the morning, napped in the afternoon. She had trouble making the simplest decisions, the white bathrobe or the blue, the seven of hearts or the jack.

"Mr. and Mrs. Conrad visited today," Sophie told Fritz one evening. "They're very concerned."

"I'm aware of that. Tom called me last night."

Fritz took Lydia to see a neurologist at Barnes Hospital, the city's premier medical center. The man ordered a battery of tests to evaluate Lydia's appearance, her judgment, her ability to understand and follow directions. "Your wife is in cognitive decline," he said when the results came back. "We think it's early-onset dementia."

Fritz took Lydia to the Mayo Clinic. He had her evaluated by doctors at Massachusetts General. He flew her to a clinic in Zurich. The diagnoses were identical. In the end, he returned her to Blenheim, and a life of sublime quiet.

The Seer of St. Louis
1953

Blenheim

*T*he one room financial firm Fritz launched was now a five-city brokerage house. Fritz M. Reinhardt & Associates managed $240 million in client assets.

Fritz's personal holdings included Lockheed, Ford, U.S. Steel, and Coca Cola. In financial circles, he was known as The Seer of St. Louis. In fact, his success was rooted in a talent for numbers that bordered on brilliance, controlled ambition, and the focused discipline of a lion tamer. One of his much emulated strategies was to invest a calculated percent of a client's holdings in what he called mop-pail dregs, out-of-favor stocks hitting new lows. The key was to find a mop-pail dreg company that was rapidly growing and paying generous dividends.

Long into the night, Fritz remained downstairs, in his study, slouched in his father's old leather easy chair, poring over financial reports, company profiles, prospectus sheets and trade publications. Anything to postpone going up to the bedroom, to the bed he shared with Lydia, to the empty shell that was his wife.

One Needn't Paw
1953

Huntleigh

*T*he Village of Huntleigh was a world apart.

The estates of Huntleigh were named at birth. Stinton Hall. Sylvan Glen. Chalk Hollow. Blenheim. For passersby, the homes came into view reluctantly, if at all, tucked at the end of long, private drives. Lawns cascaded down gentle hills, pausing here and there at a sinuous flagstone wall, a decorative coach lamp, a copse of stately oaks. Deepwater pools gleamed like sapphires. Tennis courts were lighted for evening play.

The husbands of Huntleigh ran corporations. They wore expensive suits and signet rings with swirling monograms. They smelled of bay rum. When they weren't at the office or on the golf course, they were reeling in marlin from the Gulf of Mexico or shooting impala in Africa. Their portfolios were surfeit. Their time was essentially their own.

The wives of Huntleigh were rigorously chic. They lunched on thimbles of chicken salad at the Women's Exchange. In the afternoon they looked over the silver at Byron Cade and tried on furs at Leppert Roos and bought suits and dresses and gowns at Montaldo's and Reinhardt & Krug's flagship store, places where one needn't paw at public racks, places where obsequious saleswomen in severe navy blue glided into dressing rooms the size of living rooms bearing armloads of fabulous things, and stayed, to zip and button and provide streaming, fawning compliments.

The boys of Huntleigh were Juniors, IIIs and IVs. They had perfect teeth and smooth complexions and the broad shoulders and strong jaws that generations of wealth bedded with beauty endows. In autumn they walked into Boyd's and left with a new navy blazer, rep ties and a fresh pair of oxblood Bass Weejuns. In spring they returned to Boyd's for a new khaki blazer, pastel polo shirts and a woven belt. At sixteen, they received a driver's license and a sports car, sometimes in reverse order. They attended John Burroughs, a 47-acre prep school that sent its graduates gliding into Harvard, Princeton, Brown and Yale. From there, the Juniors and IIIs were assured employment at their father's corporation, or his bank, or the family foundation.

The girls of Huntleigh displayed all the benefits of selective breeding, as well. Their pony tails were pert, their flips perfect. Their closets were filled with pleated skirts and pert round-collar blouses and ballerina flats in luscious colors. They attended Villa Duchesne and went on to Bryn Mawr, Smith or Wellesley. In due time, their mothers took them to the Designer Room at Reinhardt & Krug, the downtown store, not the branches. They stepped onto a pedestal and preened into a three-part mirror while a seamstress knelt at their feet, pinning the hem of a snowy Veiled Prophet gown.

The scions of Huntleigh did not need summer jobs. Girls did not babysit other people's children. Boys did not mow the neighbors' lawns. The scions summered in Michigan or Wisconsin, Maine or Vermont, at private camps with mellifluous Indian names and long-standing traditions. Camps at which campers arrived with one-hundred dollars in spending money, and with footlockers filled with shorts and tees embroidered with the camp logo. Camps where campers bunked in picturesque cottages nestled under soughing pines, canoed pristine lakes, rode English style on thoroughbred horses, posting to the trot, and after lights-out snuck off to the woods to smoke cigarettes and tongue-kiss.

Not every Huntleigh scion camped, of course. Some whiled away the summer at St. Louis Country Club, the Bogey Club, Topping Ridge, Glen Echo or Bellerive, cultivating caramel tans at the pool, perfecting their backhand on the courts, taking golf lessons from the pro, ordering burgers and cherry Cokes at the snack window and signing their father's membership number.

Brentwood was six miles east of Huntleigh, and another universe. In summer, the children of Brentwood babysat, mowed lawn, pulled weeds, clipped hedges, painted fences, swept out garages. Brentwood kids swam in public pools, played kick ball in the street, lounged on davenports and watched "Search for Tomorrow," and yearned for a window air conditioner.

Everything in Huntleigh was light-years better than anything in Brentwood, or so it seemed to Jane and Grace Mitchell, Brentwood girls giddy at the prospect of spending a weekend with their Reinhardt cousins. At Blenheim.

Blenheim, the most glorious of all the glories of Huntleigh.

A Spectacular Universe
1953

Brentwood

*A*ll was always well at Blenheim and nothing was as it seemed, at least as it seemed to Madeleine's daughters, Jane and Grace.

Madeleine's husband, Paul Mitchell, was a chemical engineer at Monsanto Company. As soon as the ink was dry on the marriage license, Phillip expected his new son-in-law to join the executive team at R&K. "Start close to the top, son, and work your way up from there," Phillip had said, in a rare jovial mood. Phillip was so certain the young man would accept his offer, he instructed his lawyers draw up a new succession plan.

Paul declined. He looked Phillip in the eye and said he valued his work. He said Monsanto valued his work, too. Privately, he told Madeleine he valued his independence.

Phillip was furious at Paul. And at Madeleine.

Jane was the oldest of the four Mitchell children, a peaked and pointy eight-year-old, all eye glasses and frizzy hair. At least once a day Jane fell to pieces, and when Jane was in one of her tizzies, the walls of the house practically bowed out.

Grace was five, a tomboy who played with dolls. Grace whistled like a cowboy at roundup, threw underhand, and taught herself how to braid a two-color lanyard. She had graduated from the baby pool at Tree Court last year and intended to swim well enough to pass the ropes at the main pool by the end of this summer.

Grace answered the phone and handed it to her mother. It was Uncle Fritz.

"Hi, Maddie Girl. I need your kids. Not all four, sorry. The top two. My Conrad and Rose are sitting around out here like beached mackerel. How about driving Jane and Gracie out to Blenheim for the weekend? Damn place is so big, nobody will even know they're here."

While the girls packed their overnight cases, Madeleine mapped the branches of the Reinhardt family, trying to explain how things seemed to have somehow skipped a generation. "Conrad and Rose are actually my cousins, so they're your first cousins once removed. I think."

Jane tucked clean socks and her white Keds into her suitcase. "I don't get it."

"Me either," Grace said. She dipped a small plastic wand into a jar of bubble mix and blew. "How can they be your cousins, Mom? Conrad and Rose are our ages?"

Madeleine shrugged. "You're the oldest, they're the youngest, oh, just hurry, girls. They're expecting us in half an hour."

Madeleine adored her uncle. When she was little, Fritz always seemed so dashing and fun. He always pretended to be surprised to see Madeleine at family gatherings. He'd hoist her over his head like a floppy doll, and when her feet touched ground again he would pull a shiny nickel from behind her ear and give it to her.

Grace ran to her mother's two-tone DeSoto, flung open the back door and crawled inside. Waves of heat rippled out into the early summer day. Grace had never been to Blenheim. After this weekend, she would never forget the times she and Jane orbited their cousins' spectacular universe.

Maximum Combustion
1953

Coach Lamp Lane

*E*ddie dashed to the patio, blinking furiously.

"C'mon you guys," he shouted, snapping his fingers at the four girls. "The McMillans are gonna shoot fireworks at the Switzers!"

Eddie was atypical, for Huntleigh. A wiry, freckled boy, his journey through puberty had been so protracted Fritz worried the kid might never punch through to the other side. In April, police officers caught Eddie and a friend toilet-papering the house of a Clayton High cheerleader. In May, Kirkwood police investigated a call about a rowdy party on Adams Avenue, and found Eddie Reinhardt in the yard, throwing up into a bird bath.

Eddie's older brother, Joe, was breezing through his teen years with the dexterity of a varsity quarterback, which he was. Joe had his Grandfather Albert's moral perspectives, his mother's dimples, and his father's gray-blue eyes. In the opinion of the girls at City House and Nerinx Hall, Joe Reinhardt was a dreamboat. Now, during the summer before his sophomore year at St. Louis University, Joe was volunteering at his old high school, helping his former coach with summer training.

As he did most every Saturday in summer, Fritz was playing golf at Topping Ridge. Carolyn was upstairs, showing her mother and Sophie photographs from her recent trip to France. She lingered over the shot of herself on the steps below Winged Victory, and breezed over the shot of her leaning far out over the railing of the Pont Alexandre III. The younger girls, Conrad and Rose, Jane and Grace, had finished lunch and were slouched around a patio table playing listless games of Twenty Questions.

A cherry bomb crackled in the sweltering sky, not far off. Conrad leaped up and raced Eddie to the fence. Grace, Jane, and Rose galloped after.

"You children be careful," Sophie called through an open upstairs window.

"You children be careful," Conrad yelled, sing-song. Conrad loved to mimic anyone in authority, even Sophie. Years ago, Sophie made the mistake of calling Conrad "Connie".

"It's Conrad," the child shot back. "I got my name from my Grandpa Tom. He's a famous fireman."

Once again, Missouri had produced a bumper crop of fireworks capable of annihilating entire subdivisions. The boys of Coach Lamp Lane were armed and ready.

That Saturday morning, Lydia had risen momentarily above the fog of illness. "Fritz," she called down the stairs, "are the fireworks stands up yet?"

"All over town, Baby."

"Well, give the boys a dollar, will you?"

Fritz peeled two tens from his money clip. Joe and Eddie roared down Coach Lamp Lane in Joe's sports car and returned an hour later. Eddie stashed three bags filled with whizzers, cherry bombs and bottle rockets in the potting shed. Joe carried a small sack to his mother's bedroom and arranged a half dozen snappers and caps on the carpet. Carolyn rolled her eyes at Sophie.

"See, Mom, nothing to worry about," Joe said, flashing Sophie a dimpled smile.

Incapable of sustained thought, Lydia tried to recall whether this boy was Joe or Eddie.

Fireworks wars were a revered tradition on Coach Lamp Lane. Although Joe was on the cusp of manhood and Eddie not far behind, the *schtt* of a bottle rocket still carried a heart-pounding payload. During fireworks wars, Blenheim was at the center of the action. Casa Brava, the Switzers' hacienda-style estate, lay to the south. Clareford, the McMillan's Tudor, bordered Blenheim to the north. White crossed-board fences marked the property lines.

The Switzers launched the attack. Rockets arced over Lydia's prized rose garden and landed in Clareford's back yard. Joe and Eddie raced to retrieve their ammo from the potting shed.

Salvos raged and sputtered through the afternoon. By five o'clock the Reinhardt forces, having fought a two-front war, were low on munitions. Joe tied a napkin to a broom pole and waved surrender.

"C'mon over," Steve McMillan shouted. Steve was the oldest McMillan kid.

McMillans were formidable foes but amicable victors. Joe and Eddie pushed through a clump of bushes and hopped over the fence. Conrad, Rose, Jane and Grace clambered after. Everybody stood around the McMillan swimming pool, waiting for something to happen. After a while, Joe kicked off his loafers and waded in. Eddie pulled off his polo shirt, did a belly flop off the board, sank to the bottom and pretended to drown.

Conrad noticed a Dyno-Mite rocket on a pool chair and picked it up. "Where'd you get this?"

"Our dad got 'em," Steve said, snatching it back. "At a place out in Pevely or Eureka. He bought the Black Cats and bottle rockets there, too."

One of the Clareford maids carried out a tray of ham sandwiches and bottles of cold grape soda. When the food was gone, Steve McMillan shot off another rocket. The Switzers returned fire, and the war was on again.

The summer sky faded in the heat. Crickets chirped, obeying timeless instincts. Eddie tossed a potato chip in the air and caught it in his mouth. Conrad and Jane sat at the shallow end of the pool and dangled their legs in the water. Joe and Mike stood around staring into the pool, mesmerized. Underwater lights cast organic shimmers onto their faces. Steve McMillan walked out on the diving board and did a set of test-bounces. "Not much left," he said. "A dozen M-80s and about ten cherry bombs."

"We still got the thunder bombs," Mike said, "and Wolf Packs and the Silver Salutes."

Joe picked up a firecracker and read the label. "Maximum Combustion. Maximum Thrust. Shoots 30 feet."

Conrad smirked. "Yeah, but how's the aim? Hey, Steve, you gonna jump off that diving board sometime this year?"

"Gonna come make me, warrior girl?"

It was dark now. Cicadas were calling to one another in plaintive tympany. The pool glowed, a suburban lagoon. Eddie proposed they cut their fingers and sign a blood oath of allegiance; but nobody went for it, and he turned away and lit a cigarette. The air was a heavy. Jane asked Conrad if she thought Steve McMillan was cute, and Conrad shrugged, as if she'd never considered the matter.

A Switzer firecracker blazed high over Blenheim, sending blood-red tracers into the night sky. Whizzers corkscrewed through the mock orange bushes. Comet tails shimmered in the dark. The combined McMillan and Reinhardt forces returned fire with ear-splitting whistlers. Switzers blasted back with spinners. Little Tommy McMillan toddled out and picked up a punk during its burning phase. Joe carried the bawling child inside.

Mike and Eddie hiked up on the fence rails and reported a Switzer forsythia bush had caught fire. The shrub was a goner, they shouted, a mass of white-hot phosphorous.

"Biblical!" Conrad hollered.

A Switzer cherry bomb sailed across Blenheim's rose garden and thwacked the Clareford pool house, leaving a plate-sized smudge on the door marked Les Hommes. A second cherry bomb landed with a plink on the rim of the McMillan pool.

"It's a dud!" Eddie shouted.

McMillans fired back with Silver Salutes that looped over Lydia's mermaid fountain and landed in the Switzer driveway. Mike McMillan climbed on the fence to see. "They're on Mrs. Switzer's Riviera! On the car hood! Rolling off!"

A sudden flash-bang sent everybody to the fence.

"It got the right front tire," Eddie said, breathing hard. "Switzer boys look mad as hell."

Dusk lingered, as if the sun were determined to see the fireworks war to conclusion. June bugs buzzed at the pool house screens. The defeated Switzers skulked over to Clareford and stood at the shallow end of the pool. The McMillan boys huddled with Joe and Eddie at the deep end. Steve dove into the pool and swam underwater the length of the pool, smooth as a seal. Conrad and Jane wandered off to chase fireflies in the yard. The Switzers got tired of hanging around, and went home.

Mike McMillan disappeared into the pool house and emerged with a Bettendorf's grocery bag. He set the bag on the diving board. Conrad pulled Jane close and whispered, "Two years ago Mike stuck a firecracker in the mouth of a frog and lit it."

"What happened?" Jane asked, wide-eyed.

Conrad rolled her eyes. "What do you think, dummy?"

Moonlight bathed the pool in a milky wash. Moths fretted at the light fixtures over the changing room doors. The air was thick with conflicting scents, phosphorous, coconut suntan lotion, roses.

Mike McMillan laid the contents of the sack on the diving board: a tennis racquet, a honeydew melon, a roll of toilet paper, and a jar of yellowish liquid.

Conrad pointed at the melon. "There's a hole in the top. What's that for?"

Mike unscrewed the lid and held out the jar. Conrad took a whiff. "Pee-eeuw," she said. "Smells like a filling station."

Joe ambled back to Blenheim.

Mike trickled gasoline from the jar down the hole in the hollowed-out melon. He poked a giant sparkler through the hole and packed toilet paper around the opening. Then he carried the melon bomb half-way out to yard, near the fence. Steve McMillan gripped the tennis racquet like a baseball bat and got into his stance. Mike lighted the sparkler. Burning flecks fell onto the damp grass at his feet.

"Wait," Steve said, slow and calm.

Mike held the melon away from his body. White-hot sparkles sizzled onto his bare feet.

"Keep waiting," Steve urged.

The sparkler was within inches of the paper wad. Conrad stood on tiptoes. Jane and Grace covered their eyes. Rose hiccupped.

"Now!" Steve shouted.

Mike tossed the melon straight up in the air and dove away. Steve swung the racquet. Its webbed face crashed against the melon. The bomb was airborne.

Eddie and the girls rushed the fence. The fireball soared as if flung by a catapult and landed with a blinding, flashing explosion.

"Zoom-bah!" Eddie yelled.

Mike stood on the fence and pointed. "Damn, didn't go far enough."

"Damn is right!" Eddie cried, sounding scared now. "It didn't get to the Switzers. That thing landed in our garden. Crap, we're in dutch."

Suddenly, the night grew quiet, eerily so, as if a thousand cicadas had ceased their longing, and were holding their breath.

Several months earlier, Palmer and Leroy had cleared a patch behind the garden's Japanese Tea House, set down a wood frame, and poured a cement foundation. On it they built a dog house out of pine planks. They painted it yellow with blue trim.

The breeder had registered the dog's name, of course: Penelope Pachelbel in Canon D. But from the first, the little chocolate lab was just Penny. By early June, Penny was old enough to leave her mother. The day Fritz brought her home to Blenheim, she bounded out of his car and careened around the garden, in rapture, ears flapping, tongue lolling sideways, tail thwacking, nose sniffing a thousand new smells. Rose had squatted at the mermaid fountain and called, "Here, Penny!" The puppy padded over and settled in Rose's lap, sweet as a lamb.

Now Eddie's face was in spasm. He turned on the McMillans: "You assholes hit the doghouse. You killed our puppy."

Eddie and the girls scrambled over the fence and raced through the rose garden. The dog house was reduced to a pile of charred boards. Embers glowed in the damp grass. Smoke hung in air, tinged with the acrid smell of gasoline, charred wood, and burned melon.

Conrad bent over, panting. She grabbed her knees and vowed: "I'm gonna kill the McMillans."

Eddie yelled, "I'm gonna kill the McMillans and the stupid Switzers, too."

"I want to go home now," Jane said, high and whiny.

The air cleared. The startled cicadas recovered their voices. Eddie and the girls trudged to the patio. Rose stayed out by the remains of the dog house, crying softly.

At the back of the house a screen door opened. Everybody looked up. Penny, bolted out the door, tail wagging, dog tags jingling like Christmas bells. The puppy bubbled into Rose's arms and washed her face with sandpaper licks.

"Wow, that was lucky," Grace said. "Somebody brought Penny inside, huh?"

Conrad raised her face to the sky. A half-moon hovered over Blenheim's roofline. "Carolyn," she said. "It was Carolyn."

A Framed Photograph
1953

Blenheim

$\mathcal{A}$t the explosion, Joe took the curving staircase three steps at a time. As he feared, the afternoon fireworks had agitated his mother. She was pacing her bedroom like a kennel dog.

"Mother, I'm here. It's all over now. See? Carolyn's here too, and Sophie. Let's get you settled."

Lydia sat at the edge of the bed and Sophie lifted her feet. Carolyn winced at her mother's legs and feet; their once beautiful topography now pale and scaly, mapped with veins. Sophie reached for the sedative bottle. Joe turned his gray-blue eyes to his mother, drawing her watery gaze to his. He cocked his head, so like his father, and Lydia rewarded him with a momentary smile.

When she finally drifted off, Joe picked up a framed photograph from the nightstand and ran his fingers across the glass. Carolyn bent to look, too.

It was an arty shot. Their mother was very young. She was wearing a spring suit and a darling cloche hat. She was faced away from the camera, and half-turned back, a coy and flattering angle.

"Light as filigree," Joe said.

"Once upon a time," Carolyn added.

Joe returned the photograph to the nightstand. Their beautiful mother was ravaged.

Aunt Doris oversaw the day-to-day operations of Blenheim now.

A Family Problem
1953

Blenheim

*G*race fumbled in the dark for the handrail. The enormous house — Blenheim — and its seemingly endless staircases and passageways were unfamiliar to her, "Where are we going?" she asked.

"To the rathskeller," Conrad said. "The garden still stinks like burned honeydew melon. Besides the mosquitoes are out. I say we build a fort in the basement. When it's done, I'll let you in on a secret."

Rose took her thumb out of her mouth and examined its wrinkled pad. "What secret?"

"You know," Conrad said, "the secret of all secrets. And stop smelling your spitty thumb."

The rathskeller was cool and dark. The girls draped old blankets and beach towels over the sides of the pool table and crawled underneath. They sat in a tight circle. Jane yawned and asked how late it was.

"Past your bedtime," Conrad said. She clicked a flashlight and shone it in Jane's face. Then, in the confidential tone of a gossip monger, she said: "Want to hear the secret?"

Jane and Grace scrooched closer. Rose rocked back and stuck her thumb in her mouth.

"Okay," Conrad said. "Here's the secret story of why Aunt Doris lives with us..."

About the time Tom and Mary Conrad gave up hope their older daughter would ever find a husband, Doris started dating a butcher she met at the Hampton Village Bettendorf's. Tom thought Bryan Meehan looked tough. Mary was delighted; after all, Doris was past forty. Two years after the wedding, Doris discovered Bryan was having a torrid affair with a checkout girl at the store.

"Aunt Doris found love notes in his jacket pocket," Conrad said clicking the flashlight on and off for emphasis. "She found lipstick on his collar, too."

Jane's eyes were wide. "What happened?"

"He came home drunk one night and Aunt Doris called him a dirty louse. Bam! He hit her in the chops!"

Rose sat up. "How do you know?"

"I heard Aunt Doris tell Dad, dummy."

What happened next filled two fat files at a South St. Louis police station. Bryan Meehan had taken a long pull on a bottle of bourbon and flung it at Doris. The bottle hit the kitchen sink and shattered. Doris ran to the bathroom and slammed the door. Bryan stormed out of the house and passed out cold in the street. It was dark, raining. The week before, neighborhood kids had shot out the street lamp. The truck was speeding. The driver never saw the drunk lying in the street.

As soon as the detectives finished their reports, Doris drove out to Blenheim.

Fritz had taken one look at his sister-in-law's swollen cheek and purple eye and buzzed for the butler. "Harold, bring a sack of frozen peas."

Fritz poured Doris a brandy and she drank it straight. When she finished, he said, "Why don't you go upstairs? See Sophie, and Lydia."

When Doris was out of earshot, Fritz had picked up the phone and dialed his brother. "Phillip, we've got a family problem …"

Phillip listened in stony silence. Doris marrying a butcher had been bad enough; Phillip had taken a good bit of ribbing from the Karlsruhe crowd about that. The family had kept Bryan at their fringes, but now this. Good God.

"I've half a mind to tell Doris she made her bed and she can lie in it," Fritz said.

"Then why don't you?" Phillip snapped.

"I don't think that's the best thing to do here."

Phillip was coming to the same conclusion. The violent quarrel preceding Bryan Meehan's death would hit the morning newspapers, he knew. The sordid details were all there, in the police report. Doris had told the police she was dodgy about what started the fight. Thank God. Even a whiff about Meehan's affair with an underage grocery girl would fuel the gossip columns for months. It was bad enough Lydia's parents insisted on living in that dinky South Side bungalow …hell, why couldn't Fritz get them to move out to Blenheim? Anyway, now it was time to circle the wagons. Fritz would have to take Doris in, control the damage before she rained disgrace on the whole family.

Fritz found Lydia and Doris in the master bedroom, in an embrace of unprecedented sisterhood.

"Doris, we love you," Fritz began. "You're family. Pack your things and bring them out to Blenheim. Stay here, for now."

Doris disengaged from Lydia and threw her arms around Fritz. When he finally broke free, he thought he saw a smile flicker at the corners of her lips.

The following day, Doris moved into a small bedroom on the mansion's fourth floor. Within a week, she had quit her clerical job and was working as an assistant cosmetics manager at the Reinhardt & Krug flagship store, presiding with a brittle smile and iron-fisted control over a fleet of pretty young sales clerks.

O

It was two in the morning. Grace needed to pee.

Disoriented, she wandered out of the Little Girls Wing and roamed the main second-floor corridor. A floorboard popped, planked oak straining to reach equilibrium as the night cooled. Grace startled, and then noticed someone else was in the corridor.

"Uncle Fritz? Is that you?"

The man walked past her without a word.

"Uncle Fritz, I can't find the …"

Abruptly, he whirled Grace around by the shoulders. "Go to bed," he said.

Grace stumbled back to the Little Girls Wing and fell onto Rose's bed. "Rose! You awake? I saw a ghost."

The two girls held hands and tiptoed out to the main corridor. At the top of the staircase, they looked out over the banister to the foyer, far below. Moonlight streamed in from the fan window over the door, casting shadows on the foyer's checkerboard floor. Grace sensed movement at the far end of the corridor, and saw the man climbing the service stairs, rounding the switchback. "Rose!" she hissed. "It's Uncle Fritz."

Rose took Grace by the elbow and marched her back to the Little Girls Wing. "You're wrong," Rose said, crawling into bed. "That's not my daddy. It's my pretend daddy."

"Where does he go?"

"To the attic, to check the mouse traps. It's okay. Go back to sleep."

Grace rolled over on her stomach and examined the French poodle wallpaper. She turned on her side and kicked off the sheet. She fiddled with Rose's china tea set on the bedside table.

Finally, Rose sat up. "Stop thinking, Grace. And don't talk about what you saw."

No one talked about it, but everyone knew. Everyone at Blenheim, down to the youngest. It had been going on ever since shortly after Doris moved to Blenheim.

He didn't knock, that night, or ever. He simply turned the knob and walked in. Surprise was elemental to the allure. He closed the door softly and approached her bed. His bed, he supposed. After all, his money bought it. He'd already forgotten about the child in the hall.

The room was small, the summer night sticky and close. A fan whirred, pushed air in sultry oscillations. He stood at the foot of the bed, lit a cigar and took a few puffs. Then he took hold of a bedpost and spread his feet slightly.

She rose on cue. She was wearing a cotton nightgown. Pin curls fixed with crossed bobbi-pins dotted her ash-blond hair. He liked that. It meant she didn't expect him that night.

She expected him. She was waiting. When the knob turned, a trill quivered through her. She'd applied fresh lipstick, Crushed Rose by Max Factor. It was new. The magazine ad had caught her eye, the man bending over a reclining woman, their lips touching, and in the foreground, an open lipstick tube with a pointy inch of scarlet wax protruding from its golden shaft.

She slid off the bed and knelt at his feet, waiting. Soon, she knew, his breath would quicken. With agile fingers, she parted his silk bathrobe and drew her long arms around him. She flattened her palms against the small of his back, raised her face and breathed out slowly through painted, parted lips. Then she took him into her mouth. It was both excruciating and arousing for him, she knew that. He tightened his hold on the bedpost and lifted his eyes to the ceiling.

After a few moments he pushed her away, though not hard. She sat back on her heels. It was always like that. He set the cigar in an ash tray forested with her stubbed-out Pall Malls. A thin plume of smoke rose in the night, filling the room with a sharp, unpleasant odor. For a moment, his mind wandered.

Dissimilar things on fire. Burnt offerings. Buddhist monks at Horyu-ji, breathing sandalwood smoke, yearning for harmony. Tibetan mystics crawling into yurts filled with the fragrance of smoke-roasted mutton. Vatican cardinals swinging censers that enveloped them in ghostly wrappings of smoke, plumes that, in the rising, symbolize Christian breasts afire with God's love.

He grasped her by the armpits and lifted her. Smoke, that dark, eternal warning, coiled above the ash tray. At the bed, he gave her a slight push and she fell face-down. She was smiling, though he could not see. Smiling. He was hers.

"Raise yourself," he said. She bunched a pillow under her belly. He stood between her legs and untied the sash of his robe. He braced his hand between her shoulder blades and entered her like a stallion pastured with a mare. She arched her neck and gasped with pleasure.

It was quickly finished.

She rolled onto her back and looked at him. She had everything she always wanted. Lydia's fabulous house is mine now, she told herself. Lydia's husband is my lover. I get dressed up and go off every day. Lydia lives in her bedroom, dotty as a March hare.

He cupped her chin and smeared her lipstick with his thumb. She made no move to wipe off the stain.

He left without a word.

Down in his study, he brooded for hours. It was always like that. By the time his conscience was neutralized, spears of sunlight were creeping across the motor court lawn, splashing across the feet of Venus, a goddess of love on a pedestal of liquid gold.

He was certain nobody knew. Not Lydia. Not the kids, or the servants. No one.

Snowballs in Martini Glasses
1953

St. Louis

*P*hillip, old man, high time the families got together. How about Christmas Eve at the M.A.C.?"

"On your tab?" Philip said, in jest. Half a year had passed since the Bryan Meehan incident. Family matters had quieted down again.

Fritz laughed. "Fifty-fifty split. Hey, remember when we'd order Michelob at Topping Ridge and sign with Dad's number?"

"Long time ago, brother. Christmas Eve is fine."

Phillip hung up and rang the Children's Department. "Send two plaid wool overcoats to my daughter's house in Brentwood. The red ones, yes. The tartans. And two of the red velvet dresses with the lace collars ..."

Madeleine opened the boxes and shook her head. Oh, Father, you'll never change, she murmured. Everyone has to look perfect, and nobody but you decides what perfection is. Phillip had sent complete outfits for Jane and Grace, a slim cocktail dress for Madeleine and a shirt and tie for Paul. The dark green dress was Madeleine's favorite color, but the tie was a bit sophisticated for Paul. Well, she sighed, Paul would just have to deal with it.

Phillip had made it clear that Madeleine should get a sitter for her two younger children. Paul was furious. "What does your father think? They'll cry, or soil their diapers and spoil the party? Theresa's three, and Charlie never makes a peep."

On Christmas Eve morning, Jane and Grace passed the time helping their mother bake thumb-print cookies. After lunch, the girls played Chinese Checkers, Go Fish and Crazy Eights. Finally, it was time to put on their new dresses.

Decades after the disastrous fire that killed many of its members, the rebuilt M.A.C. reigned as the city's premier downtown club. As a founding member, the late Albert Reinhardt was memorialized in a gallery of oil portraits marching along the lobby wall. In a few years, Joe, his grandson, would hold a junior membership in the club.

The sky was lead-gray. The metallic scent of snow filled the afternoon air. A few dry flakes blew in circles on the driveway. Jane and Grace piled into the car and cast exultant waves to Theresa, staring disconsolately at the front window. At Market Street, Madeleine pointed out the giant candy cane decorations affixed to each telephone pole. Paul stopped at Reinhardt & Krug so the girls could see the display windows, elaborate dioramas of Santa's Workshop. When they reached the M.A.C., Paul handed his car keys to a valet.

"Daddy," Grace said, her face puckered with concern. "Are you giving him our car?"

Paul laughed. "No Gracie. He's just going to park it for us."

"Like, crazy, man," Grace said.

Paul shot his five-year-old daughter an astounded look. "Where'd you pick up that line?"

"Cindy brings her transistor radio when she babysits us. KWK plays the coolest hits."

Madeleine stifled a laugh. "Cindy's teaching Jane the jitterbug."

Grandmother Florence was waiting at the top of the stairs. "Oh, girls, let me look at you!" All her life Florence had been a handsome woman, tall and willow-thin, her hair arranged in an elegant French twist that swept neatly away from her face. For the holiday party, Phillip had dressed his wife in a Pierre Balmain gown.

"How lovely my two girls are," she said, holding out her hands to Jane and Grace, "and so grown up. Would you like Grandmother to show you the ballroom?"

Round tables in the club's Missouri Room were set with crystal goblets and silver. Atop each gold-rimmed dinner plate was a take-home gift tied with a red bow. A fourteen-foot tree dominated the room, and glowed with lights, tinsel, and ornaments.

At the far end of the room, a cellist began to play "Silent Night." At the first liquid notes, the murmur of genteel conversation fell away. When the song was finished, Grandmother Florence and Jane tiptoed off to a smaller private room reserved for the Reinhardt party. Grace stayed at the entrance to the room, hoping the man would play "Ring, Silver Bells," her favorite carol.

Carolyn and her fiancé, Bill Hadley, were the last to arrive. When she saw Grace in the hallway, Carolyn gave Bill a quick hug and said, "Darling, would you be a dear and go on ahead?"

"One of the cousins?" Bill asked.

"Second cousin. First cousin once removed. Something like that. Cute little thing, isn't she?"

Carolyn rested a hand on the Grace's shoulder, absently fingering the child's lace collar. "Have you heard a cello before, Gracie?"

Grace looked up with a dreamy smile.

"It's a Bach suite," Carolyn said. "Isn't it heavenly?"

You're heavenly, Grace said to herself.

Carolyn wore a long column gown of black Chantilly lace spattered with jet beads. Her chestnut hair fell in smooth waves to her shoulder, pulled back at one side and held in place with a rhinestone barrette.

"We'd better go, Gracie, I hear the chimes."

"You smell good."

Carolyn beamed. "Do I? It must be the Chanel No. 5. If I tell you something, will you promise to keep it a secret?"

"Cross my heart and hope to die."

"Somebody once asked Marylin Monroe what she wears to bed, and she said 'two drops of Chanel No.5'."

Grace looked perplexed.

"It's a secret mixture," Carolyn went on. "Jasmine and sandalwood and rose, oh, lots of things. It was made especially for Coco Chanel."

"That's a funny name."

Carolyn could have listened to the cellist all night. When she was in the first grade she begged her parents for a toy piano. That Christmas, she awoke to find a Steinway baby grand in the living room. Lydia hired a piano teacher. Week after week the man grimaced while little Carolyn plinked out scales and two-finger tunes. After three years of failed piano lessons, Fritz bought Carolyn a flute. When that fizzled, he bought her a violin, and then a cello.

Carolyn majored in home economics at Fontbonne, a women's college near Forest Park and Washington University. She studied fabric arts, nutrition, baby and child care, history, sociology and anthropology. In the spring of her junior year, she volunteered to help pass out fliers for Fontbonne's annual music festival. The choral director gave her a stack of fliers and asked her distribute them in the Washington University quadrangle.

Bill Hadley was preoccupied that day. His research paper on diseases of the kidney was due, overdue, in fact, and the professor was a total jerk.

Bill skipped his morning jolt of coffee and raced from his apartment on Pershing Avenue the few blocks to campus. Half-awake, he tacked across the quadrangle heading for a quiet reading room. He checked the time on the Brookings Hall clock and chuckled at the words inscribed on its face. *Cedunt Horae, Opera Manent*. The Hours Go By, the Work Remains.

"No kidding," Bill said to himself.

Laughing at the private joke, he took a few awkward steps backward and plowed smack into Carolyn. Fourteen pages of kidney research and two hundred music festival fliers sailed into the air and drifted down like confetti.

At the M.A.C, Carolyn found the private party room and immediately showed everyone the engagement ring Dr. William Hunt Hadley had slipped on her finger that afternoon. Even by Reinhardt standards, it was impressive: a 2.6 carat Van Cleef & Arpels diamond surrounded by twelve smaller baguettes. Fritz choked back tears, thinking of Lydia at home, unable to share in the joyous news.

After the meal, waiters bladed crumbs from the tablecloth and brought trays of the club's signature holiday treat.

"Snowball Sundaes!" Conrad shouted.

"What's that?" Jane whispered. It was Jane's first meal at the M.A.C. Ever since Paul Mitchell had turned down his father-in-law's offer of an executive job at Reinhardt and Krug, Madeleine and her children had led a quieter, more financially restrained life than her upbringing would have indicated.

Conrad cut Jane a smug look. "They put a scoop of French vanilla ice cream in a martini glass. Then they drizzle white chocolate sauce over the ice cream and sprinkle shredded coconut over that. That's a Snowball Sundae." Conrad plucked the maraschino cherry off her sundae and popped it in her mouth.

"Everybody likes Bill," she told Jane. "His name is William Hunt Hadley II and he comes from an old Philadelphia family."

"Cool," Jane said, wishing she had an older sister like Carolyn and older brothers like Joe and Bill Hadley.

Conrad leaned closer. "Last summer when Bill finished medical school and Carolyn finished at Fontbonne, you know what my dad did?"

Jane couldn't imagine. Uncle Fritz's reputation for gift-giving was legendary.

"Dad had a keg of beer delivered to Bill's apartment, and he sent a case of pink champagne to Carolyn's sorority house."

"Wow, cool," Jane gushed.

"Yeah, but Carolyn told the delivery guy to take the champagne to Bill's place."

"Why?"

"It was so-o-o Carolyn," Conrad said. "She sticks a note on the box that says —" Conrad shoveled a dollop of ice cream in her mouth and went on in a high, sing-song voice: "'Bill, be a dear and take this champagne to the maternity ward at Barnes. I want each new mom and dad to go home with pink champagne.'"

Conrad licked the last of the sundae from her spoon. "I heard Bill kept one of the bottles and his buddies got soused on beer and champagne and Carolyn found out."

"Was she mad?"

Conrad scoffed. "Carolyn? Heck no."

"Was your dad?"

"My Dad? You gotta be kidding."

Last summer, after graduation, Carolyn had traveled to France with a sorority sister. She returned in mid-June and moved into a two-bedroom apartment in The Moorlands, Clayton's tree-lined enclave of colonial and Tudor apartments. Carolyn filled the apartment with R&K's most modern furnishings, a low orange sectional sofa and a kidney-shaped cocktail table, turquoise lamps in organic shapes, and scads of flat throw pillows. She signed up for French cooking classes and attended Junior League meetings. She took her mother and Sophie to the Missouri Botanical Gardens. Carolyn did what young women did in the brief, expectant interlude between a graduation trip to France and marriage to a fellow with Roman numerals after his name.

Each time she returned to Blenheim, Carolyn made it a point to bring along small gifts. Dusty-pink cubes of Double-Bubble gum for Conrad. A football magazine for Joe. Baseball cards for Eddie. A Mister Potato Head Game for Rose, and movie magazines for her mother, Sophie and Aunt Doris. In October, Carolyn had brought her father a book and left it in his study.

Fritz found the gift that evening. "What was she thinking?" he wondered.

Carolyn had given him *Dancing on Wall Street*, an investment guide written by Fritz M. Reinhardt.

"That girl is a treasure," Fritz said when the butler came in, "but she gives and gives, and never stops to think."

Torch Red
1955

Ladue

*E*ddie knew exactly what he wanted. A Torch Red Thunderbird convertible.

Eddie had followed news about the new sports car with apostolic zeal. Ford's naming competition. The 5,000 entries. The winner who came up with the iconic name "Thunderbird" received a $95 suit, including spare trousers.

Eddie laid his plans. Every June, a month before his birthday, Topping Ridge held its annual father-son golf tournament. This year Eddie made sure he and his dad were paired with Bice Finlay and Bice Junior.

On the tee box, Bice and Fritz sealed the first wager of the day with a handshake. The father with the longest drive off the tee gets $100 from the other father. Sons exempted.

Fritz teed up, waggled his driver, and moved seamlessly into his take-away. At the top of the backswing he reversed and began powering down. When the club face was an inch from the ball, Eddie shouted, "Thunderbird!" Fritz's driver scoured out a divot the size of raccoon. The ball skittered sixty yards down the fairway and dribbled into a stand of cattails. Bice doubled over laughing.

Fritz pointed the club head at Eddie. "Damn, son!"

Eddie walked onto the tee box. "A Thunderbird convertible, pops. Torch Red. Birthday coming up, remember?"

Fritz motioned to the caddy for his scorecard. With the stub of a pencil, he wrote: "Eddie. Ragtop. Red."

Bice Junior and Eddie took their shots. On the walk back to the golf carts, Bice Junior whispered: "Now I know why you bet me a ten-spot your old man would shag the first drive."

On Eddie's sixteenth birthday, a Torch Red Thunderbird convertible appeared on Blenheim's motor court. Fritz hadn't blinked at the price tag, $2,765. But he resented like hell the $100 bet he lost to Bice Finlay at the golf outing.

Fire Blight
1956

Huntleigh

*H*untleigh had changed in the seventy years since Leatham Smith and the Louisiana lawyer rode out from the city in a rented buggy. On that autumn morning, Leatham had brought a light lunch along. While he paced the meadow, he finished a delicious Bartlett pear and dropped the core to the ground. It disappeared among the Queen Anne's lace, goldenrod, and purple coneflowers. In the buggy, the lawyer munched a Flemish Beauty. He tossed the flimsy core into the meadow.

The seeds had germinated and set down tap roots. Saplings grew in the tassel grass. In time, the trees pollinated one another and blossomed. In 1897, they bore first fruit. Late that summer, Leatham prepared a picnic for his neighbors, the church-goers who had given him his start. He roasted chicken and corn, poured sugared lemonade, and set out jars of Nickel-Plated Pistol Pear Relish.

Leatham taught his son, Brooke, everything he knew. About horses, tack, and feed. About patching an old barn. About the proper care of the land they both loved. One day he brought his boy out to the small orchard and showed him how to prune the pear trees, how to lop the weak central branches and thin the clusters by pinching a stem so it stays attached to the spur. Time and weather eventually fissured the original pear trees, but in 1956 their offspring stood eighteen feet high at the crown. Each spring Brooke's pear trees burst with showy blossoms, and in fall they bore fruit, all but one, a Bartlett that went into decline purely by chance:

Brooke was slicing a peach onto corn flakes one morning, not watching closely enough. A photograph in the morning newspaper had caught his attention. The Joint Chiefs of Staff were meeting somewhere, soft-jawed officers with their fingers laced in repose on a table. The cutlines said they were strategizing about the Korean Conflict. Brooke looked closer. Their uniforms were immaculate, festooned with beribboned medals.

During World War II, Brooke had served as a ship's mechanic aboard the *USS Enterprise*. In the screaming hell that was Midway, Brooke was at his station, below decks, but he took pride in playing a part, however small, in sinking the *Kaga and Akagi*.

Brooke tossed the newspaper to the floor. His hand glanced off the counter. The knife blade sliced his thumb. At the emergency room, they told him he'd severed a flexor tendon, the ropey cable that slides in and out of a thumb as it bends. "You'll live," the doc said, "but you probably won't be able to grip."

Brooke took on a hired man to help out at the stables. Rusty drank some, but he'd do. One afternoon Rusty lifted a pair of lopping shears from a wall peg and went out to snip an old chain from a paddock gate. He had to squeeze the handles hard. The steel chain fell away, but it had nicked the lopper's beaky blades and thrown the tool a fraction of an inch out of alignment. Rusty went on to trim a Pyracantha bush near the barn. Before he returned the lopper to its peg, he snipped a drooping limb on one of the Bartlett trees.

The Pyracantha had been infected with fire blight. Bacteria clung to the lopper blades as Rusty trimmed the pear tree. Infection smeared across the ragged wound. By the spring of 1956, the Bartlett was engulfed in disease, its trunk nearly hollow. A swarm of honeybees discovered the musty cavity and took possession. Within minutes they fanned their wings, aerating their new home, emitting scent from their abdominal glands that directed late-comers to the tree. Soon, Brooke's tree was home to hundreds of drones, thousands of workers, and a single queen.

By June, the workers were scouting for food to feed the young. They flew the neighborhoods around the stables, powered by veined wings that beat seven times a second. They saw with compound eyes evolved with thousands of facets. Their jaws were mighty enough to pulverize wood. Claw-tipped legs allowed them to cling upside-down to surfaces. They were protected with a single, ultimate, suicidal weapon.

That summer, the summer of 1956, most of the worker bees in Brooke Smith's pear tree had a while longer to live. Most, but not all.

A Brazen Shade of Pink
1956

Blenheim

*M*issouri was cruel to roses. A brief winter warm snap had coaxed the buds out of dormancy, and exposed them to sleet, snow, and freezing winds. The following spring served up ungodly heat and black-spot disease. The dense soil clogged delicate roots. Spider mites nibbled at the leaves.

Palmer and Leroy babied Lydia's roses. Her beloved Ispahans and Boules de Neige were healthy. Her Fantin-Latours were hearty. Her Grootendorsts and Souvenirs de la Malmaison were alive and well. Huge wedge-shaped beds of La Ville de Bruxelles skirted the mermaid fountain like a tutu. In the garden behind Blenheim, just down the road from the Leatham Smith Stables, Lydia's spiraling beds of Bruxelles were especially gorgeous; thousands of voluptuous blossoms bobbed on five-foot canes, enticing honeybees to come, come and gorge.

A Rare Five-Gaited Show Horse
A Summer Friday, 1956

Huntleigh, 1 pm

*M*adeleine glanced in the rear-view mirror. "Girls, remember, this is only the third time you've been to Blenheim. Don't let Conrad get you in trouble."

Jane slouched in the back seat and covered her face with her Cherry Ames book. "We won't, Mom. You're pestering."

When they pulled up the long drive, they saw Conrad waiting on the motor court. "Hi, the car!"she yelled.

Grace called out, "Hi, the cousins!"

Conrad started to neigh and prance. "About time you got here. The horses are hungry."

Jane closed her book and tucked it in her overnight case. "Darn," she said, getting out of the car, "we didn't bring carrots. Conrad, can you lend us?"

"Sure. I've got carrots and apples."

Grace saw Rose peek out from behind one of the portico's seven stately columns. Rose poked her thumb in her mouth and toe-kicked the plinth, a greeting of sorts. Minutes later, the four girls were prancing like Lipizzaners around the Venus statue. Sophie came out to chat with Madeleine.

"How's my aunt? Any better?"

"About the same," Sophie said. "How are your two little ones, at home?"

"Noisy. Rambunctious. Doll clothes and Lincoln Logs all over the carpet. Is she awake?"

"I'm afraid not. Even on a gorgeous day like this, she naps after lunch. How old are the girls now?"

"Jane's eleven, that awkward age, and Grace is eight."

Conrad was grabbing the overnight cases out of the car and tossing them into the foyer. A passing housekeeper allowed herself a disapproving "tsk" and then carried the cases up to the Little Girls Wing.

"Okay, gang," Conrad shouted, "let's go see the finest horse in the world." Jane, Grace and Rose followed, down the lane and out onto Old Post Road.

Leatham Smith Stables had become an island of country in a sea of suburbia. In winter, Brooke could hear traffic whizzing along Manchester Road. He boarded a few horses, but there wasn't enough business to keep the riding school going. The show ring had gone to weed. The Bavarian-style barn his father had built by hand had faded to a dusty rose. On windy days, the weather vane creaked as if arthritic. The old stone church had been shut and locked for a good long while. Gravestones listed in the prairie grass, their inscriptions worn smooth. Wind, rain and time had consigned the dearly departed to anonymity.

Leatham was in his seventy-first year and a widower when a brain tumor took him, hard and ugly. That was back in 1936. He'd left everything to Brooke. The small house in Maplewood was hardly worth a hill of beans, but the horse stable on twenty acres in Huntleigh was practically priceless. Still, Brooke couldn't bring himself to sell.

When the weather was decent, Brooke dragged his father's old wood chair out to a sunny side of the barn and sat a spell. He tired easily. Last winter a doctor ran tests. They diagnosed a rare form of cancer, treatable but incurable. The oncologist advised a regimen of nitrogen mustard chemotherapy. Brooke said thanks, but no.

When the girls got to the stables, Brooke was in his favorite chair, snoring like a camel. Rusty was trying to rake the show ring. The girls broke into gales of laughter. Rusty was fence-post skinny, with a bobbing gullet and a wandering glass eye. His cowboy hat and his ears appeared to have been designed for a much larger man.

Conrad slid open the double doors and walked into the barn, squinting at the abrupt transition from blazing sunshine to twilight. Grace and the others followed, rubbing their eyes until the cavernous space came into focus. Grace saw a small tack room near the front, a long center aisle lined with half-door stalls, and a shaggy hayloft at the far end.

Zing! A steel box sent slashing blue light across the floor, hissing with electric fury. Jane and Rose screamed. Grace stood her ground behind Conrad.

Then a second box crackled with blue-white current.

"Cripes," Grace muttered.

Conrad clamped a hand on her hip. "Don't be ninnies. They're just the fly zappers."

Grace looked up. Sparrows were soaring through the network of rafters, flying out the hayloft doors and back in through the dovecote. She caught a whiff of ripe manure and wrinkled her nose. The air was hazy. Motes of horse hair, oat flakes, blanket wool and boot scrapings drifted in sun shafts that angled down from cracks in the roof. Jane started to sneeze.

Zing! Another box flapped its louvers. A mouse scurried between Jane's feet to a chew-hole in the wall. Jane danced a terrified jig. A barn kitten levitated and ran off. Birds whooshed from the rafters, and horses shuffled in their stalls.

"Stop it, Jane," Conrad scolded. "You're making the horses mad."

Grace scowled at her sister and turned back to Conrad. Grace idolized Carolyn, and she had a crush on Joe. Eddie she could take or leave, and she pretty much ignored Rose. But Conrad, dashing, fearless Conrad was the cousin Grace admired.

"Follow me," Conrad said. "I've been taking riding lessons at the Missouri Stables. I come here lots, too. Brooke lets me ride bareback whenever I want."

Jane stayed near the door, with Rose.

Birth order and a neurotic timidity conspired to keep Rose the family's baby, an identity the child showed no inclination to discard. She spoke so rarely that she was never expected to, and she was so coddled by siblings and servants that she rarely needed to. Unlike Carolyn's gazelle-like beauty and Conrad's robust vigor, Rose had the slight build and sallow look of a picky eater. Her stringy, wheat-colored hair fell from a low part across her face, forming an efficient wall between Rose and the world.

Conrad ran down the barn's center aisle and hiked up on the half-door of the last stall. "It's Shadow! Come see."

Grace followed Conrad and hiked up, too. A few moments later, Jane and Rose appeared at their side.

Conrad held out a slice of apple. "His name is Visible Shadow. He's a rare, five-gaited show horse. He weighs a thousand pounds and stands fifteen hands high. His sire is Quick Emotion and his dam is Mystic Madam."

Grace screwed up her face. "He stands on his hands?"

Conrad went on as if she didn't hear. "Rusty told me Mystic Madam placed a solid third at Belmont as a three-year-old. He said that accounts for Shadow being fast and feisty."

Conrad jumped down and strode back to the tack room. She returned with a bridle, saddle and blanket.

"You're not supposed to," Rose said.

Conrad lifted the door latch and walked into the stall. Grace closed the half-door behind her cousin and then hiked up and scrabbled for a toe-hold on the cross-buck trim. The monster horse had pinned back his ears. His eyes were bulging like black marbles. Grace shivered.

Conrad kept jiggling the bit until its metal bar fell in place behind Shadow's back teeth. She tossed the blanket over his withers and eased it back. Shadow stamped hard and skittered sideways.

"Knock it off," Conrad muttered.

Grace felt a thrill of danger when Conrad tossed a slim English saddle over the blanket. Shadow stamped again and whinnied.

"Is she safe in there?" Jane whispered.

Grace folded her arms across the half-door and rested her chin on her wrists. "Sure. I think so." Neither she nor Jane noticed that Rose had walked off, toward the barn's entrance.

The stirrups clinked into place. Conrad struggled to pull the belly strap taut, but Shadow was beside himself now, tossing his head, stamping furiously. He rose on his back legs and crashed his hooves against the stall door and for a nightmare second Grace found herself staring at his great veined belly.

"The saddle's too tight," Conrad shouted. "Grace, get in here and lift his front leg so his shoulder goes back. Then I can feel under the pommel."

"Don't do it!" Jane hissed. "I'll tell Mom."

Grace lifted the latch and crept in. Swallowing hard, she grabbed Shadow's off-leg with both hands. "It won't move, Conrad."

"Hold lower!"

Grace grabbed the fetlock and yanked again. Shadow raised his head and reared. As soon as the horse was down, Grace bolted from the stall. Jane slammed the half-door behind her sister.

Conrad planted her hands on her hips. "Jane," she said, her voice dripping with sarcasm, "since Grace is such a chicken, you have to help me."

Jane had crossed her arms over her chest. She was chewing her lower lip.

"I'll help you up," Conrad coaxed. "All you have to do is sit there."

Conrad opened the half-door. Jane edged in sideways. Shadow pinned back his ears and swished his tail.

"Give him some apple," Conrad said.

"I've got some," Grace said, passing a slice of fruit over the half-door.

Shadow peeled back his black lips and clicked his bricky teeth at her fingers.

"Hey, he tried to bite me!" Grace shouted. She swallowed the urge to cry.

The stallion was snorting now, hollowing back. Conrad was dancing alongside him, patting his flank and holding out a stirrup for Jane. "Hike up, Jane, now!"

Jane took a couple of awkward hops. Conrad sighed. She dropped the stirrup and stomped to the front of the stall. She stood face-to-face with the panicked horse and grabbed his bit with both hands. In the scant moment Shadow was calm, Jane hiked up. As soon as she lowered herself to the saddle, all hell broke loose.

Shadow lunged. Conrad slammed against the stall door. Jane tumbled off and landed in a pile of hay. Grace screamed and opened the door a crack, and Jane scrambled out.

"Get ... out ... of the way." It was Rose, her voice dead-flat calm, as if she were reading a phone book.

Rose unlatched the half-door. She glanced down at Conrad, crumpled on the floor just inches from Shadow's thrashing hooves. Surreally calm, Rose walked into the stall and started chanting a strange, tuneless song.

> *Possession whithers fades saith Marcel*
> *Drink stream water endless*
> *Breath, wind, essence*
> *Kalends Nones Ides Beware!*

The horse shied until his rump hit the back wall. Still singing, Rose gazed into Shadow's depthless eyes and offered him an apple slice. The horse ran a tongue across his rubbery lips and bobbed. Finally he took the apple. As he chewed, Rose dug in the pocket of her shorts and pulled out a grooming brush.

So that's where she was, Grace thought, in the tack room.

Rose drew long, smooth strokes down Shadow's damp flank. "Open the door," she told Grace. "Pull my sister out."

At the entrance to the barn, a stick-thin figure stood in silhouette, backlit by blazing sunlight. It took only a moment for Rusty to size up the situation, and by then he was racing down the aisle, elbows and knees bobbing like a string puppet.

Two Aspects of the Same Life
Friday, 6 pm

Blenheim

*T*he four girls raced back to Blenheim, hair flying, legs and arms pumping, bathed in sweat and gasping for breath. They rocketed through the June heat as if rabid dogs were nipping at their heels. At the motor court, they flopped on the grass, gasping for air. Jane whined about a stitch in her side. Rose started hiccupping and couldn't stop. Conrad kicked her in the leg, hard, and when Rose protested Conrad shrugged and claimed she was just trying to help, a good scare chases the hiccups away. After a while they made their way to the Hawaiian Room. Conrad opened the game cabinet and took out Clue. They hunkered around the board, moving the little candlestick and plastic rope, the revolver and lead pipe from room to room in silence, the way kids do when they know they're in big trouble and they're biding time until they find out how big.

At about six, Fritz walked in and headed straight for his bar. His butler knew to keep the Hawaiian Room's small bar refrigerator stocked with bottles of Budweiser. Fritz glanced at the girls. He noticed they looked a little glum, and thought no more of it. Conrad got up and turned on the television. Douglas Edwards was reporting a story out of Egypt. "Gamel Abdel Nasser has just been elected …"

Fritz and Carter Stanton had almost come to blows after Fritz told the architect to tack a Hawaiian Room onto the south side of the classically formal home. Ordered to come up with papasan chairs, tiki lamps, and decorative fishnets, Mssr. Mathieu swore in French and experienced a month-long eye tic. Fritz couldn't have cared less; it was his house and he damn well wanted a Hawaiian Room. With tiki lamps. And a kidney-shaped wet bar. And a wall devoted to one of his most prized possessions, the magnificent trophy fish he'd snagged off the coast of Morocco. What an endurance contest that had been. Two hours. The charter captain said he'd never seen a white marlin so big, and a white man so tenacious. The trip was Bice Finlay's idea. Bice had had a decent day, but his four-foot Wahoo couldn't compare to Fritz's marlin. Bice had picked up the dinner tab in Mohammedia that night.

Fritz walked over to the console television set and turned the channel dial to the early evening news. Conrad rolled her eyes. Jackie Gleason was bawling out Alice, threatening to send her to the moon. The studio audience roared.

Fritz took a long pull on the bottle of beer and eyed the girls skeptically. "You kids are flat as freeway frogs. What you need is a good joke." He was at the part where the minister, the friar and the rabbi were knocking on the Pearly Gates when the house phones jangled. A moment later, the butler appeared at the Hawaiian Room door. "It's a Mr. Brooke Smith, sir. For you."

"Who?"

"He says he's the man from the horse stable, sir."

Conrad jumped up, ready to bolt. Fritz pinned her to the sofa with a sharp finger-snap. He picked up the telephone behind the bar and listened in silence a long while. The girls figured he was hearing about Conrad and Jane going into Shadow's stall. Brooke went over that, of course, but he also told Fritz what Rusty said had happened after the girls ran off...

When the girls were out of sight, Rusty had filled two pails with water and oats. On his way to Shadow's stall, a louvered box snapped. He barely paused. Bug zappers were part of the ambient sounds of summer at a horse stable. The box continued to flash, though, and caught his attention. At first he assumed it was on the blink, or dispatching a particularly hefty insect. Big flies gave the boxes trouble. He watered and fed Shadow. He was giving the horse a rubdown when he noticed a saddle blanket crumpled in a corner of Shadow's stall. He picked it up and shook it. Dust billowed into the air. A horsefly fell to the floor.

It was over an inch long. One lacy wing was sheared off. The other wing was cracked. The body was flat as a stomped-on raisin.

Rusty knew horseflies are drawn to large dark objects in motion. He figured this one flew into the barn and drifted above the stalls a while, searching for food. When Shadow hollowed back probably the horsefly navigated along the wall and landed in the hollow of his back, unseen. Rusty pieced together what happened next. Working its mouth like a scissors, the large fly had burrowed through Shadow's coat and slashed an opening in the skin. It was gorging on horse blood when Conrad tossed the blanket onto Shadow's back. The insect had panicked and dug deeper. Conrad dropped the saddle onto the blanket. The extra weight shoved the bug's knife-edged mouth farther into the wound. Then Jane hiked up in the stirrups and sat, and Shadow reared in pain.

"My man Rusty said he'd never seen such a nasty bugger," Brooke told Fritz.

"Thanks," Fritz said. "I'll handle it from here."

The television show had cut to a commercial break. Conrad turned up the volume and danced a jig to the Oldsmobile jingle. Grace picked at a scab. Rose hid her face behind a throw pillow and sucked her thumb.

Fritz stalled, thinking about the phone call. He popped open another bottle of Bud and poured salted peanuts into a bowl. He wiped down the bar top. He knew the girls were waiting. So? Let them wait.

Fritz's concept of parenthood was to provide a home, food, education, recreation, and an abundance of love. He left the hard stuff up to the nuns and Jesuits. It occurred to him now that he might be in default. He drained the bottle and tossed it in a waste can. He picked up a fresh can of peanuts, pulled off its slender key and pried back the lid with more care than necessary. My Conrad, he thought, my dauntless, fearless child. In his mind's eye, he saw Conrad lying unconscious on the barn floor, saw hooves thrashing around her skull. The thought sickened him. And Rose, his Sweet-Baby. He saw Rose walking trancelike into a horse stall, a death trap, saw his timid child hold up an apple to snapping teeth. How could she have done that, he wondered. How could a child too shy to ask somebody to pass the salt take on a rearing stallion.

The televised droned on. Fritz remembered a dog-faced priest back at the Academy who thought the philosopher Schopenhauer hung the moon. Fritz had barely passed the course, but one of Schopenhauer's theories had stuck with him. In a life-threatening crisis, Schopenhauer believed, some people entirely shed their individuality and instantly see themselves and the person in peril as two aspects of the same life. The rescuer's identity is temporarily fused with the victim's. Family, job, even a sense of self-preservation all evaporate. According to Schopenhauer, that explains the soldier who crawls out of a foxhole and into enemy fire to save a wounded buddy. Back at the Academy, Fritz's old teacher had said that type of boundless compassion occurs frequently. Fritz hadn't believed it, until today, until he heard how his baby Rose, trance like, had calmed a wild horse and saved her sister's life.

"Schopenhauer," Fritz murmured, lost in thought. I assumed the tether that bound me to my kids was a chain. It isn't. It's a thread. It's so fragile the blade-wing of an insect could sever it. What a world. Any minute you can be walking along, going about your business, and something flies out of the sky and changes you forever. It happens. It's almost inevitable. We can't prevent it, only react.

Fritz snapped out of his reverie. "Jesuits," he chuckled, shaking off the deep thoughts. "They pump philosophy into a kid's head and it stays there forever."

Conrad turned off the television. The room was suddenly quiet.

"You girls know what you did?" Fritz boomed. "There was a horsefly under the saddle blanket. Horseflies bite so hard they draw blood."

Conrad rubbed a finger up and down her forehead. Rose spindled a hank of hair and stared at the floor.

Fritz's voice softened and he broke into the old crinkle-eyed smile. "All right then, where was I? So the minister says to the rabbi…"

Crickets in Gold Boxes
2 am Saturday

Blenheim

*T*he night light in the master bedroom had burned out. Fritz felt his way around in the dark. He tossed his summer robe on Lydia's chaise lounge and heard it slip to the floor. The air was sultry, the curtains unstirred. He felt sticky. Why the hell hadn't Sophie turned on the window air conditioner? It was June — two more months of this heat, at least. He peeled off his pajamas and sat at the edge of the bed. Lydia was snoring again. He stretched out and clasped his hands behind his head, trying not to jiggle the mattress.

The tightness across his shoulders began to relax and he closed his eyes. In the garden crickets struck up a fresh chorus. His thoughts wandered. He'd been reading in the study earlier. *National Geographic*. An article about the Ming Dynasty had included an artist's sketch of an emperor's bedroom. It showed a carved rosewood bed, ornate lacquered chests, even a silk sleeping robe embroidered with dragons. According to the magazine, members of the Chinese nobility kept crickets in gold boxes in their bedrooms so the rhythmic chirping would lull them to sleep. Fritz yawned. Soon, his vision of gold boxes and emerald dragons blurred like water colors.

She was turned toward the wall, as always. Her words should be muffled, incoherent. They weren't. They were needle-sharp. Brought forth from some secret still-lucid vault, they sliced through the air like spat-out glass.

"I smell it on you," she said.

Fritz sat up, stunned. "What did you say?"

"I smell my sister's sex on you."

Mr. Perfect
3 am Saturday

Blenheim

No sooner had Lydia spoken up than she began to snore again. Stunned, Fritz shrugged into his pajamas and a robe and returned to the dark study. Guilt washed over him like breakers lashing a pier. I'm Mr. Perfect, he said to himself. The guy with a new joke. The guy in the Santa suit. The guy who slips a twenty to the caddy and makes a fortune for himself and his buddies. Here's the thing though, Mr. Perfect and his sister-in-law rut like animals. His wife is so sick she can't even dress herself, and he's upstairs with her sister. Christ.

He rose from the chair and stood at the Palladian window, grinding his knuckles against his teeth. A string of coach lamps shone along the dark lane, areolas at driveways of named estates, at Casa Brava, and Clareford, Chalk Hollow and the others. He sat in the leather easy chair, excoriating himself, running a knife into his heart, coring his soul.

He remembered the day Phillip told him about the little tart in Chicago, the Gold Coast mistress. He remembered thinking their father would be crushed if he found out. I'm worse, Fritz told himself. I've made a cesspool of my home. I live in my own excrement.

For hours he wallowed in melancholy and shame. At dawn, he got up and rubbed his stubbled cheeks. Outside the study window, an oyster sunrise was streaming up the lane. He turned to the mahogany bookshelves, searching for a particular volume.

Rosa Xanthina
10 am Saturday

Blenheim

*G*race awoke to the clatter of breakfast dishes and the whrr-whrr of a push-mower, far below. In the breakfast room, Jane, Conrad and Rose were already forking pancakes onto their plates.

Aunt Doris stood in a doorway, fanning herself with quick snaps of the morning paper. "Hot as Hades, and it isn't even noon."

"Isn't even noon," Conrad chanted. "Isn't even eleven. It isn't even ten-thirty."

"Enough! Girls, eat your pancakes. There's no lunch today. Your father's planned a big family barbecue later on."

Rose raised her hand as if she were still in a classroom. "With watermelon?"

"Oh, sure," Doris said. "You know your father, never does a thing half-way if he can do it twice as big. Two watermelons, two bushels of corn, six racks of ribs. Carolyn and Bill are coming, too."

Lydia shuffled into the breakfast room, a lost ghost. Her housecoat gaped. Coils of clay-gray hair dangled from messy pin-curls. "Who?"

"Carolyn and Bill are coming. Lydia, what are you looking for?" Doris glared at one of the cooks and the woman led Lydia back upstairs.

Conrad shoved half a pancake into her mouth. "I'll bet Carolyn's big as a house," she said, spraying bits of food across the table.

Doris held a match to a cigarette and took a long drag. Then she picked up the morning paper again and rattled pages until she found the daily horoscope. "I should hope Carolyn's big as a house," she said, "she's due in a week or two. The baby's dropped already."

Rose's fork clattered to the floor. "Carolyn dropped her baby?"

"It's an expression, Rose. It's normal. Finish up and get on outside. Conrad, I want you to dead-head as many roses as you can this morning. Rose, get a couple of grocery bags from under the cutting room sink and help your sister. Jane and Grace, you go, too."

"Don't Palmer and Leroy do the gardening?" Jane whispered.

Conrad punched through a screen door. "Doris likes to see us slave. Hey, want a Popsicle? Race ya!"

The carriage house bays were dark and cool. Grace gawked at the luxury sedans and sporty cars, peered down into the shallow service pit. Jane studied the tools hung on a pegboard, each in its place, neat as a museum display.

Three Kenmore freezers hummed away. Conrad opened a lid and leaned into the cool mist. When the vapor finally cleared, Grace and Jane gaped at the cartons of Popsicles, Fudgesicles and Dreamsicles. Conrad scraped her initials in frost riming one of the boxes. "Pick a flavor, quick," she said. "And let's get started before Doris has a cow."

Out in the garden again, Jane read a small plaque stuck in one of the flower beds:

Rosa Xanthina forma hugoniss —

Circling a Mermaid
10:30 am

The Garden

Conrad moved around the beds snapping off spent blooms. Rose followed with a paper sack. Jane checked the underarms of her blouse for perspiration stains. She sniffed, and silently chided herself for forgetting to pack a jar of Mum. "Why can't you just let the dead flowers fall off?" she asked Conrad.

"Har-dee-har-har, Jane. It's like this, Doris the Drip makes us do a different chore every weekend. She says it reminds us how privileged we are and how lousy other kids have it."

The morning dragged on. At each flower bed, Jane read the plaque. Grace wandered over to the fountain and what she saw surprised her: long, colorful fish circling the lowest basin. "Jane, come look!"

Jane skipped over and dipped her hand in the water. A bright orange fish glanced off her wrist. "Ick! It's slimy!"

"Ninny," Conrad scoffed, swatting away a bee. "The fish don't bite. Here, I'll show you." Conrad slipped out of her moccasins, stood on the rim of the basin, and jumped in feet-first. Water sloshed over the rim.

"Don't," Rose pleaded. "You're scaring Mom's fish."

Conrad stomped around the basin, whipping the water into stormy foam. The koi retreated to the far side and swam tight reverses. Rose wailed so long and loud that finally Conrad climbed out and sat on the lip, pedaling her feet in the air, flicking the drips at Rose. "How about a game?" Conrad said. "No-Peek Hide and Seek. The fences are the boundaries. No going inside the house. No going out front. You guys hide and I'll count to ten."

At a little before noon, a car pulled up the service drive and parked near the carriage house.

"Hello! Hel-loooo! We're here!" It was Carolyn and Bill.

Ever after, everyone would remember the morning as idyllic. Racks of spare ribs were soaking in marinade. Watermelons were chilling in tubs of ice. Old Garden roses were bobbing on five-foot canes. Tangerine koi were circling a mermaid. Water lilies dotted a Japanese pond. At the shore, flanked by slender stands of iris, a stone Buddha sat cross-legged in sublime tranquility. And Carolyn, shining Carolyn, had come home to Blenheim.

Ruminations
Noon

The Study

*F*ritz tried to remember how long it had been since his last confession, and could not. He sent his kids to Catholic schools – if you were Catholic and lived in St. Louis, that's what you did — but he hadn't taken the kids to Sunday Mass in years. He didn't have a clue what his children believed. He wasn't sure what he believed.

He found the book he was looking for. His father's Bible. He opened to a random page and read. Paul was finger-wagging at the Galatians again, warning them about sins of fornication, warning that fornicators would never see the kingdom of God.

Fritz grimaced.

Snowballs in Summer
12:15 pm

The Patio

*J*ane tore her gaze from Bill Hadley and whispered to Grace. "Doesn't he look like Senator Kennedy?"

Grace shrugged. "Who's Senator Kennedy?"

"And Carolyn is the spitting image of Jackie," Jane gushed, "only pregnant."

Eddie jogged out and made an unsuccessful grab for Bill's car keys. "Glad you and Carolyn finally got your butts out here," he said. "Wow, Sis, you got a beach ball under your shirt? Bring any records?"

Carolyn opened the glove compartment and handed Eddie a slim square envelope. "I haven't heard it yet," she told him, "but the guy at Record Bar said it's got a good beat."

Eddie sprinted back to the Hawaiian room and cranked open the louvered windows. Soon, "Don't Be Cruel" was blaring across the patio.

Bill rubbed Carolyn's back. "You need me, hon?"

"Desperately, completely, eternally, but not this minute. Go keep Eddie and Elvis company in the fishnet room."

Conrad tugged at Carolyn's elbow. "Anything for me?"

"You? Gee, I forgot about you, Conrad. I'm so-o sorry." Carolyn's dimpled smile blazed, a dead give-away. She dug in her straw handbag and took out two giant-sized Tootsie Rolls. "One for you and one for Rose — hi Rosy-Girl — and share with Jane and Grace."

"That all?" Conrad said.

"I brought another treat, but it's for later."

Joe walked out to the service drive. He was jingling Bill's car keys. "Bill says there's a cooler in the trunk."

Conrad jumped up and down. "What's in it? What, what?"

Carolyn rolled her eyes, as if trying to remember. "Let's see. I made them this morning. They're cold. They're white. And they're in martini glasses."

"Sundaes! Snowball Sundaes in summer!" Conrad danced around the car. "Dibs on the biggest."

Carolyn rubbed her belly. "Hey girls, want to feel the baby kick?"

Carolyn's pregnancy was nearing term. Her unborn son was twenty-one inches long. He weighed almost six pounds. When he kicked, Carolyn felt it. She lowered herself to a patio chair and placed Conrad's palm on her belly.

"I felt a thunk!" Conrad shouted.

"That's your niece, or nephew."

Joe lugged the cooler to the carriage house and deposited the sundaes in one of the freezers. Back at the patio, he started to sit on a wrought iron chair. The seat was hot as a stove top. He leapt up, annoyed, "You girls are sure schmaltzy about that baby," he barked.

Disappointment flickered across Carolyn's face. Joe immediately regretted the remark. "Aw sis, hey, sometimes I need a knuckle sandwich, you know?"

In the Hawaiian Room, Eddie stopped the turntable and flipped over his new record. He lowered the needle again and cranked up the volume.

You ain't nothing but a hound dog
Cryin all the time

Joe pulled Carolyn to her feet. "Madam Very Pregnant Lady, may I have this dance?"

The previous summer, Carolyn had taught her brothers how to fast-dance. Eddie had trouble getting the hang of it, but Joe had picked up the moves quickly. Now Joe gave his sister an easy twirl and released her hand. Carolyn stood off to the side, clapping to the music while Joe did a fast pivot on the ball of his foot, whirled 180 degrees, brake-turned, and reached for her hand again.

"You are radioactive!" Carolyn cried, laughing hard, hugging her belly. "I have to sit. The sun is blasting."

Bill called out from somewhere in the house, "The kitchen wants to know if we're ready yet."

"I don't know," Joe answered. "Ask Aunt Doris, or Dad."

"Nobody's seen them," Bill said. "Why don't we light the charcoal?"

The kitchen staff started ferrying snacks to the patio, huge bowls of pretzels, popcorn, and potato chips, Joe's favorite dip, dried onion soup mix stirred into Smetina sour cream. There were sweaty pitchers of limeade and lemonade, bottles of root beer and Vess cream soda, platters of pickles and olives, carrot rounds, cucumber rounds, radish flourettes and more.

Palmer and Leroy had been mowing lawn since breakfast. At a few minutes past noon, Palmer decided to take a lunch break. He mopped his forehead and ate a sandwich in the shade of the carriage house. Leroy said it was too hot to eat. Instead, he walked around the edge of the patio to the house, and with a courtly bow, held open a screen door for the parade of kitchen workers carrying out platters of food.

Bill grabbed a bottle of grape soda and offered it to Carolyn. Her cheeks were flushed, he noticed. Her neck was blotchy, too. It was the heat, he knew. He looked at her with a doctor's eye and saw her respiration was elevated, her lips were parted, and she was breathing through her mouth. Bill kissed Carolyn's damp forehead.

"You're not really kissing me," she scoffed, pushing him away. "You're taking my temperature."

Bill eased Carolyn out of the patio chair. "How about you go inside and lie down? We'll call you when the food's ready."

"All right, William Hunt Hadley the Second. Doctor knows best."

At that moment, Sophie was passing through the back hall. "Coming in for a quick nap? No need to go all the way upstairs, dear. Why don't you use your father's study? It's cool in the front of the house, and if you close the door around, it'll be nice and quiet."

At the knock, Fritz emerged from his long fugue. His teeth felt fuzzy. He was still in his robe and pajamas.

Carolyn knocked again. "Dad, you in there?"

The Apollo Line
1 pm

The Rathskeller

With unbounded affection, Fritz watched his eldest daughter lower herself to the study's small sofa. When she was settled, he bent to kiss her forehead. At the study door he glanced back. Carolyn was tucking a small pillow between her knees. Her eyes were already closed.

Fritz left the door open a crack and shuffled around the house, aimless. Chatter on the patio bubbled in through open windows and doors and fell discordant on his ear. He didn't want to see children, didn't want to see anyone. He retreated to the basement. In the rathskeller, he picked up a pool cue and lined up an easy bank shot, but he put too much spin on the ball and it rolled wide.

He found a radio and turned it on, twirling through static until he heard the familiar voice of Cardinals announcer Jack Buck. It was the top of the second. Kenny Boyer popped up. The shortstop bobbled the ball and Boyer slid into first. Stan the Man smacked a fly ball over the outfield bleachers. Buck went nuts.

Fritz sank into a butterfly chair. Stupid looking contraption, he thought. Comfortable as hell though. He turned his hands palms-up and examined them with dissembled interest, unaware of anything beyond the cistern of guilt at his innermost self.

He remembered something odd that had happened years ago. He'd bought circus tickets for the kids at the colored orphans home. On the spur of the moment, he decided to go along. Late that afternoon he'd ducked into a fortune teller's tent. The woman wore a turban and hoop earrings. Bracelets jangled along her ropey arms.

"Thirty cents," she said. Her voice was dry as sand.

He laid two quarters on the table.

"Give hand here. For you, I tell extra."

She traced the line on his palm that swooped around the base of the thumb. "Life line," she said. "You gonna see improvement in your love life."

He'd chuckled. "How could there be? "It's perfect."

She pointed to a crease down the middle of his palm. "Fate line. You self-made man." Then she traced a line near the top of his palm, "heart line," and told him he had a romantic nature.

Finally she traced a line from his ring finger to his wrist. "Apollo line," she said. "Not everybody got one. You do."

"Terrific. What's it mean?"

"Apollo line tell if you have happiness, a fortunate life. But…"

"But what?"

She released his hand. "Your line patchy."

"Meaning what?"

The woman hesitated and finally spoke up. "Patchy good fortune."

Fritz hoisted himself out of the butterfly chair. His body felt like dead weight. He decided to sit awhile in the sauna he'd had installed in the basement when Blenheim was built. The cubicle was dark and smelled of cedar. He took off his night clothes and wrapped a towel around his waist. He sprinkled water on the rocks. Clouds of steam hissed into the air, drenching him in sweat and remorse.

It was 12:50. Lydia was resting in the master bedroom. Doris was on the fourth floor, idly running a brush through her hair. Sophie was on the service drive, chatting with kitchen staffers as they shucked ears of corn onto pages of newspaper spread at their feet. Fritz had given the butler and the housemaids the day off, and they had gone downtown to see "King and I". Palmer had finished his lunch and was mowing long, arrow-straight lines in the motor court lawn. Flecks of grass puffed up from the rotary blades and clung to his trousers. Leroy was out front, too, dusting the teardrop lindens with a rod-and-bulb sprayer.

Conrad and the girls were in the garden playing hide and seek. Joe and Eddie were standing guard over the chimney barbeque at the edge of the patio, snapping tongs at racks of ribs sizzling above the live coals. Bill Hadley sat at a patio table, inspecting the hors d'oeuvres. He reached for a sweet pickle and yanked his hand quickly back.

"Damn bee," he said. "I hate those things."

Eddie burst out laughing. "Look who's all ape. The daddy-to-be is scared of a bug."

"Stop rattling the guy's cage," Joe said. "Bill's allergic."

Who Else
2 pm

A Fourth Floor Bedroom

*D*oris dropped her cigarette butt in a toothbrush glass. "You must have heard wrong," she said.

Fritz groaned. Jesus, he thought, she's going to drag this out all afternoon.

"My sister hasn't said anything intelligible in two years. Her brain is what our grandmother used to call 'slob'."

"Well your sister is my wife, and my wife made an intelligible observatioin last night. Christ, Doris, it broke my heart. She knows. And if she knows, God knows who else knows."

"Nobody. We've been careful."

Doris lit another cigarette and blew a stream of smoke out her nose.

He turned away. To him, she looked like a dragon. "That isn't the point," he said. "I can't do it anymore."

Her tone changed. "Sure you can, chum. Know why? Because it still feels good."

"It never felt good, Doris. It used to feel ... necessary. Now it just feels filthy."

He walked to the window and gripped the sill. Far below, Palmer was mowing grass. Doris was talking, going on and on, but all Fritz heard was the steady, familiar sound of Palmer's mower.

Balancing on the Edge
2:20 pm

The Reflecting Pool

*E*ddie turned up the volume on his transistor radio full blast. "Ain't That a Shame" sent the sound of heartbreak rock crackling across the patio. The day was cloudless, the sky boneyard white. The air was thick with the scents of barbecue smoke and Old Garden roses.

"… nineteen … twenty," Rose called. "Ready or not, here I come."

Behind the potting shed, Grace flicked a spider from her shoulder. She peeked out. In the distance, she saw the mermaid fountain towering above what seemed like a sea of pink blossoms. She could see Rose, too, meandering along a path that led to the reflecting pool.

Nine years ago, a lifetime ago, an eye-blink ago, the white marble reflecting pool was the setting for Blenheim's renowned Camelot Gala. Fritz and Lydia had dressed as Arthur and Guinevere. Three hundred "courtiers" gathered in a white silk tent lined with life-size plaster statues of Merlin, Lancelot, and knights of the Round Table. Waiters passed out mugs of mead and barley wine. At midnight, servants lit torches and the crowd moved to long tables set up around the reflecting pool. Everyone dined on spit-roasted lamb, joints of beef, and flax bread dipped in oil. Afterward, jugglers and fire-eaters, falconers and archers performed feats of skill. The party went on past dawn.

"Where are you?" Rose called. She tiptoed along the edge of the reflecting pool and spread her arms, a wobbly tightrope walker. When she tired of that, she roamed past beds of rhododendron and azalea, poked her head into her play house, meandered to the Tea House and dallied among the stupas and spiky iris.

Grace swatted a mosquito. Stupid Rose, she whispered. She's never going to find anybody.

Sawing Flesh
2:45 pm

The Fourth Floor

A quick, surgical amputation. That's how Fritz had envisioned the breakup with Doris when he was sweating out his transgressions in the sauna. Snip the Gordian Knot.

Doris was having none of it. She was lost in a tunnel of dark memories. Walking into a wedding reception in a pea green bridesmaid gown, and seeing Lydia dancing with her date. Kneeling off-stage in the Rosati-Kain auditorium and watching Lydia bask in the spotlight, in the limelight. Playing with her jacks and hearing an unguarded conversation after a birthday party. "Lydia's the pretty one. She'll make the better match." A lifetime of living in her younger sister's shadow had filed Doris to a sharp point. Fritz might want to break it off, but Doris was having none of it.

"You're a taker," Fritz was saying to her.

She flinched. "And you're a user, Fritz. A rich bastard who thinks he's above —"

"I'm not. You know that." This isn't a quick amputation, he told himself. It's sawing flesh with a dull blade.

Doris droned on. "You knew damn well that for a girl like Lydia, the Reinhardt money was a lubricant."

"You're wrong," Fritz said.

She wasn't. He knew that, of course. He'd known ever since his wedding night, when Lydia made it clear she regarded making love to him as an obligation, a pesky little task, the price of her triumphant marriage to a Reinhardt.

Doris stubbed out her cigarette. "You thought, 'Well now, two Irish micks. I'll take the pretty one right off her Da's front porch, and when Lydia's all used up I'll have the other one.'"

Strangely Calm
3:10 pm

The Garden

*T*he afternoon air shimmered under a relentless sun. The children tired of their game. Grace watched a bee bury its head in the rapture of a gladioli blossom. She thought about giving up, but decided not to.

"Everybody come out!" Rose shouted.

Sweat trickled down Grace's back but she stayed where she was, crouched behind the potting shed. She spat on her finger and rubbed a pencil-line of grit from the fold of her elbow. A mosquito whined at her ear, loud as a Kamikaze plane.

Joe pronounced the ribs almost ready to eat. Bill Hadley and Eddie looked up and then continued their debate about the merits of Pat Boone versus Bill Haley. The kitchen staff brought out steamed corn, baked beans, dishes of raw vegetables, more chips, more soda and beer. Leroy held open the door for them.

"What happened to the tunes?" Joe said, clicking the barbecue tongs like castanets.

Eddie raised the radio antenna as far as it would go. He shook his head. "Battery must be shot. Anybody seen Dad?"

"Haven't seen him all day," Joe said. "Conrad! Rose! Food's ready!"

Rose swished her hands in the mermaid basin and called again, louder: "I give up! Olly, Olly in free!"

Grace knelt at the corner of the potting shed and peeked out again. Conrad and Jane hadn't surfaced.

The garden grew strangely calm, as if it had slipped into the space between one second and the next. A spotted frog hopped into the reflecting pool, but there was no splash, no sound. Songbirds sat on limbs, struck dumb. Crickets cowered in the verges, mute. A forest of thorned canes oscillated under the gorgeousness of empurpled blossoms, and then stilled their clacketing.

The scream cut through the afternoon like a dagger.

Scattered Clippings
3:11 pm

The Fourth Floor

*H*e was suffocating. If Doris didn't shut up he'd hit her. His thoughts ran in circles. His heart hammered. He really thought he might hit her. He wondered if he would stop at a single blow, and feared he wouldn't.

"You have to leave," he said, twirling his wedding ring.

He turned away and couldn't look at her. He pressed his forehead against the window and gazed down at the Venus statue, four stories below. Palmer had left the push mower in the motor court, he noticed. It would have struck him as odd, if it had truly registered. A few moments later, he noticed a bushel basket of grass clippings laying on the ground, on its side. Mowed grass had spilled out across the lawn, as if Penny had come along and knocked over the basket, or Palmer had suddenly dropped the basket and run off. What the hell was going on down there?

He turned away from the window and decided to reason with her one more time: "We're living in sin, Doris. For God's sake."

She had had her back to him, but now she whipped around. "Oh good, Fritz. God spoke to you? God flew down on a fucking cloud and told you to kick me out? Jesus, Fritz, you've got connections."

He was frowning now, barely hearing her, trying to piece together the connection between a push mower sitting idle on a half-mowed lawn, an overturned bushel basket, and scattered clippings. Trying to figure out where his yard man went, and why.

"So you're kicking me out?" she was saying. She sat down at a small dressing table and ran a brush through her hair, brisk, hard strokes. "It's Lydia we should put to pasture, you know —"

"Not another word. God, you're a cold-hearted bitch."

A Hollow Reed
3:11 pm

The Garden

*T*he barbecue tongs clattered to the ground. Joe, Eddie and Bill Hadley squinted, scanning the garden with concern.

Then came a second scream, a raspy screech that sounded as if it began in the belly, raced up the throat, and blasted out an open mouth. Waves of alarm shot across the grounds. The back hairs on Grace's neck stood on end.

A third cry trickled out, thin and gaspy, as if forced through a hollow reed.

Joe, Eddie and Bill raced headlong down brick paths, flaring out across the garden, calling Jane! Rose! Grace? Conrad?

Joe aimed for the pond. He shoved aside cattail spears and swatted down the spiky Japanese iris scribbling along the shore. Eddie ran to the reflecting pool, peered in, saw nothing, and headed for his old play house. Bill was running to the carriage house when Conrad sauntered out, quizzical at the fuss, sucking the whited husk of a Popsicle.

Thirty seconds passed. Forty.

Joe backtracked to the sprialling beds of Bruxelles, each triangular bed the size of a sailboat's spinnaker. He was almost at the mermaid fountain when he heard a weak gurgle. He skidded to a stop and bent to listen. Another gurgle. He dropped to his knees. Barely visible among the thick glossy leaves, he spotted a child. Her back was to him, but he thought it was Rose.

"Here!" he shouted.

Joe pulled off his polo shirt and wrapped it around his arm. Pushing aside the tall canes, he crawled deep into the bed. Thorns snagged his bare back. "Hey, Sweet-Baby," he said, using his father's term of endearment. "What are you doing in here?"

Bill Hadley was right behind Joe. Soon, drops of blood stood out along his arms and legs, like strands of rubies.

Joe reached the center of the bed and swatted aside the last canes. There was Rose, sitting cross-legged in the damp mulch. She was facing away from him, rocking, humming a tuneless melody. Joe inched closer. He reached out and touched her shoulder. "Rose?"

Rose twisted around and looked at her brother with dreamy, half-closed eyes. Joe sat back, stunned. Jane Mitchell lay motionless on the soft soil. Rose was cradling Jane Mitchell's head in her lap.

○

A feral bee had left the hive. Soon its antennae had picked up an enticing scent: roses, La Ville de Bruxelles, on the wane but luscious still. Guided by timeless instincts, it flew from the hollow pear tree at Leatham Smith Stables to the rose garden at Blenheim, a journey of a minute, maybe two. On any given summer day, it would make ten round trips, gorging on nectar, collecting food for the young at the hive.

Had it lived out the day, which it did not, the bee would have continued these journeys for a few weeks more and then it would have died, spent, its passing of scant consequence to a species in which millions fall each day.

On currents of humid air, it flew from the stable orchard to the lane and from the lane to the rose garden. There, it busied itself doing what its kind has done for a million years: tiptoe across mealy stamens, drink in nectar, gather pollen. Eventually, it landed on a flower near an eleven-year-old girl who had crawled to the center of a bed of Bruxelles, a girl who crouched there and ignored the prickly thorns, a girl determined to not be the loser in Conrad's hiding game. At the buzzing, the girl had clamped her hands over her ears. The bee lifted off effortlessly and wafted toward another blossom, a flight path that took it directly over the girl's head. She flapped her hand. She made glancing contact.

Jane Mitchell was five feet, three inches tall and weighed eighty-six pounds. The bee was less than one inch long, its weight best calculated in milligrams. For the bee, Jane's swat packed the concussive effect of a bomb blast. Mortally wounded, deeply angered, the bee plunged its stinger into the soft flesh below Jane's jaw. Poison shot into the wound through the insect's hollow lancet. Studded with barbs, the stinger was a one-way weapon, impossible to withdraw.

Jane flinched in pain and smacked at it. The attack tore away the bee's body but drove the stinger deeper. For the thirty seconds, venom leaked into the wound.

Jane had been stung the previous summer, in Brentwood. Her mother had squirted Bactine on her arm and tried to calm her histrionic daughter. The mark was small as a pea. The real damage was deeper, however, invisible, systemic. That first sting had prepped Jane's immune system to hyper-respond to a new sting in ways both instant and grave.

After the sting at Blenheim, histamines flooded Jane's body. Her lungs went into spasm and she cried out, gagging. Her tongue began to swell. Her head felt hollowed-out. Soon, her throat was closing. She wheezed and cried again. Itchy welts began to rise on her neck and chest, but she couldn't scratch because she couldn't seem to move her arms. Vomit collected in her throat. Jane's world went black.

"Let's pull her out!" Bill shouted. "Now!"

Bill Hadley was among the one or two people in a thousand who are allergic to bee stings. When he was a boy, Bill nearly died after experiencing a severe reaction to a sting. He carried an anti-venom kit everywhere he went.

"Put her on the path. Now get out of the way. Let me see her."

Grace ran from the potting shed breathing hard. "What's wrong with my sister?" she wailed.

"Anaphylaxis," Bill said. "Eddie, run to my car. My case is on the back seat. Bring it here. Fast. Go!"

Jane was chuffing, every shallow breath was a gasp through blue lips. Bill ran his hands down her arms and legs, searching for the sting.

Joe took Grace in his arms. "She'll be okay," he said. Grace buried her face in Joe's shoulder.

Bill was thinking like a doctor now. "Her pulse is fast and she's pink. Not good. Too much histamine. Eddie, where's that Epi? C'mon!"

As soon as Eddie returned with the medical kit, Bill pushed an injection of epinephrine into Jane's thigh.

Jane's papery eyelids flickered. Bill dug in the bag for his stethoscope and barked out orders. "Joe, go inside and dial the operator. Tell her you want the emergency room at Barnes. Tell Barnes I'm on my way with a patient recovering from anaphylactic shock. Got that?"

"Got it."

"Eddie, Conrad, find your dad. Have him call Jane's parents. They should go straight to Barnes, not Blenheim."

Eddie scratched his head. "I haven't seen Dad all day, but I'll look."

"Gracie, can you find a blanket for your sister?" Bill said, his voice softening. "See if Sophie's got one, will you?"

Grace nodded solemnly and ran into the house.

Bill carried Jane to his car and laid her across the back seat. By then, Sophie had heard the news and was rushing out with a blanket and pillow.

Conrad and Rose ran to the Little Girls Wing to throw Jane's clothes into her overnight case. They found Grace sprawled one of the beds, her face buried in a pillow.

"Your sister's gonna be all right," Conrad said. "You'd just be in the way at the hospital, anyhow. You stay here."

Rose patted Grace's hand. "Want another Popsicle?"

The Valley of Sleep
3:12 pm

The Study

*D*ozens of bees feasted in the garden that sunny summer day. Eventually, one found its way into the house. It lingered at a spray of gladioli on the drum table, then vectored off to a vase of hydrangea in the dining room. It detected a sweet scent, brown sugar sauce, whooshing through an open transom, but the clatter of pots seemed too great a risk. Besides, it had picked up signals that were far more tempting: the scent of jasmine, rose, ylang-ylang, and lily-of-the-valley.

When Carolyn made her debut, Fritz had given her a bottle of Chanel No. 5 and told her the story behind the fabulous scent. A perfumer had created six mixtures for Coco Chanel, the fashion designer. The fifth was sublime. Each day, Carolyn dabbed a golden drop of Chanel No. 5 on her wrist.

The study was warm and dark, the door to the foyer slightly ajar. Despite the commotion in the garden, the huge house was quiet. Carolyn slept on. In her dream, she was lying on a bed of snowballs. Her newborn baby was asleep in a cradle beside her. His tiny hands were curled into fists. His lips bubbled with milk-breath. Bill was watching over him; his stethoscope tubes drooped over the pocket of his lab coat, as always. Beyond the tall window, she could see Palmer and Leroy mowing the snow. The Venus statue bent down and handed Conrad a cherry Popsicle. Eddie was singing, sharing a microphone with Pat Boone and Elvis.

Carolyn stretched out on the cool snowballs and drifted deeper into the dream. An airplane was droning overhead, pulling a blue banner. She smiled in her sleep. Isn't that just like Dad? He rented one of those advertising planes to let everybody in St. Louis know about his first grandchild.

The humming grew louder. Carolyn cracked open her eyelids, or thought she did, for she was still half-dreaming. It was night. The plane was flying figure eights. She rested a hand on the cradle and peeked over the edge. The mewling baby was sound asleep. She gazed at Bill. Frown lines creased his forehead. What was wrong? Through the beautiful window, she saw a last star race across the brightening sky, as if fleeing the press of dawn.

The humming was impossible to ignore. Carolyn crawled up from the valley of sleep. Perspiration ringed her underarms. She felt woozy. She tried to stand, got halfway up, and sat down quickly. When her thoughts cleared, she realized the buzzing wasn't a plane. It was a bee.

Instinct is a powerful force. It resides in the cells of the body and in the mysteries of the mind. It finds a home in every one of us, yet it is unique to each. It passes from grandfather to father to son, from mother to daughter. It outlives infancy, childhood, puberty, midlife, old age, senility, even insanity. It imprints itself on every waking minute of the day. It is irrevocable.

In crisis, it prevails over reason.

Carolyn was a rare young woman. Born to great wealth, she was by instinct generous. Bestowed with incandescent beauty, she was unblemished by vanity. She was neither scholarly nor artistic, yet her presence exalted every gathering. Viewed through two prisms, what she did next was either heroic or impulsive.

The moment Carolyn saw the bee she reacted instinctively, as if it posed a mortal and imminent threat. She was wrong. The insect was not the enemy. Instinct was the enemy.

Nevertheless, her brain registered danger. In a matter of seconds, she hurtled from the serenity of sleep to the anarchy of flight-or-fight response. She picked up a magazine. On the cover, Mickey Mantle was batting up, an American hero in a ball cap and pinstripes. She rolled the magazine into a tight tube and tracked the bee as it sailed furious circles around the ceiling. After a while, sunlight lured it to the Palladian window. It dug its claws into the top arch and hung there, upside down.

Carolyn moved quickly to the door and closed it. Her heart was pounding like a pile-driver. She found two fat books near her father's leather easy chair and set them on the seat of a wood chair next to the window. Her hands felt disconnected from her, for they were shaking in short, involuntary movements.

Heavy with child, she hiked up onto the chair and stood on the books. Floaters dazzled across her field of vision. She turned to face the glass. The bee was four feet above her head. She rolled the magazine tighter. She told herself she could do this. Piece of cake.

Years ago, Carolyn's Aunt Florence, Phillip's wife, had taught her to play tennis. Florence and Carolyn had often volleyed on the shady courts at the Ladue house. Carolyn had learned fast. Her topspin power serve had been the pride of the Villa Duchesne and Fontbonne tennis teams. After thousands of games, sets and matches, the connected movements of a power serve were embedded in Carolyn's muscle memory.

Facing the window, she gripped the magazine as if it were her Wilson racquet. She drew her forearm back over her shoulder and flexed her feet. Instinctively, without thinking, she bent her knees and uncoiled. Her body drove upward. Her legs straightened to full extension. For a fraction of a second, Carolyn saw Venus beyond the window glass, a marble goddess, a rendering of female loveliness embraced by teardrop lindens. A summer ago, a lifetime ago, Carolyn had traveled to France and visited the Louvre and stood entranced before the original. A tour guide had pointed out that, although grand and graceful, the statue's twisting posture is anatomically improbable. "Try it," the young man had said. "You'll fall."

A clock struck the quarter-hour. Earth spun on its predictable axis. The top of the world basked in endless day. The bottom in endless night. The sun traced a high path along the Tropic of Cancer, pouring out luminosity. Carolyn lost the bee in a universe of dazzling glass.

But the attack was in motion. With her arm near vertical, Carolyn leaned forward and flexed her wrist. In full-body torsion now, she slammed the magazine at the bee. The pages grazed the high frame, off-target. Her body continued to angle forward in the perfect, practiced follow-through of a tennis player during service. Her right arm slashed diagonally across her huge belly. Her right foot lifted and swung forward, just as it should were she at match point on Florence's dappled court.

No one but Carolyn heard the slap of the magazine, or what followed. Her mother was dozing on the second floor, oblivious to sound or fury. Her father was on the fourth floor, urging his affair to a nasty conclusion. Everyone else was in the bee-stung madness of the garden.

Carolyn was carrying a baby in its thirty-sixth week of gestation. Her balance was badly compromised; her center of gravity had shifted over her pelvis, farther back, higher. She groped for purchase where there was none.

The descent commenced and concluded in a second. One blink of an eye. One swing of a clock pendulum. In the time it took Carolyn to fall out of this world and into the next, seventy thousand thunderstorms broke out around the world, moon glow traveled to the Taj Mahal, twenty-four frames of *The King and I* splashed across a movie screen, the heart of each person in the theater beat once.

It is an enigma, time, a human construct, not of the natural world. What we know is that it is irreversible, unidirectional, and fundamentally nonrestorable. It cannot be taken back, cannot be relived. History's most evolved minds — Newton, Galileo, Einstein — labored to understand it.

Time is misty and willful. It dawdles like the snail crawl of eternity and races like the wingbeat of a moth. A second, an instant, a moment, an eternity. Who's to say which is longer?

As she pitched through space, Carolyn's forehead smacked the edge of the window frame. The impact cracked her skull like a knife-struck egg. Bone fragments pierced her brain and still she fell. Her belly slammed the wall, a catastrophic insult. The placenta, the ephemeral organ that joined Carolyn and her child, tore. She hit the floor hard and died within seconds. A few ticks of a clock. A few blinks of an eye. An eternity.

The infant boy was fully formed, awaiting the first maternal wave that would launch his journey into the breathing world. Curled within Carolyn's womb, his heart stopped soon after hers. Beneath the veil of an undelivered caul, his dulcet face shimmered.

Pretty Sure
4:10 pm

Barnes Hospital

*B*ill was at the emergency room when the Mitchells arrived.

"Jane's going to be fine," he told Madeleine and Paul. "If the docs think she needs a second antihistamine injection, they'll give it to her. Maybe a shot of steroids. But the worst is over."

Madeleine tugged free a handkerchief tucked in the belt of her dress. "Are you sure?"

"Pretty sure, yes. They'll keep her here for a few hours, and then you can take her home."

Paul shook Bill's hand vigorously. "Can you stay awhile? Just until things settle down?"

Bill wrung the back of his neck. He was starving. And what he really wanted to do was drive back out to Blenheim and gorge on barbecued ribs. "Sure thing. No problem."

It would be hours before twilight soothed the blistered day. Hours before moths fretted at coach lamps and cicadas bestirred themselves to song, before fireflies twinkled the air, competing with stars for adulation.

It was twilight by the time Bill drove up an allee of teardrop lindens at Blenheim, and by then it was too late.

Seven Hours
11 pm

The rathskeller

Grief is a changeling. It shakes its fist at a cloud-scuffed sky and wails at a windswept grave. It festers in silence. It casts blame everywhere, begrudges everyone, everything. It shuns what is ready, solace, and craves the impossible, retribution. It picks at fresh scabs. It pours out its heart. It tears itself to shreds. Grief curses and prays, dissipates and endures, destroys and empowers. It is a changeling.

Eddie roamed the house, turning on lights. Conrad followed, switching them off. Rose cuddled her dog and sucked her thumb. Fritz ghost-walked to the Hawaiian Room, dumped ice in a glass and watched it melt. Phillip arrived with a bottle of Scotch, and joined his brother. Bice Finlay walked in without knocking. The three men drank in silence, standing, staring at the floor.

Doris drove to South St. Louis to give the news to her frail parents.

In the apartment above the carriage house, Palmer washed plates that were perfectly clean and wished to God that Leroy would stop bawling.

It was after eight when Bill finally got back to Blenheim. He drove up the motor court and saw the ambulance, the police cars, the hearse. His heart raced. He tasted the metal tang of fear.

Joe had thought to phone two of Bill's friends from medical school, guys who had been groomsmen at Bill's and Carolyn's wedding and who were young doctors now. They raced out to Blenheim and arrived a few minutes before Bill. One of them brought a syringe filled with a tranquilizer. They intercepted their friend a short way from the house. In halting half-phrases, under the saffron glow of a coach lamp, they told him what had happened to his wife, to his child. Before they finished, Bill sank to his knees in the grass. The sounds that came from him were more animal than man. One of his friends raised Bill's shirt sleeve and the other drew out the syringe. By the time they carried him to their car, he was wrapped in a blanket of oblivion.

Word spread fast. Miss Foley called. Fritz's brokers and clients called. Reinhardt & Krug people called. The managers at Topping Ridge and the M.A.C. phoned to say the club flags would fly at half-staff. Carolyn's sorority sister sobbed, dropped the phone, and hung up. The *Post-Dispatch* asked if anyone could verify Carolyn's middle name, the year she made her debut, the size of her engagement ring diamond. KSD-TV called to ask if foul play was suspected?

Police took statements and wrote down the names of the servants. The coroner remained in the godforsaken study. Men from Kriegshauser Mortuary wheeled a steel gurney into the foyer, onto a checkerboard marble floor laid perfectly on the diagonal. A steel gurney, at Blenheim.

Mrs. McMillan stopped by with a casserole still warm from the ovens at Clareford. The Switzers' cook brought over a pineapple upside-down cake and invited Conrad and Rose to stay the night at Casa Brava, if they wanted.

○

Joe grabbed the banister and glared at the upward sweep of steps, his features set with the stony determination of a mountaineer about to test the mend of a shattered bone, which he was not.

Joe. The most handsome of Lydia's five handsome children, the easy one, she often remarked, beaming at him, the radiant mother, the winsome boy. That was some time ago, a lifetime ago.

At the summit, Joe knelt beside his mother's bed. He touched her shoulder. The light tap provoked her to an involuntary quiver, like a drowsy mare shaking off a horsefly. Her skin was papery, he saw, her darling freckles gone to pale; angel kisses, she called them, once upon a time. With a low grunt, she rolled over and turned her slack face to him, wondering: Who is this, now?

"Everybody thought Carolyn was taking a nap," Joe said, his voice reedy. "When we found her, she was on the floor of Dad's study."

Each word struck her like a cudgel blow. She scrunched her eyelids to make them go away, the spittle words trickling down the boy's chin, the viscous ink words staining his clothes, his tennis shorts, his polo shirt the color of ripe apricots, the color of summer sunsets, the color of shrimp curling over the rim of a cocktail cup, the color of …

"She was already dead, Mom."

He was pleading now, pleading with his tormented eyes and his high, whiny voice. Who on earth was this simpering boy?

"There was nothing we could do."

The words were making an oily puddle at his feet but the boy didn't seem to notice. How could he not realize there were words -- words! -- pouring down his polo shirt and blazing white shorts and he simply *would not stop* talking.

"Bill was gone by then. I tried to do CPR, like they taught me at camp."

She pursed her fissured lips and watched the puddle grow wider, a stormy pool of sewer water words spattering the room, her bedroom, her universe.

"And Mom, oh God, the baby died too."

The young man sank beside her bed, mired in a cistern of words.

Her darling angel princess daughter, dead? Carolyn and her unborn child dead?

"She was at the front window. We think she wanted to kill a fly or a bee, something like that. She'd climbed on a chair and then she must have slipped and fell. She hit her head."

Lydia gazed off to the middle distance where a dulcet face slept, placid, beneath a pale caul, a curled breathless infant drowned in the womb water that had cradled him and the words were spilling across her ivory carpet now, fouling the pristine underpinnings of her much reduced life. Tributaries fingered off, each droplet a spider word prancing on pointy toes, climbing the gorgeousness of her Scalamandre wallpaper, dancing across vertical sheets of chinoiserie, lily ponds and tea houses and gilded pagodas, Ming Dynasty or perhaps Yuan, and skittering to the floor again, yes! marching straight back to her bed, a vile parade of spider words.

Joe dipped his face into cupped palms, weeping in ragged gasps.

"The police came. They're downstairs, taking statements. The coroner's here too. Can you get up, Mom? Please?"

The spindly words undulated across her silk coverlet. Python words with flicky tongues and they were licking her ankles now, yes! slithering up her thighs. Black mamba words coiling her flaccid belly. Clammy pit viper words twining 'round her from hipbone to breastbone, a living corset laced tight, closing the bellows of her lungs, casting into arrhythmia the thrum of her heart, chambers opening and shutting like the doors of a carnival fun house.

Sun blasted through Venetian blinds, laying prison bars across the silken bed. A bee fretted at the window, trying to get in. On the nightstand, a dainty clock marked time with precise indifference. Joe rested his head on her shoulder.

Lydia scanned the room, eyes glittered and darting. The words had skittered off to their hidey places. Under the bed. Behind the chiffarobe. They were secreting themselves, she knew, lurking in the accordion pleats of lampshades, burrowing in the slats of electrical sockets. Breathing. Waiting.

She traced dry fingertips across the back of the young man's neck, arose, and walked past him. In the bathroom, she slipped out of her gown and climbed into the waterless tub. Words bubbled up from the drain.

There now, she said, reaching for her razor, time for a nice, long soak.

Sophie kept vigil outside the bathroom door. Some years earlier, Sophie had removed the blade from Lydia's razor. Lydia had never noticed. At dusk, a housemaid offered to take Sophie's place. No, she said, I belong here. At ten-thirty, a cook brought up toast and tea. Sophie called through the door and jiggled the knob. Lydia had locked herself in.

By then, Joe was in the rathskeller. He lowered his tall frame into a butterfly chair and stared into space, as if thinking back, reliving the afternoon, trying to get to the spot where he could have, should have, done something, said something, been somewhere else that would have, might have…

After a while, Joe rose and rummaged through knotty pine cabinets until he found his father's movie projector. He set it up on the pool table, found the screen, and rattled its balky legs until they splayed.

Seven hours. For seven hours Joe sat in an underworld of sorrow, slumped in a butterfly chair, watching Reinhardts frolic across a frosted screen. When the projector went dark he replaced the bulb. When his eyes screamed, he rubbed them and went on, transfixed by the blithe spirits of the past.

There. A grainy soundless image of Carolyn, a toddler in an heirloom high chair painted with storybook scenes. She's in the old kitchen at Portland Place. Carolyn is swinging her long legs, playing pat-a-cake with Grandmother Reinhardt. There's Esmie setting a little roll on the high chair tray. The baby picks it up, holds out her dimpled hand, offering the treat first to Esmie, then to Grandmother.

The film fluttered. Random scenes. Then, there. Carolyn perched on Grandfather Albert's lap, turning the pages of a story book. She lifts the cover to the camera. *Twas the Night before Christmas*. Grandfather Albert finishes the story. He closes the book and kisses the top of Carolyn's head. She turns to him, covering his face with little kisses, setting his wire spectacles askew. He closes his eyes and smiles, his scholarly features the picture of bliss.

Joe took another roll of film from the stack of canisters. There. Carolyn in her Easter dress. Yellow dotted Swiss. It's the annual egg hunt at Topping Ridge. Carolyn is skipping around the club lawn, offering marshmallow chicks from her basket to the littlest tots, the ones who can't find any colored eggs.

Conrad and Rose couldn't sleep. Eventually, they shuffled downstairs and sat cross-legged under the pool table, staring at an elegy to goodness, black and white images flashing across a blinding, shining screen. "She was so young," Conrad said, and then, "Look at her cute little purse. What's that on her socks?"

"Bunnies," Rose whispered. "They're bunnies."

Joe changed the reel. They watched a few minutes of Eddie's First Holy Communion and then, there. Carolyn, taller now. A leggy girl rocketing serves over a net. A game of tennis on a sunny court on a golden, forever-ago day.

Rose stuck her thumb in her mouth, curled up on the floor and rested her head in Conrad's lap. Conrad stroked her sister's hair. It was after midnight. The projector shot a funnel of light through the room, splashing Reinhardts onto the crystal-dust screen like so many tossed diamonds, and they, all of them, drenched in celluloid happiness, larger than life.

The projector ground to a stop. Joe inserted another reel. There. Carolyn, a few years ago. At R&K, the flagship store. She's standing on a low roundel in a satin dressing room with button-tufted walls. It's the final fitting of her Veiled Prophet gown.

"Who's filming?" Rose wondered aloud.

Joe looked under the pool table. He hadn't realized the girls were there. "Sophie," he said. "I remember Dad told Sophie to go along that day and bring the movie camera."

The seamstress finishes pinning the hem. She sits back on her heels and gazes up, pleased. Carolyn is twirling now, all glossy pageboy, swan neck, creamy shoulders and clouds of tulle, snow globe ballerina virgin angel princess goddess sweetheart. And there. Lydia, her mother, sitting on a dainty gold bamboo chair, looking vaguely off to the side. And Sophie, captured in the mirror's reflection, beaming at Carolyn, at Fritz and Lydia's first-born, their luminous best thing.

Eddie made his way down to the rathskeller, found his brother and sisters, and pulled up an empty butterfly chair. Joe fit another reel onto the sprocket. Film whirred through the projector.

There. Carolyn in the garden. She and Sophie are snipping Bruxelles for Lydia's morning bouquet. There's Palmer in the background, pulling weeds. And Leroy, raking mulch into a bed. Leroy grins, a goofy, brick-toothed smile, and starts bowing.

"What's he doing?" Eddie asked.

Joe thought a minute and then said, "I heard he and Palmer worked at a hotel in San Francisco a while back. I think Palmer was an elevator operator and Leroy was a doorman. Vice versa, maybe. Looks like the camera caught Leroy pretending he's a doorman again."

Upstairs, one of the maids insisted Sophie take a break from her vigil at the bathroom door. Sophie put on her bathrobe and slippers and padded down to the rathskeller, and stayed to watch, spellbound.

There. Carolyn in Chantilly lace at the M.A.C. Christmas party. She's plucking the cherry from her Snowball Sundae and popping it into Conrad's mouth. They burst out laughing, the dazzling older sister, the bedazzled middle sister.

The final reel, shot last summer. Carolyn on the patio. She's wearing a halter top and Bermuda shorts. Mile-long legs. She's saying something to Joe, pointing to Eddie's transistor radio. Suddenly, the picture jumps around and goes sideways. Conrad cocked her head.

"I took these shots," Eddie mumbled. "She asked me to turn up the radio, play the song loud. I must have put the camera down." When the picture on the screen finally pivoted right-side up, Carolyn is pulling Joe to his feet.

"I remember that day, too," Joe said.

Eddie wiped the heel of his hand across red-rimmed eyes. "She was teaching us how to fast-dance."

Joe switched off the projector. The reel stuttered to a stop. The spear of light disappeared and the screen went dark.

In the front yard, Venus lay down her shadow on fresh-mowed lawn. In the garden, the mirror surface of a marble reflecting pool shimmered with images of a forever ago evening, when once upon a time Arthur and Guinevere danced in a spun-silk tent.

High clouds skimmed a coin moon lingering over the Tea House. Stars spangled the heavens. Along the lane, coach lamps flickered like altar candles. Soft night air held the scent of pink roses. The earth spun like a top, as if nothing had happened, nothing at all.

Epilogue
1995

St. Louis

*G*race never saw Blenheim again. Never watched comets flare over crossed-board fences or fed apples to an ebony stallion. Never hid behind a potting shed built to the specifications of Marie Antoinette or glimpsed a ghost strolling a midnight hallway.

No one talked about that terrible weekend, no one in the family, at least not within earshot of Jane and Grace. There were no more family reunions. Years passed, slow as the tolling of bells, swift as the flight of a gazelle. And then, on one of those perfect football afternoons, Grace ran into Joe.

St. Louis University High was up by twelve over DeSmet. Grace scanned the bleachers for her daughter. Leslie and her friends went to every SLUH game. Grace and the other mothers took turns carpooling.

The Rev. Joseph Reinhardt, S.J., was cheering from the sidelines of a field where he once starred as quarterback. Joe was 61. His hair had gone to gray, but the fabulous eyes and deep dimples were handsome as ever. A lifetime of athletics had kept him trim. After the game, he and Grace chatted in the banal way people do.

"You don't have a boy here at SLUH, do you?" he asked.

Grace shook her head. "Three girls. I'm picking up the middle one, Leslie, and her friends.

"St. Joe girls?"

"You got it. My alma mater."

He chuckled. "How's Jane?"

"She's good. Lives in Denver. She and Kevin have twin sons. They all ski."

They looked off, searching for another neutral topic.

"Do you teach here?" she asked.

"Got here last May," he said. "I was at Rockhurst. Then SLUH called and I jumped at it. Freshman Theology. Believe me, it's the wrath of God." Joe flashed his famous crinkle-eyed smile.

They watched the teams sprint to the locker room. Fans began to drain from the bleachers. There wasn't much left to talk about except the thing that was on both their minds. Autumn wind scoured the field. Grace shivered.

Leslie and her friends had walked to the minivan and turned on the radio. Mariah Carey was sending "Fantasy" up and down three octaves. Boys from SLUH and DeSmet stood in clusters on the parking lot, lining up rides, flirting with girls from Nerinx Hall, St. Joseph's Academy and Ursuline. Grace dug her hands in the pockets of her jacket and took a deep breath.

"Joe," she said, "what happened after that day?"

Joe tucked his head down, and she immediately regretted asking him to dredge up grievous memories. "Listen, Joe, forget it. It was wrong of me to ask."

He tugged a tuft of grass from the field and opened his hand. The blades blew off, summer secrets loosed to an autumn breeze.

O

After leaving the rathskeller, Sophie had buzzed for Palmer. It was two in the morning. Conrad and Rose were finally asleep. "Bring a hammer," Sophie had said. "And a screw driver. For the hinge pins."

Palmer had removed the bathroom door and set it to the side. A safety razor lay on the floor, flanges gaping. Lydia was supine in the tub. Somehow, she had found Fritz's hidden packet of blades and she was deftly running one of the thin black razor blades across her wrist. Palmer lifted her like a broken-winged bird and carried her to her bed. Sophie phoned the doctor.

A week after the funeral, Fritz summoned Palmer and Leroy to the Hawaiian Room. A week after Carolyn's funeral Palmer barely recognized the man, though he'd known Fritz for almost thirty years. Known the young husband who chased a cloche hat in Grant Park. Known the brilliant financier and the guy who took orphans to the circus, the father who gave car keys on birthdays. The lion of a man Palmer had known for thirty years looked bitter now, defeated, and old.

"It was a bee," Fritz told him, staring out the louvered windows. "The coroner found a bee in the study. He thinks she was standing on a pile of books, going after it." After a long pause, Fritz added: "All those goddamned flowers."

"Yes sir."

Fritz face was set with stony determination. "I want a bulldozer."

"Yes sir."

A few days later, Fritz stood at a window watching the machine tear at the earth. He smiled, watching its bucket lift Bruxelles into the air, shedding petals like bloodied flakes of snow. He watched workers take jack hammers to the reflecting pool, take sledge hammers to the Tea House and the mermaid fountain, and haul away truckloads of detritus. He watched Palmer and Leroy rake the soil smooth and sprinkle grass seed, and by September he was satisfied, for the great house rose from a stark, featureless landscape.

By then, Lydia had repaired to some vague interior world, anesthetized against reality, numb to sorrow. Phillip convinced Fritz to look at a private nursing home in Creve Coeur, a short drive from Blenheim. After a tour, Fritz signed the papers. He asked Sophie to stay on, as Lydia's personal assistant. You know, he said with a sad chuckle, you're her first and only French lady's maid. Sophie moved to an apartment not far from the nursing home. She was finally living on her own in a big city. Once, that had been her dream, but that was a lifetime ago.

The rhythm of Lydia's days seldom varied. In the morning Sophie gave her mistress a warm sponge bath and then read Dear Abby aloud. Afterward, she wheeled Lydia to the atrium. Sometimes Sophie brought along a framed photograph. "There's Joe, remember Lydia? And there's little Rose. There's Eddie and Carolyn, see? Lydia?"

In February of 1960, a young man visited the nursing home. His grandmother occupied the room across the hall from Lydia's room. He had a headache and a scratchy throat, but when he left he kissed the old woman goodbye. On his way out, she asked him to leave her door open.

Dusk came early. Sleet prickled the nursing home windows. The grandmother felt a sneeze coming on. She tried to cover her mouth with withered fingers. Invisible droplets blew into the air as if shot from a cannon. Across the hall, Lydia was asleep, breathing deeply from her diaphragm. Bacteria lodged in the moist tissue of her throat and traveled the short distance to her lungs. Too listless to cough, she became congested, and then fevered.

At the St. Louis Basilica Cathedral, Archbishop Ritter celebrated Mass for the repose of the soul of Lydia Marie Conrad Reinhardt. A fleet of limousines conveyed the family to Calvary Cemetery. The imposing Reinhardt crypt was not far from that of Auguste Chouteau. Lydia was laid to rest beside her beloved daughter, Carolyn. Inscribed above the vault were the words, "God grants his angels charge over those who sleep."

The morning was gray and gusty. Hoarfrost rimed the monuments. After brief prayers, members of the gathering hurried on to Topping Ridge, where a crackling fire, hot toddies, and brunch awaited.

Sophie and Fritz lingered among the stone archangels and obelisks. He's thinner, she saw, and hollow-eyed. He reminded her of a man alone in a lifeboat staring forlornly at a sinking ship. Branches rattled in the wind. A crow cawed and flapped off. For the first time, Sophie breached the unwritten code defining her role in the Reinhardt universe: she gave Fritz a hug. His chin sank to her shoulder, and he wept without a sound. It occurred to Sophie that all the man ever wanted was to make the people he loved happy, as simple a thing as that.

They crunched across the frozen grass, leaving a trail of dark footprints. Without a word, Fritz handed Sophie a small packet and then folded himself into a waiting limousine. He told the driver to bypass Topping Ridge, he wanted to go home to Blenheim. Twenty minutes later, the vehicle moved slowly up the drive between the allee of teardrop lindens. The staff had formed a solemn line across the portico. Leroy had placed his hand over his heart.

Back in her apartment, Sophie put a kettle on and tossed an old sweater over her shoulders. Inside the packet she found a stack of mature Series D savings bonds. A pension. It would be enough, she thought, thank God. A small booklet slipped out and she turned the pages in disbelief. The day Sophie had arrived at the house on Lake Forest Drive, Fritz had opened a savings account in her name and seeded it with $100. Ever since, he'd made monthly deposits. The account stood at $344,350.

He knew from the beginning I'd stay till the end, she murmured. He knew it before I did.

Sophie returned to Hannibal. The old house on Bird Street was for sale. After she bought it, she opened a small bed and breakfast hotel. She named it "LaChine Inn".

The day after Lydia's funeral, Phillip had Doris transferred to the Crestwood branch store. For three years, until her retirement, Doris rang up bottles of Arpege perfume and Yardley soap at a counter just inside the main doors, a locale that ensured she froze in winter, sweltered in summer, and was peppered with questions by customers needing directions. Once a month, Joe would drive to his aunt's apartment in Maplewood and chat a while, for he rightly suspected her evenings were long and lonely. Doris would bring out a bowl of Jiffy Pop or a dish of peanut brittle and they'd watch "Candid Camera."

Eddie had been a marketing major at Mizzou when he fell for a Golden Girl. Dressed in brief, sparkly costumes, the Golden Girls pep squad twirled batons and cheered for the stadium crowds during football games. Eddie and Muffy were childless when, after two rocky years of marriage, they divorced. Eddie decided he'd rather die than continue working for his Uncle Philip, so he took a job with Marshall Field's, moved to Chicago, and was promptly and legally eliminated as the last best hope in R&K's family succession plan. One day Eddie was driving to Midway Airport and, on the way, he stopped at a South Side sandwich shop. He got to talking with a young woman behind the counter. She was shy but friendly. It wasn't long before Eddie got the impression her uncle owned the café, or her uncle's cousin, Eddie wasn't sure. By the time Eddie finished a gyro sandwich and ordered a second, he'd learned her name —Josie, she told him, Josie Gibaldi.

Soon after Josie and Eddie married, Eddie landed a better job, in Little Rock, with Dillard's. When Dillard's bought out R&K in the mid-1980s, Eddie came out smelling like a rose. After one hundred years, the Reinhardt name disappeared from America's retail landscape.

The September after Carolyn's death, Fritz sent Conrad and Rose to board at the private school they had been attending as day-students, Villa Duchesne. The nuns did their best to bolster Rose's confidence and contain Conrad's bravura, with marginal success.

In 1964, Conrad rocketed from the cloisters of Villa to a more peppery zeitgeist: Madison, Wisconsin. For the next two years Conrad organized campus protest marches. She joined sit-ins and boycotts. A photo of Conrad flipping the bird to a National Guardsman made the front page of the Madison *Capital Times* and was carried over the AP wire. Fritz dispatched his chauffer to bring Conrad and her love beads back to Missouri. Conrad bought a Plymouth Fury with 80,000 miles on the odometer and enrolled at Mizzou's prestigious School of Journalism. She crashed at an off-campus pad that reeked of weed, drank Budweiser at the Old Heidelberg, played "Hey Jude" endlessly, the long version, and wrote a fine series of investigative pieces for the *Columbia Missourian*.

After graduation, Conrad packed a duffel bag, flew to Saigon, and waltzed unannounced into United Press International's office. The bureau chief looked her up and down and pointed to the door. She came back day after day until the man finally snapped a pencil, scratched his balls, and hired her. Before long, Conrad was asking for the riskiest assignments, the ones that took her up treacherous rivers and deep into the jungle. She ran into

Bill Hadley once. He was volunteering with Doctors Without Borders, providing basic medical care to refugees.

Conrad made international headlines after she sneaked into Cambodia to report on a secret phase of the war there and was captured by Khmer Rouge troops who bound her wrists and ankles with p'dou vines and interrogated her at gunpoint. When she didn't crack, they tossed her down a hole and left her to rot. A week later, Conrad stumbled onto a dirt road, half-dead. American journalism schools circulate her gutsy dispatches as examples of stellar war reporting.

Rose did not open up, as hoped, at Villa Duchesne. When the child's bouts of homesickness threatened to lead to physical sickness, one of the young nuns sought permission for Rose to spend weekends at home, at Blenheim. Each Sunday evening Sister Bernadette waited on the dormitory stoop, and spread her arms in welcome the moment she saw Rose waving from her father's car.

Rose went on to Maryville College, a women's school not far from Huntleigh. As her school days drew to a close, Fritz proposed she take a vacation. "Go anywhere in the world, Sweet-Baby. Take a friend."

"Blenheim. I want to go to Blenheim."

Fritz shook his head. That afternoon he phoned a travel agent.

"I have just the spot," the woman said. "The Kahala Hilton in Hawaii. John Wayne stayed there. Frank Sinatra and Eva Gabor, too."

"Rose won't give a hoot about Eva Gabor staying there, but book it anyway. Two first-class tickets on whatever airline flies there."

"For Rose Reinhardt and …"

"And her friend, Sister Bernadette Schaeffer."

The resort was just as Rose had expected. Bikinis and Speedos. Cocktail huts and spiked fruit drinks. Sister Bernadette suggested they attend a seminar at the dolphin lagoon.

"Welcome, everybody, I'm Simiran." The young man was deeply tanned, with dark brown eyes and a flashing smile. "Simiran means sun shining on water, but I'm not Hawaiian. I'm from Kiribati. Abemama, to be precise."

"I've heard of Kiribati," Sister Bernadette whispered to Rose. "It's the Gilbert Islands."

Simiran stuck his hand in a pail and pulled out a blob of tentacles. "Who wants to feed our beautiful dolphins today? How about you?" he said, pointing to Rose.

A year later, Simiran returned to Kiribati and married Rose under the stars in a traditional island ceremony. In the cool of the morning, Simiran launches his small fishing boat and heads out to sea. Rose gathers panadus fruit and hibiscus spinach. Their older daughter tends a low fire near the sleeping huts. Their younger girl stirs the papaya simmering in coconut milk. Sometimes, Rose is called to one of the nearby huts, to the bedside of a sick neighbor. Among the islanders, Rose's strange, soothing incantations are known to drive minor ailments from the body and to calm a distressed soul.

In the late afternoons, Rose and her daughters walk to the shore and sit under palm trees listing to sea. The girls weave mats and scan the horizon. As soon as their father's boat comes into view, they jump up and wave. Warm breezes flutter their dark hair. At sunset, Rose, Simiran and the girls cross the soft sand and return to a village of simple huts. They sleep the slumber of angels, lulled by the wash of tides.

Ten years after Lydia's funeral, Fritz had suffered a mild stroke. The doctor had told him to sell the brokerage firm, give up cigars and beer, and play more golf. Fritz nearly died of boredom. A second stroke sent Fritz into a steep decline. Twice a month, a cleaning service came to rearrange the dust. The St. Martha's Agency dispatched kindly caregivers in round-the-clock shifts. By then, a landscape service was tending the featureless lawn, a squadron of youths wearing headphones zooming back and forth on riding mowers.

When bare lawn replaced Blenheim's lavish gardens, Fritz had offered Palmer and Leroy a pension and a house. "Buy yourselves a place of your own, go pick one out," he'd said. They settled on a brick ranch in Hazelwood. Palmer thought the place was pretty darn nice, except the yard, three-fourths of an acre, seemed dinky as a soda cracker. Leroy said, "No, brother, a oyster cracker." Every so often they drove back to Blenheim and chatted on the service drive with the chauffeur or the kitchen maids, catching up.

One day LaVerne, a caregiver from the St. Martha's Agency, invited Palmer and Leroy to come on into the kitchen for lemonade. The following week LaVerne asked if they might like to say hello to Mr. Reinhardt in the Hawaiian Room.

"Can't," Leroy said. "Us was outside help."

"Don't matter now," LaVerne said. "Follow me. I warn you, though, the man can't hardly be understood."

Eventually the brothers grew accustomed to Fritz's twisted face and garbled speech, but it took a long while for them to feel comfortable about their new status as visitors. They talked to Fritz about anything and everything. The Cardinals' chances for a play-off spot; Leroy liked Lou Brock, Palmer was a Bob Gibson fan. Leroy mentioned he'd taken a ride to the top of the Gateway Arch. He claimed he felt it sway in the wind. Fritz had widened his eyes at that. One day Palmer asked if Fritz wanted to hear a story about a Honeydew Girl. Fritz brightened, thinking it might be a new joke.

"Well sir, this was a long time ago, when we was in N'Awlins. There was this girl, the Honeydew Girl. Prettiest little thing you ever seen —"

Leroy cut in. "She was skinny as a beanpole!"

"Sweetest, gentlest chile —"

"Brother, that Honeydew Girl was a hellcat!"

"She and me was in love."

Leroy held his tongue.

Neither brother had married. Leroy hadn't minded so much, but he knew Palmer would have had a wife and kids if he hadn't had to look after a dopey brother. Leroy appreciated Palmer's sacrifice and gave back what he could: loyalty, companionship, and the occasional reminder that they were businessmen.

In the spring of 1978 Fritz was felled by a third and final stroke. Lilacs scented the air on the morning of the funeral. Joe sprinkled holy water over the graves of his father and mother, his sister and unborn nephew. He ended the funeral Mass with this: "For of his God he got the grace to live in mirth and die in peace."

Fritz's will was clear. Upon his death, Blenheim was to be leveled and the barren property sold. All proceeds of his estate, including investments, were to flow into the Fritz and Lydia Reinhardt Charitable Foundation.

O

Grace looked away, lost in thought. Out in the parking lot, a boy was leaning against the side of the minivan, talking to her daughter.

"Who's that, Joe?"

"Him? Great kid. Straight out of Nowheresville."

"What do you mean?"

"After I got here in May this kid shows up at the guidance office, asking for me. He says he's from Mississippi but he's got no family back there anymore. I'm ready to call social services when the kid hands me two pieces of paper. One is all wrinkled and yellowed. The other is splotched with food stains. The writing's faded but legible. On the yellowed paper somebody had written our name, 'Reinhardt,' and a street-by-street map to my grandfather's house on Portland Place. On the other piece of paper was a recipe for cinnamon rolls."

"What!"

"I know. It's weird. The kid said his great-aunt had passed the map and recipe down to his mother, and his mother to him. I can't imagine how he found me, but he did."

"What's his name?

"Ted. Theodore Hobbs. When he turned eighteen, he aged out of Mississippi's foster care system, and he took off. Ted's smart. I found him a place to stay, got his school records from Mississippi, and finagled a full-ride scholarship to St. Louis U. He comes to all the games, follows me around like a puppy."

So, Grace said to herself, my daughter has a boyfriend.

They sat a minute in companionable silence. Then Joe said, "You know, it was years before I learned the truth."

Grace was intrigued. "What truth?"

After a long pause, Joe continued: "I get this call one day, back when I was at Rockhurst. It was Palmer. He tells me Leroy's at DePaul Hospital. He says Leroy's asking for me. So I drive across the state. By the time I get to the hospital, Leroy can hardly breathe. The guy never smoked, his nurse, nice girl named Shirley, tells me Leroy's got this aggressive form of pulmonary fibrosis. I bless him and ask if he'd like to make his peace with God. He's got this oxygen mask over his face so he can't talk, but he looks at Palmer and sort of nods."

Grace looked at Joe, curious. "What was that all about?"

"Leroy was a little off, you know? Always making these grand gestures, saluting, bowing, hand over his heart, goofy stuff. So here's what Palmer tells me: The day my sister died, we were out back getting ready for the picnic, right? The kitchen staff was bringing all this food out to the patio, remember?"

"Sort of. That isn't the part that sticks in my mind."

"Leroy decides to be gallant, be a doorman. He must have opened and closed that screen door a dozen times. At some point, he saw a bee near the door. He flapped his hand at it, trying to get it back out to the yard, but he accidentally swished it into the house instead."

"Good God," Grace said. It was common family knowledge that Carolyn had been trying to kill a bee when she fell to her death.

"Leroy felt bad, so he didn't say anything to anyone that day. In hindsight, he felt he should have gone inside, gone after the bee himself, but of course he was forbidden to do so."

"He was?"

"I heard all this from Palmer, at the hospital. Apparently my mom's decorator was at Blenheim one day, right after we moved in. Mssr. Mathieu. God! Anyway, he saw Palmer and Leroy in the kitchen and he was pretty rough on them. The guy was a snob. He gave Palmer and Leroy a real education about the wall between indoor staff and outside men."

"Everybody's got to have somebody lower."

"I guess. Anyway, all those years Leroy felt responsible for Carolyn's death, but he was too ashamed to tell anybody until he told Palmer at the end of his life."

"Grace shook her head. "I can't think of a thing to say."

"Leroy had no reason to feel guilty," Joe went on. "The chain of events was forged long before that."

"What do you mean?"

"You could say a bee killed Carolyn, brought on my mother's final breakdown, caused my dad's strokes. You could say it made Conrad reckless and made Rose retreat. You could say it ruined our family."

"Didn't it?"

"Yes and no. Conrad went on to be a phenomenal war correspondent. Rose and Simiran have an idyllic life. Eddie's about where he should be now. I became a priest. Bill is with Doctors Without Borders. That's a pretty good outcome."

"I guess so."

"Carolyn was our true north. She showed us what goodness is. When she died, it ripped our hearts out. Mom and Dad never recovered. But the rest of us made something of our lives. Things come zinging out of the blue, Grace. People crumble, or they pull themselves up and go on."

Grace followed Joe down the risers. In the parking lot, Leslie and the boy from Mississippi were still talking.

Joe seemed to be temporarily lost in his own world. "You know, Dad's only grandchildren are two little girls on a Pacific island. It's the end of an era."

"And the beginning of another," Grace said.

One of the players had left a football on the field. Joe picked it up, spun it in his hands, and then sprinted to the end zone. The sun was melting into the far trees, casting Joe's shadow on the grass behind him, a likeness scissored in silhouette, shape without substance, as visible and unreachable as loved ones engraved in memory but lost to time.

Grace jogged to the forty yard line and waited. Joe faked, drew back his arm and threw a Hail Mary pass. The ball spiraled into the autumn air, impossibly high, as if Gravity, vanquished, had at last bequeathed old burdens to the xanthous sun.

Acknowledgements

In gratitude, I would like to acknowledge:

Dennis John Fitzpatrick, who happened to cross my path in college and has been at my side, steadfast, ever since.

Claire Fitzpatrick Gould, who offered prescient advice. "Mom, novellas don't sell. Either chop it so it's a short story or expand it so it's a novel."

Meg Fitzpatrick, who listens to me read everything I write.

Daniel E. Gould, who sometimes lets me win at Scrabble.

Jenny Lewis McMahon, fille de sa mère, qui était toujours près avec l'encouragement.

Tom Underhill, who drove me around old Chicago, and Steve Olszewski, who gave Tom and me the grand tour of Mt. Olivet Church.

Ken Underhill, author of *Jack Fell Down*, who draws out the word Cath to four down-swooping, upsoaring syllables, which I like.

Pamela Underhill, who long ago, a lone voice, assured me I could write.

Michele Derus, who refused to let go.

Kathleen M. Arenz, Carol S. Cole, Jeff Fister, Rose Marie Kinder, Kelly O'Connor McNees, Karen K. Marshall, Eric Sandweiss, and Kris Radish, who wrote endorsements as gracious as they were eloquent.

Nancy Sturino, who slogged through Drafts One and Six, fretting over verbless phrases doing business as sentences.

Mary Jo Goodwin, who recommended more plot-connecting threads and more sex (in the novel).

Colleen McCarrier, who famously read and annotated Draft Two (once) and Draft Four (twice).

James F. Dowd III, who buffed and polished Draft Five.

Bob and Cheryl Underhill, James and Sue Underhill, Marcia and Tom Flanagan, Mary and Tom Domer, Pat and Izzy Matusiak, Peg and Bill Schaaf, Diane and Tom McGinn, John Lohre, J. Miles Goodwin, Santo Sturino, Whitney Scott, and Mary Ann and Jeffrey Sussman, who believed in me.

Anita Lamont, whose sense of humor made me laugh years ago, and does so still.

Shellie Blumenfield and Mary Pat Lohre, who in the depths of winter steeped herbal tea, listened to me read chapters, and sighed at all the right parts.

Wendy Randall and A.Y. Stratton, who in the dog days of summer sipped iced tea, swished away patio bees, and gifted me with sympathy and empathy.

Amanda J. Parr, who through her book, *The True and Complete Story of 'Machine Gun' Jack McGurn*, gave texture to McGurn in mine.

Rebecca Alm of Legacy Imaging, and Susan Van Dyke, who painted my words.

Ojash Shrestha, who designed a millionaire's web site, amatterofhappenstance.com, on a pauper's budget.

Annie Rooney Regenfuss, who urged me to finish the novel and get started on the chick lit piece.

Donna B., who urged me to finish the novel and get started on the 9-11 piece.

The staff at Office Depot in Mequon, who made a zillion copies and tried (without success) to teach me the mysteries of the self-serve copy machine.

Lesley Kagan, author of *Whistling in the Dark*, who provided snippets of fortitude. "How many queries have you sent out? Fifteen? That's all? Blast those queries out! Somebody will fall in love with your book."

Susan Bright, poet/publisher, who fell in love with my book.

About the Author

Catherine Fitzpatrick grew up in St. Louis County, the second of six children. Her maternal great-great-grandfather launched a family furniture manufacturing business on the streets of old St. Louis that thrived from 1874 to 1959.

After graduating from the University of Missouri-Columbia School of Journalism, Catherine worked as a feature writer at metro daily newspapers in Hannibal, St. Louis, and Milwaukee. On Sept. 11, 2001, while on assignment to cover New York Fashion Week, Catherine filed real time eye-witness dispatches from the streets of downtown Manhattan. Her award-winning coverage of the terrorist attack was among the stories about journalists chronicled in "Running Toward Danger" (Rowman and Littlefield, 2002). A *Milwaukee Journal Sentinel* edition carrying one of her 9/11 stories is among the front pages memorialized in Washington D.C.'s Newseum.

Catherine and her husband, Dennis, divide their time between Mequon, WI, and Bonita Springs, FL. When she is not writing and revising, she enjoys biking, swatting golf balls into sand traps, visiting her daughters and son-in-law in Chicago, and plotting her next trip.

In Praise of
A Matter of Happenstance

A Matter of Happenstance is a wrenching family saga that examines the uniquely American collision of self-determination and destiny. Catherine Fitzpatrick takes us from a New Orleans brothel to Capone's Chicago to a gilded St. Louis mansion, all the while examining lives of privilege and lives of desolation. I raced through each page to this novel's startling conclusion.

Kelly O'Connor McNees
Author of *The Lost Summer of Louisa May Alcott*

Catherine Fitzpatrick skillfully and beautifully evokes time and place while weaving together the lives and destinies of a cast of charming and not-so-charming characters over several generations. Haven't we all wondered at one time or another how life would have turned out if we had done just one thing differently?

Karen K. Marshall
Former feature writer, *St. Louis Globe-Democrat*

Catherine Fitzpatrick's book, *A Matter of Happenstance*, is an exquisitely orchestrated exploration of the vagaries and vanities of American life. She has glided gracefully from career journalist to first-time novelist.

Michele Derus
National award-winning journalist,
Retired business writer, *Milwaukee Journal Sentinel*

I reveled in this romp through early 20th Century American history as it played out in cities like New Orleans and St. Louis, and hamlets like Hannibal and Chattooka.

Framed in carefully crafted language that was a pleasure to read, the characters in this drama were so compelling that I missed them when I was away from the book.

Kathleen Arenz
RSVP Social Columnist, retired
Milwaukee Journal Sentinel

Happenstance rings true with the voice and personality of 19ᵗʰ Century St. Louis. It was enjoyable to get a glimpse into our city's history from such varied perspectives.

The scenes of the 1904 World's Fair were fascinating, and truly reflective of the time.

Jeff Fister, publisher
Virginia Publishing Company

LaVergne, TN USA
17 September 2010
197413LV00001B/5/P